## ADVANCE PRAISE FOR
## *EVERYONE KNOWS YOU GO HOME*

"A beautifully written story that illuminates the complex allegiances of family and the costs of denying the past for the exigencies of the present. Told with great warmth, humor, and wisdom, Natalia Sylvester brings the border to vivid life in this timeless journey deep inside the human heart."

—Cristina García, author of *Here in Berlin* and *Dreaming in Cuban*

"I was charmed by this novel from the start, and when a character from the afterlife shows up—and when no one in the book thinks it unusual or strange—I was smitten. This is the tangled history of one family's past and present both here and beyond. Sylvester's gift is that she's able to infuse it, in more ways than one, with extraordinary spirit and life."

—Cristina Henríquez, author of *The Book of Unknown Americans*

"*Everyone Knows You Go Home* is a deeply satisfying read, beautifully illustrating how love and obligation shape our lives and give them meaning. Life on the borderlands—between Texas and Mexico, news reports and real life, history and memory, the living and the dead—creates an immersive world for exploring the mysteries that we all are to each other, bound as we may be by shared blood, shared love, and shared grief."

—ire'ne lara silva, author of *flesh to bone*

"*Everyone Knows You Go Home* is a rich and moving story of love and secrets. Natalia Sylvester beautifully explores borders both physical and metaphysical."

—Ramona Ausubel, author of *Sons and Daughters of Ease and Plenty* and *No One is Here Except All of Us*

"Sylvester charms with a family saga that is both epic and intimate in scope, delivering an unforgettable tale of the boundless power of love and redemption. *Everyone Knows You Go Home* is a dreamy spell of a novel, a new window into the magic and mystery of the natural world and beyond."

—Patricia Engel, author of *The Veins of the Ocean* and *Vida*, a *New York Times* Notable Book of the Year

## PRAISE FOR *CHASING THE SUN*

"Sylvester's debut novel depicts the strained marriage of Andres and Marabela Jimenez, a wealthy couple in Lima, Peru, in 1992. When Marabela fails to come home after running an errand, Andres suspects she is leaving him for the second time. Instead, he finds a note explaining that three men have kidnapped her. The kidnappers seek a ransom in American dollars, demanding more money than Andres has. His mother, who dislikes Marabela, initially refuses to help. Each phone call between Andres and the kidnappers increases the tension, as does Andres' struggle to soothe their children, Ignacio and Cynthia. Sylvester creates a world of nightmarish suspense, not only for the Jimenez family but also for the city of Lima itself, with its curfews and unpredictable guerrilla groups. Marabela is held by her captors for 17 days; in the novel's second section, Days 17 and On, Sylvester portrays the pain of survival and recovery. The writing is clear, exact, and powerful, maintaining subtlety in spite of its dramatic subject matter, and the ending is smart and unexpected."

—Jackie Thomas-Kennedy, *Booklist*

"Sylvester debuts with a page-turning novel that strikes a balance between austere domesticity and suspenseful, life-altering trauma."

—*Publishers Weekly*

"Sylvester is a fine writer with a knack for crafting situations that externalize the characters' internal struggles . . . her ambition to reach beyond the traditional kidnapping thriller into something richer is commendable."

—*Kirkus Reviews*

"Love the mystery and suspense of *Gone Girl*? *Chasing the Sun* keeps you nail-biting as Andres tries to solve the mystery of his missing wife."

—*Cosmopolitan for Latinas*

"Sylvester deftly tells the story of Andres and Marabela, a married couple with an already complicated relationship that is put to the test when Marabela is kidnapped and held for ransom . . . a page-turner."

—*USA TODAY*

"It is a mature work of literature, one that—while it has the pacing of a thriller—offers fully drawn characters who suffer through an act of violence that was all too common in Peru during the 1990s: the kidnapping of a loved one. Based on both research and family experience, Sylvester's novel is an important and moving addition to the literature chronicling the brutality suffered by Peruvians during President Fujimori's decade in office."

—Daniel Olivas, *Los Angeles Review of Books*

"A fascinating, brooding depiction of a kidnapping in Peru and how the price of a happy marriage is much higher than any ransom."

—Jamie Ford, author of *Hotel on the Corner of Bitter and Sweet*

"In *Chasing the Sun*, Natalia Sylvester paints an intimate portrait of a Peruvian businessman whose wife is kidnapped and held for ransom. The story resonates with every tortured breath of a loyal husband caught between money and family, a troubled marriage, and an aching heart."

—Leslie Lehr, author of *What a Mother Knows*

# EVERYONE
# KNOWS
# YOU
# GO HOME

ALSO BY NATALIA SYLVESTER

*Chasing the Sun*

# EVERYONE

# KNOWS

# YOU

# GO HOME

## NATALIA SYLVESTER

Little
a

Text copyright © 2018 Natalia Sylvester

Published by Little A, New York

www.apub.com

Amazon, the Amazon logo, and Little A are trademarks of Amazon.com, Inc., or its affiliates.

ISBN-13: 9781542046374 (hardcover)
ISBN-10: 1542046378 (hardcover)
ISBN-13: 9781542046367 (paperback)
ISBN-10: 154204636X (paperback)

Cover design by Faceout Studio

Illustrated by Hannah Perry

Printed in the United States of America

First edition

*To Ceci*

*La memoria guardará lo que valga la pena. La memoria sabe de mí más que yo; y ella no pierde lo que merece ser salvado.*

—Eduardo Galeano, *Días y noches de amor y de guerra*

*My memory will retain what is worthwhile. My memory knows more about me than I do; it doesn't lose what deserves to be saved.*

—Eduardo Galeano, *Days and Nights of Love and War*

# CHAPTER 1

## November 2, 2012

## The Big Day

They were married on the Day of the Dead, el Día de los Muertos, which no one gave much thought to in all the months of planning, until the bride's deceased father-in-law showed up in the car following the ceremony. He manifested behind the wheel, then stretched his arm over the back of the passenger's seat as he turned to face Martin and Isabel.

"Beautiful ceremony, mijo," he said.

The couple's smiles froze. It seemed to take an eternity for either of them to speak, and when they did, they had little more than mumbles.

Her whole life, Isabel had heard stories about spirits who spent this one day of the year with family. As a child she had built altars for her great-grandparents, vibrant tributes made out of open shoe boxes adorned with paper flowers and pictures of religious figures that looked a lot like the dioramas she created in grade school. In her teens, her family congregated around her great-aunt's grave to clean it; one year, her mother even brought a battery-operated vacuum for the stone. *"Today we remember our dead,"* her mother always said. *"We honor them."*

Martin's father looked more frazzled than dead, as if he was running late because he had been caught in traffic. Isabel looked to her new husband for guidance and was shocked to realize he seemed annoyed. Not afraid, because honestly her father-in-law looked harmless, just like in the few pictures she had seen of him. No, Martin looked like he had simply bitten into a pepper that was hotter than anticipated.

"Did you know this would happen?" she said.

"No, but it's typical of him. Typical. Only someone so shameless would show up to a wedding uninvited."

"Martin, please!" She hadn't expected him to be so rude. She hadn't expected any of this at all, but her instincts to remain polite and respect her elders were deeply engrained—even more than her assumptions about life and death, apparently—and so her efforts to understand the situation were quickly overridden by her desire to make everybody feel comfortable.

It was the first time she had met her father-in-law. She smoothed her white dress, which was bulging into every inch of the seat, and straightened her veil over her shoulders. "Aren't you going to introduce us?"

The old man sat quietly, waiting.

"I'm not talking to him," Martin said.

"Martin, you can't be serious."

At this, her father-in-law smiled and leaned toward her, through the small space that separated the front and back of the white Rolls-Royce they had rented. "He is, I promise you. That kind of stubbornness runs deep in our blood. Isabel, I'm Omar. Though I hope they at least told you my name?"

"Of course. Encantada," she said.

In ordinary circumstances, she would have leaned in to kiss him, hug him even, but these were not ordinary circumstances. She didn't know what laws governed the dead. Could they touch? Feel? Hold? Omar seemed as if he might shift the car out of park any moment now.

Instead he placed his hand over hers, and she felt not a solid touch but a vibrant warmth, like gentle electricity. Her eyes lit up, but Martin scoffed and turned away.

"Omar," she said, letting his name empty her lungs. "Will you be joining us for the reception?" What a foolish thing to say.

"You're very kind to ask, Isabel. Thank you." He stepped out of the still-open door of the car and began walking toward the church gardens. Neither Isabel nor Martin attempted to follow.

She didn't know how, but she knew she wouldn't see him as she and Martin shared their first dance or cut their wedding cake. The whole evening, she didn't have to glance over her shoulder to see if her father-in-law had arrived. And because the last thing she wanted to do was upset her new husband, she acted like it'd never happened.

She couldn't fall asleep on their wedding night. The newlyweds made love distractedly, as if the act were nothing new, and of course for them it wasn't. They were not, by the Church's standards, good Catholics. Before today neither had been to mass in years, and they had slept together on their third-and-a-half date and had used condoms and contraceptives and spermicide, sometimes all at once.

If not new, though, she had imagined their wedding sex would feel different. Husband and wife, joining their bodies, and for the first time it wouldn't matter if someone heard them or walked in on them or if the condom broke in eight places. They were married now. They were together for life.

Martin struggled with the perfectly round buttons that climbed, one impossibly close to the next, all the way up her spine. Isabel hadn't realized until her dress was undone how the corset had constricted her all evening. She had to take a moment to catch her breath, and the indentations that the boning left on her skin, now exposed, itched.

She had wanted to make love to him in new ways, she really had, but more than that Isabel wanted to lie next to him, close her eyes, and open them to find Martin still there the next day, and the next, and the next after that.

When it was over, and they untangled their bodies, the newlyweds stared at the ceiling. She sighed. *"That was wonderful,"* she had meant to say, but the words that came out instead were, "What's wrong?"

Martin brought his hand to his forehead. "I didn't know he was dead."

It suddenly hit her that she hadn't either, but the whole encounter had been so surreal there'd been little time to process the logistics. She had long thought of Martin's father as gone. What little Isabel knew of him she had learned from Claudia, Martin's younger sister. "My father left us years ago," she'd said the first time Isabel had asked, during third-grade recess.

"You mean like, dead or to another town?"

Isabel lacked tact and tolerance for ambiguity at eight years of age. Claudia had looked so hurt that Isabel thought their friendship wouldn't last past lunch, but she recovered quickly, and Isabel resolved never to ask again.

She looked for clues, of course, whenever she went to Claudia's house. There were no pictures of a father anywhere, and she never got the impression that his absence was felt with any sort of longing. The closest she got to an explanation was the day a particularly persistent telemarketer got on Claudia's mom's last nerve.

"I don't know when he'll be back!" Elda had yelled after the fourth call. "He walked out on us years ago, so your guess is as good as mine." She had hung up, looking pleased with herself. Isabel had stared at her bowl of cereal, pretending she hadn't heard.

Years later, Isabel could still easily recall the cadence of the family's denial. When she and Martin got engaged and invited Elda to their cake tasting, the baker had asked if they should wait for the father of the groom as well.

"My father-in-law is no longer with us," Isabel had said.

She waited to see if Martin would correct her; if maybe, after all these years, a wedding would be cause enough to make amends. He proceeded to ask about the differences in frosting, and that was the end of that.

Except now, Martin's eyes grew satiny, and his gaze, wide, fixed on the ceiling fan as if he hoped the air would spare him the embarrassment of tears. When this seemed to fail, he buried his face in Isabel's neck and stretched his arm over her stomach.

She'd never seen him this way. She knew she should be sharing in his sorrow, but a part of her felt vindicated. A part of her thought, *This is what is different now, this is what it means to be married.* There would never be anyone else Martin could be so vulnerable with, and it made Isabel want to be strong for him.

"At least now, you can get closure," she said. "It could've been worse. He could've died and been gone forever, and you would've never known."

"I don't want closure. I don't want to see him or speak to him. Just—stay away if he comes back, okay?" His words landed hot against her skin. "He ruins everything."

"Nobody's ruined anything." She ran her fingers through his hair until he fell into a deep sleep. Sliding out from under him, she got up, dressed, and headed to the small lounge area in their bridal suite.

There Omar was again, slouched on the paisley couch with his hands together in his lap. Isabel felt a gasp catch in her throat. "You scared me."

Omar shrugged apologetically. "Boo."

"That's not funny."

"It is a little."

"Have you been here the whole time? While we were—"

"God no. Nothing like that."

"But you knew then, when to come back? How?"

"I just knew."

She shot him a confused expression, and after a few mumbles and false starts, Omar seemed to find the words to explain. "When you're dead, you sense all the things you missed when you were living. Moods, timing, a person's state of mind. Not their thoughts," he added quickly. "But in a way we're more alive than we ever were before."

She wandered closer to him. There was nothing about this man that didn't intrigue her. As she walked around the wooden coffee table and plush white love seat that stood between them, she wished that this were a less fancy hotel, the kind that has coffee makers with individual-sized bags of ground coffee wrapped in plastic. But this was the kind of place with twenty-four-hour room service. Even with the wedding being on a Friday to lower costs, they had gone way over their budget to book the suite. She imagined explaining the spirit of a dead man sitting in the living room to the hotel staff. It almost made her laugh.

"What's so funny?" Omar said.

"I wasn't laughing."

"But your mood shifted. You were scared just a minute ago."

"Not really scared. Startled." She sat across from him. Even with the lights off, she could see his deep features bathed in the coolness of the streetlights that shone through the windows. Now that she had a moment to take him in, she was struck by his resemblance to Martin, or rather, Martin's resemblance to him. He had a full head of white hair and a thick, salt-and-pepper beard. Martin's hair was pitch black, and he was always clean shaven, but his cheeks got all prickly by midafternoon. As a result, both men's skin looked thick; their huge pores gave them a rugged, worn appearance that she had always found attractive. Omar was slightly shorter than his son, with a wider build. He was the perfect example of the *after* to Martin's *before*, an almost uncanny representation of the natural progression of time.

Of course, there was the minor difference in mortality. Earlier in the car she had been too overwhelmed to notice that Omar's stillness wavered. When she looked directly at him, he seemed as solid as any other being, but the instant she glanced away, and his image shifted into her periphery, it stuttered, like a video call reloading over a weak connection.

She felt an urge to wake Martin, to hold him and let him anchor her to their world. But she resisted, remembering what her husband had asked before drifting into sleep.

*Husband.* Even thinking it felt like a revelation.

Omar crossed his legs, then slid his ankle up to rest atop his knee.

"God. Even your gestures are the same," she said.

"Is this too strange for you? I can leave."

This time, she didn't bother suppressing a laugh.

"You're right. Of course it is," he said.

"The only thing that could possibly be stranger than you being here would be me asking you to leave now that you are."

"I have a feeling my son would disagree," he said, lowering his voice.

"I have a feeling you're right. But you don't have to whisper. An earthquake couldn't wake him right now."

"The sleep of a very happy man."

She didn't bother arguing with that. Outside it had started to rain, quiet drops that don't tap at the window but hiss as cars skid over them through barely wet streets.

"I didn't expect you'd be back after this afternoon."

"I wasn't planning on it. I tried to visit Elda and Claudita before the reception started, but they wouldn't see me."

"That's strange." She had always suspected Elda would give Omar a mouthful if she had the chance. "They didn't seem at all bothered this evening." On the contrary, Claudia had been uncharacteristically chipper.

7

"I'm glad I didn't spoil the party, then."

"Why wouldn't they be happy to see you? Why wasn't Martin? You'd think, after all these years."

"Time doesn't make feelings go away. It just makes people more willing to push them aside. Not them, though. I'd have to die eighty deaths before they'd be happy to see me, and even then they'd simply relish the chance to see me die the eighty-first."

"I doubt that's true."

"You don't know my family like I do."

His words stung, though she wouldn't have expected them to. Immediately, he seemed to regret it. "I shouldn't have said that. It's insensitive of me to point that out on your wedding day."

"But you don't deny it's true?"

Omar said nothing, and Isabel felt the last bit of the day's adrenaline seep out of her. In just minutes, he had exposed the one blind spot in their relationship she had spent the past few years ignoring. Whenever Martin pretended his father's absence was not a big deal, she would pretend to believe him. She felt embarrassed, like she'd been caught telling a lie.

"Forgive me," Omar finally said. He looked at the clock as the minute hand twitched its way closer to midnight. "I shouldn't have said that either. In my rush to prove a point I sometimes forget my manners."

"It's okay. It's just that I suppose I've lost all opportunity to make a good impression with you. A more loyal wife wouldn't ask questions. She'd respect her husband's wishes not to speak with you."

"He told you not to speak with me?" Omar sat up, as if flattered his son had spoken about him at all. Isabel said nothing more, afraid she had already betrayed Martin's trust.

"If it makes you feel better, I've never been impressed by people who don't ask questions," Omar said.

She couldn't help smiling. "Me neither. I'm sorry to be so frank, but it's just that . . . you're asking me to start my marriage by going behind my husband's back."

"Please don't ever apologize for being frank."

"You know what I mean."

"Yes. I'm more and more proud of my son each minute that passes."

"Thank you," Isabel said. She stood up and took a deep breath, pulling her robe tighter. It was the kind of silence she thought was socially universal, that purposeful, heavy pause at the end of the evening when guests realize it's time to go. If Omar recognized this, he didn't let on. A flush of panic came over his face. She waited a moment longer and cleared her throat.

"I'm sorry. I'm only here a few more minutes. Can't we just talk?"

She sat back down and crossed her hands over her lap, sitting up straight.

"About what?"

Her directness seemed to confuse him. Perhaps the question was too simple to be answered simply.

He smiled and brushed her cheek with the tingly tips of his fingers. "You tell me. Ask me anything you want. Anything you're comfortable with."

"All right. Why are you here, Omar?"

"With you? I told you. Elda wouldn't see me, so I came here."

That wasn't exactly what she'd meant, but Isabel let it slide.

"And why is that?"

He shrugged. "You'd have to ask Elda."

"What about Martin?" Her patience was wearing thin.

"I was surprised he saw me at all." Omar shook his head in bewilderment. "But then again, it is his wedding day, and I'm his father, even though—"

"Even though you left when he was seven?"

"Ah. What else has he told you?"

"Enough to make it clear why he wouldn't want you here." This was not entirely true. Martin had a way of answering questions with no answers at all or (if he couldn't completely avoid it) with answers to completely different ones. It'd been charming when it came to trivial things like how his day had gone, but as soon as the topic turned to his father or his childhood, he would offer up a cheerful family anecdote in place of any real substance.

"What else would you like to know?" Omar said.

She wanted to prove she knew his family more than he thought she did. She remembered one of the only stories Martin ever shared that included both his father and mother.

"Tell me about the time you played hide-and-seek, and he hid so well no one could find him for over an hour."

"What?"

"He was four. In the closet? He won a ribbon. He loves telling that story."

"When we lived in the little apartment on Pecan?"

"Yes, that one."

"I don't . . . I'm surprised he remembers. We'd only been here four years. We'd sent for my family in Mexico. First my parents, and then my cousin Julio. We never should have helped him. He'd been trouble since we were kids, and I don't know how I got it into my head that as an adult he'd be any different. We were all naive then. We all thought coming to this country changes everything, and maybe it does, but not in the way you expect. Elda knew, though. That's why she insisted we offer him our couch, but only for a month. That's all the time he'd have to find a job and a place to stay. One day, he was helping me fix a leak in our bathroom when we realized we'd need a different kind of wrench. But I had to go to work, so he offered to drop me off, take the car, and fix the sink. We agreed he'd pick me up after my shift was over. I wasn't really thinking when I gave him the keys. Hours later, I'm still waiting for him like a fool. I take the bus home, and Elda's waiting up with a friend, but no Julio. Of course we start imagining the worst. He got in an accident, or a fight, or he got himself pulled over and deported. And we would never know. It's not like we could call anyone, you know? So we just waited. Finally we heard sirens in the distance, and then real close, and then you know that moment when they get extra loud and you wait for them to pass because you know they'll just keep going? They didn't. The red and blue lights started flashing into our living room, and Martin woke up wondering what was going on, and we had no idea but we knew it couldn't be good. Elda said, 'You take care of your cousin, I'll take care of our son.' So I go outside and I see Julio getting pulled over not even fifty feet from our apartment entrance. He's getting one of those walk the line tests and failing, and I'm thinking this is it, he'll get sent back, and maybe I'll see him again in a few months if he manages to raise the money to cross back over. And I'm thinking they'll find all of us, and we'll all get sent back. So I stop halfway through the parking lot and pretend I'm going to the vending machine for a Coke. Like I didn't even know him, my own flesh and blood. And he probably didn't recognize me either; he was so drunk he couldn't tell a cop from a clown. I got my soda, and I went back into the house and turned off all the lights, and we waited for the cops and Julio to disappear. It was more than an hour. Martin was in the closet the whole time. Elda spent much of it pacing the house, from nerves is what I thought, but I guess she was pretending to look for him. She told me that's how she protected Martin from the truth that night. I didn't know about the ribbon."

"That's . . . that's not how I thought that story would go," Isabel said. She sat back down on the couch.

"How does my son tell it?"

"It's one of his first memories. He talks about it like it's an early triumph. He remembers how late it was. I guess that's part of the excitement. A kid up way past his bedtime, and he gets to play hide-and-seek, and he sets a family record and gets a prize."

"Ay, Elda. Always so good with him."

"And what about you? Were you good with him?"

Now it was Omar's turn to stand up and cue his exit. He stretched his arms, and Isabel wondered if his bones cracked, if his limbs tired, or if the motion was simply a habit.

"I guess it depends who you ask."

"I'm asking you. I'll ask him later," she said, raising her eyebrows toward the bedroom.

He looked at the door with longing. "I thought I was. I tried to be. But sometimes our best intentions become our worst mistakes."

Something in the way his voice traveled away from her, as if he wished he could hide this confession, struck her. This was worse than helplessness; it was injustice—worse even than robbing a man of his dying wish. Here he was, aching to say things he never got a chance to say, but her reluctance to hear had reduced the man to riddles and veiled truths. She wished she could do more for him.

"Tell my son I'll try him again next year." He kissed her on the forehead, soft as a breeze. She smiled and closed her eyes, and when she opened them, he was gone.


In the weeks following their wedding day, Isabel and Martin discovered that married life was not very different from premarried life, and they delighted in telling people who asked, over and over, "How's married life treating ya?" that it was the same.

"But that's a good thing, or else I wouldn't have married her," Martin would say after an awkward pause. He loved setting up this joke, and occasionally Isabel would humor him by appearing to be just as shocked as the person hearing it, then join them in an outburst of laughter.

"How long do you think before people stop asking us?" Martin said one night. They were walking to their car from Claudia's apartment, carrying a half-finished bottle of rum that her boyfriend, Damian, had insisted they take back to their place for next time. To Isabel's relief, the guests had been a mix of teachers from Damian's school and flight attendants Claudia worked with. They asked the usual questions people ask to get acquainted with one another, but eventually the living room became a teacher's lounge, while Claudia's friends sipped wine and shared passenger horror stories in the kitchen. Isabel mostly listened, laughing at their airline jokes even when she didn't understand them. It was much easier than trying to have a real conversation with Claudia, who had been keeping her at arm's length ever since they'd reentered each other's lives.

"At least a year," Isabel said, happy to turn her thoughts elsewhere. "Or until someone else gets married. I don't really mind."

"You put up with my joke, so you must not."

"It was in my vows. Put up with husband's dumb jokes."

"How'd I miss that?"

"Subtext. You were never good with subtext."

"I see." He walked around the car and opened the passenger-side door for her in a theatrical fashion. "As long as we're playing the good husband and wife."

Isabel laughed as she stepped into the car, her legs slightly numb from her three glasses of wine. Moments like these, she marveled that they were even together. Despite her knowing him as a child, Martin often caught her by surprise. They had only reconnected in the last couple of years over a series of odd encounters at mutual friends' parties, during which they had felt sparks of interest at the worst possible times.

The first time they ran into one another, Isabel almost didn't recognize him. He had a wide chest and stood several inches taller than she, so that his jawline was right at eye level. His dark hair fell in one swoop over his forehead, and his eyes (which she had always thought too big for his face) were now perfectly punctuated behind thin-framed glasses. Everything about him was the same, just more settled and refined. She was happy to see he had outgrown what she and Claudia once secretly called his Kenny G phase, and for a moment debated telling him this. She opted to ask about the family instead.

They stood chatting in the narrow hallway of a friend's two-bedroom apartment, waiting for the bathroom. He made a joke about how people spend half of a relationship concealing their most basic human functions, yet they're perfectly content to stand outside a bathroom complaining about how long the line is, as if all they plan on doing once they get to the front is admire the shapes of the tile. "Or the soaps," Isabel had said. "I'm always hoping they're seashell shaped."

He had smiled and tried to say "seashell shaped" three times fast, but couldn't. They laughed, and the bathroom door opened, and Isabel realized Martin had been waiting for his girlfriend.

Some four months later they ran into each other again. Isabel was single. She recognized Martin's girlfriend before she saw him, and as she took in the woman's long legs and wide hips, Isabel doubted she would ever be Martin's type. She told herself she probably wouldn't want to be. They ended the evening playing Scattergories, and she and Martin called out the same answers so many times (Things people throw away: Lives) it became a personal mission to outdo each other.

By the time Martin was single and asked her to dinner and a movie, Isabel had been dating one of the pharmaceutical reps from her hospital for nearly a year. She was caught so off guard by his invitation that she misunderstood it to be for a double date.

"Richard's been dying to try out their new menu," she said, too late to back out of her mistake. The evening became awkward the second Martin's date asked how he and Isabel knew each other.

"We've known each other most of our lives," Martin said.

The truth was they barely did; they only wanted to.

Months after they had finally seized a window of opportunity to start dating, Martin admitted he'd decided he disliked Isabel's ex before the two couples even finished dinner. "Every time I was trying not to look at you, I'd catch him looking away from you. It's like he had no idea what he had."

Their relationship had been a crazed, rushed thing. There was no need to introduce her to his family; the first time she saw them again, Elda acted like Isabel was a daughter who had just returned from a long trip. Claudia, on the other hand, greeted her with the indifference of someone who hadn't even noticed she'd been gone. At first it barely registered; Isabel mentioned it to Martin, and he reassured her that his sister was just a bit aloof. Not that she had needed the reminder, but this was different. It was always Elda, not Claudia, who asked to get caught up on the details of Isabel's life after ninth grade. Claudia didn't dare steer the conversation toward the past, and soon their history as BFFs seemed almost inconsequential, serving no other purpose than giving Isabel and Martin a head start in their romance. They began dating in the summer and were engaged soon after the new year.

"I knew it," Claudia said when they told her.

"Thanks." Isabel couldn't tell if she was happy with the news or the fact that she had seen it coming.

"I always hoped you'd end up together," Elda said.

Isabel heard Martin stifle a laugh, and she knew they had both been thinking the same thing: one morning after the girls had had a sleepover, Elda chastised Martin for coming into the kitchen wearing nothing but boxers, shooing him away to put on some clothes and insisting that Isabel would not be so easily impressed by the cuatro pelos on his chest just yet.

"Mom, you embarrassed me in front of Isabel every chance you got," Martin said.

"It's because you were too young to think such things."

"We weren't the ones thinking them."

Moments like these, when Isabel felt like the only one who hadn't forgotten her and Claudia's friendship, it was always Martin who remembered.

But he didn't remember everything.

"You ever wonder why your sister and I stopped talking?" Isabel asked. She watched the car's headlights turn the abyss ahead of them into road, her head heavy and swaying with each curve the car took.

"I thought you just drifted apart. After you switched schools."

She caught his shrug in the window's reflection. "You mean after my dad died."

"I didn't realize that had anything to do with it. I'm sorry."

"You wouldn't, I guess."

"What does that mean?"

"Nothing. It's just that, your sister didn't seem to think it was a big deal, so why would you? It all makes sense now."

"What does?"

"The way you all cope. Or don't cope."

There'd been a few moments, during their honeymoon and ever since they had gotten home, in which Martin would grow quiet, and she would know he was thinking about his father. Each time, she'd ask if he wanted to talk about it, and each time, he'd kiss her on the forehead, as if she were the one in need of comforting, and say, "There's really nothing to talk about." Once, when she pressed him, saying she doubted this was true, he added curtly, "He left us without a word. Why would I give him more than that?"

*"Give* me *more than that,"* she had wanted to say, but she had left it, like always, for later. Now her frustration had grown like a plant left in the dark, sprouting high as it searched for the light.

She leaned into the headrest and turned to face Martin. "Our wedding night after you fell asleep, your father came back."

"Back? To our hotel?"

They stopped at an intersection just off a frontage road. The Texas lone star etched onto the highway retaining wall loomed over them, and the lights beneath the overpass glowed blue and then pink, lining the edges of Martin's face in neon. She could tell by the way he pressed his lips together that he was trying to control his emotions. Disbelief and anger, perhaps. Or a feeling of betrayal.

"When were you going to tell me?"

"I was waiting for the right time."

"Jesus, Isa. What did he want?"

"Just to talk. He said he'd wanted to see your mother—"

"My mother?" He started rubbing his hands against the steering wheel.

"And your sister, too, but it didn't work out. So he came to us. I was the only one awake," she added, her voice trailing off upon stating the obvious.

When they finally pulled into their complex, he shot her an expectant glance. "Well, what did he tell you?"

"Nothing important. We just . . . got acquainted with one another."

A small huff escaped his nose. "How nice for you both." He got out of the car and grabbed a few things from the trunk; everything shook as he slammed it shut. The lights inside the car dimmed, as if no longer sensing that Isabel was there, and she let herself, for that small moment, blend into the quiet parking lot. She saw Martin look back at her from the door of their duplex, but she wasn't in a rush to catch up.

By the time she went inside, Martin was in bed with an unopened book in his lap. He pretended not to notice as she undressed, washed her face, and dabbed the skin around her eyes with cream.

When she finally climbed into bed, he fanned the pages of his book and sighed into their breeze. "So you like him?"

She shrugged. "I barely know him."

He looked down at his lap and nodded, as if this were something he understood. "My mom used to tell me stories about my great-uncle on her dad's side, how he died on a night there was a blackout because they hadn't been able to pay the electric bill, and so that Day of the Dead and for years after, they would set up his altar and turn on all the lights in the house. They wanted him to be at peace. They wanted him to know they were all right." Martin laughed, bringing his hands to his mouth. "I don't know what kind of peace my father thinks he deserves now. But he's not going to get it from me, or my mom and sister. And if he thinks he can use you to get to us . . ."

"That's not what he was doing," Isabel said, picking at the lint on their bedspread. "No one called to tell you he died?"

"Who would've? When I tell you he left, Isa, it's like he might as well have died. One day to the next, the guy was gone. Nothing. It doesn't matter now anyways."

But it did. "He said he'll be back. To try to speak to you again."

Martin laughed. "He'd have better luck coming back to life."

"So that's it? You'd turn him away? After all he went through to see you?"

"This is exactly what I was afraid of. Why are we still talking about him? Why does everything have to be about him?"

"Because nothing is ever about him!" The words shot out of her. The silence between them trembled, failing to mask the shock of it. She placed his hand in hers, turning onto her side to get closer.

"Is it really so much to ask? That I love you and I want to know all about you?"

"I'm not my father, Isa. And he's not some cheat sheet into who I am. I can't believe you even think you'd need one."

This idea struck her as both painful and sweet, but that she didn't know how her husband intended it only underscored what she had meant to say. Maybe this is what Martin had meant about his father. Some people trail nothing but trouble into others' lives, and everyone is better off once they are gone.

"This whole thing is ridiculous," she finally said. "I'm sorry to dwell on it."

Slowly, he raised the back of her hand to his lips, giving it a cold, moist peck. "Don't be. Just promise me you won't tell anyone. I don't want my mom finding out about him."

"You think he'd hurt her?"

"I don't know."

"Did he ever?"

"I don't know. Most people would have a yes or no answer to that question, but I have no idea. I'd believe it either way."

In time, she forced herself to push away the memory of Omar. Sometimes when she drifted off to sleep, and her thoughts went back to the night of the wedding, she wasn't entirely sure if he was a memory or a dream. She would wake up and tiptoe to the kitchen, serve herself a cup of warm milk, and check her emails and read the day's news on her phone. This act made her feel like she was replacing one kind of thought with another, the more ethereal with the more concrete, but when she finished, she always felt unsettled and unfulfilled.

She tried to find subtle ways to ask Claudia about her father, but every time Isabel got up the courage to call, she got her voicemail. Call me when you land, she would text her, but Claudia would only text back, everything ok?

Just calling to say hi.

Thanks. Super tired can we talk at my mom's? But they rarely did.

With the coming of the new year, Isabel resolved to focus on her life ahead with Martin: now, next year, and the next five after that. They created plans, budgets, goals.

They were driving to a movie one Sunday when Isabel saw a handwritten "Open House" sign and yelled for Martin to make a U-turn. She had nearly missed it among a sea of signs for the latest model-home development that had broken ground on what used to be a citrus farm.

"We'll miss the movie," Martin said, but it was a statement, not a protest.

A young real estate agent handed them flyers as soon as they walked in. The place was a relic, untouched since the early '80s, but it had good bones. It felt familiar in a way that the scattered strip malls and gated neighborhoods that had sprouted in McAllen never could. Here—within these sun-yellowed walls and slanted ceilings that peaked like the perfect triangle in a child's crayon drawing of a home—would be where life happened.

# CHAPTER 2

## March 1981

"Everyone carries their own water," he told them, and then, when all he got in response were confused glances in his direction—six skittish sets of eyes refusing to make contact—he repeated himself slowly.

"Agua. Cada uno carga su propia agua."

The migrants nodded in near unison. The two men stood up from the carpet, dragging their feet as they made their way to the small dresser in the motel room to collect a canteen for each member of the group.

The coyote tried not to look at their cracked, dirty hands wrapping themselves around the shiny metal. The canteens, aside from the gas money he had paid a friend to drop him off on this side of the border, were his biggest expense. He had been told the migrants would likely bring their own, but anything could've happened to them during the long trek behind them. Some were robbed, others simply lost their belongings, too exhausted to keep track. So he brought extras. He would collect them upon arrival, along with the rest of his fees.

The men returned to the corner of the room where they had all been huddling, each holding two canteens of water. One of the men's wife, girlfriend, whatever, looked up at him with her arms crossed, mumbling something about bringing two more for their friend. Of the group, she was the only one not paired with a man. Instead, she clung to her little girl, who couldn't have been more than five or six.

He had said no children, and here there were two. At least the other was a boy, a few years older, who looked about the same age as he had been when he first started working the fields. *Boys can endure the heat,* he thought, turning away from the little girl and the two women. Ninety-nine degrees in the middle of this desert, and they looked like they were freezing their asses off.

It was 4:25 in the morning. He had already made them use the bathroom before they left. Soon he would check out of the motel room, and they would follow him seven blocks toward the highway. They would turn north, hugging the edge of the road before merging into the brush well ahead of the river. The rest was deceptively simple, miles and miles of walking and enduring what he knew they could not yet imagine. He had done it countless times, but today was the first trip he was leading alone.

"Texas is not like back home," he said, this time trying not to look at them. "It's like being in an oven. Keep moving and you won't bake."

This, the coyote didn't have to repeat. But just as he placed his hand on the doorknob, he heard the deep voice of one of the migrants behind him give a few words of encouragement to the group. The migrant paused when he noticed the little girl also listening. He knelt to look at her and urged her to drink from his canteen.

"Ready for a little adventure?" the migrant said to her.

As if he had asked all of them, the group nodded.

The migrant stood up straight, no taller than two or three inches above the rest, but leaner, with a much more athletic build than the other man among them. He wore a blue-and-gray-striped shirt and a black backpack that rested high against him, its top loop nearly touching the base of his neck.

*Mr. Hero,* the coyote thought, and he knew that the nickname would stick, if only in his mind, because this was the one the group would follow.

Himself, he was just the guide, the one who knew the way, and to cross they would need more than directions. It always happened this way: hope and strength had to spring from somewhere. He was just relieved to see it surface so soon.

He watched them gather their canteens and plastic bags full of photos and clothes. As they stepped through the motel door after him, he counted their brown-haired heads. Six. He had been told to expect seven, but he knew better than to ask after the missing. He did the familiar math, counting the days and the hungry stomachs of his children waiting back home. Six could still be enough, so long as another group soon followed.

"Vamos," he said, louder than he should have in this kind of darkness.

# CHAPTER 3

## November 2, 2013

### Year One: Paper

On Saturday, the morning of her one-year anniversary, Isabel woke thinking of Omar. She doubted she would see him again, or at least, she convinced herself that she doubted she would see him again, because she knew that when one expects something it never happens, and when one doesn't, it does. She rolled onto the center of the bed and placed her arm over Martin's chest. Martin's agency was shooting a commercial for one of their newest clients, and this was his first time managing such a big account on his own. Isabel hadn't gotten the day off either, but she was grateful not to work an overnight shift so they could celebrate their anniversary in the evening.

"Good morning, husband." The sound of it hadn't gotten old. Older couples were constantly warning them that marriage is hard work and full of surprises. Their first year had seen both. In April, the house flooded; in June, the raise Martin was counting on fell through; and in August, they had a pregnancy scare they never thought they would consider a scare.

"Hold on tight and you'll come out of it stronger." That was what Elda loved to say. Isabel no longer brushed this off without a second thought.

They got ready for work as usual. Their bathroom sinks were crammed so closely that they were constantly bumping into each other as they reached for a towel or a comb. Martin took the chance to punctuate each slight encounter with a peck. A kiss on the neck. One on Isabel's shoulder. A tug of her arm as she put away her toothbrush, and he pulled her into a quick embrace.

Normal mornings, there was no time for these things. But if she got no other gift for their anniversary, Isabel was grateful that her husband understood true romance is about infusing small moments with simple bliss.

She waved goodbye to Martin as he backed out of the garage, then began gathering her things. She reached into the refrigerator and nearly dropped her lunch bag as she caught sight of a dark figure behind the door.

A shriek scratched her throat. "Mother fucker!" she yelled, then cupped her mouth, eyes wide with embarrassment upon realizing it was her father-in-law.

Omar burst into laughter, his Adam's apple bobbing up and down at her crudeness. "I'm sorry. It's just that hearing you curse is like catching a ballerina farting."

"God, Omar." She tried to hide a smile as she stood over the sink. Her arms felt conspicuously still—it didn't seem right to hug him, but it didn't seem right not to. They had only met one day, exactly a year ago.

"I know you're late for work," he said. "I just thought I'd catch you alone, just a minute or two."

"I didn't think you'd be back." She wondered if Omar could sense white lies, if there was a tangible difference between them and deceit.

"You're in a hurry. I understand. Go, go."

"Where will you go instead?"

"Oh, you know. Maybe haunt some old girlfriends. Help a couple of friends cheat at poker."

One tremble of his lips was enough to make Isabel call in sick. Everything else seemed unimportant. Not giving Omar a few hours of her time would be like turning down a beggar's plea for the pennies she had found along the sidewalk. How unfair that we dispose of the indispensable.

"Give me a second, okay?"

After she finished dialing work, her first instinct was to offer him something to drink.

"Ten years ago I would've asked you for a scotch, straight."

"But you can't drink anymore?"

"Can't, don't need to. The body becomes unimportant, you know. I'm not sure how else to explain it."

"Can you not feel anything?"

He smiled. "On the contrary. Sometimes I think I feel too much." He pulled at his shirt collar, loosening it as he twisted his neck side to side. He was wearing a thin, long-sleeved shirt that reminded her of the pages of an old library book, and worn, dark jeans with a brown-leather belt that had a buckle the size of his fist. There was not even four feet of space between them, and as she watched his movements, she realized they were muted. No bones cracking. No clothes scratching against themselves or even the small release of a sigh, though she could see his chest expanding as he looked into her eyes.

"Does it hurt? Coming here?"

He paced their living room, tracing the perimeter of their wooden shelves and the glass doors that led to the backyard. It was ten in the morning, and the sunlight bathed the room. He passed framed pictures from their wedding, honeymoon, a Sunday dinner at Elda's with the family, and a snapshot of Isabel and Martin sitting on the grass at an outdoor concert. Each image held his attention for a few seconds before he moved on to the next.

"It seems to take an eternity while I'm gone and passes in a flash once I'm here," he said. "But I guess that's no different from life. Tell me what I missed. How was your year?"

If anyone else had asked, she would have said, "Great," and she would have been satisfied with this simple word substituting for a conversation of any substance. Sometimes it was just easier than being honest.

"I guess when we look back at our first year, decades from now, we'll only really think of one or two definitive moments. The rest will be a blur. It's sad, if you think about it."

She served herself a cup of juice and moved to the couch, hoping he would do the same. But he seemed determined to keep some space between them, the way a stranger maintains his distance in a crowded line.

"So tell me, what are the one or two moments that come to mind for this year? Don't think too hard about it. Just the first two that come to mind."

Of course she couldn't just give him her thoughts, unfiltered.

"When we moved from our apartment, the day we had to turn it over to the landlord, I took the day off from work, but Martin couldn't. So we rented a truck the night before, and since he didn't want to leave it full of all our belongings overnight, we woke up at four in the morning to load our boxes and furniture. I don't know why I think of that now. We were so careful to keep quiet. It felt like we were thieves, stealing our whole lives away. The sun was just rising by the time we finished. I remember watching Martin stretch his arm to pull down the truck door and being amazed that this is all we amounted to."

"Amazed or scared?"

"Both," she admitted. "I was scared that we could leave it all behind. But it was comforting, too. The idea of just us and a clean slate. That it would still be us no matter where we went." She remembered watching him latch the lock on the truck door, with baby rays of sunlight hugging his back. "Most days I think of Martin as an extension of me. It's an oversimplification, but just in the everyday, when I think of us as a whole, we're this unified front."

Omar nodded, as if he could already see where she was going.

"That morning, I could see he was this whole other person. I don't know his thoughts or feelings. Not really. I'm essentially living my life with a stranger I trust more than anyone in the world."

"It's a beautiful trust."

"It is."

She stopped there. No sense in telling Omar how fleeting the moment was. Later that morning, she had stood in the empty apartment and painted the walls back to white. She had watched their home become a blank canvas, and she had cried alone within it.

"But it makes you sad. Why?"

"It's nothing. Just the ups and downs. Not every moment can be precious."

"Oh, mija. Even the shittiest ones are. One day you'll look back and mourn the pain of it, how alive you were."

She grasped her drink, feeling her neck sink deeper into her shoulders. "You'd rather have the pain than nothing."

"I'd rather have the pain than forget. Or be forgotten." Quickly, he added, "What's the second one? You said there were one or two."

She smiled, wrapped in a new memory. "It's just the first time we had everyone over for Sunday dinner."

Omar looked surprised. "Here? Not at Elda's?"

"I couldn't believe it either." It was a weekly tradition that stretched back years; Isabel was only nine the first time Elda welcomed her to the family table. Her mother had been running late to pick her up, and Isabel feared she might be drinking again. Elda only smiled and asked her to help set the table, handing her an extra place mat and set of silverware.

"It was her idea, after we bought the house. I asked her if she was sure, and she said, 'How else do you make a house a home?' So we had the whole family over. It was like something out of a grocery store commercial." Everything had felt so natural that Isabel thought she and Claudia might become close again.

She led Omar by the hand to the dining table, thinking how nice it would have been to have him there. The feel of his skin warmed her palm, but then Omar let go.

"What's wrong?"

"Nothing. I just realized I haven't wished you and my son a happy anniversary. What's the first year? The gift?"

"It's supposed to be paper."

"Ah, right."

"I wrote him a love letter. Thought it'd be romantic."

He grinned, but she could tell by the way his eyes looked through her that he wasn't listening. Isabel felt her heart sink. She couldn't help wanting Omar's attention and approval, even if no one else cared for it.

He stepped back and rubbed his forehead. "I'm sorry. You're upset. You have every right to be."

She began to feel unsettled. "I know you were hoping to see Martin. I'm sorry you missed him."

"That's not the problem." He placed his hands behind his back and began walking the length of the table, his eyes fixating on the grooves of the wood. "The problem is, he doesn't miss me, so he won't see me."

"I'm sure there's a part of him that misses his father."

"You don't understand. Do you know what keeps the dead from really dying, Isabel? It's just memory. Longing. Being held in the hearts of our loved ones. Last year, I didn't get it. It was a miracle Martin saw me at all. Now he's moved on. Now he really doesn't want anything to do with me, and I can't blame him. But as long as he feels that way, I don't exist to him. Or to Elda or Claudita. It's why I wasn't able to speak with them."

"You said they turned you away."

"I said they didn't see me. There's a difference. I can't go where I'm not wanted. I'm starting to think the only thing bringing me here is you." He placed a hand on her shoulder, stopping short of rubbing it, and she felt a jolt in her gut.

"It can't be just me," she said, half-laughing.

"Why else would I show up only after Martin's gone?"

"That's not fair," she said, but just then the air conditioning clicked on, its hum harsh and intrusive, and she wondered if he'd heard her at all. "I can't be the only reason you're here."

"Of course not. But you are how I'm here. I'm very grateful for that."

"And the why?" At the very least, she deserved to know this.

"Why else but redemption? A second chance. Isn't it always?" Omar smiled and shrugged, surrendering to the ordinariness of it all.

They stood around aimlessly, wondering what to do next. She thought of the summer she turned fifteen and her mother signed her up for the Boys & Girls Club because she had nowhere else to put her. In the pool, between rounds of Marco Polo and races to the deep end and back, she and the kids would catch their breath. They would tread water, wondering if they should keep playing or dry off. Isabel always agreed with whatever the other kids decided. It was odd to keep her face so unaffected, her breath so even, while below the pool's surface her arms and legs paddled, grasping at any bit of mass that would help keep her afloat.

"What are you going to do now?" Omar asked, the way a neighbor might say as he meandered out the door. She reassured him she had no plans, that Martin wouldn't be home until the evening. He seemed in less of a hurry then, like a tired man finally admitting he needed to rest.

They spent hours together. It was a gray fall day, and the sun felt stagnant, stuck behind so many clouds that it became hard to tell time. She asked him if he would like to rest.

"No, I don't need any more of that."

When he laughed, he sounded just like Martin. She told him as much, and he seemed pleased. "I have an idea," she said. "Wait here."

Just because his family wouldn't see him didn't mean he couldn't see his family. She went looking for old photos and shoeboxes full of mementos, trying to piece them together into a cohesive narrative. Some of them she had seen: Martin at prom, Martin dancing as part of the court for a friend's quinceañera. There were collages she and Claudia had made in junior high out of pictures of them at the mall or on the cheerleading squad.

Others she saw as if they were new. In photos from Claudia's birthday parties, she caught glimpses of a younger Martin in the background. He had been an awkward specimen to her back then, with his budding mustache and khaki pants, when everyone else was wearing faded jeans. Though he was three years older than she, Isabel thought him a bit of a nerd, but she never had the heart to make fun of him.

"He was like a little grown-up," she told Omar. "Always trying so hard to be mature for his age."

Omar smiled but remained quiet. When they got to the ones of her and Martin, she was stunned to realize how young they looked not even three years ago. Their faces were fuller, but somehow smaller; their features held more tightly in place.

She was on her laptop now, clicking through her Facebook albums, when Omar asked her to stop at a picture of Elda. All this time, she had been on the other side of the camera, snapping their childhood pictures. But last Mother's Day, they had taken Elda to lunch to celebrate. Their waiter took several pictures, each milliseconds apart, so now when Isabel clicked between them they seemed to move: an elbow shifting, a turn of the head, a strand of hair blown out of place. In the center sat Elda, smiling and then laughing, eyes squinted shut as her mouth widened, her head tilted toward the sky.

"She looks as beautiful as I imagined when I thought of us growing old together." They were sitting at the kitchen table with their elbows resting against the wood. Twice already, Isabel had caught Omar mimicking her movements.

"She has a grace about her that's strong and soothing." It was the first time she'd said this out loud, though she had noticed it years ago, shocked to know mothers could be this way.

He nodded slowly, his eyes on the still image of Elda, as his hands curled into a soft grip.

"What's wrong?"

"You keep asking why I'm here. Isn't it obvious?"

They stared into Elda's eyes. It seemed she was looking right back at them.

"Will you help me?" Omar said.

"Help you what?"

"Help me get her back. Help her see me next year."

She busied herself brushing dust off the tracking pad.

"I know it's a lot to ask."

"It's just that, I don't know that anything I could say would make a difference. And I promised Martin . . ."

"You're right. Forget I mentioned it," he said. "Tell me. What are your plans for next year? Travels? Kids?"

Grateful for the change in subject, she gave the same answer she always did, which applied sadly to one question and happily to the other. "It's not in our plans for a while."

Omar crinkled his nose and smiled. "Plans are just silly attempts to control the tricks of time."

That evening, after Omar left and Martin arrived and they began dressing for their night out, she looked for ways to tell him his father had stopped by. She preferred to think of it as something she could mention casually, something that'd be received in kind. *"You just missed each other,"* she wanted to say, as if he were a neighbor Martin would normally avoid. Or, *"We chatted and caught up,"* as if she were recounting lunch with an old friend.

She studied Martin's reflection as he combed his hair, titling his head toward the mirror. Though he was not the type to brood over his looks openly, he was particular about his hair. At least once a month Isabel caught him aligning the mirrors in the bathroom so he could check the back of his head. When he was a child, Elda had told him stories about his grandfather, a man so bitter he had refused to speak with her after she had come to the US against his wishes, and who had gone bald by the time he was in his thirties. The prospect of early hair loss had haunted Martin ever since.

"You're looking very handsome," she said.

He looked down at the sink, embarrassed that she had caught him. She'd once told him it was silly, that she would love him even if he went bald as a cactus, but he hadn't thought it very funny.

"Sweetie, you worry too much." She sat on the edge of the bathtub, fidgeting with a bobby pin she had left on the counter. "Did you notice that head of hair on your father? And he must've been what, at least sixty?"

"Sixty-two." He set down his comb and kissed her on the cheek. "Maybe you're right. Maybe that's the only good thing the bastard left me." He laughed, but it did little to hide his anger. "I'm sorry. I told myself I wouldn't think about him tonight." He took a deep breath and put his hands on her shoulders, smiling like he was about to give her something. "Tonight's just about you and me. I promise."

# CHAPTER 4

## MARCH 1981

*It is not so bad,* Miguel thought. Not yet as grueling as they said it would be. The climate was stiff and breezeless, but at this hour nothing more than uncomfortable. His brothers and sisters were just spoiled from living across the border so long. They had forgotten, after years of air conditioning, how brutal the heat can be back home, how it multiplied with so many bodies in one room.

That was why they had warned him away, he decided as the group crossed the highway. They were being selfish, not wanting one or two more. Miguel had seen their living room—a room in which no one sleeps!—in pictures they had sent along with boxes of new shoes, new clothes, soaps and shampoos, all with the price tags still on them. *These were not gifts,* he had thought, *this was charity.* When the items arrived, his own children looked at him like it was Christmas. They did not bother thanking him because they knew their father could never give them such things.

Everything he had provided was taken for granted: a roof over their heads, two meals a day. Even he thought it was never enough, and on days when the rain slipped through the ceiling, soaking the mattress his family slept in no matter which corner of the house they moved it to, he knew it was not enough. They would not survive on mold-filled beds and rice and eggs and sugar-water. His wife and children got hungry not even two hours after they ate. Despite taking the kids out of school to help her sell postcards and sewing kits, when they added up the day's earnings with his own from the factory, it was gone as quickly as it came. The cost of living had started to feel like a debt he could never repay. It grew with each breath they took. Not even the air was free.

"¡Apúrense!" The coyote yelled them off the side of the road, and they picked up the pace as a truck's headlights approached.

*It's not la migra,* he thought. La migra would slow down. This one sped past and tossed a warm gust of air in their direction.

He looked at his boy, already dragging his feet on the perfectly paved road. "Don't start now. We're almost there."

"Almost where?" Tomás asked. "You said the same thing five days ago."

"That's because we hadn't reached Tamaulipas yet. We've crossed four states already. Just this one more."

"And then what?"

"Enough. You don't talk back to me." If Miguel had done the same as a young boy, his father would have whipped him for days. "Don't make me regret bringing you." It hadn't even been his idea. When he had lost his job and decided to go north, his wife insisted he take their son along.

"Two of us can stay at my mom's house, and then we don't have to worry about rent," she had said, referring to herself and their seven-year-old daughter. "But three of us, and when Tomás can already work . . . we all have to do what we can."

His son had been more excited about the trip than he cared for. To Tomás, el Norte was mythical, a land where everything was brand new and even the dogs got clean water to bathe in.

"That's not why we're going," he had said, explaining that the toys and clothes his aunt and uncles sent were luxuries. If they had really wanted to help, they would have sent cash, cans of food.

All those pretty gifts they could do without, and they had done without, ever since his sister wrote that things had gotten harder because she had lost one of her jobs.

One of her jobs. Even the women get them like they're handouts, he thought.

They turned right at a narrow, dusty road ahead and eventually came upon a barbed-wire fence that said "PROPIEDAD PRIVADA." Someone had clipped a hole wide enough for a dog or a small child to slip through.

"Quickly," the coyote said. "Over or through."

Miguel went first—climbed to the top, then jumped to the other side. He turned and extended his arm for his son to follow, but instead the others made their way, first the little girl, then the women, and only when the other man in the group insisted that Tomás go ahead of him did his son crawl through the dirt like a possum.

"You stay by my side next time," Miguel said. These people, with their desperate eyes and fear-filled whispers, were not people he would trust.

# CHAPTER 5

## June 2014

There were clouds that hung in the sky unnoticed, and clouds whose shadows crawled over the earth's surface, blocking out the sun. Isabel watched the ocean turn gray as she stood chest deep in it. The salt twinged her cracked lips, and she had to blink each time a wave kissed her face.

She let herself sway along with the current and climbed onto Martin's back. Monkey, she liked to call it. On days the ocean didn't pull their bodies apart, she would attach herself—legs wrapped around his waist, arms over his shoulders, cheek pressed against his upper back—and they would stand together in the water, weightless.

The moment passed as quickly as the clouds, stretched apart in the sky like a spiderweb. They had driven an hour and a half from McAllen to South Padre cloaked in the last bits of dawn, giddy as teenagers. Last night, Martin's office had flooded from a busted pipe, and with Isabel working 4–10 shifts at the hospital, they had found themselves with a wide-open Friday. *"Freeee-day,"* Martin had sung, sweetly into her ear. He had packed everything—towels, chairs, cans of soda in a chest full of ice, with ham-and-cheese tortas at the top, a bag of chips, and a soccer ball she was sure they had never used. All Isabel had to do was put on her bathing suit.

The island was nothing new to her. It'd been her family's weekend-RV spot before the divorce, the place where she learned to swim. It'd been her college friends' spring break mecca, the place where, at twenty-one, she had first bungee jumped from a crane two-hundred feet in the air, making the giant-shark entrance to the souvenir shop look tiny.

Still, when her feet touched the sand this morning, she marveled at the surprise of it.

"This is the last thing I expected to do today," she said.

Martin kissed her elbow, which was just below his chin. "I told you we'd have more days like this. A promise is a promise."

To their left, in the distance, was the pier where Martin had proposed. It hadn't been as empty as it was now, but the few tourists and fishermen present had been kind enough to pretend not to notice, and so the moment had remained private instead of slipping into spectacle. She remembered how, when Martin got down on one knee and even before she saw the ring, she worried it would fall through the planks of wood. She had gotten down on her knees, too, because she had wanted to see him eye to eye, and she'd cupped her hands beneath his, as if water might slip through his fingers.

"I never took that literally," she said now.

"I know. But if we made time before we can make time again."

He made it sound like something they could replicate, something not at all finite.

They walked back to their towels. It was so hot that in the time it took for them to eat their sandwiches, the moisture evaporated from their skin. The sand was firm, packed so densely that Isabel's foot cramped as she tried drawing her name in it with her toe. Birds loitered just a car's length away from them, each keeping watch with one eye for stray crumbs. By early afternoon, they were surrounded by island kids still in their school clothes, middle-aged tailgaters celebrating early happy hours, and leather-skinned retirees who had left their condos with nothing more than a mat to lie on.

Soon, she was hungry again, and just like that, Isabel decided she was ready to go.

In the car, Martin's phone indicated several missed calls and voice-mail from an unknown number; the notifications stacked one on top of the other.

"Probably a telemarketer," he said, dimming the screen. "Play them, if you want."

She resisted. If it were an emergency, whoever it was would text. They stopped for fish and chips at a dockside restaurant on their way off the island. It wasn't until they had been on the highway for nearly an hour, close enough to home and all the routine that came with it, that she began playing the messages on speaker. The first was a young, deep voice in Spanish, likely a wrong number.

"Play the next one," Martin said.

It was a variation of the first. "*Tío. I'm here. In McAllen. They said to call you when I got here, to pick me up.*"

The next, more urgent. "*I'm right off the expressway and Second Street. At a store called H-E-B. I'm in jeans and a dark blue shirt with a tiger on it.*"

The last, as if it had only then occurred to him to say, "*It's Eduardo.*"

"Shit," Martin said. "How could nobody tell me?"

"You know who it is?"

He switched into the left lane and asked her to replay the last voicemail. He was speeding before the boy could repeat his name. "It's Sabrina. Her son, I mean. I haven't spoken to him since his thirteenth birthday, but that's him."

She tried to remember which one Sabrina was, but it had always been difficult with Martin's family. There were so many aunts and uncles, she could never keep them straight, and even more who were back in Mexico whom she had never met.

"Sabrina is—"

"My aunt, on my father's side."

"Omar's sister?"

He was too focused on weaving through traffic to answer right away. "We'll figure this out," he finally said, and only then did the possibility begin to dawn on her. Behind them she could see the sky was nearly black and misty along the horizon. They had left the beach just in time to avoid the storm.

The parking lot of the H-E-B was clogged with a five-o'clock rush of cars, all idling as customers popped in for last-minute groceries before the weekend. Near the back of the lot, a police tower was perched atop a white crane that lifted it into the sky. It didn't look big enough to fit more than one or two officers, and there was no way to see inside with its black-tinted windows. Isabel had never given it much thought—she assumed they kept watch for drug dealers or petty car thieves—until now.

"How could nobody tell us?" Martin said again. He stopped at the outdoor furniture display on the outskirts of the market, where a black fence laced with vines cordoned off the sales section. Behind it, once she looked closely enough, was a boy. A teenager, perhaps. His cheeks and forehead looked burned, and parts of his clothing were torn. When he saw Martin get out, the boy picked up a large bag off the ground and darted for the car. There was barely time for the two to hug or say hello before he scooted into the back seat. If he saw Isabel, he didn't let on. He pulled the seat belt out from underneath him, brushing it aside as if it were a nuisance.

"You have to put it on. It's the law here," she said in Spanish, louder than she had intended. He gave her a startled smile. "Do you want a Coke? We have some in the white cooler behind you. There's a sandwich, too."

He reached for them and mumbled thanks. Through the rearview mirror, once they had stopped at the exit, Martin finally introduced them. Without staring too much, she tried to take him in; he was full of scrapes and bruises, and she wondered how soon they might be able to get him to her hospital.

"What time did you arrive?" she asked.

"Two, three hours ago."

She nodded. In the ER, when a child like him arrived conscious, she would ask his name, the year, his birthday, whether or not he had brothers or sisters. She learned long ago that asking the date or what town they were in was too specific. If the child couldn't say, there was no way to tell if he had a concussion, was disoriented, or just didn't know. She didn't ask any of these questions now, afraid to get real answers. She turned away and gave him his privacy.

"Does your mom know you're here?" Martin said.

Eduardo wrapped him arms tighter around his belongings. "Not yet. But it was her idea. She told me to call you."

"We'll call her, then. When we get to the house." His tone was steady, and his voice, slow; a cadence Isabel recognized. Martin had a tendency to hold the air inside of him whenever he was trying to remain calm.

When they got to the house, Eduardo asked to use the shower. Though they were only a few steps from the bathroom, Martin placed his arms over the boy's shoulders and walked him to the door. Isabel brought him two fresh towels, a bar of soap, and a set of Martin's clothes that were on the small side. The shower hissed and the plumbing crackled as it pulsed through the walls. Still, Isabel and Martin kept their voices down, their bodies huddled close in the corner of the kitchen.

"I wish they'd called," Martin said.

"What does it matter now?" She hadn't meant to snap at him, but he had been repeating himself since they had gotten the first message. "We just need to talk to his mom," she added, rubbing Martin's arm as she spoke.

"He must've left months ago."

Months ago, Isabel had treated a teenaged girl and her six-year-old brother for dehydration. They had spent more than a year hopping the trains, trying to cross not one, but three borders from Honduras to Texas, and were detained and sent back more times than the boy could remember. She hoped Eduardo hadn't tried to ride atop The Beast, too, but she didn't mention this to Martin. Instead she started a pot of coffee, while he searched the drawers for the little phone book with his family's numbers.

"It's been so warm this summer." Outside the kitchen window, in the yard next to theirs, the wind spiraled a gust of dry dirt into the air, and the setting sun colored the sky blood orange. She thought of Eduardo's burned cheeks, how the baby fat on his face seemed misplaced on his skeletal body. "How many miles between here and there?"

A pause, and then the frantic, manufactured click of fingertips tapping a touchscreen. "Six hundred seventy-three miles," Martin said.

She took a deep breath. "Remind me again. Sabrina is the middle one?"

"The youngest. Of the seven, and the only sister."

She tried picturing the family tree. Martin's paternal grandparents were buried in McAllen, though he had never expressed interest in visiting their graves. All she knew about Sabrina was that she was the only one of his father's siblings he had ever met. "Wait . . . that makes Eduardo your cousin, not your nephew."

"I'm old enough to be his uncle. That's how he sees me. That's what he calls me. You know how it is."

"Not really. You're always assuming our families are so alike."

"Right. I forget."

"Forget what?"

"Nothing." He had found the phone book and leaned back into the kitchen counter as he flipped through its pages. "I know my family's messed up, but that doesn't make yours better than us."

"I never said that." She wished he would look at her so he could see how much she meant it.

"But you think it. Every time people ask you where you're from, and you laugh and say your family's been here since Texas was its own country."

The shower shut off.

"It's a joke. You know that's not what I mean."

They could hear Eduardo's small movements in the bathroom; the scrape of the shower curtain being pushed open, the rustle of a towel against wet hair. Martin lowered his voice and pulled her close. "I'm sure everything will make sense after we've talked to his mom."

"Ready?" he said when Eduardo came into the kitchen.

He dialed the number and pressed the phone to his ear, then pulled it away to check the screen. He pushed end and dialed again. When that didn't work, he began turning the pages of the little book again. "This is the number, right?"

Eduardo shook his head. "That's the restaurant. She had to close it years ago." He scribbled another number in the phone book, in handwriting that made him seem far younger. "That's our neighbor."

They tried it three times, but no one picked up. "We'll just try again later. No big deal."

She wished Martin hadn't said that. He was a terrible liar.

"We would've called sooner, but my mother didn't want to worry you."

"It's fine," Isabel said.

"The important thing is, you made it here safe." Martin embraced him, and the sides of their heads came together, their bodies stiff and unyielding.

It occurred to her, as he asked after Eduardo's mother as if he had seen her only yesterday, that this was the baby Martin had held when he was just a newborn. Martin would have been seventeen then, the first and only time he and his sister visited Michoacán with his mother.

Isabel remembered the trip well because when they got back, Claudia had shown her the pictures of them playing with Eduardo. She told Isabel all about their aunt, who was unwed and had just given birth to the child of a man who had abandoned her. She said their mother tried convincing her to come to the US, but she refused. *"My home is here,"* Sabrina had said, over and over. That was fifteen years ago, not long before everything between Claudia and Isabel changed.

"You must be tired." She searched Eduardo's light green eyes, glistening like marbles against leather, and tried to see herself and her home through them.

"We have an extra bedroom where you can rest up," Martin offered.

*Rest up,* she thought. The words seemed newly foreign. Rest up before you're on your way again? Rest up in this extra room that might become yours for nights, weeks, years?

There was so much to discuss, but it wasn't yet the time. As a nurse she knew trust was earned not by the words she said, but by silencing those her patients didn't want to hear. How and why things happened, how they would deal . . . these were things they eventually shared of their own accord. The patients who told her everything were the hardest to say goodbye to. *"I like you, so I never want to see you again, got it?"* she would say. They would always laugh as they left.

Without staring too much, she tried to assess his wounds. "I have bandages and ointment in the bathroom. Why don't you help me set up the room, and I'll clean you up?"

She led Eduardo down the hall and stacked the first-aid kit on top of the clean linens. He offered to carry them as they made their way to the guest room.

It was a simple ten-by-ten-foot space, with nothing new except the carpet, which the previous homeowner had replaced. Since they hadn't had guests yet, this room was their last priority. The walls were painted beige, and the mattress stood naked in the center of the room, on a metal frame that jiggled if you tossed around too much.

"It's not—" She stopped herself. Maybe this room *was* much, compared to where he had been staying before. "It's not every day we get guests, so we haven't had a chance to make the bed or anything."

Placing the comforter and first-aid supplies on the floor, Eduardo tossed the fitted sheet over the mattress. They stood on opposite sides of the bed, watching as the linens filled with air, parachuting over its surface.

"My mom used to let my sisters and I jump on the bed to push the air out," Isabel said.

"Mine, too."

When they were done making the bed she asked him to sit.

"Roll up your sleeve for me, please?"

She warned him it would sting, but he didn't flinch. The cut was fresh but not deep. The blood had yet to dry so it looked bright and sugary, like a jam sandwich sliced down the middle. It ran about five inches across his triceps toward his elbow. Isabel cut a square sheet of gauze in half and asked him to hold it in place while she taped it against his skin.

"Are there any others?" she asked.

A nod. He rolled up his left sleeve and brought his hand to his shoulder, lifting his elbow toward her face. It was a small scrape, the kind that exposes not blood but white, stinging skin that refuses to heal. She dabbed it with hydrogen peroxide but said nothing as she smoothed on a Band-Aid. He turned around and raised the back of his shirt, exposing a gash similar to the first. Twisting his neck back, he looked at her face.

She simply nodded matter-of-factly and got to work. One piece of scarred skin after the other, he showed her the souvenirs of his journey. He kept his eyes on hers, looking for a reaction. When the fresh wounds had been tended to, he showed her the others: yellow-greenish bruises, weeks old, a spot of skin on his head where hair would never grow again, a half-torn toenail inching its way back.

Isabel knelt and held his bare foot in her hand, spreading the toes apart to examine them.

"It'll take a while, but it'll grow back," she assured him.

Eduardo shrugged. "The cops raided The Beast when it slowed down outside of Monterrey. Even took my shoes. I just ran. I didn't notice the nail was gone until I saw the blood on my sock. It didn't hurt," he added, as if to comfort her.

# CHAPTER 6

## MARCH 1981

Back home they called her gorda. Vieja. Fea. Because when your husband calls you these things in front everyone, you become the joke. And everyone loves to be in on a joke.

She almost wished he could see her now. This fat, old, ugly body, walking away from him. Walking for miles and days and weeks, crossing mountains and rivers, putting space between them that was even bigger than his rage. The only thing she regretted was missing the look on his face the day he would finally wake—probably well past noon, his face sticky from drool, his breath and sweat still dripping alcohol—and realize she had left him.

Finally. Gone. Basta.

It still hurt, though. Not just the gash in her abdomen, but the thought of him, this man for whom she had endured so much. It would have been easier if she had grown to hate him, but Marisol couldn't help that she still loved him. Most painful of all were moments when she missed him. When she would daydream that he was out getting groceries or flowers, instead of puteando like he always was, dipping himself in dirty women and then coming home to force himself on her, like she was nothing more than a toy for him, always open. And then, when she had blacked out a few times from his pummeling, thinking she would finally die, she would wish he would join her.

What kind of love was this? What kind of woman dreams of killing her man? Sometimes she would look at her daughter in fear that what she felt for her husband and what she felt for her child came from the same place. What if the devil inside consumed her, and there was nothing pure left for Josselyn? She would never forgive herself then. She would not become the worthless shit her husband said she was.

Except now, along this invisible trail, she wondered if there was no escaping it. For the first five days of their journey, they had taken three different bus routes. On the sixth, as she realized she needed to ration her money, they stopped at a church for food and rest. The nuns sent them off with full bellies, prayers, and two and a half gallons of water. Two gallons had been all she could carry, so she had to ask her daughter to carry the extra half.

On the tenth night, on the bus that would carry them halfway across the country, Marisol felt a man's body begin to push against her, his cracked fingers pulling at her scalp. Everyone was asleep, even Josselyn, who was curled under the blanket they shared. No one would have thought Marisol's cries beyond the ordinary, but she feared the struggle would wake her daughter into a nightmare she would never recover from. Quietly, like a beetle turned upside down, she writhed. She had at least learned quickness from her husband: when there's no protecting yourself, make it harder to catch you, to hurt you, to hold you down. This had backfired, obviously, the day her husband took a machete to her stomach. She had been lucky that he was drunk and too weak for the blade to penetrate more than her skin. A neighbor sewed her up and told her next time, the stitches wouldn't be enough to save her.

How could she have known that the next time, the attack would come not from her husband, but from some monster on that bus? How could she have known that all the strength she wished she had had years ago would finally manifest in the moving darkness?

It happened faster than she could process. Even now, all she could remember were the man's eyes, how in trying to pin her body down he had pulled the blanket away, and his hungry gaze had shifted to her daughter. And then how his eyes had felt, warm and rubbery, as Marisol pressed them deeper into his skull. No one stirred as the man stumbled away from them, stunned and in pain. Sometimes she wondered if she'd dreamed it, this nightmare still beating in her chest.

That had been the first ten days of their journey. Now, with the desert stretched before her, time sank back, stagnant.

"Mamá, I'm bored," her daughter said, tugging at the old shirt she'd tied around her waist. This had been Josselyn's chief complaint since they had left. Not, "How much longer?" Not, "I'm thirsty," or, "I'm scared," or, "When will we eat?" Josselyn was only eight and already wise beyond her years. Her greatest pain came not from hunger or danger, but from having nothing to do. Perhaps her daughter was right. Perhaps pointlessness was the most life-threatening of all. To live but have no purpose. To exist without being visible. To leave everything you've known and risk everything leaving you.

She looked down at the ground. Her ankles and calves were swelling. Her feet felt as if they could burst out of her canvas shoes. All she could hear were her own breaths and gasps.

"I know," she told Josselyn. "Let's. Play. Which. Nopal. Loves. Me. More." Each word was suffocating.

Her daughter's face brightened at the mention of their favorite game. Even the woman walking a few feet apart from her, the one who had joined their group just a few days ago, smiled. The woman's name escaped her now, but the kindness in her eyes had become familiar.

"Me first, me first," Josselyn said.

The child's steps turned into skips the closer she got to the nearest cactus. It was a short, stubby-looking thing. Not like those tall, tree-like ones depicted in cartoons. The prickly green disks sprouted in clumps. She pointed at one that was asymmetrical: two half-circles stuck together like conjoined twins. One had grown taller and thinner, as if trying to stretch away from its chubby partner.

"This one loves me a little," Josselyn said. A few more steps forward, and she waited for her mother to catch up. The rest of the group was far ahead of them, close enough to stay in their sights, but not within earshot.

"This one . . ." She bent close to a prettier one now. The shape was almost right, but its skin was cracked and beige. ". . . loves me more."

"This one loves me not at all," she said a few seconds later. They had come across a plant that looked like it'd been run over. It had been torn in half, and now each side was twisted in opposite directions.

Marisol smiled and told her daughter to keep looking.

Josselyn shrieked, so loud that the coyote turned and yelled back at them to keep quiet. The sun had started to rise, and the sky was between darkness and light now, not bright enough for them to see much, but not dark enough to hide their shapes against the horizon.

"This one loves me most!" Josselyn said, victory in her loud whisper. The nopal she had chosen was a perfectly shaped, perfectly undamaged heart.

# CHAPTER 7

Eduardo slept. Though he said he didn't need to, his body knew better than he did. Isabel left the door ajar and walked quietly to her bedroom, where she found Martin on the bed with his laptop. She sat next to him, and he looked up, startled to find her there.

"Thanks for taking care of him." Martin placed his hand over hers, then covered his face with the other, stretching his cheeks and bottom eyelids. "I'm sorry you had to deal with it."

"*We're* dealing with it," she corrected, thinking of his earlier comment about their families. His thanks was not the best substitute for an apology, but then again, he had ignored the fact that she had snapped at him not even minutes before. "It's been a long day. Why don't you turn that off and we'll go to bed?"

He shook his head and turned the screen toward her. Its white light made her eyes sting, but when they adjusted she saw that he had several tabs open: mostly immigration resources, but also a pediatrician's website, and Martin's old high school.

"This is all papers and lawyers and"—he scoffed in disbelief—"that same, constant fear, all over again."

She thought he was overreacting, and it made her feel like a decision had been made without her. "This isn't permanent. Let's just wait till we've spoken to the neighbor. Tomorrow."

He took a deep breath and held it. "The neighbor's line is dead. I didn't want to say anything in front of Eduardo."

"So we try the other ones," she said, sitting up on her knees. "What about all the cousins and aunts and uncles in that phone book? I've seen how thick it is. You can't tell me Sabrina's is the only number."

"It's mostly addresses, or phone numbers for my mom's side. On my dad's, there was only the one number to Sabrina's restaurant. They almost all worked there. If it really closed, then I don't know where they went. I don't get why nobody told me."

"When's the last time you spoke with any of them?"

He took off his glasses and massaged the bridge of his nose. "The point is, he has no one else. We're it."

It was like she'd been caught in some twisted game of tag, and now everyone had left the field, tired of playing.

"I'm so sorry, Isa. But we can't just turn him away."

"I never said that."

"Then what? I know this isn't what we planned . . ."

She needed him to stop talking like this.

"Let's just give it a few days. Things have a way of working out."

When Martin said nothing—just went back to his computer—she curled onto her side and listened for a lull in his typing that never came.


It didn't matter that Eduardo barely woke the next day. It gave them the illusion of calm, but it only lasted until late in the afternoon, when Martin and Isabel realized they had to go in to work early on Monday, and they couldn't leave him alone.

They called Elda, never expecting she would say yes. They thought she would send Omar and his entire family to hell, but her curiosity got the best of her. "Sabrina sent him? After all this time?"

"You'd think she doesn't believe me," Martin said, recounting the conversation to Isabel. "Like she swears I picked up the wrong kid."

"But she'll watch him?"

"She and my sister will be here first thing tomorrow."

Isabel felt her stomach wind itself into a small knot. It stayed that way all evening and into the early morning, when they all found themselves crowded together in the hallway to say hello.

"Look at you, taller than your mother now," Elda said, brushing off the formalities. She embraced Eduardo slowly, as if worried she might scare him away. When Claudia only extended her right hand to him, Elda said, "The last time you saw Eduardo he was just a baby. Chubby, always giggling. You cried when it was time to leave."

"I don't even remember." Claudia shook his hand and shot them a sarcastic, tight-lipped smile. There were some things the years hadn't changed a bit.

By contrast Elda was a daily revelation. For the first time, Isabel was seeing her as a person and not just as her friend's and husband's mom. She had a quick, urgent energy about her, never spending more than a second or two on any decision. Nearly sixty, she wore a variation on the same ensemble every day (black, flowy pants and a gray blouse with a matching cardigan) and spent her weekdays at the movies with friends or teaching free financial literacy classes at the library. Since she had retired from the school district, the only invitations Elda ever turned down were from men interested in more than friendship. "Love's too complicated," she once told Isabel. "It's a young people's game."

Elda had arrived with a reusable bag full of puzzles, snacks, and books that she emptied out on the living-room table. "For later. But first, tell me." She led Eduardo to the couch. "How's Sabrina?"

Isabel noticed she didn't mention any of Omar's five brothers.

"I don't know," Eduardo said. "Have you heard from her lately?"

They all shook their heads, and Martin offered to call again this afternoon. Elda stared at the boy sitting across from her, searching his face—for what, Isabel couldn't guess. It made her feel like she was a little girl again, an outsider trying to feel her way into the family.

They left him with Claudia and Elda in the living room while they resumed their morning routine, getting their breakfasts and lunches ready in a hurry. Through the partition in the kitchen, Martin told Eduardo about the new high school. The student population had outgrown its campus, so the older grades were moving into a new location this year while the intermediate and middle schoolers took over the original buildings.

"The new campus is beautiful, you'll see."

Everyone looked confused, unsure what to do with this information.

He turned back to his coffee tumbler. "The problem is, with the campuses so far apart, cars back up for blocks with parents picking up their kids. Soon it'll be traffic all day. Did you notice when we picked up Eduardo, Isa? They broke ground for more condos across from the H-E-B."

She had been too distracted, replaying Eduardo's voice messages, to notice anything at all, and she was surprised to hear Martin bring it up now.

"Who dropped you off?" Elda asked, with the gentle authority only an educator could carry in her voice.

"Some guy. One of the kids I crossed with, he had a friend who picked him up."

Elda stretched her lips into a delicate smile. "And before that? Did anyone bring you over?"

"You mean, like a coyote?" He shook his head. "Mom said we didn't have that kind of money, but it'd be fine because Omar knew the way. Or at least he did, before we got separated."

"Omar?" Claudia said. The way she said his name made it sound like an accusation.

Isabel shut off the faucet and left her dishes in the sink, noticing that Martin, too, had grown quiet. All this time and Omar never once mentioned him. She imagined him smiling that mischievous grin that always seemed to know more than she did.

Elda crossed her legs, sinking further into the couch. "When was that? The last time you saw him."

"I don't really . . . I dunno. A while ago. We got separated. I tried looking for him. I got off the train and went back."

"It's okay," Isabel said. She had moved close to him, but stopped short of placing her hand on his shoulder. "There was nothing you could've done."

Elda cleared her throat and excused herself, mumbling something about the restroom while Claudia followed. But the hallways concealed nothing. They heard Claudia ask Elda if she was all right, and they didn't bother to keep their voices down as they began arguing in English.

"*I'll be fine. I just wasn't expecting this, that's all.*"

"*You don't have to do this, Mom. You don't owe him anything.*"

"*We can't just leave him alone.*"

"Why not?" A voice, a different version of it, caught everyone by surprise. "I can take care of myself," Eduardo said. He spoke louder in English, as if compensating for keeping it to himself for so long.

"I didn't realize . . . when did you learn to speak English?" Martin said.

"Omar taught me. After I started school he said it'd be good for me." His accent was thick, but there was no hesitation in it.

"He was with you all this time?" Claudia said.

"Just since I was little." He shrugged as if it wasn't a big deal. "Not all my life. But most of it."

Elda marched back into the room, her face bright red as she packed up the books she had brought. "Of course. That makes sense. I assume he taught you to read, too?"

He nodded. Isabel and Martin exchanged quiet looks of panic; they were already running late, and there was no way either of them would get the day off so last-minute.

"Good," Elda said, gathering her purse. "We'll go to the library and get you some books in English. And you two? What are you still doing here? You'll be late for work. Go."

Isabel had left in a daze that clung to her all morning. At the hospital she could think of little else but Elda, Omar, and Eduardo. They were like a light she kept dimming as she sprinted across the ER—focusing on paperwork, making sure she didn't write Bed A when she meant Bed B—then switching back on in moments between the chaos. By noon she was on her second medication error report of the day when a coworker suggested she take an early lunch break. Isabel made her way to the cafeteria and dialed Elda's cell.

"How's it going?" She tried to keep her voice down.

"Oh, we're just out and about. I thought we'd get a burger or something."

Right away she knew something was wrong. Elda was never the type to speak ambiguously.

"And how's that going?"

"Great. We're just . . . we'll probably be another couple of hours or so." A tiny, exasperated breath escaped her, a moment's hesitation.

"Elda, what's wrong? What happened?"

"I just . . . Isabel, I don't know where he is. We went to the library. We dropped Claudia off at work and went for burgers. One minute I get up to grab our food, and the next he's gone."

As she sped from the hospital to the burger stand, Isabel's mind raced. He had been kidnapped. Arrested by ICE. He had decided to run away. He had gotten distracted, wandered off, and couldn't find his way home. He had been killed, and soon all they could hope to find was a body. There would be canines and neighbors volunteering to search and Isabel would not even have a picture of Eduardo to guide them.

She arrived just as Martin did, and they decided to split up, reasoning that he couldn't have gotten far on foot. Isabel would check nearby stores while he checked the professional offices across the street. Elda would circulate the neighboring homes in her car.

"It's going to be okay," Martin told her.

"We're wasting time just talking about it."

"My God. And we can't even call the cops," he said, clutching her hand as they said goodbye.

For the next hour and forty-five minutes, Isabel wandered the aisles at Marshalls, then checked every tent and sleeping bag on display at the sporting goods store. She charged through the automatic doors at Michaels and came up with nothing but the smell of potpourri stuck in the back of her throat. By late afternoon, she could think of only one other place there was hope.

Isabel drove home without telling anyone. She pulled into their empty garage, pushing back tears that turned her words into whimpers. "You're okay, you're okay," she said to herself, to Eduardo, to Omar if he was listening.

The house carried a heavy solitude, and as she made her way to the back-door patio, she got the sense that it no longer belonged to just her and Martin. Her breath caught at the sight of Eduardo's hunched-up silhouette against a lonely patch of grass in the backyard. He was hugging his knees, his head down in his crossed arms.

"Hey!" She rushed to his side and shook his shoulder, but he only looked at her with an expression she had seen many times on Claudia—like Isabel had gone slightly crazy and he couldn't understand why. "Are you okay?"

He scooted a few inches to his left, and she sat next to him. "I thought you and Elda had gone to lunch."

He nodded. "Is she back yet?"

"How long have you been waiting here?" She couldn't believe he didn't realize what he had put them through.

"Ten, fifteen minutes."

"Why didn't you both come back together?"

He pulled a couple of blades of grass from the ground and picked at them until they were confetti in his palms. "Because the police came," he said matter-of-factly.

"And? Did they do something to you?"

Again with that look. "No. But why would I wait around until they did?"

She studied his face, trying to make sense of what she could be missing. "Back home," she said, choosing her words carefully, "do you always leave when the police arrive?"

"Pretty much. You don't want to be around when trouble's starting."

"That's true. But what if you're with friends or family, and you get separated? How do you find each other?"

"Everyone knows you go home."

# CHAPTER 8

## MARCH 1981

*Remember this,* he thought. *Not the air that dries your insides, or the breaths that steal your life. Remember the timidity of the sun's rays, how they're barely kissing her face. How her beauty defies nature and her spirit is stronger than this desert.*

*How she will be the one who survives.*

The young man stretched his back, standing taller the more he repeated these words to himself. They had become his prayer.

"What do you think he'll do to the ones who can't pay once we arrive?" His wife's voice, soft but unshaken, was a welcome interruption to his thoughts.

"Why do you ask? We'll be fine. We have everything we need."

She sighed and smiled. "Ay, vida." It stunned him that even now, when the world felt like it had abandoned them, she could still talk as if this moment were small enough for just the two of them. "I wasn't thinking of us," she said.

"You shouldn't worry about things we can't control." He wrapped his arm around her shoulder and pulled her close for a quick peck on the forehead. It was a clumsy motion; they were still walking and their bodies collided gently like muffled wind chimes.

"And if I can't help it?" Her neck strained over his shoulder in the direction of the woman and her young child trailing behind. "She's so alone. And the girl reminds me of your sister. ¿No te parece?"

He shook his head. Ever since they had joined this group, he had been trying to convince himself it was just his imagination. Just the trickery of longing and sadness. His little sister looked nothing like the girl, but there was something in her energy, in how she sprinted and skipped and rested, then started up again, recharged.

"I don't know. Maybe. Maybe that's Sabrina in a few years," he said, knowing he wouldn't be around to see it. When they had said goodbye, he had promised to send for her when she was older. She had only cried and wrapped her arms around his leg, and though it had been days now since he had left, those first steps out the door still weighed on him.

"At least they have each other," he said, worrying that his words sounded selfish, not full of hope as he'd intended. "Like we do." But it was hard to pull hope from such thin air.

So many hours had passed and nothing had changed. Not the piercing foliage all around them, nor the plumes of dirt their feet kicked up as they moved. Not the sky, which still burned with the same fervor it had in the early morning. It was as if the earth were rotating beneath their feet, erasing any progress.

If not for his wife squeezing his hand every half hour or so, telling him, "Soon, mi amor. Soon," he would no longer have any sense of time. They could walk for the rest of their days, die among the barren rocks of the desert, and never know how old they had turned, how much life they had sacrificed for this new beginning. He had always thought crossing the border would be hardest, but now he suspected it was this, the in-between, the stretches of miles for the forgotten, where they could become lost but never mourned, or found but tossed back, turned away as if they had never arrived.

He tried to squeeze her hand back, but her balmy skin slipped from his grasp. Never would he have imagined needing distance between his own body and hers, but this was the cruelty of the desert: it could make you feel trapped when nothing but emptiness surrounded you.

"Toma," he said, handing her the canteen of water.

"I'm not thirsty. You drink."

"Please. If not for you, for our child."

She took the warm metal container but rolled her eyes at him. "You won't be able to use that forever, you know."

"More reason to use it now." He slowed and rested his hands on his knees, letting his head hang over them. When he looked up he saw her just a few feet ahead, waiting for him. For a moment he thought he would cry, but instead he gave out a parched sob that shook his body once, hard. He would never understand what his wife saw in him, but in moments like these he prayed that whatever it was, he would never lose it.

If Elda walked the rest of the way one step ahead of him, Omar could traverse the length of five deserts put in front of him. Didn't she know he only lived to follow her? He willed himself to catch up and pulled her close again. For now, he could protect her and their child in one place and time. It was the only thing that kept him going.

# CHAPTER 9

Life was reduced to waiting. Worse, Isabel didn't know what for. Sometimes Martin's phone would ring, and she would run to it as if that call could solve all their problems. The sound of Sabrina's voice—though she had never spoken to her, only imagined it, sweet and polite with an undercurrent of irritation—would run through Isabel's mind as she answered and tried to anticipate what she would say. Other times, she would come home from work to find the guest bedroom unoccupied, the bed tidily made, and think, *He decided to leave.* Having worked past her ten-hour shift, the realization felt logical; she was away for such long stretches that something drastic was bound to happen in her absence. Always, she would dig her cell phone out of her purse to alert Martin that Eduardo had gone, only to find a string of unanswered texts.

at the grocery store with eduardo. need anything?
picked up eduardo & went to get the car washed. home in 20.

On nights they went to bed together, Isabel and Martin exchanged stories and conversations, trying to piece together the bits of Eduardo's past they had gathered. They pruned these anecdotes from him slowly, and never more than a few at a time.

"It was the gangs," Martin said one night as he sank into his pillow. "That's why he left."

"He told you that?" Despite her exhaustion, she lay completely awake now.

"I asked if he wanted to call any of his friends. He said most of them are gone. One was beat so bad his family fled to California to live with his aunt. Another ended up selling drugs for the gangs so they wouldn't kill him."

Another evening, as they both took a shower: "He found that picture his mother sent you years ago, the one of him waiting tables at her restaurant." It had been in a drawer with their old DVDs, and Isabel had told Eduardo to look for a movie when he had gotten bored watching Netflix. Martin and Sabrina had kept in touch over the years sporadically, on every other birthday or Christmas, ever since that one trip to Mexico.

"That's the last one she sent. He must've been eleven or twelve," Martin said, leaning his face into the steaming water.

"He said that's about the time things got bad. Sabrina didn't want people knowing they had family up north. They'd had neighbors get extorted by the gangs. Every month. Can you imagine?"

In this way, they began to get a better picture of him. When they were all together Isabel felt partly relieved and saddened, because she knew that Eduardo was safe but couldn't help wondering at what cost.

Some evenings they would stream old reruns of *Friends*. ("I only ever saw them in Spanish," Eduardo told them, and the novelty of the actors' real voices made him laugh at the oddest parts.) She would hear the low rumble of the train billowing past, just a couple of miles from their home, and she would find herself staring at the back of Eduardo's head, resting against the couch from his seat on the carpet, and she would try to place him there, sleeping and stirring on top of the train, but it was like coming up with a character and a situation for an improv show: too absurd to be believed.

At any given moment, she was either trying to heal his wounds, or worrying that they might pain him again in the future. The present seemed to pass through her like an aroma. Each night, she would think back to the day's events and realize she could only grasp a faint whiff of them, unsure if they were real or imagined. She would forget things she tried to remember and remember things she would rather forget.

Martin, on the other hand, seemed alive with an insatiable desire to make everybody happy. It made him fretful and impatient, unwilling to leave anything for later. If they were cooking and realized they were out of rice, he would rush out to get some. One evening, Eduardo asked about his job, and within minutes they were all in the car, headed to his office, Martin insisting that he see the game room the company had set up for their lunch breaks.

It was as if the stillness had gone out of Martin's life. Isabel often found herself struggling to catch up, exhausted yet grateful for the constant motion. Whatever she was feeling, she knew they couldn't both sink into it. She suspected this was Martin's attempt at buoying her.

"Do you think he's liking it here? With us?" she said one night. She still spoke about him as if he were visiting. They were in their closet, she dressing for a late shift while Martin loosened his belt and took off his shoes. They had gotten into the habit of speaking about him without mentioning his name. The light bulb had died yesterday evening, so they stood in the dim light of the sconces that trickled in from the bedroom, the amber warmth barely reaching them.

"I think expecting someone to like a place they had to go to, but didn't choose, is a lot to ask."

"He misses home," she said. "Of course." She had been so obsessed with making him feel comfortable, welcome, and safe, it hadn't occurred to her that what he longed for was already gone. Ever since she had found Eduardo in their backyard, she had convinced herself that this was where he wanted to be. "He seems to have fun with you, though."

Martin gave her a sideways glance. "It always feels like I'm forcing him to. Like he'd rather be left alone."

It wasn't surprising. These last few days she had come home from work at ten in the morning and found Eduardo still sleeping. He got up an hour, maybe two after her arrival, and seemed relieved when Isabel apologized that she needed to sleep. When she woke, he was often still in bed, staring at the ceiling as if he had given up on what to do with himself.

There was a time when she had felt the same. She had been just a few years shy of Eduardo's age when her father fell ill. At first he had asked Isabel not to tell her mother—he said he didn't want to worry her until they got the test results, but she knew he had been afraid she would try to gain full custody if he got sick. The doctors had started by ruling things out. It was not a viral infection, or a thyroid issue, or diabetes. When they finally learned he had a tumor that was causing Cushing's disease, they had rushed him into surgery. Isabel's mom had refused to take her to the hospital, so Elda had driven her instead. Claudia had brought her homework assignments on the days that she missed school, and when the doctors released her father, Isabel had refused to be away from him, not even on the Wednesdays or weekends she was supposed to be at her mother's.

"What are you going to do? Report it to the courts?"

Her mother hadn't bothered arguing with her, and that was when it struck her that her father's illness might not pass.

She had started taking the bus to school instead of having her father drive. In the afternoons, he would give her a hand with her homework while waiting for radiation treatments, quizzing her with flashcards or pretending to check her math problems. Two days before Christmas break, they learned the tumor was not gone. "And all those bills, taking a life of their own," her mother had said when she heard the news. The next few months of Isabel taking care of her father were grueling; the only thing more difficult than the endless days and nights was when they suddenly stopped. Everything felt empty. There was nothing more she could do for him. There was nothing more she could do.

Isabel felt the piercing sadness of those days rush back at her. "He's in mourning." *Of course.*

"Probably, yeah. Think of all he left behind."

"When's the last time he asked you to try calling Sabrina again?"

Martin took a moment to think back. "A week, maybe a week and a half."

There'd been a time when he asked and they tried calling every day, but the attempts had grown sparse as the weeks dragged on.

"He told me she would've called by now if she could," Isabel said. "When he was looking at the pictures."

"That's probably true."

"But it's the way he said it: 'If she could.' And if she can't, what does that mean? What could possibly keep his mother from calling all this time?"

They stood in the dark closet, afraid to acknowledge what was becoming clear.

"Then we're all he's got," Martin finally said. She had heard him speak like this before, but it was the first time she truly believed it. She thought of that day at the beach, how she'd stood by the shore with her arms around Martin's waist. It'd amused her then that her feet had sunk deeper into the sand with each passing wave. Now she thought, *This is all we'll have left of it, that sinking, paralyzing feeling.*

He put his arms around her, and she curled into his chest, making herself small enough for him to rest his chin on top of her head. She felt him nod as he said, over and over, that they would be okay.

When she got back from work the next morning, she found a note from Martin next to her sink: a list of child psychologists he had narrowed down to two, and the name of an immigration lawyer a coworker had recommended. She stepped into the closet to change out of her scrubs and was startled by how bright it was now that Martin had replaced the bulb.

# CHAPTER 10

## March 1981

"This isn't a walk through Disneyland," the coyote said. "Pick up the pace." He looked at Elda when he said this, and she knew he hadn't directed it at all of them. He passed her and Omar and began hurrying toward the migrants behind.

To the little boy and his overprotective father, she heard him say, "¡Ándale!" To the little girl and her mother trailing them, she heard him whistle as if they were cattle. The sky was not yet completely dark, but already the ground looked like a black sea. He called them over silently, urgently, with a flashlight that he waved over his head twice. From that distance the woman's body was just a round figure that limped along; her daughter, by comparison, was spry. She was a ball of energy orbiting her mother.

Once they all caught up, the coyote didn't stop walking. "See those lights?" He pointed at a lone shining beacon above the horizon. She thought it was an early evening star. "That's the other side of the border."

She squeezed Omar's hand, letting the air empty out of her. For a moment she thought she would cry from the relief. It was so close. So close.

"That's our checkpoint. If you can't get there in the next two hours, the truck leaves you. It doesn't wait for anybody. Understand?"

They all nodded, and she looked down at her feet, swollen in her once-blue shoes. They looked like a pair of sponges left to soak too long in the water—whether this was from the walking or the pregnancy, she couldn't tell. Before they had left, Elda's mother had tried to tell her everything she would need to know about bringing a child into the world, but they'd had so little time.

*"You'll grow slowly, and then all at once."*

*"Remember how you used to blow bubbles into your drink through a straw? That's how the first few kicks will feel."*

*"After you give birth, every inch of you will be exhausted and in pain except for your heart."*

*"When he cries, remember your body used to be his whole world. Cherish the moments he cries for you, but let him go a little more each day."*

She had felt like a child then—felt, for the first time in years, a longing to stay protected in her mother's arms. But it was no longer safe there. Her mother admitted as much just hours after she had told her parents about the baby, and her father had stormed out of their house.

He hadn't said where he was going, but her mother knew in the way only wives know about their men. "He'll call the doctor and have him come in the dead of night."

This gave them only a few days. The doctor was a couple of towns over, and he visited their town only once a month, always in the last week, and he saw patients in a back room of the town's church. Mothers and children would stand in line overnight with bags of avocados or bunches of tomatoes to supplement their payment.

Elda couldn't accept that her father did not want her to have this child.

"With this poor excuse of a man?" he had shouted, pointing at the only man who had ever stood by her side and stood up to her father. He told her he would never give them his blessing to be married. They had been planning to leave ever since, but not this soon. Not before she had had a chance to say goodbye to her friends, to the few cousins she knew she could trust, and to her mother, who would have wed them yesterday if she could.

Instead, they were married on the fifth day of their journey, in a town 250 miles north of their birthplace, at a church that offered rest, a few warm meals to travelers, and countless prayers from the nuns.

*"May God always follow you, wherever you go."*

She looked again to the light. She no longer knew how much time had passed since the coyote had pointed at the horizon, nor how far they had come. There was no strength left inside her to walk faster.

No one spoke. Night had fallen, and the sky was pitch black; the moon, hiding behind dense clouds. They all followed the coyote's flashlight, which he pointed at the ground. Its dim circle shook with each step.

She heard rustling behind her and didn't know if it was someone in the group or an animal. She felt scratches at her ankles and wondered if she had brushed up against a plant or a rock. When the wind picked up, she turned and expected it to be a car coming after her.

Sometimes she heard the sound of running feet, and she knew they didn't belong to anyone in their group.

Twice she thought she heard people's voices, could sense the speakers were far away. She pretended not to hear them and hoped they were doing the same.

Finally, they reached the river. She sank into the cold water, quiet as a lone raindrop, until the ground disappeared beneath her, and all there was left to do was swim.

She could sense that this part of the journey was the most critical. It was in the way the coyote mimed to them, uttering not even a whisper when hours ago he would have shouted. In the way she could see nothing, and therefore felt like she was nothing, traveling through nowhere. There was no longer any going forward or back. Not to the home she had left. Not to the place she was headed. Yes, they were deep in the border now, a place so dangerous even maps had no names for it. She pictured them all then, tiny black dots blending into a thick-lined border.

Even crossing and reaching the first checkpoint—two large hatch-backs parked miles from the towering light that had been guiding them—did not assuage her fears, but rather confirmed them. She had not been cold for long (the air sucked her clothes and bones dry), but still her body trembled.

"In, everybody in. Three here and there," the coyote said. He waved the little boy in the direction of the girl and her mother, and they squeezed into the trunk of an old four-door car.

The boy's father didn't protest, only mumbled something about the gorda taking up enough room for two grown-ups.

"You three in here," the coyote said.

Up close, the trunk seemed too small for even one of them. She looked down at it, hesitating.

"What are you waiting for, tía? Room service?"

Omar pressed close to the coyote now. "Some respect, please." But the man was too busy clearing out the space to listen.

She climbed in first, her husband behind her, and lay on her side. If she closed her eyes and let her body surrender to the exhaustion, she could pretend she was sleeping.

"It's okay. The worst is behind us now." His words landed warmly on her hair, but he had said them so many times now.

She felt the car dip abruptly with the added weight, felt the space around them constrict now that a third body had joined. Before she could even attempt to turn her head, a blanket fell over them. It was thick and itched her arms. It made her breath bounce back at her face.

Somebody slammed the door shut over their bodies, jolting them toward the ground and back up again. Outside, all sounds were muffled. Inside, their hearts and lungs pounded. The car started, and they began moving. The vibrations of the engine seeped into her body, aching like a million little needles.

It seemed useless to pray. Who protects the invisible?

# CHAPTER 11

The trouble began in the fall. Summer was hazy; its heat evaporated any semblance of permanence. Even as Isabel and Martin tried to make Eduardo feel settled in, there was the illusion of him soon leaving.

The days became a perpetual trade-off of shifts. Eduardo was a teenage boy, but to them, he was a newborn. They took note of when and how much he ate, how often he slept, and how well. They tried to keep him entertained any time he so much as glanced in their direction. They rested only when he did.

"Is he still obsessed with that Sam Smith song?" Claudia asked one afternoon. She was never in town long enough to watch him, but she called from time to time to ask how he was doing.

"How'd you know about the song?" Isabel asked. He had been blasting it as if it were an anthem for days. It was a typical, desperate ballad, and the chorus was just the singer pleading someone not to leave, over and over.

"Mom's always singing the chorus. And then it gets stuck in my head, too."

"He'll get tired of it eventually," Isabel said, making her way to the laundry room.

"I hope. It's really annoying. And depressing."

"Well, he's going through a lot." She opened the washing machine and poured detergent in hurriedly, letting the water scorch her fingertips.

"I guess. I don't know how you do it."

"Well, lucky for you, you're never around." The lid fell forward and slammed shut, punctuating her words. It was the truest thing she had said to Claudia in years, and surprisingly gratifying. She tried imagining her on the other line: the shock and shame of it.

"It's just work is crazy right now." Claudia grew quiet, more subdued. "You know how it is."

"I sure do." It was hard for Isabel to stop, knowing she was in the right.

"I have to go. Tell Martin I said hi."

"Yup. Sure thing."

On her way back to her bedroom she stopped to ask Eduardo about the books Elda had lent him a few weeks ago. All his peers were reading from the same list that summer, and she had thought it would help him transition into his new school.

"I already finished them." In his right palm he squeezed a stress ball Isabel had gotten from the hospital. It was blue, with the logo for an antianxiety medication in white, and he kept his eyes on it as he spoke.

"Which was your favorite?"

The ball wheezed in his hands as he thought it over. "The short one." When Isabel didn't respond, he added, "I'll give them back to her. I promise."

It was ten till seven, and Martin would be home soon. She decided to change the subject and asked if he had any clothes that needed to be washed.

Between patient rounds and on her lunch breaks, Isabel often scoured the Internet for answers to questions it seemed no one had ever asked. Not even Google autopopulated the blank search bar when, in a moment of desperation, she typed, how to handle immigrant child's unaccompanied arrival. The list of lawyers and therapists was bookmarked on her browser, visited only online, because when they had finally approached Eduardo about it, he said he wasn't ready.

*Give him time* was the blanket advice. They did what they could to help him adjust, rarely giving much thought to whether or not they were adjusting at all. They could hardly see through the fog of their exhaustion. It wasn't that Eduardo had taken over their lives; it was like they had taken over someone else's, and no one was coming to reclaim it.

Two weeks before the new school year, they went to Target and bought Eduardo a backpack full of fresh pens and pencils, a stack of notebooks, a set of highlighters, and a three-ring binder. As usual, the total came out to more than Isabel had expected. It was the same crazy math that was taking her by surprise recently at the end of month when she saw the water bill, the electric bill, and the credit card statement.

In the car, Eduardo thanked them and said it was too much, that he didn't need so many school supplies. But Martin insisted.

"You're going to be a Green Jay. And a junior," he said, as if Eduardo needed reminding. Isabel had hoped the administrators would place Eduardo in tenth grade, a year behind his age group, but they hadn't felt it was necessary.

"We just want you to have whatever you need to feel ready," Isabel added.

He just stared out the window and chuckled as if he had remembered an old joke. "Being ready's like learning to swim without water."

"Worthless until you're drowning," Martin said. He took his eye off the road for a quick moment to look at Isabel. "It's something my father loved to say."

"Really?" It was the first time Martin had mentioned Omar since the day Eduardo went missing. She twisted in her seat to see if Eduardo also remembered. "Like when?"

Martin cut Eduardo off before he could answer. "Ever since I was little. He refused to put training wheels on my bicycle. Said I'd learn more from the fall than the safety."

Eduardo looked like he wanted to say something, but just then the railroad crossing down the road lit up, its bells and red lights going off in tandem. A group of joggers along the sidewalk bobbed in place, and Martin put the car in park. They all grew quiet, watching the train approach.

"Who can guess how many cars will pass?" Martin said. "I bet forty-eight."

Neither Isabel nor Eduardo felt like counting. It seemed the cars were being dragged, so very slowly, down the tracks. Out of the corner of her eye she saw Eduardo's head turn to follow them.

"Omar was right, you know. The first time we tried getting on the train together, I told him it was going too fast. He said the train would be gone by the time we were ready. He said the only right time to jump is when you think it's too soon." Eduardo rested his elbow on the door and his chin in his hand, his fingers stretched casually over his lips.

"We don't have to talk about this if you don't want to," Martin said.

Isabel unsnapped her seat belt, sending it flying across her chest and against the window. She shot Martin a perturbed look and turned to Eduardo. "But if you do, we're here to listen."

She could tell by the way his head moved that Martin had rolled his eyes at her. Eduardo turned away, which shouldn't have been surprising. Of course he would follow his uncle's lead.

"There's not much more to tell. That's it really." The train finished passing, its cars uncounted as the trio headed home.

In their bedroom, Isabel turned on the radio and waited for Martin to step into their bathroom. It was the point farthest away from Eduardo's room, and she didn't want to risk him hearing them.

"How could you shut him out like that?"

"I was just trying to make him comfortable."

She hated how innocently he said this. "You made yourself comfortable."

"Didn't you see him? The kid's torn up into little pieces." He rubbed his fingers together, as if he were sprinkling confetti over the bathroom counter. "Whatever happened with him and Omar fucked him up."

"He's not the only one."

"What the hell's that supposed to mean?" They were speaking in whispers now, quiet, calculated daggers.

"There's something you're not telling me. I'm not an idiot." When he didn't respond she thought of how much about him she didn't know, and it made her voice shake as she chose her words. "Until you can work through whatever issues you have with your father, you won't be able to help Eduardo. Not in any way that's meaningful."


In October the school began preparing for Halloween. Cheerleaders hung ghosts made from pillowcases on tree branches, and students lined the entrance with fake cobwebs. The long, narrow pickup area by the side of the building needed no such decorations; it was packed with cars, teachers, and students all seeming to know where they were going. Every time it was her turn to pick up Eduardo, just the sight of the campus filled Isabel with dread. She would spend the drive home asking him if he had learned anything new, or what homework he had been assigned—any question that didn't warrant a one-word response. There was no predicting Eduardo's moods. One day he told her that they were decorating his history classroom for el Día de los Muertos. His teacher had draped a band of marigolds over a fake gravestone and hung strings of papel-picado cutouts in pink, orange, and blue along the windows. He smiled and showed her the sugar skull he had made, but when she asked if they would be making altars, too, he just shrugged and stared out the window.

They asked Elda what she thought about his behavior, and she suggested he see the migrant counselor at the school. "Trust me. I worked with high school students for more than twenty years." (She always said this.) "His situation may not be exactly like the migrant kids'. But just because he's not missing months at a time to work the fields doesn't mean he's not struggling with fitting in, on top of everything else he's been through."

All Eduardo ever said was that he would think about it.

Eventually, Martin began emailing his teachers and cc'ing Isabel in all his messages, which were riddled with the type of urgent but nonchalant corporate clichés that made it easy for everyone to not bother responding. The one teacher who got back to them answered in short, unspecific anecdotes that weren't much help at first.

Eduardo keeps to himself, as can be expected for a new student, Miss Cantú wrote. A week later, I notice he seems more comfortable drawing attention to himself. And then, Mr. and Mrs. Bravo, it'd be helpful if you spoke to Eduardo about the right time and place for jokes. If he's not careful, I worry he could be expelled.

The next day, Isabel and Martin somehow managed to move their schedules and arrange a meeting with Miss Cantú in person. It turned out Eduardo had become the class clown. On a day the students were particularly rowdy, she had told them they were acting like misfits, and he took it as a cue to tell them that this was nothing, that his last teacher had gotten held up at gunpoint in the middle of a lesson and never came back.

"That crossed a line," Miss Cantú said. She was probably two years out of college but had the voice of a middle-aged smoker. "I told him next time, I'd have to report him for threatening a teacher. Gun violence is not taken lightly around here, and I won't have my students making up stories just for popularity points."

Like any parents would, they promised to speak with him, but they were more afraid that he might be telling the truth. That afternoon, they had him sit across from them in the dining room as they held each other's hands under the table. Martin's palm was sticky and dewy, but Isabel gave him a gentle squeeze and he exhaled.

"We spoke to Miss Cantú. She thinks you're lying to the class to get attention."

"Why would I do that?" Eduardo sat back in his chair and crossed his arms. His foot bumped into Isabel's as he spread his legs across the floor, and he mumbled an apology.

"We know you wouldn't," she said. "But maybe you just have to be careful about the things you tell people. Bringing up guns in school . . . it's not okay here. It can be taken the wrong way."

"That's funny. I thought the wrong way was holding a gun up to your teacher so you can kidnap a bunch of students and make them sell drugs for you. But I guess it's just talking about it that's wrong."

"That's not what Isabel meant. It's complicated."

She watched Eduardo pick at a dried-up grain of rice that'd slipped between the cracks of the wood. When he couldn't get it out with his nail, he took a pen out of his jeans pocket.

"No shit. Because one minute everyone's like, I'm too quiet, I should try to make friends, and the next no one wants to hear what I'm saying." He pushed the rice around with the ballpoint, hunched over as if he were writing.

"Miss Cantú says the students like you," Martin said.

"Yeah. They're always laughing at my stories. They think it's funny." The grating of the pen grew furious, and then it stopped as he lifted his head to look at them. The room was so quiet, Isabel could hear the silence ringing in her ears. She tried to put herself in his place, in a new high school with no friends and nothing but a classroom full of strangers who heard you, but didn't listen. It was not so hard to imagine, after all. Just a simple matter of remembering.

"Maybe you don't need a lot of friends," Isabel said. "Just one or two really good ones."

Eduardo raised his eyebrows and gave her an incredulous smile. "You think I don't try? What's the point, Tía? I'd just rather be alone than feel alone."

He excused himself, and they watched him slink away to his bedroom, as if he worried they might call him back and force him to sit across from them, studying him until some small part of him made sense.

# CHAPTER 12

## March 1981

Her body was begging her: rest. But the air was burning her lungs. She tried to lift her head from the rough surface of the car's trunk, thinking a new angle might get her more air. This only set off a wave of explosions in her vision; the darkness became peppered with dots of red and yellow flashes. They reminded her of buzzing bees, the way they trembled and disappeared. She tried chasing the flashes of light with her eyes, but each time her eyes moved, so did the light. It didn't surprise her. No one ever waited for la gorda.

"Please. Just for a moment. Please stop."

"¿Mamá?"

Marisol heard a voice from somewhere far away. She felt a tiny body press close. She tried to move her arm from under her, but it was tingly and so heavy, the effort was excruciating. Her body had begun to fall apart, just as she had feared. Her arm was a branch that had reached too far and snapped.

She knew what she had to do. *Pick it up. Pick it up with the other one before it's gone, too.*

"Mamá, I'm scared." The voice was persistent. It grasped at her shoulder and shook her whole body. Tears. Sobbing. She knew that was all it could be. When she was twelve she had watched her grandfather get buried in a wooden casket, watched as the thin plank of wood slid over his face, and she had tried to stop them, cried, *"But he's all alone!"* Even after her mother and aunts and cousins explained that death is not a sleep, but an awakening, she couldn't forget how perfectly sized the box had been, how neatly tucked away his body was, forgotten.

In the coffin he had lain on his back, hands over his abdomen. A tidily wrapped package, easier to send. It would be best if she positioned herself the same way, but when she tried to turn from her side onto her back, there was no space. *It's the wrong size. Oh God, it's the wrong size.*

A shriek. It was like a cat whining. "You're hurting me, Mamá. Please, I can't move." It sounded so much like her daughter. She wanted, more than anything, to comfort the sound, but she knew she couldn't. The voice was nothing more than the residue of her deepest longings, her only tie to a world that had slipped away.

"Please, Mamá. Please wake up."

And then, another voice, deeper, gruff, came from beside her daughter's.

"It's okay. You just have to stop crying. Just hold still and try to stay calm. Try to slow your breathing."

*Yes,* she thought, *this is a good idea.* She must go slowly, peacefully. Within moments the space around her shifted, and she felt the wall pressed against her back give way, just an inch. The box vibrated and hummed, as if pummeled by millions of particles of dirt. *All alone. Like I said.*

"Mamá, please." It was smaller this time, farther away. A spot of warmth the size of a hand landed on her arm, became a blanket as it traveled up and down its length.

Gently. Yes. This is how it happens.

"We're almost there, I promise. Just hold on a little longer." It was a whisper in her ear, and then it was quiet, because it was true.

*Not much longer.* The flashes of light stopped and the ground went still and the air left silently. She thought of her daughter. She let go.

# CHAPTER 13

## November 2, 2014

## Year Two: Cotton

There'd been death in the ER tonight, in the early hours past midnight, when the weekend partiers hit the road heading home with too many drinks in them. They trickled in slowly at first—the tipsy and clumsy who had broken an arm or hit their head—but once the bars closed and Isabel still had hours to go of her shift, the EMTs kept coming. The waiting room swelled with the stench of vomit and vodka; she barely noticed when the fluids spilled onto her clothes as she helped pump her patients' stomachs. She'd hoped this was as far as it went, but inevitably the criticals arrived. Tonight there were three, their bodies partly charred from the car that had flipped off the highway and burned.

When they lost the first patient, Isabel imagined the soul joining Omar's. She searched the mourning faces of the loved ones left behind in the waiting room. She could spot them by the criticals' items that they held in their hands: a bloody sweater, a purse, a torn hat. Their pale faces were drenched in tears and sweat. She wanted to believe there was still hope left for all of them, that soon Omar and all the night's lost lives would reappear.

It was nearly six when Isabel finally stumbled through the quiet of her house. She felt raw and sore. Her hair was dripping wet; she had showered at the hospital and rushed home. She grabbed a set of matches from the kitchen and stepped into the backyard.

When they had first closed on the house, Isabel had complained that the toolshed was wasted space; all the tools they possessed fit into a yellow toolbox. They were not a power-tool couple. They paid others to mow their lawn and repair appliances. Any furniture they had ever assembled came with the usual Allen wrench from IKEA. The toolshed was dark and musty, housing only hardware, a spare tire for Martin's car, and a pile of empty ceramic pots.

Which is why, since the middle of October, Isabel had been using this lonely appendage on her property to build an altar for her dead.

It was a small, understated tribute. At first, she had thought to make it for her father and Omar, but as she'd gathered remnants of their lives (black-and-white school pictures of her father, the silver pen he had used to write checks, a stack of Nancy Drew books he had read to her when she was a child) Isabel realized she had come up short of the equivalent for Omar. She had no pictures of him, and she didn't want to raise Martin's suspicions by asking. She had none of his personal belongings and no idea what he had enjoyed doing for fun.

In an attempt to mask her ignorance, she kept the altar vague and unspecific. Atop a large cardboard box covered by a green bedsheet, she had placed a couple of sugar skulls she had bought at a meat market down the street. A framed art piece from Bed Bath & Beyond created a focal point for the arrangement; in restaurant-style cursive against a chalkboard background, it read *A Father Is a Superhero Without the Secret Identity*. She'd filled a mug with coffee beans, rationalizing that all fathers enjoyed a strong cup of coffee, and by this same logic, the next day, she had bought a small bottle of whiskey.

She sat on the floor and scattered a set of candles across the altar, lighting a new match for each one. She was so dazed from the lack of sleep, that by the sixth candle she performed the task mindlessly.

"You know, some fathers also like cars and poker." Omar's voice didn't startle her this time; it slipped into the silence as if it were thoughts.

"How did you do that?"

He smiled; the edges of his lips and the corners of his eyes stretched toward each other, squeezing everything in between. "I'm not really sure. Did you ever have pet fish as a child?"

"A couple. Why?"

"When you bring one home from the store, you're supposed to leave the fish in its bag when you place it in the tank until it's acclimated to the new temperature. Remember?"

She nodded.

"That's the best I can describe it. You listen and you wait. You feel out the water until the moment feels right. Until you can jump in without the shock of impact."

"It's always a shock to see you," Isabel said.

"I'd say the same thing about you, dear." He tilted his head at her as if lifting an invisible hat. She returned the gesture.

"You didn't have to go through all the trouble." He waved his hand at the altar, taking in the forty square feet of space around them. "Or maybe you went through just enough."

"It wasn't easy. If Martin found out about any of this . . ." she said.

"I'm sorry. I shouldn't joke. It's kind. Very kind. I'm honored you would rest my memory alongside that of your father." Omar sat down next to her, leveling his eyes with hers, and she could tell he was being sincere.

"The two of you would've gotten along. It makes sense."

"Ah." He put his hands in his pockets, taking in the contents of the altar. "How long ago was it? When he passed?"

"Fourteen years," she said, without having to count. She had been keeping time since the day he'd gone.

"He was young then, when he died. And you, too."

She wanted to say the same thing about him, but she wasn't ready to change the subject.

"He was sick. I spent months trying to care for him, but he still—"

"You spent months. That's all that matters. You spent months knowing. If more people knew when a moment was a last—a last breakfast, a last kiss—we'd leave with less regret."

The problem was there had been too much knowing. Each time she would hold her father's hand, she would wonder if it would be the last time she felt his pulse against hers. They had compressed a lifetime of conversations and confessions into weeks: every bit of fatherly advice, every apology she could think of. When she had told him she still regretted once lying to him about going to the movies with a boy, he had only shrugged and said, "That wasn't you. That was youth."

Until he was gone, she had never known it was possible to feel too young and like she had aged a lifetime all at once.

"You'd hoped he would be here," Omar said. "And you got me instead."

"It's not that."

"It's not a bad thing. It means he's found peace, and that is so fragile. We have to let it rest when we get it. I'm sorry you're stuck with me, though."

"I'm happy to see you. I'm just baffled, by all of this." She gestured at the altar, trying to hide her disappointment.

"You, too? I thought between us, you were the smarter one."

"You're funny."

"Not enough to make you laugh. Last year, my jokes were faring much better."

"A lot has changed since then." Isabel reached for one of the candles, which had burned out, and struck a match to relight it.

"So it has."

"When were you going to tell me about him?"

"When was there time?"

She shot him a knowing look. "I was all ears. You're the one who didn't talk."

"I'd hoped he had already made it, last year. But when he didn't, I was afraid to assume anything."

"But you gave him our information. You could've warned us, at least."

"Sabrina gave him your number, not me. And I didn't realize family required warning."

"You know what I mean. We could've been more prepared."

"I don't believe in being prepared."

"So I've heard."

Outside the thin walls of the toolshed, the wind bellowed. It sounded like a storm, like south-Texas breezes always do—bigger than they are.

"How is he doing?" Omar asked.

"I have no idea." It was a truth she hadn't admitted until now. "I'd like to think he's better off than before, but . . ."

"He is. He might not see it, but it's true."

"I don't even know what that means. Sometimes I look at him and it's like staring at the ocean. I can't trust the surface."

"He's a good boy."

"Is that thanks to you? All those years you spent raising him?"

"Instead of Martin and Claudita?"

She sighed. "I didn't say that."

"I did. I spent half my life wishing I could change things. But why would they take me back? They won't even talk to me now that I'm dead. Or will they?"

She didn't have the heart to tell him things were probably worse than before. "Eduardo always has you in his thoughts." No sooner had she said the words, it dawned on her. "He looked for you for months, after you got separated. Does he not know?"

Omar shook his head. "It's not that simple. I told him if we ever got separated, we'd meet at the border. If he knew I was dead, would he have kept going?"

"You're right." She rubbed her eyes, trying to fight off the sleep that was finally taking over. Eduardo usually slept in on weekends, but Martin would be wondering why she hadn't crawled into bed yet. Lately, those few hours when their sleep schedules overlapped were becoming scarcer.

"Just wait here," she said, and she blew out the candles.

But when she walked into the kitchen to make a pot of coffee, she found Omar. He stood by the refrigerator, reading the grocery list stuck to its side.

"Please don't do this. You'll wake Martin and—"

"You said so yourself: he won't see me."

"It's not just that." She could hear her husband getting out bed, pushing hangers around the closet. Through the walls of Eduardo's room, she thought she heard the low bounce of voices. Had he gotten a new radio?

"You should give Eduardo some space today," Omar said. "He'll want some time alone with his mother."

"Sabrina?" She was only half listening as she began pulling cereal and spices for eggs out of the pantry.

"Yes. Seeing her for the first time will be difficult."

Isabel stopped, and her breath quickened. When she closed her eyes and focused in the direction of Eduardo's room, the noises became clearer. They were not just any voices, they were two: one calm, the other crying.

"What do I do?"

Omar shook his head, but then his eyes landed on the space behind her and lit up with pride. "My son."

But he had been right. Martin didn't see him or hear him. He looked only at Isabel, with the sweet nostalgia of reliving a moment that, at only two years old, seemed ages ago. He kissed her, and just for this moment, she wished Omar would leave. She searched the kitchen for him, and he was gone.

"Happy anniversary," Martin said, leading her back to their bedroom.

"Right now? But Eduardo—"

He shushed her and ran his fingers gently over her eyes. "Put your hands out."

There was the sound of tissue paper crinkling, and then a small container landed in her palms. Cold and grainy, it felt like a ceramic pot, no bigger than a tea kettle.

"Open your eyes," Martin said.

A single dark brown twig stemmed from black soil, with three white buds sprouting like miniature clouds. "Cotton flowers? They're beautiful."

"Second anniversary is cotton. I thought it'd be nicer than a T-shirt."

"I hope they'll grow here."

"I'm sure they'll thrive under your care." He gave her a long, soft kiss.

"Thank you." Her hands cupped the space below his ears and around his neck. If she just held on to him, she wouldn't have to face her father-in-law or the mourning child hiding a few walls down. She closed her eyes and took a deep breath. "Wait here, okay?"

They had planned to spend the day together; it was the first Sunday Isabel had gotten off in weeks. After she rested, they'd have an afternoon picnic at the park and go to an improv comedy show that evening. Martin had said they were both in need of a good laugh.

She stepped out of the bedroom, making sure to close the door quietly. Omar was lying face up on their couch, his hands placed on his abdomen.

"Omar . . . this just isn't the right time."

He stood. "I know. I'm sorry. But it's the only time I have."

"I know. But I'm so tired. And I can't just drop everything, not today. Either tell me what it is you need, or go. Please."

He thought about it. She could tell because he twisted his bottom lip between his fingers as he stared into the yard and considered. Just like Martin.

"Can we go somewhere else?"

It'd been nearly twenty hours since she had last slept, and her joints pulsed, begging for rest. But her curiosity pulled harder. She went back to the bedroom and told Martin she'd forgotten something at the hospital. She made it sound mysterious and like a surprise, even though his gift was hidden in her car.

"Can't you go later?"

"I'm up now. Might as well go before my energy crashes." It crushed her, how easily he believed it.

She gathered her keys and purse in the living room.

"Don't feel bad, mija. You did it out of love," Omar said. "And love is never simple."

She pretended not to hear this. "Where to?"

"Wherever you'd like. I'm tethered to you, remember?"

There was only one place that made sense today. On their way to the garage, out of instinct, Isabel headed toward Eduardo's room first.

"Give him his space," Omar said. She felt a warm numbness spread over her arm as he held on to her, holding her back.

The cemetery was teeming with life. She circled it twice before pulling into an empty stretch of curb by the main gate. Isabel was struck by how jumbled the gravesites looked—not perfect rows, as she had remembered, but scattered plots blooming like wildflowers with altars.

Children flew kites and chased each other while women passed out small plates of food. Others held still and knitted or read a paper, as if life were going on as usual.

She looked down the long, palm tree-lined road that led straight to the airport. An airplane soared just above them, and she thought of Claudia driving to and from work, passing the graves of her grandparents every week, probably without even a prayer.

"Do you come here often?" Omar asked.

She shook her head. "For a while, I thought of looking for you here. But then Eduardo told me what happened, and I realized you were probably buried in Mexico."

She didn't know why she had brought them here, and she noticed he didn't ask. The last time Isabel had been to a funeral it was her father's. She had been fourteen, and just a few days before, she and Claudia had gone to the mall to meet a couple of boys from school. They had tried on beer-bong hats at the gag store and joked about getting their ears pierced at Claire's.

"My dad would kill me," she'd said. The doctors had put her father into a coma four days earlier, and it was the first time she had left his side. Her mother had arranged for Elda to take her and Claudia to the mall, insisting that her father would want her to be happy if he were awake.

Isabel had pulled a neon necklace from the piercing display and turned the long plastic tube up and down. She shook it, expecting the lime-colored liquid inside to move, but it seemed to be frozen solid.

"He'd totally freak," Claudia had said.

She thought of her father and the tubes connected to the backs of his hands. It'd felt satisfying to watch the liquid drip and rush through the clear plastic, but Isabel always panicked as the droplets floated closer to his skin. She had wished he were see-through. She had wished they all were, so their bodies could have nothing to hide from anyone.

As the girls pretended to debate which body part they would pierce and the boys pretended they found any exposed piece of flesh hotter than any other, Isabel's dad had already died.

At the funeral, she sat next to her mom, trying to make out Claudia's and Elda's faces from among those of her relatives. She could barely see the polished wood of his coffin through the crowd of people gathered to see his body.

"My dad asked to be cremated," she said now to Omar. "He said a body is too heavy to carry."

"He was probably right, though I wouldn't know. I never got a chance to bury my parents." After a moment, an air of optimism came over him. "Maybe they're here."

They got out of the car and wandered through the cemetery at a steady, unhurried pace. Dry, brown leaves covered the ground but made no sound as Omar walked over them. Every once in a while, he stopped at a grave and studied it, like it was a painting in a museum. She tried to see what he saw, wondering if every grave was connected somehow, if they all existed on a plane that the earth could never fathom.

"Someone you knew?" she asked. He lingered longer than usual on a stone the size of a book.

"It's just the years," he said, shaking his head slowly. "This one had so few."

*Seventeen,* Isabel realized. The boy who lay here had died before Eduardo was even born. Omar walked for several more rows until he found his parents. He ran his fingers over their names in the stone, and Isabel looked away, wanting to give him some privacy.

"You haven't seen them? Where you are?" she finally said.

"I haven't seen anyone. It's not that simple, you know. Here and there. Them and us." He jutted his chin at the families celebrating. "I envy their dead, their peace."

They got back into the car, but she didn't start it. "What's it like over there? The rest of the days?"

For the first time since they had met, he seemed afraid, unable to look her in the eyes. "I don't know where I am. I'm just drifting. I think I'm here because I have nowhere else to go."

They didn't speak the rest of the way home. They got a red light at every traffic signal, and she felt the minutes stretch, wasted like rubber bands sent flying through the air. He sat staring at the dashboard, looking both embarrassed and disheartened. It wasn't until they were a couple of houses from home that she noticed the red car parked in her driveway. Isabel slammed on the brakes, startling Omar out of his muddled state.

"What happened?"

But it was too late. Omar grasped Isabel's arm at the sight of Elda, and she felt him reverberate against her skin like a pulse, so powerful it made it hard to breathe.

"Omar, please." He let go, and she saw that he had vanished. She found him outside the car, standing several yards in front of her, immobile.

Elda looked past him and waved, hiking a paper grocery bag up her hip. The sun danced with her hair as she stepped through the grass to meet Isabel.

"Oh, thank goodness. I was beginning to worry. Martin said Eduardo wasn't feeling well, so I stopped by to check on him. I thought you'd be sleeping."

"I've . . . been trying to." She worried Elda would hear her heart beating when they embraced, but it was like they had splintered into two worlds—Elda stepping inside the house, whispering so as to not disturb Eduardo, and Isabel following behind, watching Omar's image flicker on and off in her peripheral vision.

"Tell her I'm here. Tell her you see me," he said as they watched her unpack the groceries. "Isabel. Please."

But she couldn't speak. She couldn't bear how much the words would hurt Elda, how much her silence would hurt him. She could see clearly now that she had been wrong; it was not death that made him vulnerable; it was this love that had been his life.

Isabel's eyes stung as they filled with tears. "I'm so sorry, it's just too much." The day's exhaustion took over in an instant. She felt herself collapse and heard voices rush to her side. She couldn't tell them apart, couldn't make out Omar from Elda from Eduardo. When she finally woke, only Martin lay next her, and all the rest had gone.

# CHAPTER 14

## March 1981

Of all the moments for the baby to kick.

Maybe the baby, too, felt he was suffocating. Maybe like her, he was no longer feeling protected, but trapped.

"My love?" she whispered. When Omar didn't respond she called for him again, this time using his favorite pet name. "Mi vida." *My life.*

"Yes?" Right away she felt his hand back on her shoulder. The warmth of his breath, once so comforting against her skin, felt damp and heavy. She had never thought it possible for their bodies to be pressed too close—*how many nights had they intertwined as if they were one?*—but she felt they were baking, expanding in this heat, and soon they might explode.

But again the baby kicked.

*Ignore this,* she thought. She reached back for Omar's arm, draping it over her side. Before they had left, on an afternoon they had watched the sun set from a hill on the edge of town, he had made her promise to tell him when the baby moved. "I want to feel him, too."

Now Elda placed her hand over his and pushed down on his fingers. "You might have to dig a little." She felt him hesitate. "It's okay." She was used to this. Before she had gotten pregnant she had looked at other women's expanding bellies and thought they were delicate as balloons. Now that she could feel her child growing inside her, she knew it was strong, but malleable. Sometimes at night when the baby moved, she would push down on her stomach with one finger, poking him back.

"Do you feel it? Two quick kicks at a time. *Boop boop.*"

"Mm-hmm." She heard his head rub against the car's trunk and knew he was nodding. Closing her eyes, she tried to imagine they were anyplace else, and she remembered how, when she was a little girl, her mother had told her to think up her own paradise to ward off nightmares before bed.

It'd been an imaginary place back then—lush palm trees, a quiet beach—but today it was a simple memory. Still holding his hand in hers, Elda recalled the moment she had met Omar, how he had first introduced himself. Fearing the moment would pass too soon, she had pretended not to hear and asked him to repeat himself.

"Is it Omar or Mario?" she had said. He had become flustered at having to say his name a third time, and she decided right then that she liked him.

"It's Omar."

"Can I call you Mario?"

"But that's not my name. That's just the letters from my name mixed up, with an extra one added in."

"For good measure," Elda added. "So that I have something to call you that's my own."

She was mischievous like that. He told her his full name—Omar Roberto Caverso Bravo. "Bravo, like the river," he added, as if that would make it final, something she'd not tamper with. She seemed to consider it. In that quick pause, she tried on his last name with her first. From then on, anytime she would introduce him to her friends she would say, "This is Mario. I mean, Omar," and the two of them would giggle as if they alone had invented secrets.

The car sped up and then decelerated. Their bodies shifted, pulled toward the back as if they were magnets. She heard a heavy thump, and then the man in the trunk with them was cursing, something about his head and some piece-of-shit drivers who didn't care if they lived or died.

"Hey. Please, man. They said to be quiet," Omar said.

"What difference does it make? There's no one to hear us for miles."

"Do you have any space back there?"

"What the fuck do you think?"

"Please, man. My wife—"

"It's fine." Elda tried to stretch her leg. Her hip bones dug into the car, and when she tried to move, the surface rubbed against her appendages like a pumice stone. She wished she could turn her body, her head, anything, but the effort only exhausted her and brought her to the brink of tears.

"You're right. We're almost there," Omar said.

She wanted to ask him, *"How do you know? How can you be sure of anything?"*

But she only nodded and said, "You're right." She moved his hand back to her belly. The baby was quiet now, and there was nothing else to do but wait for him to start again. She tried to think of this moment as nothing more than a pause between heartbeats, the stillness before movement. "If it's a boy, we should call him Mario."

"Don't you mean Omar?"

She prodded him gently in the ribs with her elbow. "Mario."

"I don't know. Is it selfish of me to want to keep it to myself?"

"Maybe," she teased. It felt odd to speak of a future when she couldn't even see an inch in front her. "We'll think of something."

Elda closed her eyes again and wondered what Omar's face looked like in that moment. She wanted to believe that if she looked into his eyes, she would find every bit of the hope she had lost still alive within him.

# CHAPTER 15

Martin said that she had been exhausted, that she had been delirious the day of their anniversary. There was no other way to explain the nightmares and the crying, or the things his mother and Eduardo said she had yelled in her sleep. They couldn't make sense of it either way; Isabel had yelled something about a dead man being trapped, another about him being forgotten. For days after, Elda insisted that she shouldn't feel at all embarrassed.

"The things you must see in that ER. It was bound to get to you eventually," she said. "Promise me you'll take better care of yourself."

Isabel worried it would always be like this—November would come, vivid and concrete, then fade into memories she couldn't be sure she hadn't imagined.

One thing she knew for certain: Sabrina was dead. It took Eduardo three days to tell them, but in that time, she recognized his suffering. On day one, they woke up to the sound of him dry heaving over the toilet, his stomach empty from a lack of appetite. On the second day, she found Martin tapping on his bedroom door when she got home from work. He gave her a look that said, *"Check on him."* "Maybe that stomachache is actually food poisoning," he said. Eduardo had barely eaten, or when he had, he hadn't been able to keep his food down.

She handed Martin a glass of water. "Give him time and keep him hydrated." What else could they do?

Finally, Eduardo told them he had reached a friend of the family. His mother's body had been buried months ago.

"I should've been there to protect her. I should've gone back, instead of crossing," he said, sobbing so hard Isabel forgot herself and held him. Their bodies curling into one another was too much for Martin. He left them alone, catching their breath in the dark as the tears subsided.

"You're not crazy," Eduardo finally said to her. "Omar really is trapped."

"Sabrina told you, then?"

He nodded. The secret swelled between them, but they didn't speak more of it for fear it would fade away.

When Martin asked who this family friend was, Eduardo claimed it was a neighbor whose phone number he had suddenly remembered.

"You don't have to explain," Isabel told him. "Stranger things have happened."

The news of Sabrina's death hit Elda hard, too. She offered to collect Eduardo's books and assignments from his teachers, dropping them off and staying most afternoons to help him with his homework until he was ready to return to school. On days Isabel got home in time for dinner, she often found them red-eyed and sullen, having exchanged stories like they were trading cards. Elda had known Sabrina as a child, and Eduardo, as his mother, and Isabel imagined it was comforting for them to remember her so completely, as if each anecdote were a spark that revived her in those short moments of discovery.

Time felt muted in those days, and in the weeks that followed. Slowly, Eduardo began living the life his mother would have wanted. Small things became routine, became everyday, became normal. Untethered by false hope, he could finally take small steps to move on. Almost daily, Isabel found herself in awe of his resilience. It was spectacular to witness him change into a teenager so ordinary.

On Saturdays he watched college football with Martin and helped him adjust his fantasy bracket. They were always hunched over the coffee table, and it wasn't long before Eduardo stopped asking if he could use Martin's iPad and started taking it into his bedroom whenever he wished. He downloaded a comic-book app and another that gave him daily workouts he did in the yard, and so many new songs that if Isabel ever shuffled their playlist, she was deluged by teen pop. One day, an icon popped up for a 3-D driving school.

"It makes sense," Martin said when she pointed it out. "Most kids in his grade already have their license, if not a car."

She knew he might never be one of them. Even if he studied, even if he got all the answers right, this was a test he would never pass. License or no license, they agreed they couldn't keep him from driving forever.

Secretly, Isabel made an appointment for an initial consult with one of the lawyers she had bookmarked months ago. Of all the websites she had saved, his was the only one that didn't include a head shot on the home page. She found this endearing. They weren't selling real estate, for God's sake.

"It's a good thing you got in touch now," the lawyer said when she told him Eduardo would soon turn seventeen. "It's pretty much out of our hands once he turns eighteen."

"We'd been trying to give him his time. But I think he's ready."

Through the frosted glass on his office door, silent silhouettes crept by. The waiting room had not been full when she arrived, but now everyone was restless, their bodies floating like atoms through the small space. The lawyer asked questions about Eduardo and took notes on a yellow pad. He had a big voice, the kind you can hear churning in a person's throat even when he's quiet, but he kept it low and monotone. She noticed he used the word "if" a lot:

"*If* he's been here for a certain amount of time."

"*If* the state considers him abandoned or neglected."

"*If* it's not in his best interest to return."

"*If* he has family members who are citizens willing to become his legal guardian."

"*If* he qualifies for a visa at all."

She kept waiting for the "then." She remembered Elda helping Eduardo with his homework last week, phrasing a list of statements with "if" and "then":

"If the cafeteria is serving pizza, then it must be Thursday."

"If George works overtime, then he will be paid time and a half."

"If Anna gets a 4.0 GPA, then she will receive a scholarship."

Eduardo had found the exercise frustrating and pointless, and Isabel hadn't immediately disagreed.

Isabel told the lawyer that Eduardo's mother was dead and that she didn't know about his father. He said death does not necessarily qualify as abandonment.

"Seriously?"

"Legally, for these purposes, no. But if his father were abusive or neglectful, say an addict, then he might qualify for Special Immigrant Juvenile Status. We'd have to prove it, of course."

"Of course," she said, then, "I'm sorry," though he probably didn't realize she was mocking him. "It's just that I don't know the first thing about Eduardo's father. I'd have to ask him."

"Talk to him and try to be as specific as possible. We need to know what kind of case we can build, if any."

She wanted to ask if quantifiable suffering was the only kind that counts. Instead she picked up her purse off the floor and checked the time on her phone. She had forty-five minutes to get to the hospital. "And if there's nothing?"

"If he doesn't qualify for anything, he's better off not applying in the first place. He crossed the border scot-free. As far as ICE is concerned, he's not even here. He never got detained, so he doesn't have a deportation trial to contest. Why try his luck?"

When she got home at half past midnight, she was surprised to find Martin and Eduardo still awake. They were standing in the kitchen, leaning against the counters, eating ice cream out of a pint.

"What's going on?"

"Tell her," Martin said through a mouthful.

"We went for a drive." Eduardo shrugged. No big deal.

"And?"

"And I didn't crash." A deep, nasal laugh escaped him. Isabel played along but she couldn't stop staring at his elbows, how they bounced up and down against the counter like lanky springs as his body shook.

"It's a bit late for all this, don't you think?"

"He has to start learning at some point," Martin said.

She had meant the ice cream. "I guess you'll be borrowing someone's car pretty soon."

"You'd let me do that?" Eduardo said.

"Eventually. If we can trust you behind the wheel, I don't see why not."

Something flicked on and off in Eduardo's eyes; he recovered so quickly, she might not have noticed if she hadn't seen it before. It was that word, wrapped in too many assumptions. It was why Eduardo had eventually pushed his textbook away and called the whole *if/then* exercise stupid. People placed too much trust in things working out the way they should, and never enough on the chance that the most meaningless conditions could change everything.

# CHAPTER 16

## March 1981

The car stopped. Omar listened for doors opening, for footsteps approaching the trunk and hands grasping at the lock to open it.

"¿Llegamos?" Elda said.

"In a little bit," Omar said. The sounds outside had changed. The car stood still, but he could hear others around them. Leaky brakes whistling as they came to a standstill. A violent vacuum of traffic speeding past in the opposite direction, trucks so large they displaced the air, causing the car to shake.

Omar closed his eyes and listened for other city noises, too—the chorus of street vendors, women and children selling baseball caps and used clothes, the cacophony of impatient car horns—but they never came. Could this muted existence be their new home? In his search for peace, he had never considered that loneliness might tag along, too.

"It's just that I have to go; I have to use the bathroom," Elda said.

"You and everyone else in this car," the other migrant replied.

"Oye, Miguel, please." Omar had grown tired of trying to appeal to this man's sense of decency. "We must be at a stop light. It probably won't be long until . . ." He let his voice trail off. He didn't know what came next.

The car started up again, then turned a corner. He could feel they were ascending, and the floor of the car jolted in regular intervals. Perhaps they were crossing a bridge, he thought. Perhaps they were approaching an immigration checkpoint.

For maybe three or four minutes, the road became smooth. Omar's arm was folded beneath his head, his elbow pressed against the curved interior of the trunk that jutted in to make room for the car's tires.

"Well, we're definitely arriving somewhere," Miguel said.

He couldn't argue with that. They had slowed and turned left, then right, and right again. The car went into reverse for what was probably a few yards, and then it straightened out. When the engine died, they could still hear its parts rattling underneath the hood, like coins trapped in a turbine.

For all the time they had spent confined, it was this moment that seemed to stretch the longest. He felt the weight in the car shift, heard a side door open and slam shut. He counted the footsteps. Two sets, six or seven steps until they stopped. The trunk opened, and a dark silhouette stood over them. Air rushed in, warm and dry but with plenty of space to breathe.

"Let's go, let's go," the dark figure said. He kept one hand on the open trunk and waved the other through the air, rushing them along. Miguel climbed out first and disappeared. Omar's turn came next; he brought his legs out, letting them dangle over the car's edge, then used his arms to catapult forward. As soon as he was out, he turned to help Elda, and that's when he heard the screams.

"Help her, please! She won't wake up!" They were coming from the car next to them, from the little girl still in the trunk, trapped behind her unmoving mother.

"Inside, now!" The coyote yelled at Omar and Elda to keep moving, but they wouldn't. The house in front of them appeared to be floating on air. It was long, beige, and boxy, and it reminded Omar of train cars or truck trailers. The view to the front door was blocked by a giant green trash receptacle that made the air sting with its smell. The coyotes began yelling at one another as they pulled the boy and girl out of the trunk.

"Take them inside!" One of the coyotes grabbed the little girl by the arm and swung her to Omar, not even looking to see where she would land.

"In there?" Elda said.

"Over here!" The boy started toward Miguel, who was already climbing the few rickety steps into the home. The boy rushed back out to take Elda's hand, and Omar nodded at him in gratitude as he ran to the second car to help pull the remaining woman from the trunk.

"¡Pinche gorda, she weighs a ton!" The coyote Omar didn't recognize, the one who must've been driving the other car, looked like he might cry from the effort.

"Take her feet," the other said to Omar. He was the one who had led them across the border, and now more than ever, Omar wanted to believe they hadn't been wrong to follow. The man leaned half his body into the car and twisted his spine to the side so he could scoop his arms under the woman's. "On three!" As they began to drag her out, five or six inches for each time they counted and pulled in unison, her head swayed. Her eyes and mouth stayed shut.

"Into the house! ¡Apúrense!"

They carried her over the grass as if she were a hammock draped between two trees. The younger coyote closed the trunk and rejoined them, attempting to grab her by the knees, by the waist, then finally, by the hands. Omar had no idea in which direction he was going; he let himself be steered by the coyote pulling the woman, and with each step, he said a prayer. Her name somehow surfaced from his memory.

"Lord help Marisol. Lord help Marisol."

The coyote told him to shut up as they made their way up the steps. *Lord help Marisol. Lord help Marisol,* he thought.

They entered the house, and Omar saw the little boy rushing around, clearing a space on one of the mattresses on the floor. The little girl's wails for her mother filled the air. He could hear Elda trying to comfort her, trying to shush her in the same way you would a child who scraped his knee.

"Is she dead?" The voice came from the corner of the room, from Miguel, who just hours ago had called Marisol fat and ugly.

Omar searched her neck for a pulse. Her skin was warm and slippery, soaked in sweat. He poked it with two fingers, moving up and down along the side of her throat, begging for it to push back. He climbed on top of her and began pumping at her chest.

"Vamos, Marisol. You've come too far to give up now." Her body only answered in jolts, refusing to wake.

He looked at Elda, who was cradling the little girl. His arms burned the more he pushed against Marisol, and he didn't know how much longer he could keep going.

"That's enough." He heard the coyote call to him, felt his hand press against his shoulder.

"I'm not done," Omar said. He pressed his mouth to hers and gave her his breath. He doubted he was even doing it right, but he kept on.

"Omar . . ." This time, it was Elda's voice begging him to stop, though she only kept repeating his name.

He couldn't make himself let go. He tried six, seven more times. Pumping, breathing. Her body shook a little less each time he pushed against her, as if she, too, were tired. He wanted to shake her, wanted to slap her, wanted to scream: How dare she leave when they had only just arrived?

"Mar. I. Sol!" With each syllable, he punched her chest.

There was a gasp. Beneath him, the mattress shifted. He was still sitting on Marisol's body, and he felt it now, expanding and shrinking like the sea as the wind rushed back in.

# CHAPTER 17

They had agreed not to make a big deal out of Eduardo's birthday (just a simple get-together with family and friends), but two weeks before the barbecue Isabel tossed a set of invitations into her cart.

They were the fill-in-the-blank type. *Who, What, When, Where.* Each envelope had *To* and *From* lines, and it occurred to her that she hardly knew anything about Eduardo's friends.

"Here, in case you want to invite anyone," she said when she got home. "They're cute, right?" There were ten cards in the pack, with a design simple enough not to embarrass a teenager. He glanced at the front and back, then placed the packet on the coffee table.

"Thanks. But I can just text them," he said.

It turned out Martin had bought him a cell phone as an early birthday present. An impulse purchase, he had called it, though it had technically been free with a new plan.

"It's for safety purposes," he said as he flipped through the user manual. A long black cable stretched over the back of the couch, charging the phone while Eduardo watched the battery-indicator light blink on and off.

"That's what I told my mom to get her to buy me a pager," she said. Senior year, Isabel's hot-pink pager had been all the rage. Her mother insisted it was for emergencies only, and for the first few months she had felt a knot in her gut whenever her mother paged.

"Remember one, four, three? I love you?" she said to Martin.

"One, two, three: I miss you," he said without skipping a beat. He turned to Eduardo. "We were the original texters. Except we used codes. And we'd each choose a number so the person could know who was beeping them. Mine was twenty-four."

"Mine was twenty-three," Isabel said. "We were meant to be together."

"Were you a cheesy couple back then, too?"

She gave him a push as she sat next to them on the couch. "Martin and I weren't really friends in high school. Besides, I transferred to another school freshman year."

"Oh, right. I keep forgetting you and Claudia knew each other first."

"Senior year, I had a boyfriend who also had a pager," Isabel said. "When it was too late for him to call the house, I'd page him and call Moviefone to tie up the line. Then I'd click over when the call-waiting beeped through."

"Sweetie, you're confusing him with ancient words like "call-waiting," Martin said. He started to program his own number into Eduardo's phone.

"I know what call-waiting is. What the hell's Moviefone?"

As she explained, she thought of the smell of popcorn and the carpet patterns in the darkened theaters. There'd been nothing else to do back then. Nothing else they would rather have done.

"What about you? What'd you and your friends do for fun back home?" Immediately, she regretted her choice of words. They implied home was not here, but there, that it was gone and past.

Eduardo didn't seem to notice. No one ever did but her.

"Random stuff. Hanging around the neighborhood. It was always hot. Sometimes we'd swim in the lake."

"The great outdoors," Martin said.

"What?"

"It's just an expression. You know, when you go camping or hiking, surviving off the land. You rough it."

"Like, for fun?" Eduardo said, and when Martin nodded, Eduardo shook his head. "Why would anyone want to do that?"

Isabel rested her head on Martin's shoulder. He dialed her number and created a new contact in Eduardo's phone: *ICE Isabel*.

"What's that?"

"'In Case of Emergency.' You've never seen it at the hospital?"

Once, maybe three years ago, she had contacted a girl's parents this way before the girl bled out from a car accident. "I'd forgotten," she said. "Here." She took the phone and changed both numbers: *A_Home Martin. A_Home Isabel.* "So it's alphabetical."

That evening she began filling out the invitations. On the "What" line, she wrote *Eduardo's Turning 17!* She set it aside and wrote another: *Eduardo's 17th Birthday Party,* and another: *Join us for a Springtime BBQ.*

It really was a stupid idea. To Isabel and Martin's friends who had never met him or barely heard of him, it'd look like a seventeen-year-belated birth announcement. Saying anything now felt awkward, like telling someone they had been saying your name wrong after years of letting it slip by. A phone call would be better, she decided. She would make it sound like a casual, but special, occasion. Isabel tossed the cards and kept the envelopes.

# CHAPTER 18

## MARCH 1981

Almost dying brought Marisol more peace than she had ever felt in her life. It wasn't that she was happy about it; the experience had frightened her daughter so much that several times every night, she felt Josselyn's finger below her nostrils, checking for air. Marisol made a point to breathe harder so there was no doubt she was alive. She even pretended to stir, wrapping her arms around her daughter's body. She would let the low undulations of her breath lull her back to sleep.

Except now, when morning came, there was no hangover to look out for. No bruises to disguise as they blossomed on her skin. Even her soreness was unfamiliar: for once her throbbing muscles felt like an accomplishment, not a punishment. Now, when she thought of her husband, she liked to think he was in a jail cell somewhere; that in her absence, he finally started a fight he couldn't finish.

She imagined him cursing everything in her name. Though he couldn't hurt her anymore, Marisol knew it'd been him in that trunk, strangling her one last time. She unwrapped a pack of peanut butter crackers and handed a few to Josselyn. The men had come back last night with a plastic bag full of food and water, mostly prepackaged snacks like potato chips and tubes of dried meat. These were new indulgences for her daughter, who ate them happily.

A man none of them recognized had said, "Be ready tomorrow morning." Though it had taken nothing more than putting on their shoes and gathering their belongings, the group had gotten ready. Morning had come and gone, and they were still waiting.

"Be ready tomorrow morning," Elda said now, dropping her voice to imitate the young man. "He doesn't know what's going on any more than we do."

It was true. Marisol guessed he was no older than eighteen; he had a nervous air of confusion about him.

"Just stay inside and keep quiet," he had said the first time Omar asked how much longer they would be waiting. He'd turned the volume down on the small black-and-white television that flickered from the corner of the room. It sat sandwiched against the wall between two mattresses; a third mattress, the one she and Josselyn now slept in, had been arranged horizontally to form a U with the other pair.

The television got one channel, and barely, but Josselyn and Omar hadn't stopped watching since they had arrived. They watched cooking show after cooking show in silence. No one could understand what the hosts were saying.

The chef on today's show was preparing a noodle dish in a giant pan. Instead of stirring the vegetables and meat, he was shaking the pan so the food flew into the air.

"What happens if he doesn't catch them?" Josselyn whispered to Omar.

He mumbled something about cooks having pets for a reason. Marisol laughed, careful to not let on that she could hear them.

Elda paced the room, tracing the thin trail the mattresses created along the carpet. Every once in a while, she scooped her belly. It was a small bump—maybe four or five months. Marisol wouldn't have even known she was pregnant if not for Elda's habit of massaging it.

It occurred to Marisol that the young woman was lucky to be pregnant on this journey. Years from now, when Elda would look back, she'd remember the growing weight of a life sharing her body. All other sensations would be secondary.

"How are you doing, mija?" This was all Marisol would allow herself to ask; acknowledging the pregnancy seemed cruel.

Elda swept her hair off her face. Thin, loose tendrils stuck from the sweat. "Maybe if it weren't so hot . . . but then again, I doubt it'd make any difference."

There was a shower in the house, but they had been instructed not to use it. Even the toilet flushes cost money, they'd been told, right before being instructed to use it in pairs. Last night, while everyone slept, the toilet had clogged when Marisol tried to flush. It was like the damn thing knew she was breaking the rules. Afraid another attempt would cause it to overflow, she had left it alone. She had been too mortified to use the bathroom all morning.

Marisol went through what little belongings she had left: an extra pair of shoes for Josselyn, a couple of toothbrushes, and a Bible. From between its pages she pulled out a pamphlet the nuns had given her.

"Here." She fanned herself a couple of times to demonstrate, then handed it to Elda.

The young woman thanked her. She tilted her head back as the tiny gusts of air hit her face and neck. After a few moments, she took a quick glance at the paper. "The Lord's Prayer," Elda said.

Marisol only knew which prayer was written on the paper because the nuns had told her. "It's brought us all this way." Of course she knew it by heart.

"What about the rest of the way?" said Miguel from one of the beds. None of them had noticed Miguel was even awake. "Got another prayer that'll get us out of this place, or is hot air all they're good for?"

"Don't start, güey," Omar said, his eyes still on the television.

Miguel propped himself up with his elbows. His son, such an energetic boy until they got here, pulled the T-shirt he had been using as a blanket over his shoulders. Marisol had considered pretending to sleep, too. Anything to make time go faster.

"You might be comfortable as cows here, but I'm tired of being treated this way. At least cattle get their shit cleaned out once in a while," Miguel said, looking right at her.

An unbearable heat rushed across her face. She hoped her skin was too burned for anyone to notice. A crack in the wood-paneled wall curled, river-like, halfway to the ceiling, and she followed it with her eyes.

"You poor thing," Elda said, shaking her head as she looked down at him. "Couldn't figure out how to use the plunger? Or are you just too delicate?"

"It's okay, mija." Marisol tried to coax her away. If there was one thing she had learned from her husband, it was how to read a man's silence. Men like Miguel didn't let things go; they collected their anger as if it were fuel.

Perhaps Omar sensed this, too, because he got up and rubbed his wife's arms. "She's right. We're all tired and cramped, that's all." In a lower voice meant for just the two of them, he added, "How are you feeling, my love?"

At this small tenderness, Elda brought her hand back to her belly and mumbled she was fine. Marisol wished she could give the couple some privacy, but all she could do was turn her attention to her daughter, still glued to the television. "What is he making?" she asked.

Her daughter shrugged and turned onto her side. "I don't know. I'm tired of being here, too. You said things would be better. Why can't we just go back home?"

# CHAPTER 19

Eduardo invited, of all people, a girl. Her name was Diana, and she arrived driving her own truck (a blue pickup that looked twice her age) and carrying a gift bag with rainbow-colored tissue. "They're headphones. I couldn't find a smaller bag," she said, as if worried he might get too excited by the presentation.

Eduardo thanked her, reaching for the gift just as she stepped in to hug him. Isabel excused herself to help Martin in the kitchen.

"They're cute together," he said, filling a bowl with salsa.

She agreed, but she couldn't help wondering if Eduardo's armpit hair tickled against Diana's shoulder. He had cut the sleeves off a T-shirt Isabel had given him last week, and though she had said he looked fine, the truth was it annoyed her. It was obvious he wanted to show off his arms; his daily workouts were molding him into a brawny guy. He was more confident now, and somehow, less innocent.

As the guests dispersed into small groups, Isabel fluttered from one group to the next. Mixing family and friends made her anxious; it wasn't so much the mingling, but the transition of leaving one conversation for another that always felt rude.

Isabel slid onto the picnic-table bench, where Elda sat across from Claudia and Damian. The couple had the whole bench to themselves, and they huddled close, their fingers intertwined as if one of them might fly away.

They were telling a story Isabel hadn't caught the start of, but from the way they took turns with lines and details she assumed it was how they had met.

"So la loca grabbed a bottle of club soda off the shelf and opened it, just like that," Damian said, much to Elda's amusement. The wind picked up just as they began to laugh, and Isabel caught Martin's eye from across the yard, where he was sharing a beer with a few coworkers. The balloons they had tied to the fence danced around like restless children.

But there was no sign of Eduardo and Diana.

She went looking for them, with her beer bottle still cold in her hand. The hot dogs and burgers were already on the grill, which seemed a good-enough excuse to interrupt the two hormonal, but hungry, teenagers on her couch.

"Plates are there. Burger toppings and condiments, here," she said as she escorted them out to the yard. They held their empty paper plates by the table. Eduardo stared at the tomatoes and pickles and mayo with the intense focus of someone making a very important decision.

Diana poked at his biceps with one finger. "Ding-dong. You there?"

He rubbed his hand over the spot she had touched. There was a bump Isabel recognized: the small piece of smooth, puckered skin left behind by a tuberculosis shot. At work, this mark told her nearly as much about a patient as a birth certificate; babies born in the United States weren't vaccinated for TB, but most born south of the United States were. She often wondered if the skin was still tender, or if, like any other scar, it'd gone numb.

"Yeah. So maybe we can go next weekend?" Eduardo said.

Diana nodded and scanned the food on the table. "I'm starving. Everything looks delicious."

With her empty plate held before her, Isabel felt like a beggar, her pleading eyes hoping for more detail. She wanted to ask what they were talking about, but they had already moved on, quite purposely, to another subject. *Maybe later,* she thought. Maybe after midnight, when it was no longer Eduardo's birthday, but there were still slices of cake left, they could pick at it with two forks as he told her how much fun he had had.

Instead, the party stretched past midnight, past the birthday song and the few gifts that friends had brought. Most of them were gift cards in envelopes that should have taken barely seconds to open. But Eduardo took his time, thanking and hugging each person after unwrapping their gifts. He seemed particularly excited to receive Claudia's, an armband for his phone, but she waved off his gratitude and joked that Damian had picked it out. He saved Diana's gift for last, and the pair sat outside next to the recycling bin full of beer bottles, listening to songs on his cell phone with one earbud each. They leaned their heads close together, as if they might hear the music better this way.

Elda moved away from the window to give them privacy. "See? You were worried he'd never get comfortable, and now you have to worry about him getting *too* comfortable." She sank into the loveseat by the television and added quite loudly, "I noticed Costco has a box of fifty condoms."

"Damn, you must be going through them fast, Mom." Claudia laughed and Isabel began picking up the last of the paper plates around the living room. The sound of polite giggles and tired sighs rose and then fell into quiet.

Martin sat on the arm of the loveseat, tilted toward his mother's frame. His eyes had turned red from a mixture of exhaustion and alcohol.

"Sit, mija. I'll take care of the plates," Elda said to Isabel, but Martin placed his hands on Elda's shoulders and pulled her back into an embrace before she could get up.

"How about everyone just sit and relax? When's the last time we were all in the same room?" Martin said.

"We had Sunday dinner when we first bought the house," Isabel said. "And before then, we had the wedding. So give or take two years." It seemed much longer. Perhaps time hadn't just crept forward, but also back as they all moved along. How else to explain the gaps, the moments they seemed to have skipped just to find themselves in a life that didn't entirely feel like their own?

"That was a magical night," Elda said.

"You think so?" Isabel took the last big sip of the wine she had been nursing since they had cut the cake. The couch was piled high with oversized pillows and the few purses and coats that still remained, so she sat at the very edge closest to her mother-in-law. "In what way?"

She could feel Martin's eyes on her, and then he hiccuped, just a little louder than usual.

"There's just something special about that many people you love coming together. It rarely happens. Or if it does, it's for your funeral. Not nearly as fun," Elda said.

A warm languor spread over Isabel, clouding the space between her thoughts and speech. "What was your wedding like?"

All grew quiet. She heard a couple of ice cubes stir in Damian's drink, and though Martin said nothing, his gaze clicked into some invisible place just shy of her feet.

"It was simple. Two witnesses, a priest, a bouquet of days-old flowers. Nothing worth remembering," Elda said.

"I doubt that's true."

"Isa," Martin said.

"Fine." She rolled her eyes and turned toward Claudia and Damian. "What about you guys? Any big plans in the future?"

"What? You mean a funeral?" Damian said. "It feels a bit early for me to start picking out caskets. Maybe we should do a hey-I'm-not-dead-yet

115

party. Tell everyone that I am, but then they show up and surprise: it's an unfuneral."

"You're crazy," Claudia said. "And everyone would kill you."

"Seriously, though, Clau." All that was left to do was jump for it, gracefulness and tact be damned. "You remember when we were little and we used to plan our weddings? I wanted a long dress with poufy sleeves, and you wanted a Jessica Rabbit dress, but in white. Your bridesmaids' dresses would be mermaid pink, and mine would be baby blue. And I always pictured my father walking me down the aisle. Of course that didn't happen, but I like to think he was there in spirit." A long pause. "You always said you wanted your mom and brother to walk you. You never wished he could be there, though? Omar?"

Right there, she knew nothing had gone too far until she said his name. It was in how Claudia's lips opened, so slowly, she could see the edges stick together as the rest of her face seemed to float apart. It was in the lights screaming and the couch cushions squirming and the air Isabel stopped breathing, knowing they were all holding back. Elda excused herself to use the restroom.

"You've always had a hang-up about my father," Claudia said once Elda was gone.

"It's just hard to believe he's not a big deal."

"That's because you *had* a father." It sounded like an accusation.

"And what? Were you jealous?" Isabel began to laugh at the thought of it but stopped. "Oh my God. You were."

"Don't be a drama queen, Isabel."

"Is that what you thought I was being? After my father died?"

"What? No. I never said that."

"You never said anything." With her dad gone, Isabel had moved to her mom's place, a small house in a new development just a couple of blocks outside of her school district. She didn't bother making friends at her new school; it was hard enough most days to breathe, let alone smile or talk to complete strangers. She took comfort only in the weekends, when she knew she would be able to sleep over at Claudia's. Then that, too, had changed. "You were so dismissive. And distant."

"We were at different schools, Isabel. People grow apart."

"I lived twelve minutes from your house! I know because I counted them. Every Friday."

"Isa," Martin said.

"No. You weren't there, Martin." She looked again to Claudia and felt a familiar shame well up inside of her. "You acted like nothing was wrong. Like I should just get over it." She remembered her last night at Claudia's house, how she had cried herself to sleep on a folded-up comforter on the floor next to Claudia's bed, afraid she would hear her.

"I was trying to be supportive."

"You stopped calling me."

"You stopped calling first."

"I was depressed."

"I was there for you. My mom was there for you. All those times she drove you to the hospital."

"You didn't even say hi at the funeral. And after that, you were too busy with all your other friends to ever hang out."

"Look, I'm sorry, okay? It wasn't easy being around you. I didn't know how to deal."

"Sure you did. You did what you guys always do."

"What is that supposed to mean?" Martin said.

"You shut me out. You shut out your father . . ."

"Don't go there, Isa."

"Why? What are you people so afraid of?"

"Don't you get it?" Claudia leaned in close and spoke to Isabel in a deep, slow whisper, like she would to a child. "This isn't about you. Or Omar. It's about her." She nodded her head in the direction of the bathroom. "When I was little I'd ask my mom about him, and it killed her, every time."

"So you just stopped?"

"I stopped because I care about her too much. And I couldn't care less about him." Claudia leaned back into Damian's arms and took a sip of her drink, her eyes suddenly smiling at Isabel over the rim of the glass as Elda came back into the room.

Isabel sat still, dumbfounded. Before she could say anything, the back door opened. The alarm chimed twice, friendly and upbeat, as Eduardo and Diana made their way through the living room.

"Good night. Thank you so much for a lovely evening," Diana said. Everyone stood up to kiss and hug, and Damian tapped his pockets for his keys.

"You're in the blue truck? I think I blocked you in. We'll head out with y'all."

Everything else felt like echoes until they were gone.

# CHAPTER 20

## MARCH 1981

She didn't want to tell Omar, but Elda thought she had an infection. Her insides burned when she went to the bathroom. It had woken her several times this evening, and she had tried to ignore it because she was afraid of stumbling through the dark, narrow hallway.

But the dreams had started again. When she was a child, Elda had shared a mattress with her younger cousin and had frequently wakened mortified at having soaked the mattress. She would dream she was swimming in a river, with no one around to notice if a small cloud of water around her suddenly turned warm. In reality, she had been wetting the bed.

Ever since, even in adulthood, Elda considered this recurring dream a nightmare. The incidents had stopped later in her childhood, but the fear remained. What if now, sharing a bed with Omar as husband and wife, she revealed herself to be little more than a child?

She got up before the dreams could continue.

It was the deepest hour of the night, when even the sleepless slip away, and being awake felt like an intrusion. Elda stepped between the mattresses, careful to maintain her balance. She could feel everything inside her shifting, readjusting, to make room for her child.

In the bathroom, she didn't turn the light on. She closed the door behind her, but didn't lock it for fear of the harsh click. The light from tonight's half-moon barely made its way through the small window over the toilet.

She regretted not slipping on her shoes. She imagined her socks absorbing the urine and sweat of strangers who had come through this house before her, and it made her long for a shower. The tub was right there, the shower curtain pulled open. No one would have to know.

She unrolled a wad of toilet paper and wiped off the seat before using it, then washed her hands and arms with soap and water all the way up to her shoulders. She tried to fit parts of her chest and abdomen over the sink, then cupped her wet hands and brought them to her face. She had been bathing like this for three days, and still it felt like the earth clung to her.

Elda tapped the wall for a hand towel. As her arm searched the air, she sensed the space around her shrink, and she knew, even before she opened her eyes, that she was not alone. She saw a dark figure behind her and felt his hand slap over her mouth. She tried to scream, but it was nothing more than half a breath. All she could see were her own eyes growing in the mirror. They traveled to the knife against her neck, then down the length of the arm holding her, then finally, the face.

He seemed so much calmer now that he was in control. His grip over her mouth loosened. Gently, he pressed his other hand against her back, folding her body over the sink. He pushed her down until keeping her eyes locked on his reflection hurt, as if they might stretch out of her skull. But she couldn't not look at him. She couldn't let Miguel do this without a witness.

His jeans rustled, shuffling down his legs. Her own legs began trembling. Rattling. She couldn't make them stop.

"Always so delicate." He traced her spine with the knife down to the small of her back, then wrapped himself around her. A gasp escaped, hollowed by the cold metal blade, thin against her belly.

"You keep acting like something's gonna fall out of there," he said.

And then she collapsed. Her legs failed her. She tried grabbing the sink as she fell, and her knees hit the tile. Her arms were still wet and sudsy from the wash, and though he tried to stop her, she kept slipping from his grasp until she heard the thud of his blade landing in the sink, and her fingers gripped around the sound. In the dark, she thrust the knife in his direction.

His flesh was thicker than she had expected.

It was painful, even to her, to push so hard and have his weight collapse back onto her own.

He rolled over and felt for the blade.

"No!" Without thinking, she pulled it out and clutched it close.

"You fucking bitch. You fucking bitch!" His rage barely reached a whisper.

Eventually, or perhaps immediately, Elda screamed.

The walls filled with footsteps. Someone turned on the lights, and she tried shielding her eyes with her hands, but they were covered in blood. She felt Omar lift her away, and she heard Marisol telling the children to go back to sleep. One of the coyotes kept calling for more towels and more pressure and once, she heard him say, "Sangre, mucha sangre," and again she looked at her hands and nodded, agreeing that yes, there was far too much blood.

She didn't notice how quiet it had gotten until she looked up. In the hallway, in the light that was coming from the bathroom, stood Tomás. Elda watched him watch his father on the floor. She knew, from the way the boy's back collapsed for an instant before he breathed again, that she had killed the man.

# CHAPTER 21

It always started the same. In the moments before they said, *"I'm sorry, it's okay,"* and meant it, they became strangers. Too polite. Isabel recognized the motions, but didn't know what came next.

It was the first time they had fought this long. They spent days after Eduardo's party staying out of each other's way. Their anger was the winter, and their moods, an unsurprising forecast, shifting but still governed by the nature of their hostility.

On the first day, Martin was volatile. He slammed doors and spilled coffee over the rim of his mug when he placed it on the kitchen counter. She, on the other hand, was tranquil, taking pleasure in how little his anger fazed her.

By the second day—by the time she'd really had a chance to think about it—Isabel was more irritable than a cat. Why should she be the one to apologize when it was Claudia who had hurt her the most? How could Martin not take her side? If he didn't want to speak about his father, fine. But ignoring Omar wouldn't make him go away.

Martin brooded over every little thing on the third day, as if he begrudged the weight of his own limbs. He grunted and hunched, a sight made more spectacular by how quickly his disposition changed when he spoke to Eduardo.

Overall though, it could've been worse. At least they were peaceful, at least they became well rehearsed at avoiding each other's eyes. They were hyperaware of their bodies and personal space, in which they each orbited without crossing into the other's. Their gravity didn't allow for touching. It was practically a new form of intimacy.

Then he called her from work for a favor.

Now, of course, Isabel knew that thirty minutes before an important pitch meeting was not the right time. And she wasn't even passive-aggressive about bringing him a clean shirt after he spilled his chocolate protein shake on the new one. She didn't ask, because she could already imagine: Martin never closed the blender properly at home, so why would it be any different in the office break room?

She laughed to herself in the car, picturing the liquid lunging out at his face and chest, but then she felt guilty and slightly protective of him. With that ounce of sympathy, she suddenly knew they would get through this.

"Oh, good. You brought the right blue one," Martin said when she tapped on his office door.

What other blue one was there? This was the one he wore most often, the one he paired with dark jeans and a jacket on casual days, and a gray suit anytime else. She had watched him try it on at the store after she had sneaked into his fitting room. There were light blue shirts and navy shirts hanging in their closet, but Isabel always knew what he meant when he said his *blue shirt*. She resented the implication otherwise.

"Thanks. You rushing off to work?"

"Not yet." She sat in the chair in front of his desk, placing both hands on the armrests. "I have ten or fifteen minutes."

Not bothering to close the window blinds, he began unbuttoning his shirt. No one in the office paid them any attention; they sat hunched in their cubicles, plugged into their headsets. "I have to head out in a few, but stay as long as you like."

"Which client is this for again?"

"The bank."

Hence the tie, which he straightened as his eyes scanned his desk. It was a perfectly symmetrical knot, and one he'd never, in all the years they had been together, asked her to help him tie.

"Who taught you to tie the knot?"

For a moment he looked confused, but he was too preoccupied searching for something under piles of papers to dwell on it.

"Your tie," she said. "Who'd you learn it from?"

He pressed his lips together and looked down. "My grandfather. When I was twelve."

"Was it hard for you?" She thought she caught the hint of a nod.

"The tie? I don't know. I don't remember. What's this about, Isa?" Perhaps he'd found what he'd been looking for, or perhaps it no longer mattered. He began piling things into his arms with a nervous quickness.

"I was just wondering. It occurred to me that there are a lot of things I don't know about you."

"Jesus. Do we really have to do this now? I'm prepping a huge meeting, and all of a sudden you don't know me?"

"I'm not saying I don't know you. Just *things*. All those stories couples know about each other because they've heard them tell them a million times. You never told me your grandfather taught you. I assumed that your father did when you were little, or maybe your mom did after he—" She had been speaking so fast she hadn't known where this was headed, and now that she did, Isabel hesitated.

"After he what?"

"Nothing."

"No, really. After he what?"

"After he left." She crossed her arms and turned her head toward the window, not wanting to see the look on his face. Her neck turned cold, her cheeks, hot.

"Is this how it's always going to be? Everything ends up back at him?"

"I don't know. I just . . . that's the problem. We're supposed to know each other and share a life together, and there's this huge part of your life that I know nothing about."

"Not huge. Seven years isn't huge."

"You know that's not all it is."

"You keep trying to make him mean more than he does."

"And what? I have no right to ask? I'm your wife." The word hissed past her lips. Out of the corner of her eye, she could see his coworkers fidgeting. They were children awakened from slumber, suddenly alert. Isabel lowered her voice. "I don't keep any secrets from you. Everything that is me is yours."

Martin came around to the front of his desk and took the seat next to her. His body fell into it, legs sprawled, back slouched, as if resigned to finally apologize. The wood creaked as he sat up abruptly, steeled. "He didn't just leave, Isa. He went to prison for killing a guy. He's no saint."

He kissed her on the forehead and left the office—a quick, hard peck, just for show. Martin's coworkers had stopped pretending not to watch them. She stretched her lips into a smile in his wake, and on her face it felt foreign, a fragile, broken thing.

# CHAPTER 22

## MARCH 1981

They had watched the coyotes fling Miguel's body into the back of the van, and it'd sounded like a bag of sand. Omar had thought it would rumble more, perhaps get tossed around as they slammed the van shut and climbed in, but the body was decidedly still.

He wrapped a bedsheet over Elda's shoulders. The air was warm and stagnant, but she was shivering, and this gave him something to do. The men had left fifteen minutes ago, and still he and Elda stood in the short hallway, staring at the locked door.

Every once in a while Elda glanced over her shoulder at Tomás. He cried in Marisol's arms, then curled up in bed to sleep. He woke, sat up, and went to the bathroom. There was a moment of hesitation as he stood at the door. Omar had to stop Elda from going to him.

"Mi amor, no." He held her closer and tighter. "Now's not the time."

"Then when?"

He didn't know. "He'll be with his family soon."

Tomás, Marisol, and her daughter all had someone who would pick them up and pay the rest of their way. They had often spoken about their futures to pass the time, and Tomás had told them about his aunt, his father's sister, whom he had never met because she had left before he was born. "She's the one who's paying," he had said, right before his father had told him to shut his mouth.

Omar and Elda were the only ones who had just each other. They had paid in full before leaving and simply had to trust that things would work out as expected.

"Where do you think they'll take his body?"

Tomás came out of the bathroom, leaving the door open. From where they stood, Omar could see the spot where the man had lain as a circle of blood swelled around him.

"Some place far. Some place where it's just another body if it's found." He winced. They had come all this way without acknowledging the shoes and sweaters and empty canteens all around them. Twice, Omar had sworn he had stepped over a human skull in the desert, but he had convinced himself it was just a rock, just the darkness playing tricks on his mind. "Come. Rest. We'll be leaving once they return."

Elda shook her head, but she let him lead her through the hallway and onto the nearest mattress. The rest of the group scooted down.

"You sure you're okay?"

Again, she nodded his question away. It had been five hours since the house had awakened to Elda's screams. Omar kissed her hand, rubbing her goose-bumped flesh. He turned it so her palm was facing the ceiling and inspected her skin.

"Did he hurt you?" It was the most specific he had been all morning. No one had bothered asking what happened. When they had come into the bathroom, Miguel's pants had been lowered halfway down his thighs.

"Now's not the time," Elda said, repeating the words he'd used only minutes ago. She kept her eyes on the little boy and lowered her voice. "He didn't, because I stopped him. Do you really need to know more than that?"

He didn't need to, but he wanted to, if only because he felt useless to not have been there. Left to his own imagination, Omar kept trying to insert himself in time. If he had awakened when Elda did, if he had accompanied her to the bathroom and guarded the door, Miguel would have never dared come near her.

Or, if he hadn't, if he'd only been stirred awake by the light slipping out of the bathroom as Miguel sneaked in to surprise her, he would've smashed his head into the tub, and it would've been Elda who held him back, Elda who pried the knife from Omar's clenched fingers, Elda who would've whispered, "It's not worth it, my love, I can't let you do this."

He would have waited for her voice to dissolve his anger. He would have let her wipe the sweat from his face and kiss it until he was convinced that she was right, that he would never forgive himself for killing a man, even if he had had no choice.

She would've told him the same thing she'd said when they had realized they had to leave home: "Just because you have no choice doesn't mean you'll be able to live with the decision."

Her gaze continued to elude him. Her fingers shook as he squeezed them between his. It should have been his that were bloodied. "I should've been with you, I should've—"

"Don't. Please. Blaming yourself won't make me stop blaming myself."

"But it's not your fault."

"I know, Omar, I know." She rubbed her eyes and took a deep breath. Instead of an exhale came words, quick and heavy like sobs. "But why do I still feel like a monster?" She brought her hands to her mouth and stiffened. "Just, sit here," she said, gesturing for him to move in front of her. "I don't want him to see me like this."

"What? Who?" Omar looked over his shoulder in time to see Tomás staring at them from the corner of the room. It made him want to go to the boy and tell him things would be all right. But he wasn't convinced this was true.

"How does someone like me apologize to a child like him?" Elda said.

Omar considered this. Through the small window behind her, the sun was beaming directly into his eyes. When he tried looking at Elda, all he saw was a darkened silhouette.

He remembered how, when he was twelve, his father had been his hero. In the mornings, while his mother scrubbed their laundry, she would complain about him to no one in particular, to the soap bubbles that floated into the air. *"A grown man, afraid of lizards, imagine!"* she would say. *"He snores and talks in his sleep about other women, and when he wakes he says it was just another nightmare." "Look at that, he doesn't even know how to wipe his own butt!"* As proof, she would show Omar his father's streaked underwear. He rationalized that his father must have simply sat on mud many, many times.

"Boys will always make excuses for their fathers," he told Elda. "Maybe one day when he's older he'll understand, but right now . . ." He was too exhausted to complete the thought. How much longer would the coyotes be? How much longer would they have to take this?

"How's our little man?" he asked Elda. "Is he moving much today?"

"Hmm?" She lifted her eyebrows, and he caught a flicker of confusion in her eyes. "Oh. Yes. He's fine today. Just fine."

Like it was habit, like it was the most ordinary thing in the world, Elda placed Omar's hand on her belly. He felt it, stronger than it'd ever been. Life kicked.

# CHAPTER 23

Omar, a murderer. It didn't compute. The fresh grief of it washed over her, thick with unanswered questions. On her way home from work, when she finally had time to think about it, traffic lights turned fuzzy through her stubborn tears. They kept flooding her vision until Isabel blinked them back. She didn't want to cry for him.

The house was dark and quiet when she entered. Not even the porch light or the small bulb of the microwave was on. Normally, Martin would have left some small corner of the house illuminated so Isabel could make her way to the bedroom, but not tonight.

She passed Eduardo's room. The door was open, and she didn't have to see his empty bed to know he had gone out with Diana. For weeks they had discussed giving him a curfew, but they had yet to agree on a time. The green numbers on the oven glowed "1:30." Too late by Isabel's standards. Not unreasonable by Martin's.

She made no effort to keep quiet as she fixed herself some cereal. She reveled in the spoon's light chime against the bowl, the buzz of her toothbrush in the bathroom, the toilet flushing. When she climbed into bed, she hoped the cold air climbed in with her. But Martin remained motionless, and after minutes of her lying with her eyes closed, exhausted and sleepless, she felt his arm twitch.

Just a jab was all it took. Her sobs came so fast they shook the bed. He sat up and turned on the lights, leaning over her curled body. His hand on her shoulder felt thoughtless and heavy. It was all instinct.

"What's wrong?" he said through a yawn.

That he pretended not to know made it worse. "How could you not tell me?"

"I'm sorry." He rubbed her shoulder in one slow, lazy gesture.

"And the way you said it. To hurt me."

"You're right. I'm sorry."

"And then you just left, and everyone was watching me. Do you know how humiliating it is to be caught so off guard? By your own husband?"

"You have to understand, Isa. I never told anyone. And when we were dating, it was never the right time."

"You didn't trust me?"

"It's not that. It was just too heavy."

"And you were embarrassed."

"No. Why should I be? But see, that's the problem. You attach me to him. You think I'm somehow a reflection of him, when he was never even around. And if you knew what he'd done . . ."

"You thought I'd see you differently."

"Don't you?"

Her hair, caught under the weight of her shoulders, stung her scalp as she tried to shake her head. "We're more than the actions of our parents."

He sighed. "That's all I've ever been saying."

"So what happened? Why did he do it?"

"I don't know all the details. Just that he stabbed a guy."

She didn't want to push him, but she was certain that wasn't the whole story. "I just keep thinking about him. It doesn't make sense."

"Isa, he's not worth this. You have to just let it go."

Even as she agreed to it, she knew it was a lie. She could never forget Omar. Not with every year reminding her how he longed to be remembered. How all he wanted was to be redeemed.

They turned off the lights and remained still. Tree branches scratched against the window, and their shadows bounced against the bedroom wall. She thought about what Omar had told her the first night they met, and she tried to imagine what it must feel like to sense yourself being cast away. Maybe it stung, or worse, maybe it burned. Maybe it was more like drowning and watching the surface of the water rise.

*Forgive me,* she thought. And then to Martin, she said, "I'm sorry."

He had not fallen asleep either. "Just promise me you won't tell anyone. My mom never wanted us to find out. She told me and my sister that he left us. And everyone outside the family just assumed they divorced. Please don't say anything."

She rubbed his arm, pulling it closer over her waist, and promised. "I should at least apologize for bringing him up like that. I feel like such an ass."

"You'll only make it worse. Just forget it ever happened."

"They must completely hate me."

"They don't hate you. Claudia will get over it. And my mom's not the type to hold a grudge."

"If she didn't want you to know, how'd you find out?" In the dark, without facing each other, the conversation seemed to float over the bed. She tossed questions into the air, surprised when they didn't fall back at her.

"It was stupid of me. I hired a private investigator when I graduated. The guy was an ex-cop, so the first thing he did was check police records. He gave me the name and address of the prison. He told me my dad had been there since '89."

"Did you go see him?"

"Yeah. But as soon as I got there, I wished I hadn't. I saw him walking toward the phone with his cuffs and his jumper, and I got up to leave. I didn't want to give him the satisfaction of knowing I'd been looking for him. But he recognized me right away. As if ten years don't even change a person. Like I was still a kid."

"What'd you tell him?"

"That I had nothing to say to him. That it was all a mistake. And before I could hang up the receiver, he banged his fist against the glass and said, 'Does your mother know you came?' I said no, and he asked me never to tell her. Demanded it, really. Like he had any right to ask me anything. He started screaming it. 'She can never know you know,' until the guards pulled him away. But he was right. It's her secret, not mine."

"It must be so lonely for her. Keeping it all to herself."

"She's stronger than you realize, Isa. She was better off after he was gone. We all were."

Isabel wasn't sure she believed that. "That first day he came, how could you have been so calm?"

He spoke as if the answer were obvious. "I didn't want to ruin our wedding."

Outside, the faint rumble of an engine grew closer until it was parked right at their driveway. She checked her phone to gauge how long it took for Eduardo and Diana to say goodnight. Twelve minutes later, the truck door opened and shut, the lock turned, and Eduardo's steps pressed softly across the hall. She knew this, too, would keep her up.

"Twelve minutes. That's enough time to do all sorts of things," she whispered, but Martin had already fallen asleep.

# CHAPTER 24

## MARCH 1981

Now that there were fewer of them, they only had to take one car. It was a dusty, white pickup truck with a hard-covered flatbed, and it was the first time Marisol had seen it. Aside from the van that had come to take away Miguel's body that morning, she hadn't seen a car return to the house more than once. There were the two cars the group had arrived in, and then a long, black four-door with angles so sharp she thought it would cut anyone who leaned on it. It had pulled up beside the house on their second day, but the driver had only climbed out to switch places with the young man keeping watch. The next day, the young man returned in a champagne-colored Toyota. Again he and the driver switched places, and so it went, twice more in the evening and the following morning, a carousel of cars.

The walls were so thin, Marisol constantly heard them mumbling as they handed over the keys. They all worried about the cars being clean. This, coming from slobs who spit tobacco out the window and never bothered showering, despite claiming they were the only ones allowed to do so. Marisol's eyes and ears were everywhere. She was relieved to finally be leaving.

"You kids, squeeze on top of la gorda," the coyote said, pulling the passenger's seat forward so they could climb into the back. "You sit next to them," he said to Omar. "And you, in the front," to Elda.

Marisol had grown tired of taking orders, but she was glad to be close to the kids. It was only because she had been sleeping next to Josselyn that she had been able to keep her daughter from witnessing the morning's tragedy. She'd had her stay in bed while she got up to see what all the screaming was about, and she regretted not asking Tomás to do the same. Now Josselyn thought the man who had been carried away had died of a heart attack, while the poor boy thought his father had been murdered.

"Things are never that simple with grown-ups," she'd told him, but this had only upset him more.

"You'll meet your aunt soon," she said now as Tomás sat on her lap. Running two fingers through his hair, she placed a loose tendril behind his ear.

Tomás looked out the window. "She's an ingrate," he said, so low she almost didn't catch it.

"What do you mean? You were so excited when you told me about her a few days ago."

"My father said it never should've taken her this long to send for us, not after all he did to help her come over in the first place. He said she spends all her money trying to keep her boyfriends from leaving her, because no man would stay with a woman that ugly for free."

"Well, she's coming now, isn't she? You have her number?"

Tomás nodded. "He made me memorize it."

"Good. There's no better place to keep something safe than in your mind." Her cheer bubbled into a giggle that even she knew sounded obnoxious.

"Mom, pleeease," Josselyn said.

"Okay, okay."

Marisol caught Omar smiling at her as he squeezed his hand through the small space between the door and the seat to rub Elda's shoulder. The car started, and she looked away, watching the road pass underneath them.

The sun was glaring, and she felt exposed. There were no blankets over them, no tarps covering the windows. The drive itself was shorter than she had expected; barely half an hour before they stopped at a gas station. It wasn't a busy road, but it wasn't desolate, either. The gas station had two pumps and a convenience store, with empty plots of land on both sides. In the distance Marisol could make out a huge, flat-looking building with a parking lot almost twice its size. A sign bearing a thick, red K towered over the entrance.

The coyote parked the truck next to the trash bin along the side of the convenience store. "Here." He placed dimes in Marisol's and Tomás's palms and pointed at a pay phone just outside the entrance. "Call whoever you need to."

"Do you want me to go with you?" she whispered to Tomás. He shook his head no.

They watched as the boy approached the telephone and dialed. Marisol prayed someone was home. She counted the seconds, wondering how many rings it was, until she saw Tomás's mouth move and his eyes squint under the sunlight. When he turned away, she shifted in her seat to face Elda.

"He's going to be all right, you know," Marisol said.

Elda looked stunned by her frankness. "I don't . . . I don't see how you could know that."

"I just do. It's not an easy start, but it'll be a new one. At the very least, he can say he got what he came for."

Tomás hurried back to the truck, and Marisol patted her daughter on the back so she would let her through. She took one last look at the crumpled note where she had written her boss's brother's phone number. Like Tomás, she had memorized it long ago.

"Here. Take it. That's where we'll be, in case you ever want someone to talk to."

Elda said nothing, but she took the number and smiled. Marisol felt sad for the couple; a baby on the way and no one to call for help. And yet, she envied the young woman—a man needed only attempt to hurt her, and she didn't hesitate to stop him.

Marisol tried to think of a time when her husband's fists came as a complete surprise, but a part of her believed what her father had said was true: it was her duty as a wife to take the beatings, to be strong for her daughter and her marriage. If only she had been more like Elda, if only the first time her husband had laid a hand on her had been the last. All she knew for sure was that she wouldn't have Josselyn, and she wouldn't trade the pain of the last six years if it meant not having her daughter.

Still, as she slid the small coin into the slot and dialed, she vowed that the future would be different. No one comes all this way to end up in the same place they started.

The call to her new employer was quicker than expected. She told him the crossroads the coyote had given her, and Sebastian (that was what he told her to call him, though it made her wince to use his first name) said he would only be forty minutes. She prayed that this man would be as kind-hearted as his sister, whose house she had cleaned these last several years.

"How long did your aunt say she'd take to get here?" she asked Tomás when they were back inside the truck.

"Half an hour."

What a relief. She had hoped to see him off for the chance of looking into his aunt's eyes.

"And it's just her coming?"

"She's bringing my cousin, too. He's twelve."

"How nice." Family he could grow up with, ride bikes with, and walk to school with.

"He's just a bastard," Tomás said.

"¡Mijo! Who ever heard of a boy your age using that language? Dios mío! Promise me you'll try to be friends with him. Promise." She lifted his chin to make him look at her. Sitting this close to her, Tomás didn't seem tough but afraid, and she let him crawl back onto her lap and rest his head on her shoulder, just as he had done that morning.

Cars came and went. She saw a pristine green minivan with a Tamaulipas license plate pull up and hoped it was one of theirs. She saw a dented four-door Chevy with a plastic bag for a rear windshield and prayed that it wasn't.

In the end, it was a white van with a wooden panel along the side that parked beside them. Marisol waited for the driver to come out and embrace Tomás. She had pictured this so clearly. But the coyote took one glance into the van's window and got out of the truck.

"Wait here."

Through the back window, Marisol could see him leaning on the driver's-side door and poking his head into the vehicle. The whole exchange lasted barely a couple of seconds. "Go on, get your stuff," he said.

The boy got out of the truck without so much as a glance back.

"Wait!"

He stopped, but she could see his impatience in the way his feet barely committed to the spot of warm pavement. Was there anything she could say that he would hold on to?

"Dios te cuide, mijo." He was in God's hands now, after all.

Marisol prayed for him as the van backed out of the parking spot. She prayed for God to protect him, but most of all she prayed that God would help him leave these past several days behind. She hoped Tomás would forget them, even though she knew she could never forget him. *Let his aunt be kind in his time of grief,* she thought as she tried to catch a glimpse of her before the car drove away. All she saw was a head of thick, blondish hair, the wiry profile of a young man reading a magazine in the passenger's seat, and Tomás, slouching in the back.

The van looked new and taken care of, the latest model and everything. Its back bumper bore a bright green sticker that said "Guerra Junior High School." She heard a sigh just then, coming from beside her. She had almost forgotten about Omar, but there he was, staring at the van as it disappeared, while Elda looked away.

# CHAPTER 25

The teachers at Guerra High School often sent kids home with forms and flyers that Isabel and Martin ignored, unless it was a report card or required a signature. The red and gray and yellow papers piled up on the kitchen counter, until eventually Isabel tossed them into the recycling bin. If Eduardo was around she would sometimes flip one over and say, "Did you go to this?" and he would look up from his phone and shake his head no.

But now that it was homecoming season, and they were seniors, Eduardo was suddenly excited because Diana was. She would slip a countdown into any conversation: that she had found a dress only a week before the dance, that she couldn't imagine the homecoming committee would get everything done in just three days.

There was talk of a group renting a limo, of tuxedo fittings and after-parties, and songs that Diana hoped the deejay would play because they were *their* songs.

"Babe." Eduardo had started calling her this, much to Isabel and Martin's amusement, after his birthday. "At least tell me what color your dress is so I can get my vest to match."

"Just wear one with a bunch of different colors and you'll be fine." She was determined her dress would be a surprise. "But don't go crazy. Nothing too loud."

"That makes no sense, babe."

It was like listening to someone else talk. It was so sweet, that Isabel barely kept track of what it would all cost, and when Martin tallied up the ticket fees and limo charges and the cash he'd given Eduardo for the requisite homecoming memorabilia, he only smiled and said, "Can you believe I bought a mum for my first crush for twenty-five dollars in '95?" Isabel thought even that was too much for the clusters of school ribbons and bows so big they stretched past the girls' knees and pulled the fabric of their gowns along with them.

"You should get one for Isabel," Eduardo said. "For her to wear to the game."

"What game?" she said.

"The football game. You guys are going, right? It's homecoming. Martin's an alum," he said matter-of-factly. As if he had always known.

Pride, relief, and a giddy sense of anticipation came over her. Isabel sorted through the stack of memos, looking for ways to get more involved with his school life. They needed volunteer chaperones for a field trip, and though it was last-minute, it coincided with her day off. Isabel began filling out the sign-up form and stopped when she reached a line that said "Relationship." She wasn't officially his guardian, and anyway, it seemed like such a cold way to describe herself. She set aside the paper and decided she would email Eduardo's teacher instead.

"So you're into birds and stuff?" Eduardo asked as they drove to school that morning. His science teacher had arranged for a guided tour through the nature preserve. In big, italic letters on the flyer, she had written: *"IT'S THE PERFECT TIME TO SEE THE MIGRATORY FLOCKS OF THE SCISSOR-TAILED FLYCATCHER!"*

"Eduardo. Please try to contain your excitement. Just a little bit. At least until I've had my coffee." She caught his smirk in his reflection against the window.

A row of buses was already parked at the side of the school, and students chattered by the entrance, clutching giant paper-bag lunches and water bottles. Everyone had been instructed to wear clothes they didn't mind getting dirty and appropriate shoes for hiking. A few wore hats and sunglasses.

Eduardo joined his friends, while Isabel said hello to the other chaperones.

"I'm Nicole, Henry's mom."

"Tamara, Jasmine's mom."

"Nick, Angel's dad."

None of their names fully registered, and after a pause Isabel blurted out, "Isabel. I'm with Eduardo." She turned away from them and pointed in his direction.

The teachers assigned each chaperone to a bus and had them do a head count once the students were settled. Eduardo's teacher, Mrs. Moyer, clapped to get everyone's attention, and when that didn't work, she pulled out a whistle, brought it to her lips, and took a back-arching breath of air. The kids grew silent, like magic. One whispered, "She's gonna blow!" and a wave of hushed giggles traveled the length of the bus.

"Guys and gals, y'all are in for a treat today." She paused for dramatic effect. "Now. I know your bellies are all aflutter with excitement for homecoming. And pretty soon the school stadium will be packed with alums flying home to their alma mater, but I assure you none of that compares to nature's spectacle as the butterflies and the birds fly away before the winter. Who can tell me what that's called?"

From the back, a student yelled, "Migration!"

"Exactly. And where're they going?"

"To get a date for homecoming!"

The group erupted into laughter. Kids clapped, high-fiving and hugging their bellies. A boy sitting on the aisle fell over in his seat, and even the adults failed to keep a straight face.

"Okay, okay. Besides that. Who can tell me where they're going?" Mrs. Moyer asked.

"South," a young girl said.

"Exactly. And what's south?"

"Mexico." This time, it was a voice she recognized. Isabel locked eyes with Eduardo, who seemed embarrassed that he had said anything at all.

"That's exactly right! They go south to Mexico, and sometimes they keep going through Central America into Panama. Pay attention, because later we'll be drawing their route on our maps."

They parked among a row of RVs just outside the park entrance. Mrs. Moyer pointed out a trailer with a Minnesota license plate, explaining that the Valley was home to so many rare species, birders trekked from all over the country to catch sight of them. A little farther down the way, a pair of Border Patrol trucks crept along the road. A jogger waved hello to one of the agents, and he lowered the window of the green-and-white SUV for some friendly banter. They moved in tandem until the road split, and they went their separate ways.

The teachers assigned each chaperone to a small group of kids for a guided hike along the trail. Each group was joined by a park ranger, who shared all sorts of fascinating facts: that the way a rock cracked could tell a story—had it been water, or the earth shifting, or both? (The river was just a few miles away.) That a bird's song could tell its name, even when all the group saw were branches shaking high above their heads.

"Nature is a mystery, and we are its observers. Detectives," the guide said.

They met back at the welcome center for lunch. It was a perfect day to be outdoors; cool gusts of wind and just enough clouds to provide cover without turning the sky gray. Isabel caught the parent chaperones touching up layers of sunscreen while their children tried to swat them away like flies. She was glad she wasn't one of them.

The parents must have sensed this. While they were cordial to her, among themselves they had long-winded conversations on subjects she knew nothing about, and they didn't seem to mind her silence. For a while Isabel nodded sympathetically as they complained about their kids' schedules, about how difficult it was to coordinate drop-offs and practices.

Isabel watched Diana lean into Eduardo's chest as they both straddled a picnic bench several tables away. He wrapped his arms over her shoulders and whispered something into her ear.

"That Diana's made a world of difference for Eduardo," Mrs. Moyer said, her voice, for the first time all day, quiet. "Opened him right up like a flower."

"She's a very nice girl. My husband and I have enjoyed getting to know her," Isabel said.

"She's whip smart, too. Definitely going places. Seems to be giving him just the push he needs." Mrs. Moyer stood up to address the group again. Lunch was over, and it was time for the kids to explore the preserve and chronicle their findings. She wished them all luck in spotting the scissor-tailed flycatcher.

Isabel's group was Eduardo, Diana, and two others. The boy, Seth, clutched a pair of binoculars around his neck, while Julia, a tall, lean, girl with the air of someone much younger and smaller, followed behind. Isabel recognized them as the stragglers. The ones who were always picked last and pretended not to mind. She slowed down so the group could stay close together.

"Cool binoculars. Have you seen anything?" Eduardo asked. She was so proud of him for this small kindness.

"Not yet. Just a lot of leaves and moss."

It was true. Strands of moss hung from everywhere, thick and long as ropes, and Isabel had to push them aside with her arms to let the kids through. The moss was dry, and it swallowed the light as they passed, but it added a sense of adventure. She could tell the kids liked it, too.

They heard a rustling of leaves overhead. Chins up to the sky, they searched the trees for the telltale signs of the flycatcher: black on top, white along its belly, a tail shaped like an open pair of scissors. Isabel looked at the group as their mouths opened in anticipation. In the distance, she saw a small group crossing over the trail they had just traversed. They seemed lost, their movements hurried but indecisive. Perhaps a few students had gotten separated from their chaperones. The leaves crunched beneath their feet, and the kids, startled, turned their attention away from the trees to the silhouettes.

The group stopped several feet away from them. They were not students or hikers at all. They were a family: mother, father, little girl. They were all younger than she. The father locked eyes with Isabel, his face dripping with mud and sweat and water, and she understood.

"Are you all okay? We were just heading back to the entrance. That way." She gave a slight toss of the head backward. "The school bus and park security will be waiting for us."

"Yes. Thank you." He placed his arm over his wife's and child's shoulders, gathering their soaked bodies into a line and turning them in the opposite direction. Slowly, they walked off the path, their bare feet stepping over split trunks and dried leaves. The little girl dropped something—a water bottle or a doll, it was hard to tell at first—and Diana lunged forward to pick it up. She was about to call after them when Eduardo stopped her.

"Be right back," he said, taking the crumpled fabric, which had been knotted to form the shape of a small child.

"Did they fall in the river?" Seth said. "Should we call for help?"

"No, they'll be fine," Isabel said. "They're just finding their way through."

Eduardo returned to the trail and started walking in the opposite direction. Isabel and the kids followed.

No one mentioned it the rest of the way. It felt important to forget, or at least pretend to forget, what they had seen. They focused on other things with the kind of enthusiasm Isabel was used to seeing in parents who were trying to be strong for their children. They smiled with their whole faces, voices pinched with cheer along the edges.

Everything around them became far more interesting. A sprouting plant cordoned off with chicken wire became poisonous or an endangered species. A trail of splattered berries hinted at deer nearby. They came upon a stream that cut across the trail, and Eduardo leaped over it, extending his hand to her and Diana. It was no wider than a sidewalk; along the way it grew deeper, and the water rushed through the earth as if nothing could stand in its way.

Isabel wondered where the water came from, where it was all headed. To think it was strong enough to carve canyons and polish rocks. To think it was simply once water, and now a border so fluid they could barely swim in it without drowning.

They merged with another group on their way back to the welcome center. Quiet disappointment spread over the students as they formed a line to board the buses. A few whispered among themselves, "Did you see the birds?" They shook their heads or answered with a low "no." As she took roll, Isabel caught Seth taking one last glance through his binoculars, scanning the sky and the miles of trees ahead of them.

"Before we go, make sure you're not forgetting anything!" Mrs. Moyer shouted. "Remember the first lesson of nature: make like a tree and leave it the same as when you arrived."

She paused, as if expecting a laugh or at least a few groans, but the students were no longer paying attention. They looked past her at something behind the bus.

Across the sky, a sheer-black blanket looked like it'd gotten caught and tangled in the wind. It grew long and thin, stretching in waves over a bed of trees.

There must've been thousands of them, and yet, they were one. The flock fanned through the air, shrinking and expanding as it flew and flowed and paused and changed direction, and the group became mesmerized into stillness, every soul afraid to move or say a word because it felt too beautiful for them to witness.

Seeing them, Isabel felt weightless. The birds turned gravity into magic, and only when one straggled and lost its place did she finally look at its wings, and she knew, as it flapped in a desperate fury, that it was no longer flying. It was just trying to keep from falling.

# CHAPTER 26

## January 1982

Elda had never been so cold in all her life. The air here was bitter and dry; it made the backs of her hands feel like an old cotton dress that'd been washed too many times. Sometimes, when she was folding Martin's clothes or pinning his diaper, the cracks in her skin would latch onto the fabric's fibers. She worried she might scratch the baby with her hands.

"A mother's touch should be soft. Gentle," she said to Omar. This place made her hands tough as pot scrubbers, but she dared not say it. She dropped a blanket over the top of the baby's stroller, hoping his breath would keep him warm as he slept. If only they could raise the temperature just a little, she would be able to tolerate these nights, but the building managers kept the thermostat locked away.

"It's because there are so many bodies here during the day. It must get warm," Omar said.

Elda couldn't imagine. By the time the three of them arrived every evening, the place was deserted. It was three floors of office space, clusters of desks barricaded by plastic, fabric-covered walls.

Elda sat at a bench by the main stairwell while Omar made his way through the maze, vacuuming and dusting and emptying trash receptacles.

The baby seemed to find the constant hum of the vacuum cleaner soothing. He would drift into a calm sleep and wake only during the abrupt pauses of silence when Omar had to switch the plug from one electrical outlet to another. Even then, Martin protested not by wailing but by stirring and whining and gurgling. It was as if he knew he wasn't really supposed to be here. Omar and Elda's boss trusted them to come every weekday evening, clean the entire building, and lock up the facility when they were done. He had no idea they brought the baby along.

She rocked the stroller back and forth until Omar finished the floor and returned. "Did you find any cheese at the end this time?" It was her little joke. Ever since she had first seen this place, she had called it the labyrinth.

"I ate most of it and gave the rest to three pretty mice I ran into on the other side. They wanted to know what took me so long."

"Did you tell them chubby old rats move slower?" She grinned, and he leaned in to kiss her as he squeezed onto the bench beside her. "See? You barely fit," she teased. In truth, she found the extra pounds Omar had gained since they'd arrived to be kind of cute, and she often told him so.

She placed her pencil and book of crossword puzzles back in her purse and got up, stretching. "Remind me what my time was yesterday?"

Omar pulled a palm-sized notebook from his shirt pocket. After three straight nights of him forgetting, she had made him start writing it down. "Ten minutes and thirty-seven seconds."

"Okay." She took the cart full of cleaning supplies that Omar had pulled out of the closet.

"You're sure you don't want me to do it? I don't mind."

Every night he tried, and every night she said no. She'd felt bad enough having Omar do her work when she had just had the baby. Now that it had been nearly seven months, she told him it was a matter of restlessness. She got too much rest, and he not enough of it.

"Stay. Admire your son for a bit. I'll be back in less than ten minutes. Ready?"

Omar looked at his watch, waiting for it to hit the minute mark. "Okay . . . go."

She rushed off, pushing the cart toward the restrooms.

By now, Elda had a system. With window cleaner in one hand and porcelain cleaner in the other, she would spray the row of mirrors first, then mist the sinks on her way back. She would stuff her pockets with newspaper to clean the glass, and with towels to wipe the faucets and porcelain. She had a similar choreography for the stalls, and at the end of it, when the bathroom walls were gleaming and the toilets had been scrubbed, she would flush them all at once, reveling in the chorus of spinning water. The floors, of course, she mopped on her way out, before moving on to the men's room. She always cleaned it last, because the urinals didn't take as long.

"Time!"

"Ten eighteen. You beat last night's by twenty-one seconds."

"That's it?" She was out of breath, and her forehead was balmy. They put away the equipment in the supply closet and headed to the stairwell, ready to do it all two more times.

"Mi amor, you have the strangest way of keeping yourself entertained," Omar said before he turned on the vacuum.

"I can't help it." It was both a relief and a surprise that he believed she was doing this for fun. She wouldn't have wanted to worry him with the truth—that making a game of it was the only way to make it go faster.

She did it because she couldn't stand the cold of the bathroom tiles. She couldn't stand how the lines between each square intersected, forming crosses just like the ones she had prayed to that night at the stash house, all for nothing. She couldn't take how even a small, dark stain or a cloud of mold in the grout made her think of the blood that had seeped, so slowly, out of her attacker's body.

What she hadn't told even Omar is that she didn't scream for help right away. That night, in the moment after she stabbed him, she had pressed her body against the bathroom wall and watched him die.

The blood had pooled out of him like watercolor on paper, perfectly round and silent. He hadn't grunted or grimaced. His entire body had tensed, as if he were trying to squeeze every muscle tight enough to seal the wound.

He never took his eyes off of her, and Elda had found she couldn't look away. He was boiling, evaporating right in front of her. It seemed vital that she not interrupt. It seemed vital that she bear witness.

She had watched his hand start to tremble, then his leg. A string of saliva formed between his lips, glistening in the moonlight like a spiderweb, when it became hard for him to breathe.

In the end, his head did not collapse onto the floor, nor did his open-eyed gaze simply go vacant. Watching him die had been like watching someone fall asleep; she counted his breaths until they faded. It had possibly been the single most intimate moment Elda had ever shared with anyone, even Omar. When he was finally gone, only then did she feel how his spirit clung to her. Only then did she scream.

Nearly a year later, she still knew by heart how long it takes for a man to die. She hadn't been keeping count, but the moment's stretch came back to her constantly, so much that it became its own unit, a measure of time only Elda could understand.

It was in her coffee, steaming and then suddenly cool enough to sip. In between the second-to-last stop along their bus route and the moment it dropped them off blocks from work. In the number of seconds Martin spent suckling at her left breast, then her right. Most of all it was in the bathrooms she cleaned night after night. It didn't matter if it took her ten minutes or fifteen. The moment expanded, filled the time. It lived and breathed and pulled her with it.

# CHAPTER 27

It was easy for her to keep her promise to Martin; Claudia blamed her work for not calling, and Isabel felt so guilty about making Elda uncomfortable during Eduardo's birthday party, that she didn't dare bring up the subject again. An odd silence reigned over the family that summer. Everyone seemed busy and happy enough that there was not much to report when they saw each other. Work was good, the kids (as Martin liked to call Eduardo and Diana) were fine. Life moved forward in that slow, steady pace that makes it hard to notice anything is changing until it has changed.

It was a Sunday, and as usual they were on their way to Elda's house for supper. They drove in separate cars, with Eduardo and Diana trailing them at a two-car distance, just as Martin had taught. Isabel watched through the rearview mirror for full stops, for eyes on the road, and for hands at ten and two o'clock. She winced anytime Eduardo's knuckles slipped below the dash.

"It's okay," Martin said. "He's got a good head on his shoulders."

"It's not him I'm worried about." In the lane next to theirs, a convertible swerved in and out, in a hurry to overtake them. "If he ever got pulled over—"

"He won't. He knows he can't goof off like most kids do."

"How do you know that?"

"Seriously? Eduardo makes Superman look like a troublemaker. He wouldn't bend a rule to save his own life."

It was true. It was hard to believe how much he had changed. Like any other teenager, Eduardo still had his mood swings and lapses in judgement, but they trusted him to make good decisions in the end.

"You're right. He reminds me of you sometimes, when you were his age. Except without the pleated pants."

"Hey. You barely knew me then."

"I paid attention. You were like a tiny adult. Always serious and helpful and obedient."

"You thought I was a mama's boy, didn't you?"

"Your words. Not mine. I would just say you were . . . innocent."

He laughed and shook his head. "I'd say spineless. I'm just glad I grew out of that phase in college."

She was about to say she liked this Martin better anyway, when they heard a horn honk behind them. She turned just in time to see Eduardo, still at a safe distance, and a truck speeding up to pass them both. It had a giant hot-pink-and-purple bear-shaped piñata strapped to its roof, and as the driver made an angry gesture, its strings flailed against the truck's windows like frantic tentacles. It cracked them up so badly, Isabel thought she would cry, then she saw Diana and Eduardo in the rearview mirror laughing along.

They pulled in to Elda's driveway, still giddy from the bizarre display of road rage. "That was crazy," Eduardo said as he helped them carry the food out of the car. "But see how calm I stayed?"

They praised his driving and alertness while they waited at the door.

"Oh good, you guys are finally here!" Claudia said when she opened it.

"What do you mean? It's barely five after five," Isabel said.

"We agreed on four, but it's fine."

"But Elda told me five," she said, trying her best to sound unaffected.

"No, I told you and Claudia four. I'm trying to eat earlier now, remember? What does it matter? You're all here, and you made it in one piece!" Elda leaned in to kiss her and whispered, "We would've called to check on you, but we didn't want to make Eduardo feel rushed."

Standing in the foyer, Isabel gazed at the tiled staircase that towered before her, wishing she could run up the steps and hide in the first closet she stumbled into. She couldn't picture the second floor of Elda's house beyond this slice of space. It was not the same home she had visited as a child, years before Elda became vice principal at the high school. Isabel had gotten a tour of the house the first time Martin brought her, and since then, there'd been no need for her to go back upstairs. The house was not particularly large; the downstairs housed a half bathroom, the living room, and the kitchen. The vague idea of Elda's bedroom hung over her, and she imagined it as an extension of the staircase—walls white as milk, thresholds and windows framed in bright Mexican tiles that repeated colors and patterns like a kaleidoscope.

"You okay?" Diana had come over while the others set the table.

"Yeah. I just thought I forgot something in the car. But I didn't, it's fine." Lately, Isabel found it easier to act distractedly instead of saying what was really on her mind. There was comfort in *I forgot*; no one ever bothered to challenge it.

In the dining room, she found Eduardo saying hello to Elda's best friend, Yessica, who always marveled at how fast he was growing. It made Isabel think that maybe he had. Maybe she was simply too close to notice.

They finally sat down. What would normally be a flurry of mixed conversations was replaced by a sudden dumbness. Elda, Claudia, and Damian exchanged glances, their lips pursed together in self-contained smiles.

"Oh, no. Don't look at me," Elda said. "Like you asked my permission in the first place." She waved her hand as if hurrying them along.

"Well the thing is, Claudia and I are engaged," Damian said.

The first thing they all heard was a gasp—Diana covered her mouth in what looked, to Isabel, like a Miss Universe impersonation, and then the congratulations and the raised glasses came, chairs screeching against the tile as everyone got up to hug the happy couple.

"You almost gave me away," Damian said to Isabel. "I'd just started shopping for rings the day you got to talking about weddings at Eduardo's birthday party." His voice trailed off, as if he had just noticed his own foot sliding into his mouth.

"Lucky guess, I guess. So happy for you two." Isabel stole a glance at Claudia just as she looked away from Isabel. She wondered how much longer they would keep this up.

"So have you set a date yet?" They had finished eating, and Isabel had followed Claudia into the living room to pick up a few wine glasses left on the coffee table. She ran a damp napkin in circles that spiraled in and out of each other over the wood, even though the glasses had left no water rings.

Claudia shook her head. "Nope. I mean, we just barely got engaged like two weeks ago."

"Right. Two weeks is nothing," Isabel said, wondering how long it had taken Claudia to tell her coworkers about the engagement. They had probably been first to see the ring and hear all about how Damian proposed. "If you need any help with any of the planning . . ."

"Thanks. But we're not really doing any of that big wedding stuff. I mean, not that you guys did. Or I mean, I guess you did, and it was great, but I just don't think—"

"It's fine. I get it." She excused herself to help Elda and Yessica with the rest of the dishes. They were standing by an open cabinet, taking turns placing a bright red bowl inside of it or in a drawer next to the oven.

"If you put it there, it's in plain sight," Yessica said.

"To you, maybe. But I'm used to it being in this drawer. That's where it goes, for years now."

"Fine. That's what I'm saying next time you call asking if I took your red bowl."

"Ay. Don't exaggerate, Yessica. That happened once."

"Three times this month!" The charms on her bracelets jingled as Yessica shook her hands in the air.

"Three?" Isabel said.

"Ignore her. She's just making a big deal out of nothing."

"You guys are so cute," Claudia said, squeezing through the kitchen door past Isabel. "You sound like an old married couple when you fight."

"Who's fighting?" Elda said.

"Who's old?" Yessica added. She took the bowl from the drawer and placed it back in the cabinet while Elda was looking away. "Mija, when you've been friends as long as we have, you keep each other young."

# CHAPTER 28

## February 1983

In his second job, Omar's favorite thing to do was refill the bowl of pep-permints by the hostess stand. It wasn't officially part of his duties. After all, being a busboy was the most straightforward thing in the world. This is what his boss, Jimmy, had told him the day he walked by, saw the "Help Wanted" sign, and inquired with his most rehearsed words in the English language: "I am interested in the job."

"Well, that was quick! I only put that sign up yesterday," Jimmy had said, his face beaming bright red. "Let me give you a tour of the place, walk you through the job."

Omar had liked the man instantly. He was thrilled that for once, he could understand such a large portion of a conversation. Jimmy was the first person he'd met in Texas who actually spoke like the man on the English-language cassette tapes he had checked out from the library. His voice was even and mild mannered, each word articulated slowly. This had been unexpected from a man in the restaurant business, but not surprising considering his age. He had explained that he and his wife, Melissa, owned the place.

"You could say we're failed snowbirds. Came here to escape the cold in Iowa for a few months, stayed the rest of the year, and bought a restaurant. Turns out we're not great at being retired, either."

Jimmy had walked him through the restaurant, pointing out the booths against the walls, which he indicated were most difficult to clean because breadcrumbs tended to get caught in the caulking that welded the windows and tables together. He pointed out the smaller tables in the center of the space and grabbed a large rectangular bucket.

"See these two-tops and four-tops? That's what we call them because that's how many people they'll seat. Anyway, just be careful when you clean them." He ran a wet rag over the blue and gold speckled surface. "See how it wobbles? Some of the legs are just the tiniest bit uneven, so you gotta just, wiggle them like so."

He had shown Omar the jukebox and pay phone near the back of the restaurant, the restrooms with the doors labeled "Gals" and "Guys." There was an L-shaped counter where lone diners sat on separate stools; Jimmy walked behind it and into the kitchen, and Omar followed. The air was filled with hot steam coming from the ovens, sinks, and dishwashers.

"Let's see. I think that pretty much covers it. Not much more to being a busboy. Maybe keep an eye out for things that need doing. Keep the mint bowl full, sort out the menus when they get all mixed up . . ."

"And the hours?" Omar had asked.

Jimmy hesitated. The job was part-time and all day shifts, which were generally less busy than the nights. It was exactly what Omar had hoped for. He hadn't wanted a job that would replace his night shifts with Elda; he had just been looking for some additional income. Back home, his family was hoping to join them across the border, and they had been asking his help with the fees.

"I'll do it," he'd said.

Jimmy shook his hand and told him his wife would be pleased they had gotten someone so fast. They agreed he would start the next day.

"I almost forgot about employee perks," Jimmy said. "The menu's half off, but the salad bar is free for employees. It's all-you-can-eat."

Omar couldn't understand why this was so exciting. It was now his fifth week working at the restaurant, and he had tried every combination of salad he could think of. He was so tired of eating lettuce and tomatoes and carrots that he gave himself a stomachache one afternoon eating nothing but hard-boiled eggs and tuna.

The next day, Elda started packing his lunch. This way was better, because he had been wanting to take his breaks in the park across the street, now that the days had gotten warmer.

"I'd make a mess eating those huge salads on a park bench."

"I don't understand. Why own a restaurant only to tell your workers that salad is all they can eat?"

It wasn't until the following week, when their neighbors invited them to a buffet-style Chinese restaurant, that Omar realized the misunderstanding. He was more amused than embarrassed, and when he told Jimmy, the man laughed so hard he let Omar have anything off the menu, on him, for the rest of the week.

Omar ordered a club sandwich with fries and crossed the street to the park, just as he had planned. He watched a family of ducks swim in the man-made pond. Not two blocks away, he could hear children's voices and the shrill blow of a whistle. Minutes later, the sound of footsteps rose out of the bushes, and he turned to see a group of twenty, maybe twenty-five, kids jogging down the trail along the pond.

They wore green shorts and yellow T-shirts, and they seemed to clump together by level of athleticism: the spry ones, far ahead of the rest of the class, while the ones whose feet barely lifted off the pavement limped at a steady pace, just a few yards from the kids who had stopped to walk or clutch at their sides.

He scanned each of their faces as they passed, wondering how old they were. When Martin was born, Omar had looked at his son's face for the first time in complete disbelief that he could hold an entire person in his arms. He still had a hard time believing the boy was walking. One day he would run just like these perfect strangers' children.

"Who do you think he'll be like?" he had asked Elda that day at the hospital. "More you or me?"

"Both. And neither. I think that's the whole point," she'd said.

Since then, they had moved out of the crowded apartment the coyote had left them in, and they had found a place much smaller, but that they had to share with no one. It was a bedroom and a kitchen and a dining room in one. The only space behind a door was the bathroom.

With their earnings from cleaning offices at night, they managed to pay for rent and utilities, bus fare, groceries, and the occasional large purchase like the mattress they bought when they moved in. But for the most part their money went to family back home and things for the baby. Even going to secondhand stores, it seemed they were never done shopping for him.

They began to cut expenses. The first things to go were Elda's weekly phone calls to her mother. They then went from speaking every other week to once a month, with Elda often crying throughout their conversations. When she would hang up, she'd tell Omar that their son was growing so fast, it seemed impossible to cover thirty days in ten minutes.

"Mamá doesn't think it's fair she should be separated from her daughter and now her grandson. She thinks God is punishing her." Elda had just finished nursing the baby, and Omar had put him down for a nap.

"For what?"

"For not standing up to Papá for me. She thinks he would have accepted us being together eventually. She blames herself and says it was all for nothing. That Martin and I should've stayed behind."

He popped open a can of soda and leaned against the refrigerator. "She just misses you, that's all."

Elda sat against the kitchen window, at the small fold-out table the last tenant had left behind. The sun shone through the curly tendrils that always seemed to orbit her forehead, no matter how tight a braid she wove. Omar thought she never looked more beautiful than when she was coming slightly undone.

"Do you agree with her?"

"With what?"

"That it was all for nothing."

She didn't look at him, just scratched at an old scuffmark on the table. "Not all of it."

He understood without having to ask. Things here were new, clean, better. But there were days when he felt he had traded his life for somebody else's and gotten the wrong size.

"And the rest of it? About you and Martin staying behind?"

She recoiled as if she had bitten into something sour. "She's crazy. To even think about separating father and son . . ." Elda shook her head and looked down at her lap, her chin pressed close to her neck. Her silence shifted into something dense, as if she were straining to carry it.

Omar bent down and placed his hands over her knee, peering up at her face. He had sensed this for so long, but had been afraid to acknowledge it. Her pain was a short pause between moments; only off rhythm if you paid close enough attention. He'd felt it when he spooned with her at night; how it took her longer to fall asleep. In the mornings she would wake as if she had never been resting in the first place. When she used the bathroom, Omar would hear her flush and wash her hands, and then he would wait. She always stepped out a few seconds after he expected her to. He always wondered how she filled that time.

"Vida. I wish I could suffer instead of you."

Her fingers found their way to his, and she squeezed his hand. "I just think about him all the time, growing up without his father. All because of me. What if he's not okay? What if I've ruined that poor boy for good?"

Omar was not convinced Tomás would have been better off with a father like his, but he didn't say so. He knew there was nothing more haunting than a *what if*. If Elda hadn't defended herself that night . . . There was no alternate ending he could see them living in. This pain was waiting for them all along, unavoidable, in one shape or another.

"Even if you could, would it help to know how he was doing?"

She sighed, her breath wet with tears. "Sometimes I want to know, and sometimes I just want to forget."

Two weeks later, Omar walked into the restaurant and got his second job.

He was wiping down one of the booths near the front of the restaurant, catching glimpses of passersby outside the window, when he saw him.

It was a Tuesday afternoon, and classes had let out half an hour ago. The school's basketball coach had brought in the boys' team for a meal before their away game. Omar counted them, scanning their faces as their clumsy bodies trickled in, then helped the hostess group several tables together for the large party.

It was their slow time of day—just a few customers who had come in for a snack or a cup of coffee—and the coach's voice filled the space as he began giving the team a pep talk. He asked them a string of rhetorical questions ("Are we gonna go out there and give our all today?" "Are we gonna stay focused and play smart?" "Who's number one?"), and the boys responded in grunts and cheers in the affirmative.

Their young enthusiasm amused Omar, who laughed as he leaned over a booth to clean it. As he looked not just at the window, but through it, he noticed three boys on the other side. One was holding his backpack open, while the other two looked inside. They high-fived over what they found. The boy zipped up his bag and swung it over his shoulder, turning toward Omar. He didn't see him at first; Omar probably just looked like a silhouette behind the glass, and the boy was about to turn away when they both paused.

"I'll be right back," Omar called to the hostess, who barely looked up from her seating chart as he walked out.

"Tomás."

His cheekbones were more pronounced than the last time he had seen him, and his jawline tensed as soon as he recognized Omar. His friends mumbled their goodbyes and walked away with a swagger. For a moment they just stood by the trash receptacle, not saying anything. Omar tucked the damp washcloth he was holding into his back pocket.

"I didn't think I'd see you again," he said.

"Were you like, following me?"

"I work here." Omar signaled toward the restaurant entrance, and the boy nodded. His eyes traveled into the space, scanning the students' faces in the center.

"Do you know those guys?" Omar asked.

The very suggestion seemed to offend him. "The jocks? They're not my friends."

"Don't you go to school together?"

"Yeah, but we don't hang out or nothing." He put his hands in his pockets and turned away from the window.

"Of course. You have your own group of friends. The ones with the sideway hats, right?"

Tomás smiled and nodded.

"And you like it? It's going good, I mean? School . . . and stuff at your aunt's?"

"Yeah, it's fine. You?"

"Things are going good."

"You like it? Cleaning up after the school jocks?"

"It's honest work. And they treat me well."

Tomás seemed to consider this. He took out a pack of chewing gum and offered Omar a stick before unwrapping one for himself. "What about your wife? What does she think about it?"

"About what?" Of course the boy would ask after Elda; he should have expected as much. But the way he did it so casually rubbed Omar the wrong way. Tomás was one of the only people who knew their deepest secret, and yet here they were, talking about nothing and perhaps everything.

"I don't know. About all of this."

"Everything is good. Life here isn't easy, but it doesn't give false promises like back home. A person can build something if they work hard enough."

The boy looked like he had already lost interest. From inside the restaurant, they could hear chairs scraping against the floor as the students gathered their bags and lettermen's jackets. He gripped the straps of his backpack and shifted his weight between both feet. "So you think you'll be here for a while? At the restaurant?"

Omar wondered what was in that bag. What would have provoked him to high-five his friends when he was a teenager? A dirty magazine, perhaps, or a pack of cigarettes, or alcohol. "I'm here from mornings until four, most days. You should come by, you know? I'll buy you a sandwich."

Tomás's face lit up at the offer. "And my friends?"

"Don't be fresh. I don't own the place, remember?"

The boy smiled. He stepped aside as the basketball team poured out the door, rushing past him and Omar toward the yellow bus in the parking lot. The bus rumbled as they climbed in. It became a tunnel of shouts and laughter as windows snapped open, and then a whistle blew and all was quiet.

Omar heard the coach's voice boom: "On three. Onetwothree!"

"GUERRA GREEN JAYS, THIS MEANS WAR!"

# CHAPTER 29

## November 2, 2015

## Year Three: Leather

The walls throbbed. The air around her pulsed. In her own silence, Isabel could hear the static of her thoughts, crackling and sparking beneath the surface.

*This is what happens when you drink like a teen in your thirties,* she thought.

Still in bed, she raised her arms and brought her hands in front of her face. They were swollen, and they itched, but when she scratched at the skin, the sensation spread down her arms like a bruise. She flipped them over: black nail polish and faded-purple ink made the wrinkles on her fingers look deep and dry. Over the course of last night, she and Martin had gone to four bars and been stamped five times—once by each bouncer that asked for ID, and twice by an overzealous doorman who probably resented all the other bars they had visited before his. Isabel's hand looked like a passport that'd run out of pages.

She got up and went to the bathroom, nearly tripping over her shoes, tossed to the side of the bed. Ignoring the light, ignoring her lack of balance, she ran the bathwater as hot as she could and pulled out a facial wipe.

If her mother could see her now, hungover with makeup still caked all over her face. It was the most she'd worn since probably her wedding, but when Claudia called insisting they come out for a few drinks to toast both her engagement and Isabel and Martin's anniversary, Isabel had gotten an urge to feel glamorous. Eduardo was on a school trip to Six Flags Fiesta Texas in San Antonio, and this time (sensing he didn't want her tagging along for his senior trip to the theme park) Isabel had not volunteered to chaperone.

With the house finally to themselves, barhopping had not been on her list of to-dos. But it felt nice to be invited, and it seemed one of those rare chances that, if turned away, would never resurface. Martin had begun ironing his shirt as soon as he got off the phone with his sister. Pressed for time, Isabel had dug a black skirt out of the closet and paired it with a sleeveless sequined top.

"Are we going someplace fancy?" Martin had asked. "I was planning on wearing jeans."

She'd laughed and said it was not like they had to match.

Of course, none of this amused her now.

She dipped her naked body into the scorching water, relishing the initial burn, how something so painful could become so soothing. It was not unlike drinking, or the first few times she had had sex. Except this asked nothing of her. In this, she was alone and warm, and she could float without feeling like she was falling. She couldn't remember the last time it'd been like this.

She tried and began to cry.

Her body, shaking in the tub, created a gentle wake. The water slapped against the white tiles. She slid her head beneath the surface, and her sobs became muffled, her outburst, just harmless bubbles.

Last night while she and Martin took one, then two and three, then countless more shots with Claudia and Damian, she had felt the world shift a little. With each drink they toasted the engagement and new beginning. With each drink, gravity seemed to loosen its grip on her, and she had drifted away, watching all the tension in her relationships sink beneath her, as if they were held down by stones.

It'd been hard to stop then. Even after Martin switched to water, Isabel kept drinking like she had something to prove. Looking back, she couldn't remember what it might have been. Worse, she couldn't bring herself to fully admit it.

They had planned nothing for today. No gifts, no special dinner. If she was lucky, she would get a peck and a happy-anniversary mumble mixed with morning breath. It felt silly to care; she never thought she was the type to bother with romance—until it was gone.

She sat up in the tub and took a deep breath. For a brief moment she thought of Omar, but he, too, seemed distant and unimportant. Last week, Martin had slipped her a copy of the police report from his father's arrest.

"Thought you might like to read this," he'd said, as if each handwritten page were a bedtime story. The report was not as detailed as she would have liked, but it painted a clear picture, nonetheless. A drug deal gone bad. Such a petty way for a person to die. Omar had confessed to everything: one stab to the left side, and the victim had bled out. Isabel studied the report night after night for nearly a week, rereading the lines, the names of the officers and victim, in hopes of catching something new.

"What is it? Not what you expected, right?" Martin finally said.

"It just doesn't make any sense. Was your father an addict?"

"I didn't think so, but that shows how much I know. Just don't let yourself get obsessed, okay?"

The next day, Isabel scanned the report onto her laptop and gave the hard copy back to Martin. She didn't ask where he had been hiding it all along, and he didn't offer to tell her. He folded the pages in half and then in quarters, then kissed her on the cheek as if to say thank you for laying it all to rest.

Except now she had more questions than she had started with, and they made her feel tainted and unfaithful. She was more determined than ever to get answers and be done with it, convinced that the truth would wipe the slate clean for all of them.

On the fuzzy floor mat next to the tub, her phone vibrated. It was a text message from Claudia asking Isabel for a ride to pick up her car. They had left it parked overnight in a garage off of Seventeenth Street, and now she was worried it might get towed.

**Martin won't pick up. Damian's at work,** Claudia wrote.

**Nice to be your last resort,** Isabel typed. But instead of sending, she deleted it and replied she was on her way.

In the garage, she cringed as the metal door slid open. Martin didn't have to be up for another half hour, but the roar of the door's motor was so loud, she was afraid it would wake him. She took a step toward her car and immediately jumped back.

It already had a passenger, sitting and waiting, as if she were simply returning from getting something she'd forgotten inside the house.

Had he ever arrived without startling her? That first time, that day in the car after the wedding ceremony, she had been frightened less by his presence than by what he represented—a gaping, invisible hole in her and Martin's relationship, one she had never seen until Omar arrived, so big that he could fit in it.

He smiled at her and shrugged. He had the look of someone caught in a lie, afraid and relieved. The car dropped a little as she rushed in and closed the door.

"This is getting old, Omar."

"Thankfully, I'm not."

"Don't do that. This isn't funny anymore. Is this all a joke to you?"

"Possibly. Is there any other way it makes sense?"

"I'm tired, Omar. I'm not here to solve your riddles. I have a life to . . . figure out. It's our anniversary today. Or did you already forget?" Taking her eyes off the road for a quick moment, she caught him crossing his hands in his lap and closing his eyes. She wondered if this helped to absolve the hands that had taken a life. "What is it? You look like you just found religion or something."

He laughed. "Please. I'm only here for one day." He put his elbow on the window and rested his chin against it, looking outward.

They got on the highway overpass, heading west. Palm fronds peeked over the edge of the road, dwarfed only by a series of strip malls and fast food signs that jutted toward the gray sky.

"I wasn't sure you'd come," she told him. "Is your mood-sense or radar thing or whatever you call it not working?"

"I don't scare off easily. And I thought, maybe it's about time I apologize."

"I'm not the one who needs your apologies." She felt sour, as if everything she had learned about Omar had gone bad inside of her.

"Maybe. But you're the only one who'll hear them."

"I don't want to. You've done nothing but keep secrets from me. You made me keep them from my family. Do you know what that's like? To feel like you're lying to them even when you haven't said a word? And for some crazy reason, I trusted you. I felt sorry for you. And you let me." She gripped the steering wheel tight, catching her breath.

"It felt nice to have someone on my side for once."

"When were you going to tell me about prison?"

Omar rested his head back. Drops of rain had accumulated on the sunroof. The clouds were clearing now, and he let the sun shine on his face, not bothering to squint or close his eyes. "Did Martin tell you? Or Elda maybe?"

"He's my husband. Did you really think he wouldn't tell me?"

"And Elda?"

"She doesn't know we know. When were you going to tell me?"

"She doesn't know."

"That's what I said. Now answer me or go. Please."

"You're not listening. Elda doesn't know. Any of it. She doesn't know I went to prison."

Isabel slowed the car, for once grateful for the red light near Claudia's house. "How is that possible?"

"It's . . . it's a lot of things." He made no effort to say anything else.

"So what, she just thinks you left her?"

"It was better that way."

"For you maybe. And for her?"

"For her, always. You don't know the half of it."

Though his words carried more sadness than anything, they were the closest he had ever come to anger, and they stung.

They passed the first two entrances into Claudia's neighborhood and turned into the third. "I need you to go now."

"So soon? I'm sorry. It's just not easy for me to talk about Elda."

"It's not that. It's just, your daughter's expecting me." She came to a full stop at the end of a thin road. There were no cars behind them. Once she made this right turn, they would be just a few houses away from Claudia's. She took a long moment to finally look at Omar.

"You're going to Claudita's?" His smile, usually so natural, looked vulnerable. "You get to see her. Just like that? Anytime?"

*Not exactly,* she wanted to say. "I'm sorry."

"I won't say anything. I just want to see her. She won't . . ." But he didn't finish his sentence.

"She's getting married soon."

He nodded. "I'll stay in the back. I won't say anything. It won't be like last time, I promise."

"Do you know what that put me through? Last time? I nearly had a breakdown."

"I just want to see her up close, hear her voice. She won't even know I'm here."

"How can you be so sure?"

He tapped his fingers against the center console; she wanted to put her hand over his to stop the tapping, but didn't. "Because I've tried. Please. I know it's a lot to ask. But she's my little girl."

It almost felt like they were talking about different people. Claudia had been many things to Isabel, but never little. Back when they had tied her bedsheets to her closet doorknobs and created a canopy under which they dreamed of growing up, it always felt like Claudia was years ahead of her. She never cried, never apologized, never bothered with crushes and hurt feelings. In her mind she was already living a life far from the Valley, while Isabel couldn't imagine calling another place home. Nothing ever fazed Claudia; she was like a giant stone, jagged and impenetrable, but also too quick to turn cold.

"Just, get in the back and stay there, okay?" She sensed his smile without looking at him, even as she lowered the window and signaled for the car behind her to pass. It sprayed a mist of rainwater as it sped by, and when she turned back to look at him, Omar had already switched seats. She sighed. He was always moving without her noticing.

She caught sight of a curtain swaying, just barely, in the front window of the house. No sooner had she put the car into park than Claudia stepped out wearing a simple blue jersey dress and gray flip-flops that slapped against her heels in quick succession. She was always power walking, always seemed to have other places to be. Isabel thought it made her look like she was racing to the nearest bathroom.

"You're a lifesaver," Claudia said. She plopped into the car and turned to the back seat. "I didn't realize you'd have company. I'm Claudia," she said, busying her hands with the seat belt. Isabel tapped the brake, and the car jolted in the driveway, as if barely missing a cat or a child crossing behind it. Claudia gave Omar a quick, cordial smile, and he stared at her, dumbstruck, perhaps a bit too long.

"I'm so sorry," Isabel said. "I just, I didn't think . . . this is—"

"Mario," Omar said. "We know each other from the hospital. Crazy luck, I ran out of gas this morning, and Isabel happened to drive by. Gotta get that gauge fixed. It sticks at a quarter tank when it's empty."

"Well, it's a good thing you ran into each other," Claudia said. She laughed in the way people do when they're trying to be polite.

"So I guess we'll get your car first," Isabel said.

"There's a gas station right around the corner."

"Oh no, no. You first. I don't want to keep you any longer," Omar said, craning his neck to look at her as he spoke. In quiet moments at traffic lights or when she slowed before a turn, Isabel could see him in the rearview mirror, glancing at his daughter. It was like watching a teenager with a crush: no glimpse or chance to say something wasted.

He asked them both general questions, but Isabel knew better than to answer most of them.

"How was your Halloween?" When he meant, *Tell me about any of your days.*

"Have you lived in this neighborhood long?" When he meant, *How has your life been, all this time I've been gone?*

For her part, Claudia didn't seem to mind. She was in such a hurry to get her car and get back to her wedding-planning that she barely looked at Omar as they spoke. When he asked, she told him that she had been working on Halloween, and that the neighborhood was nice because it was mostly full of young professionals. "No loud kids on the street, but lots of baby-making noises next door. So I guess we'll wait a few years and see."

"Do you have kids?" Now he was posing questions he knew the answers to, just to keep her talking.

"It's just me, my fiancé, and our dog."

Isabel saw him smile at her in the mirror, even though it was lost on Claudia, because by now they had pulled into the garage, and she was looking for her car. They went in circles from one level to another, and she wondered aloud whether it had been towed. "That's the last thing I need today." She scanned the lot while Isabel's and Omar's eyes remained fixated on her messy brown bun. It'd been maybe ten minutes since she had gotten in the car, and Claudia hadn't recognized him. She hadn't paused to ask if they had met before, hadn't mentioned that something about him felt familiar.

Was it time or absence that disguised him? Perhaps she simply had no memory to match him to.

"There it is!"

Isabel had driven right past the blue sedan.

"Thank God." She leaned in to Isabel for a half-seated hug and grabbed her purse. "It was nice meeting you, Mario. Get that gas gauge checked soon, all right?" As she walked the few steps to her car, she gave them both a small wave. They idled, and Omar mimicked her gesture, wiggling his fingers while his palm stayed still.

"See her left foot? How it tilts out a little?" he whispered.

Isabel nodded.

"She's always done that. It was worse when she was three . . ." He paused to wave again as his daughter drove away.

"I know. She went to physical therapy for it, and when that didn't work, the doctors had her try Rollerblading. It straightened both feet out, for the most part." She hadn't realized she was interrupting until it was too late. They were both so eager to claim a part of her, they had forgotten this was not a casual conversation.

"Thank you for this."

"I'm sorry—"

"I mean it. You didn't have to let me stay."

"I didn't think she'd see you. Or at least, you know."

"Elda really never talks about me, huh? Not that it'd help. I imagine to Claudita I'm barely a faceless memory."

"But she saw you this time."

"That's true. Maybe barely is enough."

Cars were starting to circle into the lot. Isabel backed into a spot and parked. "What's so different about this time?"

Omar shook his head in wonder.

"Come on, enough already. Why come all this way if you won't tell me anything?"

"It's funny you think that. I always feel like I've told you too much. There are so many things you shouldn't know, and it's nearly impossible to pick apart what I can't tell you from what I must."

"Must?"

"The first time I came, I was just so happy to see you and Martin. I didn't think much about why. And I thought I had so much time. I thought she would, anyways."

"Who?"

He laughed like it'd always been obvious. "Elda." For a moment he said nothing else, just let her name stand on its own. But when he spoke again, there was a desperation in his voice she had never heard. "I have next year. Maybe the one after. Maybe."

Isabel couldn't tell if he was talking to himself or to her. Suddenly he was all mumbles and pauses, torn over what to say and what not to say.

"Slow down. You're not making any sense."

"I can't." He brought his hands over his mouth. He looked small to her then, like someone she would probably never notice in a crowded room. "You know how they say that one person's paradise is another person's hell? The idea of this unflawed eternity . . . unflawed for who? It's not perfect. It has gaps and holes and spaces we can get lost in. Everyone there, we're just memories. All we know is what we remember, what we choose to hold on to."

The warmth of the morning's bath came over her, rushing into every small part of her, then turned piercing and cold. She remembered as a child drawing heaven, a simple blue line between earth and sky. Aside from a few clouds and birds, it was blank, a vast nothingness she could never picture. When her father died, she imagined him painting it for her, adding color and texture and sound. She closed her eyes and tried to think of it, but everything was littered with dark splotches, places where her sight and memory failed.

"Why are you telling me this?"

"I never wanted to."

"Then why?"

"You haven't noticed? Sometimes, even when I can't see her, I can tell she feels lost. She doesn't remember, or she remembers the wrong things at the wrong time."

Isabel's mind was still hazy from last night. She could feel her heartbeat climbing her chest to her throat. "Elda?"

"Who else?"

And she understood. Who else had ever mattered? "I hadn't noticed."

"She's always been good at keeping her secrets."

"What are you getting at?"

"If she goes without knowing the truth, then she never will. It'd just be her without me. Always. Two sides of the same coin."

"If she goes? You don't mean that she's—"

"I'm not saying it's soon. I don't know, actually. I can't see the future, just what's in front of me. I never wanted to have to tell you."

Beyond the cement enclosures of the parking garage, the horizon was nearly black from a far-off rain that was fast approaching. It was time to head home, but she couldn't will herself to move.

"Is this about the man you . . . went to prison for?"

He crossed his arms and nodded. The AC was set just above low, but he shuddered as if he were cold. "Martin thinks I did it?"

"You confessed," she said, as gently as she could muster.

He looked down at his hands, wrinkled and pale as school paper. She could tell he was picking his words, tossing some, keeping others. "Tell her I did it to protect her. I can explain the rest, if she'll let me."

"Omar, I can't . . . I promised Martin I wouldn't say anything."

"Then tell Martin to tell her. Tell them anything."

"And even if I did, why would they believe me?" She thought, *Why should I believe you?*

"Maybe she won't. But maybe it'll be enough."

They headed home, the rain, mixed with hail the size of raisins and marbles, rattling against the car. Pedestrians ran across the intersection, carrying bags and coats over their heads, and on the highway cars sped home, as if nature were chasing them away. Isabel kept her hands tight on the steering wheel. The car kept slipping past her grip, sliding over layers of rain and pavement. She couldn't see more than ten feet in front of her, just road and yellow lines dashing beneath them. She could hear nothing but the rain engulfing them. It was so loud, Omar had to shout when he next spoke.

"I have to go. Please don't let her forget me."

She was too worried about the car swerving out of control to turn away. She tried to tell him to stay a few minutes, that they would be home soon and under cover. As she got off the highway and stopped at an intersection minutes from her neighborhood, she felt her hand turn hot and balmy against the car's interior.

Looking down, she noticed Omar's hand on hers. It was covered in veins and freckles that seemed to be fading. She couldn't take her eyes off them; it was like his skin was reversing time, growing smoother and lighter until it blended with her own and was gone. She looked up to find the seat empty, and when she placed her hand on it, the leather was still warm.

# CHAPTER 30

## April 1983

No one ever seemed to stand still in the United States. People in lines glanced over the shoulders of those in front of them. Mothers sitting in buses bounced children on their laps, as if the roads weren't bumpy enough already.

Elda had observed the rhythms of her new home silently when they first arrived, not wanting to complain despite the exhausting noise. The contrast was striking: back home, the big cities had been all car horns and police whistles, and even the smaller towns carried the voices of food vendors and gossiping neighbors from one end of the village to the other. But in between there were always moments of nothingness. Beggars napped. Housewives cooked batches of tortillas over the comal. Children, resigned to boredom, kicked rocks down hills of dirt.

Here there was time for none of that. The roads were eerily quiet and controlled, but the drivers were like ticking bombs; swerve a few inches into someone's lane, and they would honk you off the road.

Elda tried not to let it get to her, but she could sense their new life taking its toll. She often thought of the walks she and Omar took along the edge of their village. On their first date, they had followed the railroad tracks up a hill to where a group of Omar's friends were gathered around a campfire. They had a few beers, played songs on the guitar, and when they walked home three or four hours later, with nothing but moonlight to guide their way, it seemed like no time had passed at all. Everything was familiar, and everything felt theirs. Elda had never recognized that feeling until it was gone.

Here, she was an uninvited guest in a home she didn't want to disturb. In public she said only what she needed to; she learned the cuts of meat she liked at the grocery store deli, the stops along her usual bus route, the forms she had to fill out every two weeks when they got paid and wired money to Mamá.

Her newfound timidity became habit. She spoke to herself and the baby more often than she spoke to Omar, keeping her thoughts to herself in his presence. With this new job he had at the restaurant, he was suddenly the one with stories to tell, so as the three of them rode the bus to their night job at the office building, Elda only listened.

There was always one about his boss, Jimmy. How it turned out he'd had a stroke four years ago, and that was why he spoke slowly. Or the hostess, Karen, who was so distracted that she often seated too many customers in one waiter's section, and once handed a menu to a blind man. There were the regulars, the ones who ordered the same thing every Thursday, the ones who tipped big, and those who didn't. Sometimes Omar would repeat a joke the cook had told him, and when Elda didn't get it, he said it was funnier in English, or that she just had to have been there.

"Maybe the baby and I can visit sometime for lunch," she said one Saturday evening. Elda leaned against the bathroom threshold while Omar covered his face in shaving cream.

"Yeah. Or maybe we can go for dinner one night when I'm off. That way things are calmer." He let his razor run under the hot water until the steam fogged the glass.

"It'd be nice to put faces to all the names."

"Mm-hmm." He pressed his lips shut to get his chin.

Elda's heart beat loudly in her chest, and it felt like her world against Omar's, constricting as his expanded, one desperate to catch up with the other. As much as she loved him, it wasn't enough. She was shrinking in on herself, each day full of less life than the last.

Omar had surprised her when he took the job at the restaurant; he claimed it would help them bring family over, and they wouldn't have to feel so alone. But Elda knew better than to place her loneliness in the hands of others, hoping it would dissipate when she wasn't looking. She needed to do it herself.

She began defying her instincts. They were small choices at first—a fuchsia-colored shirt instead of her usual gray or white, the radio turned up a notch louder as she cooked with the windows open. Her accent be damned, she started practicing her English with store clerks and bank tellers. Most spoke to her in Spanish as soon as they sensed her struggling, but she persisted. She found that with strangers, she could be anyone.

One afternoon, she ran into someone she thought she knew at the grocery store. At first she couldn't place the woman with the baby boy at the end of the aisle, but she was smitten by the possibility that they might lock eyes and not look through one another. That they might lock eyes and not look away.

Elda pretended to read a box of cereal as she watched her—and then she remembered: Elda had lent this woman a quarter a couple of weeks ago when she had spilled her change all over the laundry facility's floor. Satisfied with her realization, she made her way down the aisle. She was surprised that the woman had a child—she wouldn't have guessed as much from the clothes in her hamper.

"Hi. I think we live in the same building."

The woman looked at her as if she were about to squint, and then her eyes widened, and her lips parted into a smile. "Yes! You saved my clothes. I owe you a quarter, at the very least."

"It was nothing."

"Créeme, mija. The viejitas in our building are the patrollers of laundry. The one time I left my washing machine unattended and came back just five minutes after the cycle ended, I found Señora Lucia tossing out my clothes like it was yesterday's trash. She kept shouting, *'Time's up, time's up,'* as if I was the one that's hard of hearing. La pobre está loca. But she's going to drive me crazy, too, one of these days."

"I'll remember that for next time," Elda said, already intoxicated by her energy.

The baby squirmed in the woman's shopping cart, which she had lined with a teddy bear-patterned blanket for him to sit in. He couldn't have been more than four months older than Martin, his legs just a few inches longer.

"You're new, though, right?"

"Yes. Well, we've been here almost two years. But we moved to the building a few months ago."

"You and the baby . . ."

"And my husband."

The woman nodded. "Well, it's not paradise, but it's a start. Of what, is the tricky part, no?" She laughed and her thick, red nails glistened under the fluorescent lights.

"It's taking some getting used to. I mean, look at all these boxes," Elda said, turning to the cereals that towered over them. "Who knew we needed so many flavors? What is a tiny rainbow supposed to taste like? Or a dinosaur pebble? It's too much sometimes." She wasn't sure why she was suddenly so talkative. Elda was often overwhelmed by choices when it came to things that didn't matter, and left without a choice when it came to things that did.

"Sugar. Pure sugar is what it tastes like. Here, try this one," the woman said, handing her a yellow box that looked like it was filled with cardboard O's. "All the moms insist it's the healthiest, and the kids like it, too." She looked at her little boy. His hair was fine and light, completely unlike his mother's, who wore her black hair in a ponytail three times the size of Elda's. "God, I sound like a commercial."

Elda took the box, thanked her, and asked for her name.

"Yessica. Or you can call me Jessica. Everybody does."

"Yessica. I'm Elda, and this is my son, Martin." She pulled him out of the cart and held him against her hip. Martin shouted sounds he seemed to think were words. "He does that a lot lately. Maybe he's trying to introduce himself to your beautiful little boy."

"Oh. No, Sam isn't my son. I take care of him during the day while his parents work. I take care of him and the house, actually." In her hand she held a sheet of paper with purple and yellow borders, filled front and back with a list written in cursive. "Today's grocery day," she said, raising her eyebrows.

They continued down the aisle together. Yessica shopped quickly, picking cans of vegetables or loaves of bread off the shelf and marking items off her list. Elda worried she wouldn't be able to keep up and they would have to part. She started reaching for the same items her friend did.

"You don't want that one," Yessica said when they got to the canned milk. "It's nearly twice the price for no reason. I get it because Mrs. Daniels insists it's the brand she likes, but here." She bent to reach the very bottom shelf and picked up two cans of the store's generic brand. "I promise you there's no difference."

They paid and said their goodbyes in the parking lot, but not before exchanging apartment numbers. The temperature had gone from warm to scorching in just under an hour, and as Elda pulled Martin's stroller from underneath the shopping cart and began hanging the plastic grocery bags from her arms, she could already feel her elbows sweating.

"You're taking the bus home?"

Elda nodded.

Yessica checked her watch. "The last one came by not even ten minutes ago. It'll take you at least an hour now."

"I'll wait. I don't have to be at work until eight."

"But it's so damn hot," Yessica said. She pulled a set of keys out of her purse. "Ugh. I'd offer to take you . . . Mrs. Daniels is not too strict, but I don't want her thinking I'm driving my friends around while I'm at work, you know?"

Elda smiled. She had been called a friend. "It's really fine. Don't worry about it."

Yessica hugged her tight. The last time she'd been held like this, Elda had said goodbye to her mother.

"You know where to find me if you need anything at all." Yessica bent over Martin's stroller and kissed him on the forehead. "Angelito. He reminds me of my son at that age. Agustín was tranquilito, just like Martin."

"Really? How old is he? Maybe they can play together sometime."

"He's ten now," Yessica said as she stood up and straightened out her linen dress. "But he's in Honduras with his grandmother." She pulled a worn picture out of her wallet, of a little boy in navy blue shorts and a button-up white shirt. He had a red lunch box with cartoon figures on it strapped over his chest. "I sent him those shoes and that lunch box for his first day of school."

"He looks like a happy, healthy boy." It was the kindest thing Elda could think to say, the only thing she imagined really mattered.

# CHAPTER 31

It was true, then, what they said about medical professionals not treating family. Perspective was only possible from a distance; up close,
where eccentricities were mistaken for personality traits and suspicions
felt like betrayals, Isabel had missed everything.

Now, the signs all clicked together, and she could no longer ignore
them. The problem was, she didn't know what to make of them, either.
Memory loss was a symptom; the diagnosis could be anything. There
were days when Isabel convinced herself it would be best to let Elda tell
them in her own time. There were days when Isabel worried they would
be out of time if she waited.

She asked Martin if he had noticed his mother acting strangely, and
he smirked as if this were always the case.

"You know what I mean," she said. "Forgetting things. Or not
being as quick lately."

"She is getting older . . ."

"Middle age is not older, Martin."

"Maybe it's menopause. That's probably it. You should talk to her."

"Me? You're her son."

"But you're a woman. And a nurse. It'd be better coming from you."

So she began looking for a window, stopping by Elda's house as
often as she could without it seeming strange. Eduardo always offered

to drive, though he, too, had ulterior motives: he wanted to prove he could be trusted with the car.

There was no licensing test he could pass or fail, just an agreement that they would let him drive alone once she and Martin felt he was ready. Isabel couldn't remember the last errand she had run on her own. The first few rides were anxiety-ridden; Isabel insisted he take the less-crowded back roads, which took twice as long.

But Eduardo was a fast learner, and more importantly, a calm one. She graduated him to main roads with traffic lights and on-ramps to the highway. Even when they got stuck in traffic, it was nice. They would sit next to each other, both with their gazes fixed on the road, and talk.

She told him about the time she nearly ran over her mother during her first driving lesson. It was an innocent mistake: her mother went to get something out of the trunk, and Isabel, thinking she was in park when she was actually still in reverse, let go of the brake.

When Eduardo spoke about home, friends, or school, she would gently prod him to tell her more, but she could never bring herself to take that last step. Always, hidden behind every question and intention, was Isabel's curiosity about Omar. There were times it would have been so easy. Eduardo pointed out the odd angle of his right thumb, the result of a soccer injury a few years ago that didn't heal right. He lamented his mother having him work at the restaurant, because that was when all the trouble had started.

Isabel could've asked, "Was Omar there?" or "Couldn't Omar have helped?" but she let him talk instead. His stories drifted to other places, to more detailed versions of anecdotes she had already heard: how most of the friends he played soccer with had either moved, had their lives threatened, or had simply disappeared. How the gangs had coerced his mother for a cut of her profits every month, until she had to close the restaurant.

Eventually, Sabrina chose to trade her own safety for her son's. That was how Eduardo put it the day they picked up Elda for a doctor's appointment. He pulled up to the driveway effortlessly, his hand stretched over the back of the passenger's seat as he straightened out in reverse and said, "My mother was convinced they'd never stop, even if they killed her."

"That's why she sent you here?" Isabel said. "With Omar?"

Eduardo nodded and looked toward Elda's front door. "Do you want me to go get her?"

The last time they'd come, Elda had told them to just honk the horn when they arrived. She didn't want to be fussed over. It was bad enough they were acting like she couldn't drive herself to a simple routine appointment. But Isabel couldn't bring herself to do something so crass. She decided to call the house instead.

"She said she'll be right out. So what were you saying? About your mom?"

Sometimes, when they got interrupted, Eduardo would lose his train of thought, or perhaps pretend to, and Isabel would be left with no choice but to play along.

"Just that she didn't see much of a way out," he said, keeping his eyes on Elda's front door.

"You must really miss her."

He nibbled on a loose piece of skin on the side of his thumb. "When I left, she hugged me goodbye, but I didn't hug her back. I wanted her to come with us. I took it out on Omar for weeks. I still don't know why he put up with me as long as he did."

"Maybe because he'd made a promise."

"That's what Diana says. That as long as I'm here, they didn't die for nothing."

At the mention of Diana, everything made more sense. She pictured Eduardo telling his girlfriend all the things Isabel would never know, and Diana asking all the questions she would never dare, as they parked in darkened lots on the edge of town or strolled through the mall having ice cream. Perhaps they wallowed, and cried, and comforted one another, in the way only teenagers could do.

He dug into his pocket for his phone and glanced at the screen. "She's late a lot, isn't she?"

"Who?"

"Elda. Didn't she say she'd be right out?"

"You're right." Nearly ten minutes had passed. "Maybe she decided to change, or maybe she's in the bathroom. But I wouldn't say she's late all the time."

Eduardo raised an eyebrow and smiled. "I don't know. Ever since I met her she's been distraída, you know? I mean, even that day we went to get burgers, like what, two years ago? Damn. Yeah, almost two years ago," he said, as if it were a lifetime. *Teen years don't pass the same as the others,* Isabel thought. They shed like dead skin, discarded as they're outgrown.

"I thought you said she just took a while. To get the food?"

"Right, because what did I know? But trust me, me and my friends eat there all the time, and the food never takes that long. Elda's just out of it sometimes. I mean, I get it. Every time I'm in bio lab my mind's somewhere else, too, you know? I can go get her."

"No, I'll go. Just wait here," Isabel said. The wind blasted tiny particles of dirt onto her cheeks as she walked the path to Elda's front door. She rang the bell once, then again not a few seconds later. On the third ring, she finally heard footsteps, slow and calm like a person who wasn't expecting company at all.

"Isabel!" Elda's eyes traveled right away to the car still running in the driveway, and her smile wavered a bit at the edges. "Come! I was just getting my purse together. You know how it is when you switch bags. Lipstick in one, wallet in the other, glasses in the pocket you always forget to check." She pulled out a light sweater from the closet in the hall and kissed Isabel hello as they stepped outside and locked the door. "It's ridiculous, these purses. You start to feel scattered all over the place."

It dawned on her that it would never be the right time to ask Elda what was wrong. She placed her hand on the doorknob.

"What is it really?"

"What's what, dear?"

"You can trust me. Memory loss is nothing to be embarrassed of. It could just be your body trying to tell you something."

The beginnings of a smile spread across Elda's face, but then it fell, and exhaustion settled in its place.

"Well, shit then," Elda said. She put her hands in the air, irritated. "This is exactly why I wanted to drive to the doctor's alone. I'm just going in to get some test results, that's all. No point in jumping to conclusions."

Isabel nodded but said nothing.

At the hospital, she waited by the gift shop with Eduardo while Elda took the elevator to the third-floor offices. "Get Well Soon" balloons drifted alongside giant pink and blue bears, and she could taste in the back of her throat the sugary scent of flowers on the verge of wilting.

"That was fast," Eduardo said when Elda returned, not twenty minutes later.

"It really was, wasn't it?" Elda replied.

Later, when they all gathered at her house with Martin and Claudia and Damian, Elda said the doctors had given her two dates: one for a surgery scheduled next Friday, and another for an expected prognosis.

She said it hadn't been a big deal at first. Just moments when she forgot herself, moments when she stepped into a room and had no idea why. When the headaches and nausea had started, she figured it was menopause. By the time she went to the doctor, she knew deep down it was something else.

"The body knows these things. The brain is just stubborn, that's all. The doctors say the tumor cells are shaped like stars," she said with a strange tenderness. "Hard to catch once they're shooting out in all these different directions."

# CHAPTER 32

## JUNE 1983

There were things in this life Marisol was proud of, and things she wished she could forget. The problem was keeping them from getting mixed up, since her biggest triumphs often stemmed from her deepest regrets.

How then could she explain to Josselyn when she asked why all her classmates had fathers who came to Parent Night, that being away from her father was one of their lives' greatest blessings? That it had nearly cost Marisol her life to get away from him, and that it would certainly have killed her if she'd stayed?

She had worked seven different jobs since they had gotten here. She had cleaned houses and tailored clothes and waited tables and answered phones at a beauty salon, often taking two or more of those positions at once. It had gotten them a place of their own, out of the maid's quarters in her boss's home.

Months after that they moved to a safer neighborhood, with better schools for Josselyn. Her latest efforts had been for a car; Marisol could finally arrive on time to her daughter's recitals and spelling bees.

It was exhausting, but the barometer for a better life always moved one step ahead of her. "As long as you're pursuing a goal, you haven't lost the race," she often told Josselyn. For the most part, this kept her little girl content, until the day came (and it always did) when the school planned a field trip that Marisol couldn't afford, or when the teachers had her make Father's Day cards.

Her heart ached, knowing what would happen next. They would assign Josselyn to another classroom for the day, doing busy work in the back. Or they told her to make a card for her mother instead, and Marisol would tuck the pieces of blue construction paper with drawings of a family that looked nothing like their own into her nightstand drawer, next to the Mother's Day notes.

She had to remind herself constantly: *One day, none of this will matter. One day, she'll understand and she'll thank me.*

In many ways that Josselyn was too young to realize, she was already repaying her mother's sacrifices. She was bright and motivated. At night when she did her homework, Josselyn read her books and compositions out loud, pointing out each word and pretending she needed her mother's help when it was really the other way around. When other parents complained about the latest assignment being too difficult, or how they had to get on their child's case about schoolwork, Marisol remained quiet.

"Josselyn is a very self-motivated child," she once made the mistake of saying. It was the end of the grading term, and the school was celebrating with a day-long activity festival.

"How nice for you," one of the mothers said, in a tone that wasn't very nice at all. Marisol had only been repeating the notes the teacher left on Josselyn's report card. She said as much, then asked if the bike shop was nearby.

"The bike shop?" the woman repeated.

"Yes. It says here that they award students a free bicycle bell?" She pointed at the coupon attached to the bottom of Josselyn's report card.

"Oh. Well, the address is right there. You can find that, can't you?" the woman said, holding the card in her hands. She took a moment to study it. "You must be so proud of her. All A's, even in English. Who would've thought?"

Marisol couldn't help it. She laughed in the woman's face, so hard that she nearly cried and ended up fanning herself with the group of papers the teacher had given her. She tried to calm down, and it was only after the woman excused herself that Marisol realized what she held in her hands. On top of a memo about resurfacing the school parking lot was a bright red bumper sticker: "Proud Parent of a Rio Grande Valley Elementary School Honor Student." She thought of how nice it would look on her new car and smiled.

# CHAPTER 33

Elda hadn't heard the doorbell ring because of the vacuum. She shouted this to Isabel when she finally opened the door, not bothering to turn off the machine. With each stroke, it painted over the beige fiber, turning it a shade lighter as she pushed it forward, then back to normal when she pulled it back.

"Do you need help?" Isabel yelled.

Elda shook her head. With all the corners she'd turned and pieces of furniture she'd circled, the cord now wrapped itself around one of her ankles, and the vacuum hose serpentined between her feet as she moved.

"How about I finish up while you get ready?" Isabel placed her hand on top of Elda's. Again, her mother-in-law said nothing but simply turned her away.

In half an hour, Claudia and Yessica would be arriving for an early supper. "It'd be nice to get all my girls together," Elda had said last week. Her surgery to remove the brain tumor was scheduled for the day after tomorrow, but she was adamant that life go on as usual in the meantime.

Over a series of texts, Isabel and Claudia had decided to keep things lighthearted and discuss wedding plans—things like dresses and catering options and color schemes.

*Just between us,* Claudia told her, *my heart's no longer in any of this planning shit.*

*When was it ever?* Isabel thought, but instead she reminded her that it'd be a welcome distraction, for all of them. Except there would be no more talk of the wedding date, which they'd had to move up by five months. Claudia and Damian blamed the change on the venue double-booking them. No one complained.

Elda shut off the vacuum and put it away. She raced to the garage and came back with a mop and a small red bucket, which she left filling with water in the kitchen sink while she sprayed the cabinets and countertops.

"Elda, let me help you with something, please."

But her mother-in-law showed no signs of stopping. She looked like she was racing someone, and each second that passed had to be spent three different ways.

"I'm almost done. Just give me two minutes," she said. Her chest heaved as she took a moment to stand by the entrance and inspect the house. She turned her head slowly, then stopped as something in the dining area caught her eye.

"No mires, Isabel. How embarrassing for you to see all my dust." From behind the refrigerator, she pulled out a white metal stepladder. It clanged as she opened it with one foot. Isabel stopped her before she could go any further.

"I'll get the chandelier." Isabel climbed up two steps and began wiping at the glass. Illuminated by the sunlight, the pieces trembled, excited by her touch.

"No, it's filthy," Elda said, as if this were a most shameful thing. "All of it. Everything. You shouldn't have come early. I hate for you to see me like this." She dusted off her clothes, looking disgusted with herself.

"Your house is spotless. On its worst day it still looks perfect compared to ours. You keep it beautifully."

*Keep.* She had never used the word this way, and it felt mismatched, borrowed from a story she couldn't place. Elda's face turned calm, and she took a seat at the dining table, looking up at Isabel cleaning. The chandelier chimed, splashing its reflections against the pale green wall, and as Isabel admired the catches of light, she remembered a story Martin once told her about the night before his eighth birthday. It was just a after his father had left, and they'd moved, temporarily, into his grandparents' apartment upstairs. The place was like a mirror of their own home, except flipped and furnished differently. The bedrooms smelled like old books and cigarettes, and in the living room there was a giant credenza filled with mismatched silverware, dish sets, and glass sculptures his grandfather had bought at the flea market.

The apartment was so musty, Martin could smell it on his and Claudia's clothes when they got on the school bus in the mornings. It was like a cave, and every time he went inside, he felt they were hiding from something.

Martin was too embarrassed to invite friends over for his birthday, but his mother insisted that nothing had to change just because they had moved. She planned a party anyway, and she used it as an excuse to clean every crevice of her in-laws' apartment.

"It was like a bomb exploded," Martin said. Every drawer and cabinet, emptied. Every shelf in all the closets wiped clean. Clothes and shoes and photo albums and cassette tapes all piled in the center of the living room like debris. His grandmother came home and told Elda she had gone mad, and the women argued past midnight, past yelling at the kids to go to bed.

Martin stayed up and listened to them through the door, and though they shouted things he couldn't understand, it was the low, menacing whispers that scared him most.

*"I can't raise them here,"* his mother had said, and Martin pictured her pointing at a dead cockroach behind the television.

*"Look all you want. There's nothing to find,"* and he imagined his grandmother overturning couch cushions, offended by the notion that their house was full of filth.

They moved out soon after, but every once in a while, Martin and Claudia would wake to find a sock drawer or a bin of toys ransacked, its contents tossed onto the floor—a message that it was time to reorganize. Even Isabel could recall a few instances, years later when she had slept over at their house, of being stirred from sleep by the sounds of Elda cleaning.

"My mom keeps house like her life depends on it. She's not happy until it's perfect," Martin said.

Now, as Elda's eyes darted from one space to another, Isabel wasn't convinced it was that simple. "You know, I never would've noticed the chandelier was dusty if you hadn't pointed it out," she said. "You could've gotten away with it another few months."

"But I would've known it was there," Elda said. She stood up and took off her shoes, placing them in the hallway closet before making her way back to the mop.

"I just don't want you exerting yourself. The floor looks fine. Yessica and Claudia will be here soon, and we just want to spend time with you."

She dipped the mop in the bucket. "That's very sweet. But I'll be done in just a minute."

"You don't have to do this, Elda."

Her strokes got faster and wider. "Maybe you don't have to in your house. But I enjoy it. It soothes me."

Isabel watched as Elda moved from the kitchen to the small square of tiles in the foyer, talking at the floor as if she were alone.

"When the house isn't clean, it makes me feel like the world knows all my secrets. And when it is, I can breathe again."

It was strange to hear Elda go from being passive-aggressive to vulnerable in just a couple of sentences. She was usually so guarded that this small bit of honesty seemed vulgar, a slimy thing that had slipped past her fingers. Lately, Isabel feared any small change in Elda's personality was actually the illness—tiny seismic shifts in the brain, evident only when they broke the surface. Sitting on the couch with her torso twisted toward her mother-in-law, she turned away and pretended not to notice.

The silence grew cruel. Elda paused by the door again in her socks. Isabel crossed her arms over the back of the couch, resting her chin on them.

"I used to help my father clean his store on Sundays. He had this tiny furniture shop. At first he sold his own pieces, and then it got bigger, so he'd take his truck across the border and come back with artisanal headboards and dining sets, painted ceramics, that kind of thing. He hired a janitor, a young guy. I think his name was Nelson. But my father insisted the store was too big for one person to clean alone, so on the weekends he and I would help. I actually kind of liked it. But one weekend I had a party, and my dad promised to take me when we were done. Nelson had sprained his shoulder somehow, and everything was taking longer than it should have, and I threw a fit. I couldn't understand why this was our job, or why my father didn't just hire someone else while Nelson recovered. He dragged me across the store by the arm and had me wait in the car. I cried the whole time. Half an hour later my father told me I owed Nelson an apology. He said, 'Some people have holes in their hearts not even time can fill, but that doesn't mean they're broken.'"

Elda sat next to her. She looked at Isabel with the same sad expression Isabel had grown used to seeing whenever she spoke about her father. It never felt right: her father had lived to tell jokes and make people smile.

"I would've liked to know him better," Elda said.

"He could make you laugh so hard you'd cry. I know you never spent much time together, but he was grateful for you. The whole family. Sometimes it's weird to me that Martin doesn't remember him. It's like he's a language only I can speak."

Elda sighed. On the coffee table, there was a stack of bridal magazines, five or six in a perfect pile. "I doubt Martin feels the same about his father," she said, her voice so low it felt like a confession.

Isabel held her breath, afraid to move or say anything that would startle her. A thousand questions flooded her mind, but none seemed appropriate.

"He never really talks about him."

"He wouldn't, would he?" Elda leaned toward the coffee table and began rearranging the magazines. "He used to, when he was little. He'd ask when he was coming back, and he'd call me a liar when I said he wasn't. He was angry with me, for months, and then one day, it was like he flipped a switch. He stopped."

"He was angry with Omar, not you," Isabel said. "I think he still is. He doesn't talk about it, but I know it makes him uncomfortable that Omar and Eduardo were so close. It hasn't been easy." It was the first time she had spoken to Elda about her marriage in anything but a positive light. Her mother-in-law's eyebrows gave a jolt, and she smacked her lips together in a sudden scoff.

"Pinche. All these years later, and Omar's still causing trouble." She shook her head, as if baffled, and announced she was going to change before Claudia and Yessica arrived. When she left the room, Isabel slid her body down the couch. She felt like she had just seen a poor impersonation of the woman she knew, a version of Elda that cursed and complained and was loose with her feelings.

With her head on the pillow, Isabel slipped her hand underneath the coffee table and ran one finger across. It was spotless.

# CHAPTER 34

## April 1986

Omar had begun to suspect that Tomás was skipping school. He couldn't pinpoint why, nor could he imagine a conversation in which he actually confronted him. During the last several months, Tomás had grown sensitive, unpredictable.

"Where's your boy these days?" Jimmy asked. He wished his boss wouldn't call Tomás that. He had met Elda and Martin years ago, when they started coming by for dinner on Sunday nights, and when Elda was pregnant with Claudita, Jimmy went out of his way to seat them himself. He asked after the family constantly, always by name, but when Omar's coworkers overheard him calling Tomás "your boy," they misunderstood. The new hostess was convinced Omar had a fourteen-year-old kid who came to the restaurant every Wednesday for a sandwich and a milkshake.

Except not lately.

Lately, Omar had eaten the soggy sandwich and melted milkshake after it sat at the counter for forty-five minutes.

Lately, he had begun to find the boy waiting for him in the parking lot, leaning against his car at the end of his shift. "You can come inside, you know."

"I can't stay long," Tomás said, and Omar wondered how long he'd been waiting for him.

He told him to get inside the car so he could take him home. It was a five-minute drive that the boy usually walked, but Omar hated the idea of him wandering the streets after dark. Three blocks west and one block south, the neighborhood changed. The car dealerships along the streets went from new to used, from displaying shiny trucks on pedestals to waving plastic-triangle flags along their perimeters. It was hard to tell which houses were businesses and which ones were homes. Tomás lived just beyond the main road.

"I haven't seen you in a while. School keeping you busy?"

Tomás nodded and pulled his sleeves over his hands, rolling them into covered fists. Omar turned the air conditioning down a notch. "Yeah. I mean, kinda."

"Kinda?"

"They gave me detention for drawing in my history book. It wasn't a big deal. Just some doodles in those blank pages in the back."

"I see." They'd arrived at his apartment building now, parked right outside the leasing office.

"Don't tell my aunt, okay?"

"I won't." Omar had never even met Tomás's aunt. Countless times, he had thought about introducing himself, but when he imagined walking up to the corner apartment with the overgrown plants and Dallas Cowboy-themed welcome mat, he always came up short on what he would say. That he'd crossed the border with Tomás five years ago, and had been keeping tabs on him since? That he's the husband of the woman who had killed his father in self-defense?

"Good. Cuz she'll use any excuse to ground me this weekend. Not like I want to go to Chris's stupid track meets anyways. They spend hours following the school bus around just to see him run in circles."

Moments like these, Omar remembered what it was like to be a teenager, how he had always been convinced the world was out to get him. Everything he did revolved around planning and plotting otherwise. Even now, he could tell by the way Tomás stared intensely at the dashboard that he was thinking one thing and getting ready to say another.

"But yeah. Now they want me to pay for the damn thing. Like I have twenty bucks for a book. Hello, I go to public school."

In the half-lit interior of the Chevy sedan, it felt like there was a version of the truth that Omar was missing. He thought of what Elda would say if she found out he had given the boy twenty dollars. How livid she would be to learn he had spent time with the boy at all.

Omar had never meant to keep Tomás a secret; he'd just been waiting for the right moment to tell her, never realizing it didn't exist. Now it was too late. Four years ago, running into Tomás could've been a coincidence, a couple of chats over lunch. He told himself he was just making sure to stay in the boy's good graces. He'd been afraid to turn him away for fear that he would blackmail his family. He knew now that Tomás didn't have that kind of malice in him, and so their encounters, however brief, had accumulated into something Omar could never explain. He couldn't say what he wanted from the boy, or what he got out of following his progress. He felt better about Tomás's future, but knew it could never change the past. And if Elda ever found out, the first thing she would ask would be, *"How long? How many minutes, how many days?"* As if he had taken a lover. As if there were room in his heart for another.

"You don't get an allowance? Anything like that?" Omar asked.

"From my aunt? Bitch is cheap as hell."

"Oye. Since when do you call women bitches? Where'd you pick that up?"

"Sorry, sorry. My aunt. She gives me the change when she shops for groceries, but only if I put 'em in the car. She says she feeds me and keeps a roof over my head, so what more can I ask for?" His voice got high and melodic, steeped in sarcasm, before lowering into a quiet sadness. "Like I'm only good enough for the bare minimum."

"A lot of people don't get even that, you know. Back home—"

"I know. You told me."

"Here." Omar pulled four five-dollar bills out of his wallet, folded in half, and held them across the center console. It was the first time he had ever offered him money; half-priced burgers and milkshakes didn't seem to carry the same weight as four green crinkled bills. The boy just stared at the money with his hands in his lap, until Omar tapped him on the shoulder. "Take it. Just this once so you don't get in trouble, okay?"

He hadn't expected Tomás to hesitate. Did he not trust him? Did he fear being indebted to him? After all this time he still found himself wondering what Tomás really thought of him. Did he ever look at him and see his dead father, or was it just Omar's guilt that tainted everything?

"You wouldn't owe me anything. Got it?"

"You said it. Not me." He gave Omar a quick, tight-lipped smile.

"Just promise me it'll go where it's supposed to. For the book."

"I promise."

"What subject is it again?"

"Texas History."

"You mean Mexican history?"

They laughed. "Something like that."

# CHAPTER 35

It was June sixth, exactly two years since Eduardo had arrived at their home. Isabel had not expected to know this. She had not marked the date on the calendar. She had not made a mental note of the previous year's June sixth.

They'd just finished a long breakfast. Martin had prepared ham-and-cheese omelets, Eduardo's favorite, and now they were rushing to get ready for his graduation. As she brushed her teeth, the significance of today's date floated gently to the surface of her mind, like it'd always been there, waiting for the right time.

When she told Martin, he stopped midshave to think about it. "Are you sure? I remember it being cooler, like maybe spring."

She understood the trick of memory: a scorching sun, replaced by the welcome warmth of sunlight. A merciless drought, washed away by April showers. "I'm positive," she said.

"Did Eduardo tell you?"

"No." But she wondered if he knew. "Do you think that day is a happy memory for him?"

"I don't know. He looked like he'd been through hell."

It was like the patients in the ICU. When they left, as they said goodbye, they always smiled. They thanked the doctors and nurses and staff. But the gratitude for surviving was not the same as the gratitude for living. No relief could erase what they had been through.

In the living room, Martin set up his camera on a tripod and corralled the three of them into a group shot. They stood with Eduardo in the middle, like a bar graph of descending units, and before the shutter went off, Isabel sneaked a look at him—remembering how his eyes had been level with hers the day he came—struck by the close view she now had of his chin.

It was a darling picture, the kind you frame and display near the front of the house, the kind that Isabel could imagine sending to Eduardo's mother if she had ever had the chance. It was a picture Sabrina should have been in. A familiar weariness spread over her limbs, and she had to sit down, leaving the image displayed on the camera. Lately, it felt like everyone she thought of was either dead or dying. Every celebration was accompanied by a sense of mourning.

The doorbell rang, and Diana arrived with Elda, whom she had picked up on the way. Elda wore a sea-blue sweater and matching silk pants, with a floral scarf that looped just once around her long neck. Its ends draped like waterfalls over the front and back of her shoulder.

Isabel thought Elda's new look was regal. The defiance hadn't escaped her—despite her short hair and the scar on the side of her head, Elda made no attempts to cover up. Instead, after her wound healed, and the doctors began chemo, she bought a new scarf for each week of treatment. There were now six scarves, and she wore them around her neck almost daily: bright, bold prints that made Elda's eyes shimmer and her skin look dewy and warm.

Elda crossed the living room toward Eduardo, who was still standing in front of the tripod in his robe and cap.

"We match," he said. They laughed like this had been the plan all along. Isabel got the sense she was missing something, as if she were only hearing the end of a story. Ever since the surgery, Elda and Eduardo had grown close. Several times a week, they went for a walk inside the mall.

Elda said it helped her clear her head, and with the brutal summer heat, the mall's air conditioning made the exercise more tolerable.

Once, Isabel asked Eduardo what they spoke about for such long stretches of time.

He'd only shrugged and said, "Just life, stuff. We have a lot of different things in common."

Elda embraced him now, keeping her hands on both his shoulders as she took him in. With her hair cut short, it was hard not to notice how the scar across her skull stretched when she smiled.

"Let's get one with you and Abuela," Diana said, fumbling with the lens of Martin's camera. The term seemed to disturb no one, least of all Elda, who only laughed and straightened her blouse for the photo.

Isabel wondered if wanting to be happy for someone counted as being happy for them. She was about to suggest taking a picture with just herself and Eduardo when Martin said they should get going. Traffic and parking were bound to be a nightmare. They squeezed into the car, Elda in the front, while Eduardo sat sandwiched between Diana and Isabel in the back. His gown stretched over part of Isabel's leg, and she straightened it out with the warmth of her palm, thinking it would have been better if he'd waited until they arrived at the convention center to wear it.

"Thanks for ironing it this morning," he said.

"Oh. It's nothing." She turned to look out the window and felt his shoulder press against hers.

"Mira. It's us." He had snapped a selfie of the two of them, an overexposed, blurry image of him leaning into the frame while she gazed into the distance, unaware that he had come in close.

# CHAPTER 36

## JUNE 1986

They were just eggs, smaller than the eye of a needle. And yet, every time Elda slid one off a long, shiny strand of Claudita's hair and cracked it between two fingernails, the sound—a low click—made her want to run out of the apartment, jump into the pool, and scream where no one could hear her. It was like something out of her worst nightmare. Her baby's soft head, populated by microscopic parasites that had her itching and crying all day.

"Mami, ica, ica," she'd say, and Martin would laugh and correct her, "It's pica! ¡Pica!"

But Elda wasn't amused. No mother wants to tell her daughter, years later as they reminisce over faded photo albums and fuzzy memories, that some of her very first words were "it itches."

Elda told as much to her mother one Sunday evening.

"Don't laugh." She imagined her voice slithering through the phone line for hundreds of miles, only to be met with the sound of her mother's chuckles. "We don't pay forty-eight cents a minute for you to make fun of me."

"Mija, that's too expensive! You can send me three letters for what it just cost us to say hello."

"Don't be silly. It's worth it to hear you. I can't get that in a letter." She pulled out one of their new fold-out chairs from beneath the kitchen table, spinning twice to untangle herself from the telephone cord before taking a seat. "Omar and I can afford a ten- or fifteen-minute call every once in a while."

"Since when?"

"Since tonight." Omar had called just minutes ago with the news. "He got promoted to shift supervisor. He'll be overseeing the staff for a new building. It's seventeen stories tall!" It felt almost impossible to keep her voice down. If Elda hadn't called her mother the second she had gotten off the phone with Omar, she might have awakened the kids just to have someone to celebrate with.

"¡Gracias a Dios! I'm so happy for you. It was time, no? How long has it been since he's worked there now?"

It'd been more than five years, but that wasn't so important. "Only two years since the last time they promoted him. And if it hadn't been for that, I would still be scrubbing toilets with him, remember?"

"I suppose that's true. But what is this world coming to with buildings taller than God made the mountains?"

"It's not that tall." Elda tried to picture it the way her mother would, windows and doors that opened to the clouds. Only she could exaggerate and minimize something at the same time. "You've seen them bigger. Remember that time we went to DF for Tía Eva's wedding?"

"Don't remind me. My sister's always been a show-off, but a wedding in DF was too much, even for her. I'm sure she loved having her husband pay for our hotel when we could've easily slept on the couch. Who puts their family in a hotel?"

"I thought you liked the place." To Elda, who had been sixteen when her aunt married and moved to Mexico City, the hotel was majestic, the most beautiful place she had ever been. It had a glass elevator with golden railings, and the rooms—with their two beds and a couch—were large enough to sleep six.

"Who needs all that luxury? That's what's wrong with cities," her mother said. "Everyone is so obsessed with living in big houses, they end up cramped together, sleeping in each other's filth. That's how kids end up with lice."

"Like you never saw a head of lice."

"You never came home with one, no."

"Besides, McAllen is not some big city. It's not even a tenth the size of DF."

"It's not the size of the city that matters, it's the population. And what's worse is all the DF drug dealers and gangs are coming into our town now."

"What?"

"I didn't tell you? Poco a poco. We hear these stories all the time now. My friend's son was mugged just two weeks ago on his way home from work. The pandillas wait for them outside the bar on Fridays. Maybe they'll think twice about drinking away their money before spending it on their family, but still. Casi lo matan."

"That's terrible."

"I know. Have you tried hot air? A blow-dryer?"

"What?"

"For Claudita's lice." Her mother had no patience for segues. She was always bouncing from one topic to another, and got annoyed when Elda didn't keep up.

"No. I thought about it, but Sylvia says the baby's too young. It'll burn her scalp."

"Oh? Well what does Sylvia suggest you do?" Since Elda's mother-in-law had moved into the apartment upstairs, Elda's mother got defensive whenever Elda mentioned her. It was an innocent jealousy, born of a mother's longing to be close to her daughter. Still, Elda decided not to mention that Omar's cousin, Julio, had arrived just a week ago and was sleeping on their couch. Today Julio had left with Omar when he went to work, giving Elda a small, rare window of privacy.

"Don't say it like that. You know you could just as easily come live with us too if you—"

"Just as easily, ha! It is not, 'just as easily,' mija. Mi tierra is like my blood. You can't just take it out of a person. That is not living. You were young when you left. Maybe that's why you think it's so easy."

"I never said it was easy. I just don't feel like being reminded every time we talk."

"You're right. It's just, I miss you. I miss the kids . . ."

Through the crackling phone line, Elda could hear her mother's quiet sniffles, the muted sobs for the grandchildren she had never met. "If things go well, maybe we can visit soon."

"What do you mean? What things?" Her mother gasped before she could answer. "No, Elda. Tell me you didn't hire another lawyer. Not after what happened last time."

Last time. Last time she had let her hopes fool her into optimism, and it had cost her two and a half years of their savings. Elda could barely stomach the shame.

"This time will be different," she said. "Esta vez es de confianza. He helped a woman at our church in the exact situation. Even Yessica is using him. We asked around to nearly everyone we know."

"And what exact situation are you in?"

"You know what I mean. The kids, they're citizens."

"And what does Omar have to say about all this?"

"Hold on." She stood to get a Coke and some leftovers, the telephone cord stretching between the refrigerator and the kitchen table. Elda heard a shrunken voice coming from the receiver.

"*Don't tell me you haven't told him! ¿Elda? ¿Estás ahí?*"

"I'm here, I'm here."

"Why wouldn't you tell him? Is it because of how angry he got last time?"

"He didn't get angry. Not at me, anyways." Elda was constantly reminding her mother that her marriage to Omar was not as volatile as her and her father's.

"This is not a little thing. A husband has a right to know his wife hired another immigration lawyer."

"And he will. When the time is right. It's too early to tell if anything will come of this, and I don't want to get his hopes up. He was so upset about the money last time, it was like someone drained the life out of him. He said everything was fine, but he can't fool me."

"Does Martin have them, too? The lice?"

That was the other thing about Elda's mother: she dropped an argument the second she realized she wouldn't win it, with about as much finesse as a tired squirrel.

"Not nearly as much as Claudita. The second he brings them home from school, they decide they like her head best."

"Well then have him stay home until that school has their lice under control. You're always talking to the teacher. Just have one of those conventions again."

"Conferences, Mamá. And I can't have Martin missing classes."

"It's just a few days."

"And what kind of example does that set for him and his sister? They have to know their education is the most important thing."

"You put too much pressure on them, mija. They're so young."

"Exactly. They're sponges now. They absorb everything."

Elda heard the delicate clatter of her mother's rosary beads and pictured her nightstand, crowded with framed pictures of her grandchildren.

"What are they doing now?"

Elda knew her mother meant not in this moment, when they were tucked away in bed, but in this life. What new development had she missed?

"Martin has become obsessed with the *Star Wars* movies. One of his friend's moms took them to the theater for her son's birthday, and now he can't wait to see the next one. He pretends everything is a sword. His toothbrush. His father's flashlight. His English is nearly perfect now. I think he's taught his sister a few words. She named her favorite doll Jenna."

"Jenna? Where did she learn a name like that?"

"I have no idea. Maybe it's one of her brother's classmates, or the TV."

"Don't let them watch too much TV. You know it only turns them stupid."

"Only a little bit. And only educational shows." Even Elda had learned a few new words from *Sesame Street*. "Claudita watches an hour in the morning while I pick up after breakfast, and then we go to the library." *Not every day,* she thought. It was more like once or twice a week, but her mother didn't need all the details. "She likes it when I read to her in the afternoons."

"And they're eating well?"

"Claudita's a vacuum. You drop a shred of meat on the floor and it's in her mouth before you can pick it up. And Martin will eat anything you put in front of him. Sopas, tamales con mole, hamburguesas . . ."

"You make him hamburgers?"

"He orders them when we go to Omar's restaurant."

"El restaurante de Omar? You talk like he owns it. Is he still busing the tables?"

"Yes, but I don't want to talk about it." The only thing Elda hated more than arguing with her mother was agreeing with her. If her mother only knew how many times she and Omar had fought about this job he insisted on keeping. Three years, and his wage had gone up by just a dollar, for a job with a title with the word "boy" in it. *"It's because even a child could do it,"* she'd once said, and tried adding (too late) that Omar was better than that.

Her mother whispered, "It's just odd, isn't it? That he likes it so much."

"He says the owners are good to him, and that that's hard to find. It's true. He and his wife are very considerate."

"And everyone else that works there? You've met them?"

"Unless they hired someone new yesterday, I've met everyone."

"No one of interest, then?"

"No, Mamá. No one. And even if Sophia Loren was waiting tables in a skirt, I still wouldn't be worried."

"Don't exaggerate, Elda. That's just foolish."

She sighed. "Tell me about you. How is your back?" Her mother had taken a bad fall last summer when she slipped and landed on her tailbone. It was the first and only time Elda had spoken to her father since they had moved, and his voice was unrecognizable. She had thought it was a prank at first; Yessica was always warning her about scammers who would try anything to get money out of immigrants worried for their families back home.

Only after he cleared his throat—phlegm and rage comingling as they always did—and yelled, "¡Puta! Is this how you repay your family? By forgetting us?" did Elda understand. They wired money for her mother's hospital bills and medications, and when the prescriptions ran out, she sent bottles of aspirin and heating pads with neighbors who traveled home.

"It's not how it used to be, but it's fine. I'm older now. Maybe it's just what God intended. I have the back of a woman never meant to carry her grandchildren." Her mother took a deep breath and tried to laugh, but it wasn't funny.

"Mamá . . ."

"You should go. Our fifteen minutes were up ten minutes ago. Kiss the babies for me and send my love to Omar. Te quiero mucho, hijita."

The hardest thing was not the goodbye, but the silence that followed. It left Elda feeling disoriented, like she had been plucked from one place and left alone in another.

It was still two and a half hours before Omar and Julio would be home. Elda ground coffee beans into the percolator and called Yessica over. It was late enough that her building was finally at rest. The neighbors' dogs had exhausted one another trying to bark through walls, and the group of teens that often spent the evenings in the parking lot, sitting on car hoods and tossing empty beer bottles into trash bins, had moved on to quieter, more intimate pursuits.

"You'd think they'd be the moaning, screaming types, with all the noise they make leading up to it," Yessica said when Elda opened the door, rolling her eyes in the direction of the dark green Mustang that rocked gently in place.

"I'm not about to complain," Elda said. She cleared Julio's bedsheets from the couch and folded them so she and her friend could have a place to sit.

"Where's Don Juan?" Yessica asked. Omar's cousin had been trying to flirt with her since he'd arrived. "I almost didn't come over until you told me he wasn't home."

"I might've gone over to your place if he was." She missed having her own space. When Omar was at work and the kids were at school and her in-laws weren't coming in and out for a meal, she would sit on the couch and read the paper. Now with Julio around, there was never a quiet moment to collect herself. "He and Omar should be home soon."

Hours passed. The first few glances at the clock were to see how much longer they had before the men arrived and Yessica would go. Soon Elda began making excuses—perhaps there was traffic, or maybe they stopped somewhere for a drink—and she knew her friend would stay up with her. There was nothing lonelier than waiting. Nothing worse than the ebb and flow of hope as footsteps approached and passed them by.

While they sipped cup after cup of coffee, Yessica told her about a sign she had seen at the management office, indicating they would soon begin fining litterers. They laughed, because management was always giving false threats and promises. They spoke of school, how ridiculous it'd become that lines of cars stretched for blocks when parents arrived to pick up their kids.

"I wish Sam could just take the bus, like Martin," Yessica said, and Elda nodded, pretending that the child her friend spoke of was her own. Yessica stared into her reflection in the cup she held with both hands. "I spoke with my mother the day before yesterday. I could hear Agustín in the background, calling *'Mami, Mami.'*"

"That's sweet," Elda said.

Yessica shook her head. "He didn't mean me. He was calling to her. Mami, cuelga. He wanted her to get off the phone and play. With his new Lego set."

Elda had gone to the toy store with Yessica to buy that Lego set. They had spent nearly an hour choosing the one Agustín would like best.

She placed her hand on Yessica's knee. "One day he'll know who's sending the toys and clothes and the money for school, and he'll be grateful."

"At least I chose a toy he loves, right?"

Before Elda could think of something to say, Omar rushed into the apartment, slamming the door behind him.

"Is he here?" He ran into the hallway, and then the bathroom.

Elda stood so fast she spilled her coffee on the couch. "Who?"

"Julio. He's really not here?" Omar lowered his voice. A long trail of sweat marked his back and underarms, and his face was flushed.

"He hasn't been back all day. I thought he was with you."

"He dropped me off at work so he could use the car."

"You lent him the car? Without telling me?" Out of the corner of her eye, she could see Yessica stirring, gathering her purse. Elda held a hand out for her to wait.

"There has to be a reason he'd take so long," Omar said.

"None are good," Yessica said, and without another word, they all understood.

Hours later, Elda woke, startled by the sound of Omar's fingertips cracking open the blinds. Somehow, the trembling *shushhhh* of the thin white metal strips registered before the sirens did. Their piercing cries seemed far away until suddenly they weren't.

"There's the car," he said, starting for the door.

Red and blue lights splashed over his face. They grew brighter and closer, one color chasing the other through the windows and against the walls, until the sirens stopped, and the lights filled the apartment.

"They're making him get out of the car," Omar whispered.

She let herself look. There were two police cars, two officers. One stood by the hood of his squad car taking notes while the other paced behind Julio, whose face she could barely make out as he leaned against the driver's side.

Somewhere behind her, she heard Yessica cooing, "*It's nothing, nothing at all.*" She heard Martin asking what was wrong.

"Stay here and don't open the door for anyone," Omar said, pulling on a jacket.

"Don't. You'll only make things worse."

"Trust me."

Elda felt a cold rush of wind and noise as he left. She twisted the lock behind him and leaned against the door.

In the living room, Martin stood by the couch, with all his sleepy weight against it and the back of his hair ruffled. He scanned the walls slowly, in awe of the lighted spectacle that'd befallen his home in the nonexistent hours of the night.

"Is it a spaceship, Mamá?"

She knelt close to him. "It's a special game, just for you. See the blue and red lights? That means we have to hide. And you can't come out until the lights are gone and I've called time. Not even if someone finds me before they find you, okay?"

Martin smiled, and she could see his wet teeth shimmering, his wide eyes plotting where to go.

"And this is very important: if someone finds me, then Yessica becomes the one who can call time. Nobody else can say when the game is over, okay? You hide until one of us says so, understand?"

He nodded and whispered, "Do we start now?"

"On three. ¡Uno, dos, tres!"

Elda pretended to cover her eyes as he ran off. She watched him dash to the hallway, undecided between the linen closet and the bathroom. Neither of those places would be good enough.

She spun, wondering aloud where he would go as she meandered toward him. He ran down the hall, past the bathroom and into her bedroom. She counted to eight and heard her little boy drop to the floor and shuffle beneath the bed.

"Ready or not, here I come," she whispered. Elda headed straight for the kids' room. She opened the closet and cleared the floor of all their shoes. She carried Claudita's sleeping body to it and covered her with a bedsheet and a fortress of dolls and teddy bears, keeping her head free so she could breathe. Her daughter could sleep through an earthquake. She prayed tonight would be no exception.

In the kitchen, she found Yessica trying to peek through the blinds without daring to touch them.

"Here," Elda said, placing a set of keys in her friend's hands.

"What's this?"

"Take them. If they come for me and Omar . . . the birth certificates are in a lockbox under the bathroom sink. The key is this little one here," she said, trying to keep her hands from shaking as she singled out the small bronze one. "Martin and Claudita can stay with their grandma upstairs at first, and then maybe . . ." She had contemplated this possibility for years, but now that she had to say it, she couldn't.

Yessica took the keys and held her. "It won't come to that. I'll see you soon."

Alone again, Elda paced the apartment, pretending to still be looking for Martin. Even after Omar returned with a cold can of soda in his hands, sipping by the window as if this were a movie he couldn't turn away from, she couldn't stay still.

She prayed that by now, Martin had fallen asleep, bored with their game of hide-and-seek. She tried not to imagine him watching her feet from under the bed, holding his breath, waiting and wondering when it would be safe to come out again.

# CHAPTER 37

The surgery hadn't worked. There were still pieces of the tumor left behind, growing with a vengeance after the attempt to out them. Isabel was the first Elda called with the results. She didn't ask what next, because she didn't have to.

"I'd like to be the one to tell Martin and Claudia," Elda said. "Just not yet. Not until I'm ready."

She sounded so small and distant, and in the silence that followed, Isabel thought of Omar. He had been right all along, about so many things.

*"Being ready is worthless,"* he would probably say. *"Like learning to swim without water."*

Isabel warned Elda not to wait too long to tell the family. "Delaying can make things harder," she said, then found herself wondering for whom. Was it the doctors? Her husband? Eduardo? She felt tiny spasms of anger bubbling inside her.

"I wish you hadn't told me," she finally said. Keeping a secret like this from Martin, even for an hour or a day, was too much to ask of any wife.

"Then I didn't. There."

Isabel stood next to the open door of the linen closet in the hallway, staring at the numbers on her phone screen as the call ended. It hadn't even taken a minute. *Perhaps this wasn't really happening,* she thought. Perhaps it was all a test she was failing.

It had been the same with Isabel's father. In the end, he grew so sick his bones became brittle as a bird's, and she had wanted nothing more than to embrace him, but feared that she would break him. Purple stretch marks and bruises that refused to heal tattooed themselves all over his body, but it was the fractures he feared most. The first time she saw an X-ray of her father's rib cage, it struck her that this was all we have to protect our hearts. His was full of hairline cracks, tiny rivulets of pain. He said it almost hurt too much to breathe.

That night, she crawled into bed and rested her head on Martin's chest, wishing she could close her eyes and find she truly believed the same things he did. That they were happy. That everything was, and was always going to be, all right.

In the inevitable clarity of morning, she was overcome by guilt. It was Saturday, and an owl hooted in double beats outside her window. A branch, stirred by the wind, made the sunlight dance in and out of her eyes through a crack between the wall and the blinds. It'd been months since she and Martin had spoken about anything but prescription doses and doctors' orders, and even if they had, she was too tired to remember it. Everything had been blown out under the glare of Elda's tumor, so Isabel tucked away any minor grievances to focus on staying strong for her. She knew she was not alone in this; anytime she asked Martin if he was okay, he nodded as if he couldn't imagine a reason why he wouldn't be. They floated around one another, breathing the same air, occupying the same space, keeping content as their lives coexisted side by side, and Elda's seemed to slip through their fingers.

What a fragile thing it was, to feel connected.

She sat up in bed and swung her legs to the floor, letting the feel of the carpet fibers against her feet turn small and needle-like. Everything was more focused now, everything impossible to ignore. She thought of the second time Omar visited, how he had asked her to pluck from memory the moments that had defined her and Martin's year. When she tried doing this now, all she had were flashes of Eduardo and Claudia, Elda and Omar. Here was the family she would never have had without Martin, without him. Somewhere along the way, she'd lost sight of him.

She got out of bed and found Martin in the kitchen, eating a slice of ham wrapped in a tortilla over the sink. Eduardo's was the only bedroom still frozen in dreams and silence.

"Let's go out for breakfast," she said, wrapping her arms around his waist and kissing the back of his neck.

"Where?"

"Anywhere. Someplace new."

"Where?" he said again, as if the question were a different one.

They got dressed, and she drove. It was the reverse of what they normally did; Martin always went for his keys, and by default she would enter his car through the passenger's side. She had told him once she missed looking out the window, and ever since they had settled into this unspoken arrangement.

Now, as they pulled out of the garage, Isabel felt the promise of adventure. Before it all changes, we'll have this, she decided. Just a drive alone, down the same roads of every night and morning, seeing what the other sees. In that moment, she felt it could be enough.

She got on the highway and rolled down the windows. Up ahead she could see a terra-cotta tiled roof shaped like a square along the frontage road, so she got off before she might pass it. The restaurant had a towering wood-and-stained-glass door that splayed open to reveal a courtyard full of white linen-covered tables and lush, glorious palm trees. A mariachi band migrated through the space, which was so large that the sound of trumpets and guitars nearly faded when they reached the far end.

"Party of two," she told the hostess. Even this felt indulgent. The morning began to feel magical and make-believe.

They were seated at a small table, pressed against an adobe wall. Its porous, uneven, beige surface made her think of a fort, the kind of place that ends up in Texas history books. The leather-clad menus were uncomfortably large.

Isabel browsed through the brunch items, trying to think of something to say to her husband. The obvious—*"It's been so long since we've done this"*—felt like a waste. Looking at him over the rim of her menu, she noticed he was sitting up straight, chest proud and rigid. To the many families and couples seated around them, she imagined they looked like they were on a first date. There was a stiffness to how they sipped their glasses of water, a delicateness as they placed their napkins on their laps. Perhaps Martin noticed it too, because after they placed their orders he leaned in close, elbows on the table as he intertwined his fingers, and just smiled at her.

Isabel felt her face grow warm. She looked down at the table, at his hands. "Did you know that how you hold your hands never changes? It's practically instinctual." She rubbed his right thumb with her own. "See? You put your left hand over your right, without even thinking."

He tried switching, interlocking right over left. "You're right. That feels weird."

It was nice to have shown him something new. It'd been so long since she had felt there were parts of her unknown to him, and she'd begun to feel like a barren field, unworthy of exploring. That was the thing about sharing your life with someone. Curiosity brought you together, but that enchantment is not infinite. There were only so many pieces left of the person Martin fell in love with that he had not yet seen. She kept them inside herself, safe and warm, knowing that when they slipped out of her they'd be gone forever, and one day she would run out, left with nothing to give him but everything she'd become, everything he already had.

"We're full of habits we never realize we've formed," she said.

He seemed intrigued. "Tell me more."

"What do you mean?"

"Our ticks. Not the annoying stuff. Like, I know I leave my socks on the kitchen counter and I'm trying to get better about it . . ."

She had noticed both of these things and thought they were cute.

"But the quirks. You know that glass of water you bring to bed every night? You ever notice you take a few sips walking over from the kitchen, but then you don't drink from it again once you put it on your nightstand?"

"No way. I get thirsty."

"For about five seconds."

Replaying every evening in her mind, she knew he was right. "You gargle to the beat of Salt-N-Pepa." She put her hands up, knowing he could never top what she'd just said.

"Wait, wait. What?"

Isabel shrugged and began rearranging the forks in front of her. "When you brush your teeth. You gargle, and swish, gargle, and swish. Always for the same exact amount of time it takes to sing the chorus of 'Push It.'"

His mouth twisted in disbelief. "Show me."

"Here? No."

"I'm not buying it until you show me." He inched her glass of water closer.

"It's just like . . ." She looked over her shoulder. No waiters coming, no diners watching them. Just a small window to explain.

She took a small sip and hummed to the beat of the chorus. Head back, gargle, pause, swish. Head back, gargle, pause, swish, swish.

By the time she mimed him spitting, Martin had lost it. He laughed so hard he clapped and sat back in his chair from the force of it. Isabel started to quiet him but couldn't help joining in. She spit a little as the air rushed through her mouth. People were staring now, and she didn't care. *Look at this couple,* they would think. *Look how much fun they have, just the two of them.*

"Your turn. Another," she said when she had nearly caught her breath. The waiter refilled her water, and she chugged it, choking back tears.

"I can't beat that."

"Oh, come on."

He traced the rim of his glass as he thought about it. "When you yawn, you squeeze your nostrils shut as you cover your mouth."

"I knew that one. It's because when we were little, Claudia convinced me that our nostrils get permanently bigger with each yawn. Next, please."

"Shit. Okay. Um, first of all: my sister is evil. Second of all . . ." He turned his head as if he had caught a whiff of something over his shoulder, reminding her of another quirk.

She gasped. "You bite the inside of your left cheek when you're thinking hard. That's three."

"Are we keeping points now?"

"Maybe."

The food finally came, the table filling with small bowls of salsa, sides of guacamole, and a large, round plate of chilaquiles that left barely any room for their eggs and chorizo. They moved their glasses and silverware around, trying to accommodate the many dishes. As the waiter left, Isabel could see the band inching their way toward them, one table and song at a time.

"So?" she said.

"I'm drawing a blank." He took a bite of his breakfast, staring blankly at the table as he chewed. "Not sure if this counts, but, is it just me, or does Eduardo talk to himself a lot? Most of the time I just catch him moving his lips, like he's reading to himself, except he's not reading. But one time I flat out heard him talking. His door was closed, so I couldn't understand what he was saying, but man, it was weird."

"He was probably on the phone," Isabel said, wanting to move on to another subject.

221

"It was charging in the kitchen. That's the other thing, you'd think he'd sleep with the thing like any other teenager. But that day, I'm positive because he'd just gotten back from his school trip to Six Flags, and he was exhausted. He went straight to bed and left his phone charging. You weren't home. You'd gone to get my sister's car. But the kid was talking to himself, Isa."

"You mean on our anniversary?"

"Yeah."

As if it were any day, and this is what he remembered most. She'd been too distressed by Omar's arrival and sudden departure to notice anything odd when she'd come home, feeling raw from everything he had told her. Until this moment, she hadn't questioned why he had cut his visit so short when he still had plenty of hours left in the day. She had never thought there might be other places he could go, other people he might see—or who would see him.

"He was probably counting his reps. You know how Eduardo is about his workouts." Her food was getting cold, and she didn't want to think about it anymore. She felt like she had crashed from an incredible high, and now all she wanted to do was climb back up, make a home there, and pretend it was just big enough for the both of them.

# CHAPTER 38

## OCTOBER 1986

It wasn't just the word, it was that she so often felt like one. On the radio, on the evening news, in headlines struck in bold, capital letters, Elda was reminded that she no longer belonged anywhere. Sometimes she imagined herself not as an alien but as an astronaut, floating between worlds so far apart that her voice got lost in the middle.

There was hope again, but she didn't want it. For more than a year the government had bounced around plans to give papers to families like hers. *Legalized,* as they called it, as if a living person breathing this air in this corner of the world were against the laws of nature. In their big house on a big hill, the men and women of the House and the Senate threw together all their ideas on citizenship and who should have it. They tossed it back and forth among themselves, fixing this, bargaining on that, until Elda felt dizzy from chasing it in the middle. She was convinced she would never catch it.

Tonight, the reporter with the perfectly wavy hair announced the government had agreed on a plan, and President Reagan would soon sign it. Elda clicked off the television, leaning against the blank screen. The set was warm, like the hood of a car, and she closed her eyes and took comfort in it. She didn't need to hear the rest of the news, which promised to outline all the requirements and stipulations for a path to citizenship. Not much had changed from the original plan, and she had already memorized the details by heart.

"Does this mean we can play now?" Martin asked.

She opened her eyes and found him in the center of the room, with Claudita just a few feet behind him on the couch.

"Only until dinner."

Martin pumped his fist in the air, and as usual, Claudita imitated his movements. She watched him in awe as he pulled out the cables and controllers from the bottom drawer of the unit.

"Me me!" she yelled.

His fingers moved swiftly as he powered on the game. A familiar, tinny tune came on.

"I play Mario?" Claudia said.

"No. You know I'm always Mario."

Elda chuckled and turned away from them as she searched the pantry for a jar of seasoning. This was probably not the best time to tell her son that they had, in fact, almost given him the same name as his favorite character. Poor Claudita would be doomed to play the thin little man with the silly mustache and green coveralls forever.

She heard some rustling and muted grunts; the children were playing tug of war with Martin's remote control. "Cuidado or I'll take it back to the store." That silly set had cost so much, Omar told the kids it was worth their next two birthdays and Christmases.

The game resumed, filling the room with its bubbly sound effects. Elda's favorite was when Mario shot balls of fire out of his perfectly circular hands—the flames bouncing happily across the screen—because the high-pitched whoop reminded Elda of her mother hiccuping. She told this to the kids as she rinsed a couple of tomatoes under the faucet.

Martin paused the game. "Nah-ah. Really?"

"Really. She goes like this." Elda imitated her mother's wide-eyed expression and covered her mouth with the tips of her fingers. "Whoop,

whoop!" she said, shrugging her shoulders. "Your abuela always acts surprised when she hiccups. Like it's the first time it's ever happened to her."

Claudita stared at her with a blank expression. Out of nowhere, she whispered, "Hiccups mean I love you."

"You think so?"

Her daughter nodded. She climbed onto the couch, her bare feet sinking into the spaces between the cushions as she puffed out her chest. "Hiccups mean I love you," she said, louder this time. She shot her arms into the air and her shirt rode up, exposing her soft, round belly.

"Nah-ah! That's stu—"

"Martin Jose!" Elda said.

"—pendous! Stupendous."

Elda narrowed her eyes at him, but she couldn't help smiling. "My little boy, using such big words."

"It means awesome. Amazing."

"Amazing!" Claudita said.

"Are you just going to repeat everything I say?"

"Are you just . . ." She forgot which words came next. Martin fell to the floor, rolling with laughter.

"Martin, ya! Enough picking on your sister." Elda handed three sets of forks and knives to her son, along with a cluster of napkins. "Turn off the Nintendo and set the table."

"Ha!" Claudita said.

"Tú también. Fold the napkins."

The children scattered. They had learned this routine long ago, always at their most well-behaved on nights when their father was at work. They had heard her say, *"Wait until your father gets home,"* so many times, his absence had become more of a threat to them than his presence.

"It's a miracle. They fell asleep after I read them just one book," she said to Yessica when she called her to come over after dinner.

Minutes later, she was setting the percolator on the stove, when Elda heard her friend's light tap at the door.

"Well?" Yessica gripped the back of a chair in the kitchen, looking like she might jump over it.

"Well what?"

"Don't tell me you didn't hear the news."

"Oh. That."

"That?! Not just *that*, Elda. *That* could change everything. *That* means I can finally visit my baby boy and bring him home."

Elda sighed, embarrassed this hadn't occurred to her sooner. "Of course it does." Yessica's baby boy was a teenager now, but she still spoke of him as if he were a child waiting for his mother to pick him up from the last place she had left him.

He'd been waiting so long now, Elda worried Agustín's desire to reunite with his mother was waning. Sometimes she would visit Yessica's apartment and catch them on the phone, and she couldn't help noticing the brief pauses, the way Yessica asked him question after question to fill the silence. The conversation was like a rope Yessica couldn't stop pulling, hoping she would find her son connected to the other end.

"Have you told him yet? Or do you think you'll wait until after you've applied?" Elda asked.

"Why would I wait to share such good news? After all this time! I'm calling him first thing tomorrow night." Friday nights had special discounted phone rates. Yessica reached across the table to Elda's wrist and gave her a gentle shake. "Anda, amiga. Don't make me celebrate alone."

"I'm happy! Really. I just don't want to get too excited until it's official."

"And when will that be? When you apply, or when you become a resident alien months after that? Or five years later, when you can finally apply for citizenship, and they hand you the papers during the fancy ceremony?"

"My point exactly. You can wait forever."

"No, mija. *You* can wait forever. *I'm* getting a bottle of tequila on my way home from work tomorrow. Promise you'll share a drink with me."

So they did. The next night, even Omar was home to celebrate. They poured shots of tequila into three ceramic mugs Elda had collected from the previous years' community health fairs. The mugs clanged together clumsily as they gave a toast.

"To good friends," Elda said.

"New beginnings," added Omar.

Yessica's eyes shimmered, their edges pinching together as she smiled. "To fucking finally!"

# CHAPTER 39

## NOVEMBER 1987

Josselyn hadn't stopped crying since Marisol had picked her up from school and they had gotten on I-2, watching their lives and their home shrink away in the rearview mirror. Marisol couldn't argue with her daughter when she said, between sobs and gasps, that it wasn't fair to have to move. Not in the middle of the school year. Not on the day before Thanksgiving break. It'd all been so last-minute, Josselyn didn't even get to say goodbye to her best friend.

Marisol had found out about the job late the night before. She had woken at dawn to collect boxes from back alleys behind grocery stores, before the workers had them destroyed. When she got home, her daughter was still in her nightgown, brushing her teeth as she paced the apartment, looking for a scrunchie to tie her hair together. Those little elastic bunches were everywhere except in their place. When Josselyn saw her mother walk in with an armload of flattened cardboard boxes, she pointed at them with her toothbrush and mumbled three syllables: "What are those?"

Marisol knew she had handled it poorly, but she was in such a hurry. It shouldn't have come as a surprise, because she had been telling her daughter for months about the job opportunities in Orlando.

All the tourism there, all the commerce. And of course the high season would be during the holidays. Of course they would have to leave on short notice.

"Opportunities like this don't wait for people like us," Marisol said, scooping the contents of her closet, clothes hangers and all, into her arms. She squeezed through the narrow hallway toward the living room, where she had assembled several large boxes. "It's a twenty-hour drive, so we'll have to leave as soon as possible. Here, this box is for your shoes."

But instead of taking the box, instead of obeying her mother like she always had, Josselyn ran into the bathroom and slammed the door shut. It sounded like a car backfiring. It was like something out of those horrible teen dramas her daughter watched in the evenings, the ones Marisol warned her were full of kids who disrespected their parents. "See?" she would say when one inevitably ended up pregnant or addicted to drugs. "That's the problem with parents in this country. They let their kids talk back to them, and then they're afraid to even lift a finger in their direction. And they wonder why they can't control their children."

Marisol had hit her only once, when Josselyn was seven, because she'd refused to pick up a book an older neighbor had dropped in the elevator. She almost sprained her wrist from the force of it, and she was glad they'd never had to repeat the episode again.

But she began to reconsider as she shook the locked doorknob. That she had to resort to yelling—"We have to go! We have no time!"—so loudly that Marisol was sure her voice traveled through the walls, ceilings, and floors was unforgivable. Was this what they meant by troubled teenagers?

"I'm not helping you pack a damn thing!" Josselyn opened the door and pushed past her mother to her room. "If you don't take me to school so I can say bye to my friends, I swear I'll sit here all day screaming till the neighbors think you're killing me."

That was the first and, Marisol resolved, the last time she ever let her daughter disrespect her.

Now that they were on the road with a trailer full of all their belongings attached to the back of her minivan, Marisol found she no longer had the energy to be cross. "Why don't you lay in the back and sleep?" she said to Josselyn. "I'll pull over so we can get the pillows and blankets out of the trunk."

They were on a long, two-lane road that cut through land that had been cordoned off by fences made of dried wooden logs and metal wires. For miles the mesquite bushes crept over the fences, nearly obscuring the "Private Property" signs. Truck after truck made the earth feel like it was shaking as they passed.

If she couldn't get Josselyn to stop crying, she might as well get her to fall asleep. *One naturally follows the other,* she thought, remembering how heavy the tears used to make her eyes on nights when she would stay up praying that her husband would come home one moment, fearing that he might, the next.

"You don't have to try to make me feel better," Josselyn said as she fluffed out her pillow. "Nothing you do would help anyway."

The hours stretched longer than the miles. It was nearly midnight when Marisol stopped for gas and coffee at a station just off the highway. She took a cassette single from the front display and asked the attendant to ring it up as well.

"How long you been driving now?" he asked.

"Almost ten hours. And we're still not out of Texas."

He flashed her a smile brighter than the fluorescent lights overhead. "Hardest part is getting out of here. All the other states, you can cross them in a couple of hours. But Texas . . . makes you feel like you're never gonna leave."

With the dead hours of the night still ahead of her, she had a hard time believing she would ever make it. Every fifteen or twenty minutes, a car came out of nowhere and passed her. Even here, on this empty, potholed road, the world seemed to have a head start.

She called out to Josselyn, who lay curled in the back seat, pretending to be asleep. She had listened to the changes in her daughter's breathing too many nights in her lifetime to be fooled otherwise.

"What do you want?" Josselyn whined.

"I was just wondering if you want to listen to this tape I bought."

This sent her sitting upright. "You bought me Tiffany?"

"Yeah. But talk back to me like that one more time, and I'll toss it out the window." She raised her eyebrows at Josselyn's reflection in the rearview mirror and caught her nodding as she climbed into the passenger's seat. Her daughter wore an oversized white shirt she had decorated with glitter and swirls of paint so thick, they reminded Marisol of dried-out spaghetti. They listened to the song five or six times, until Josselyn no longer bothered rewinding it to the beginning. She tucked her knees close to her chest and pulled the shirt over her legs.

"¿Tienes frío?" Marisol asked.

Josselyn nodded. "I thought Florida was supposed to be warm."

"It is. But we still have to make it through Mississippi and Louisiana and Alabama, where it's cold." She leaned into the steering wheel, hugging it as she tried to stretch her lower back.

"You okay, Mom?"

"Just tired. And I don't know how much further we have until the next rest stop."

"So just pull over and rest. There's no one on the road anyways."

"It really feels that way." She sighed. "We walked along roads like this once. It was just as dark, and the cars were going too fast to see us." She didn't know why she said it. Perhaps she was feeling nostalgic. Guilty. How difficult it had been back then to arrive. How easy now to leave.

"I remember," Josselyn said. "When we left the hotel, I remember thinking we were going to look for treasure. Like it was some big adventure."

Marisol hadn't expected this. Their trip across the border was certainly not a secret, but they had always spoken about it as something that simply happened, one day to the next, with no specifics or recollections worth dwelling on.

"What else do you remember?"

Josselyn shrugged as if she didn't even have to think about it. "Random stuff. The plastic bag with our toothbrushes and clothes. The nuns. How they made us that really yummy cinnamon oatmeal? And that room we slept in a few nights, with the TV that was always playing cooking shows. That's why I always put milk in my eggs."

Marisol had forgotten about the nuns. She wondered what else Josselyn had held on to, but when she took her eyes off the road to look at her, she was staring into the darkness out the window.

"I always thought you'd learned to make eggs like that from Tricia's mom."

Josselyn laughed. "When did I ever have breakfast at Tricia's?"

Marisol had allowed her daughter practically everything except for sleepovers at friends' houses. It didn't make sense to sleep on the floor of a stranger's home when she had a perfectly comfortable bed under her own roof. For years, Josselyn had begged not just her mom for permission, but her grandmother, presenting her case each time they spoke long-distance on the weekends, hoping she would in turn convince Marisol.

"Is it true she probably has just a few weeks left?" Josselyn said.

It always shocked her how their minds traveled to the same places when they shared silence. As if whatever they had been talking about before were a door that swung only one way.

"That's what your uncle said. The doctors are just keeping her comfortable now. Your abuela has even made her own arrangements for the funeral. She knew exactly where she wanted to be buried. Típica. It's just like her, really."

"Maybe we'll go someday. To visit."

"Sure." But Marisol couldn't stand the thought of her daughter returning to her birthland, only to step on the graves of their dead. She watched their headlights, how they swallowed the white, crooked stripes on the road. Up ahead they beamed onto a sign that welcomed them to Louisiana. Josselyn reclined the passenger's seat and began to fall back asleep.

"Mom?" she said, her eyes still closed. "Do you think that's what it's like for the little boy who crossed with us? He can't ever visit his father's grave either, can he?"

"I guess not, mija." It pained her to admit it out loud. She had tried tracking Tomás down once or twice, back when they still lived in the corner bedroom of the first house she had cleaned. Elda, la pobre, had called out of the blue, saying she had found the slip of paper with Marisol's phone number, and she wanted to say hi. But it seemed the poor girl had much more on her mind. When Elda asked if she had kept in touch with anyone from the group, she sounded disappointed that Marisol hadn't. She called Elda a few weeks later to tell her about her failed attempts at locating the boy.

"But who asked you to do that?" Elda had said. "He'd probably rather forget us all. Déjalo en paz."

That was the last time Marisol and Elda spoke.

She stole glances at her daughter as she drove, wishing she could let her gaze linger. The lights from the dashboard illuminated the smallest grooves of Josselyn's face, and Marisol wished, more than anything, that she could trace her softness with the ridges of her fingertips in circles and figure eights and mindless swirls that would make them both forget.

# CHAPTER 40

Nothing would ever be normal again.

When Elda told them the tumor was back, she begged them not to lose faith. She made them swear they wouldn't treat her differently.

But you can never look at a person the same way once you fear they'll be gone. Every moment became a special occasion, sandwiched between alerts for Elda's countless medications. The doctors couldn't risk surgery, because the tumor was too close to a major blood vessel. They suggested a more aggressive round of chemo than the last, but after two weeks spent either paralyzed from the pain or vomiting, Elda told them she was done. She said the only one being attacked was her, not the disease.

"I'd rather stop while there are still pieces of me left intact."

Privately, they couldn't help mourning her. She was different now, more irritable than not. Elda would snap when Claudia noticed she had lost her train of thought midsentence. If she repeated a question she had asked not twenty minutes ago, she would say no one had given her a good-enough answer.

The only person she was always happy to see was Eduardo. He had registered for community college and was looking for apartments with Diana, and hearing about his plans excited her.

"You live your life," Elda would tell him, squeezing his hands in hers. Her skin had grown thin and transparent; each day she disappeared small bits at a time. When Isabel saw her and Eduardo side by side, she'd think of how they'd soon both leave her, and she would feel a motion sickness, teetering between relief and sorrow.

Her thoughts seesawed between the memory of Omar and the promise she had made, now empty, as she failed to find the right time to say anything. It was all lopsided. He wasn't supposed to still be here. He was the piece that made everything wobble.

That Sunday afternoon, Isabel suggested they take Elda and Eduardo to the livestock show. They walked the grounds without hurry, which only served to make Isabel feel like she was forgetting something. The summer heat had begun winding down, and even the cattle seemed tired of swatting away flies with their tails.

Isabel rested her arm on a metal bar that separated her from an old longhorn, just as the animal buried its head in a back corner. So much for a good picture. She waved Eduardo and Elda over anyway.

"Look at its coat," she said. The longhorn was a light baby brown covered in shimmering white, as if draped in fresh snow. Isabel watched its sides fill with air, slow and limitless, then recede.

"Five feet, eleven inches," Eduardo said, reading the handwritten placard hanging from the gate. "Tip to tip, that's how long her horns are. Her name's Margaret."

"That's taller than any of us," Elda said. "Imagine walking with those things on your head."

"What else does it say?"

Martin, who, despite the animal's positioning, had snapped a few candid shots, placed his hand on Isabel's waist and pulled her toward him. He puckered his lips at a sign she hadn't noticed she'd been covering.

"Descendants of the first cattle brought over to the New World by Christopher Columbus on his second voyage in 1493," Martin read.

"Early Texas settlers mixed Mexican cattle from the Nueces Strip, the borderland between the Nueces River and the Rio Grande, with their own cattle to arrive at the longhorn we know today."

Eduardo came closer to reread the sign. "Río Bravo," he corrected.

"Órale," Elda said.

Across the border, the river was not called the Rio Grande but the Río Bravo. Not grand or large, but harsh and unforgiving. The Río Bravo was ill-tempered and fierce; the brave ones were those who crossed it.

Sometimes, when Isabel remembered the day Eduardo arrived, it felt less like a memory and more like a story she shouldn't forget. To think she had been soaked in sea water, sitting on a towel, while he was completely dry, having waited for them for hours. To think they had all just been swimming.

She looked at him, and he smiled.

"What? Bravo's a better name," he said.

Of course. Because it was theirs. But unlike Eduardo or Martin, she hadn't grown up sharing a name with something so much bigger than she.

"I bet no one ever picked on you with a name like that," she said.

"It didn't make any difference." Eduardo moved on to the next pen, where a calf the size of a Great Dane nursed on its mother. He placed one foot on the lowest bar of the fence, tapping it back and forth so the bar jiggled against the lock.

"I got picked on all the time," Martin said. "Kids saying I should change my name to chicken, stuff like that."

"I almost didn't take the name," Elda said. "And then I thought about changing it back to my maiden name after Omar left, and once all my papers got sorted out. But I didn't want there to be any confusion for the kids."

Elda stared at the cow nursing her young. Her giant glassy eyes were fixed on the two women, and then she blinked, slowly and lazily, as if from pleasure or sleepiness.

"I almost didn't take the name either," Isabel whispered. "But I liked the bump up in the alphabet." She wiped at her forehead with the back of her sleeve; the air, laced with the smell of hay and droppings and deep-fried anything, stopped short inside of her.

Martin had moved on to the shorthorn station. A boy, no older than twelve, posed for pictures by the pen, holding a bright blue ribbon close to his chest.

Martin pointed it out to his mother. "It's like the ribbon you made me."

"What ribbon?"

"The one you made the night Tío Julio left and you had Martin hide from the cops." The words escaped Isabel's lips before she had a chance to taste them. She cringed, and everyone looked at her skeptically. She was making no sense to Martin and perhaps too much sense to Elda, and she felt the familiar trappings of questions she couldn't answer sinking into her chest, squeezing out what little air she had left.

"What are you talking about?" Martin smiled the way people do when they don't understand a joke.

"Never mind. You meant the time you won hide-and-seek. Right?" She rubbed at her temple and blamed the heat for her confusion, saying she had gotten it mixed up with a story a patient once told her. As they walked away, Elda placed her hand on Isabel's elbow.

"Who told you that?"

"What?"

"About Tío Julio."

The words wouldn't come. A million lies raced through her mind, but all she managed to say was, "Omar."

Elda's grip on her arm went loose. She studied Isabel's face—every crevice and wrinkle and blink—as if it were the first time they had met. Crowds parted around them, and voices boomed through the PA system.

Isabel blinked back tears. "He told me."

"Who did?"

"I did." From nowhere, Eduardo's voice cut between them.

Elda let out a deep sigh, bringing her hand to her chest. His appearance seemed to amuse her more than it startled. She fanned the dead air over her face, pretending to laugh as he explained.

"Omar told me years ago, and I told Isabel a while ago. I thought everybody knew."

"Not Martin. And I'd rather he not find out." She gave them a stern look and went searching for her son.

"Why did you do that?" Isabel asked, half grateful, half resentful of the interruption.

Eduardo kept his gaze on Elda's small figure shrinking away in the distance. "You can't just tell her he's been coming. Not like this."

So it was true, then. He had been visiting Eduardo as well. He was no longer a secret for her to keep, and the small part of her that thought she was his only hope began to dissolve. "How can you be so sure that's what I was going to tell her?" she said.

"Just be careful, okay? He's not everything you think he is. Not even close."

Maybe it was the heat, or the overlapping conversations that surrounded them, swallowing her thoughts and concentration. Maybe it was that Martin had gone on to the next station without her, not bothering to wait or ask where she had gone. Or maybe it was Eduardo's young smile, that one teenagers give adults when they're convinced they know more than the adults do.

Something inside her snapped. "I don't even know what to think anymore."

She turned around and walked straight out of the tent, barely registering the sight of Martin holding up a young yellow chick in front of his mother's face, or the sound of their voices calling after her. The carnival grounds were uneven and muddy in places, and out of pure instinct she hopped over spots to keep from falling, even though she felt like the earth was no longer solid beneath her.

# CHAPTER 41

## December 1987

Today of all days, there was sunlight. Omar lay on his side with the pull of sleep still heavy on his body. His eyelids opened and closed, like breathing. He placed his arm over Elda's waist, beneath their pale yellow comforter. Elda always slept like the dead. He often joked that waking her was like watching an egg hatch—it takes time to see movement beneath the surface.

There was a twitch, and then the pop of a knuckle. He sat up and watched Elda's hand search for him under the sheets.

"Don't make a sound," he said. "If we hold still, maybe they'll sleep through the whole day." She smiled with her eyes still closed. Soon, there would be balloons to blow up, gifts to open. Songs would be sung and games would be played. All would become splashes of color and bursts of sound, but for now Omar wanted to stay in Elda's calm. Just a little longer.

"What time did you get home last night?" Elda whispered.

"Two thirty."

"And my kiss good night?"

"I kissed you. You started sleep talking. You said, 'Cover the roof with sugar and come to bed after you've showered.' What I wouldn't give to be in your dreams, mi amor."

She pulled him closer, and felt the tips of his chest hair brush against her back. "Who says you aren't?"

"There was a time when my kisses were enough to wake you."

"And now your lips are as intimate as my deepest sleep."

"Don't forget sweet. They must be, with dreams of sugar and showers."

She stifled a giggle. The kids were constantly on alert for such noises. "And how do you explain my dreams about the radios riding bicycles?"

"Mmm . . . that one is easy. Estás loca."

"Careful!" She sat up and lifted her pillow, making like she was about to hit him with it, and he let out a yell. They paused and listened. Claudita's footsteps were the quickest and loudest, accelerating by the millisecond. Martin's were five confident stomps.

"You woke the monsters! What did you do?" He looked to Elda, who only shook her head and laughed.

"We're being invaded. ¡Socorro! ¡Socorro!" She lifted the sheets to let them crawl under.

"No one can save us now. Except for la cumpleañera!"

"Yes! The super birthday girl," Elda said. "But where is she?" She propped herself up and scanned the room, her hand over her forehead like a visor.

"I'm here! I'm here!" Out popped Claudita, wearing the end of the comforter like a cape, her feet bouncing so high off the mattress she seemed to fly.

Omar caught her and kissed the back of her head. In just the last few months, her hair had changed from a fine mist of light brown to black silky strands of night. When he pressed his lips against her, he could still feel the softness of her skull cushioning his kiss. He wished all children would stay like this, never hardening.

"Who wants their gifts?" Elda pointed beneath their bed, and Martin dove under, pulling out several boxes wrapped in checkered paper and an impossible amount of tape. Omar shot her a confused expression, but he could tell she was trying not to look at him.

"These three are for Claudita, one for every year. And this one is for Martin, for being a wonderful big brother."

Claudita opened her gifts slowly and quietly, as if they were made of glass. The first was a set of tablitas. She tried holding the wooden tablets together in one hand, but a whole group of them, held together by thick strips of red, green, and purple cloth, slipped from her grip and cascaded onto the bed.

"Mira, así." Elda restacked them and held the top tablita between two fingers, lifting it into the air slowly as the rest dangled beneath it. "Now, pay attention." She bent her wrist to fold the top wooden tablet over the one directly under it. It toppled, sending the others flipping over one another until the very last one shook like a fish just pulled out of the water. "Try it. Fold it in this direction. See? It's like magic."

It seemed that way to Omar. He couldn't understand where the gifts came from. They had agreed they couldn't afford any, and as the kids moved on to the next boxes, Omar studied the tablitas more closely. He smiled and caught Elda's eyes as it dawned on him. They were old coasters, and the strings were ribbons from a bow Elda often wore in her hair. The satin was dull and stiff from the dried glue, but he remembered the color combination, how Elda had bought the ribbons years ago, saying they reminded her of home.

The rest were toys the kids didn't recognize, because Elda had disguised them as new. Fresh strings of yarn for hair and a dress made out of an old blouse revived a forgotten doll. A bent clothes hanger with a mesh laundry bag attached to its rim formed a butterfly net.

His wife was a marvel. Omar hoped their son would be equally amused.

"Open it," he told Martin after his sister was done, and Martin ripped at the paper, revealing a blue thermos with a *Star Wars* label wrapped around it. It looked brand new. He was so excited, he leaped off the mattress and ran to his bedroom to find his matching trading cards. Claudita quickly followed.

Elda explained. "Yessica sent a package of school supplies home to Agustín, but it was going to be too much weight, so she separated the lunchbox from its set and gave us the thermos." She shrugged and smiled, as if it were no big deal, though they both knew it was.

In the afternoon they went to the diner. Jimmy had insisted the meal would be on him and told them not to worry about a cake, either.

"Birthdays are special, especially when kids get to three," he said as he gathered the menus. "That's when they start remembering things you'd never expect them to."

Which was strange to think about. All Omar and Elda seemed to worry about was how to build a life for their children. Every effort, every decision, revolved around protecting them from grief, exchanging it for moments of happiness. He had forgotten that each time he embraced Claudita or made a face to get her to laugh was a moment he couldn't guarantee she would remember. Would her memory start today, surrounded by nothing but smiles? Or would she hold on to him at his worst, with his "not nows" at the end of a long day, the attention he gave in scattered fragments?

As she blew out the candles of her strawberry-shaped birthday cake, Omar wished for the strength and energy to be a better husband and father. His family, and nearly everyone in the diner, burst into applause, and Claudita bounced so hard in her seat that her pigtails slapped against her cheeks. He laughed as he caught Elda's eyes from across the booth, but was quickly distracted by a small figure pacing outside the restaurant. Its silhouette floated back and forth across Elda's shoulders.

Probably just a customer waiting for someone to join him for dinner. When he looked away and let the figure slip into his peripheral vision, he recognized its cadence, the slight limp that Tomás liked to affect, as if he were carrying an old wound in his side pocket. A numbness came over him, a peaceful recession of his breath and heartbeat, as if one could stop and not miss the presence of the other.

Omar patted at his pants, the pockets of his shirt. "I think I left my wallet in the car. I'll be right back."

"But Jimmy said—"

"What if someone breaks in?"

Outside, the air was wet and piercing. Tomás had stepped away from the window and was pushing all the buttons of the vending machine to the side of the entrance.

"Tomás. ¿Qué pasó?" He tried to sound casual and unbothered, not wanting to provoke the boy into an argument. They'd had so many lately. Tomás was always putting words into Omar's mouth, convinced that, like his aunt, Omar was trying to rid himself of the boy, because life would be easier without him. "Is everything okay?"

He could tell he had been crying. The tip of his nose was red and bloated, and his eyelashes clumped together from catching tears. "I came by yesterday, and they said you'd be back today." Tomás leaned over to look through the window. They could see the side of Elda's face over the top of the booth, and her right hand, wiping the frosting off Claudita's mouth. He nodded in their general direction. "That her? Your wife?"

Omar wondered if he really needed to ask—had it been long enough for Tomás to forget?—or if he was simply trying to match her face with the one that haunted his last days with his father.

Omar placed his hand on Tomás's shoulder. "What's really going on?"

"My aunt wants to kick me out of the house."

"Is that it?"

"What do you mean, 'Is that it?' That's not a big enough problem for you?"

"I mean, what else happened? She doesn't want to kick you out for nothing, does she?"

"She's been waiting long enough for an excuse."

"Tomás. What'd I tell you last time?"

He stopped short of rolling his eyes, but said nothing.

"I'm serious. ¿Qué te dije?" Omar knew he was pushing his luck, but he didn't have time for games, with his family waiting for him.

Tomás kicked the bottom of the vending machine in one clumsy, weak motion. "You'll help as long as I tell you the truth."

"Okay. So tell me what happened."

"It's not a big deal. My cousin started it. He's always rubbing things in my face, and he got this new stereo he always plays super loud like he's deaf or something. And my friends threw a party the other night, so I borrowed it."

"You borrowed it?"

"Yeah I borrowed it. I even invited Chris and everything, okay? But he shows up with all his friends, like I fucking stole it or something, and he turns off the music and ruins the whole party. My friends didn't like that."

"¿Qué pasó? Did they hurt him?"

"His friends started it, okay? And he goes and tells on me, like a little bitch."

"So your aunt kicked you out?"

"Not yet. But the stereo broke. And she says if I don't buy Chris a new stereo, I better start looking for a new place to live. That thing cost like three hundred bucks."

"That's a lot of money."

"That's how spoiled he is." Tomás rubbed his hands together and blew into them. The sun had started to set, and the flaming sky made Omar feel exposed. He could see his breath in the air, and he thought of how much warmer he would be, how much safer things would feel, if he were back inside the restaurant where he belonged.

"I'm not asking you for money, all right? I just . . . I just thought since you always know what to do . . ."

Omar shook his head, trying to piece together his thoughts, but he was tired. Tomás was always making excuses and putting blame on whomever was nearest.

"You know, after a certain point, I don't believe in bad luck. I don't believe in bad things always happening to people for no good reason. I want to help you, but . . ."

"I can work for it. You're always talking about how I need to learn responsibility. I'll do it. I just, I really need to get that stereo back."

"I'm sorry, Tomás. I have to get back inside."

"Maybe ask your boss. Just to see if he's hiring."

Someone opened the door, and for a brief moment Omar heard Martin's voice come and go, a fragment of his laughter. He began stepping toward it and stretched out his arm to hold the door. "I'll try. I can't promise anything."

Tomás nodded and stepped away from the light of the restaurant. "Thanks, man." He ran away, looking so much more like a child getting lost than a teenager looking for trouble.

"¿Lo encontraste?" Elda asked when he rejoined them.

"It was in my jacket the whole time. I guess my wallet is just so light, I forget I'm carrying it."

Elda didn't laugh. She kept glancing over her shoulder. After a few seconds she sighed and pushed a plate of cake toward Omar. "Claudita didn't want to finish her slice without you." She turned to their daughter and smiled. "It was practically like waiting forever, wasn't it, mija?"

When they were done eating, Omar stacked the dishes on top of one another and gathered the spoons, forks, and cups.

"¿Qué haces?" Elda asked.

"Sorry, it's a habit."

"See? ¿Qué te dije? You've been doing this too long, amor."

She had told him this countless times, and it always ended with Elda saying he was too good for it. Tonight, she only placed her hand over his and rubbed it with her thumb while she turned her attention to the kids.

And then it hit him: she was done dwelling on the idea of something better for him.

Omar stood up and excused himself. He made his way to the kitchen, wordlessly looking through the steam and the mist rising off the water hoses, the shelves stacked with white plates and bowls and saucers, all crooked and ready to fall at any moment. He found Jimmy where he always did, hunched over his desk with a calculator in one hand and a pile of diners' tabs in the other. When he gave his two weeks' notice, Omar offered to stay however long it took to train his replacement. He told him Tomás was interested in the job.

That evening, after they had tucked the kids into bed and sung them to sleep, Omar stood across the bed from Elda, undressing, and told her about his decision. She nodded and raised her eyebrows as she unbuttoned her blouse. She took some time to think before saying anything. Omar couldn't take the time to wait.

"I thought that's what you wanted."

"Of course it is." She gave him her most encouraging smile. "It's just I'd always thought we'd talk about it first. Plan things out a little better. Are you sure they'll give you more shifts at the new office building?"

"That's what they've told me all along."

"I just don't want any surprises. Every time I think I've got our bills under control, the car needs new tires, or Mamá gets sick, and we have to start over. It's like that toy the kids play with. The one you shake, and it erases all your drawings? That's how I feel every day. Like I'm just waiting for the shake."

"I didn't know." Omar was always working on nights Elda balanced the checkbook. When he got home, and she was already sleeping, he would see a tidy stack of bills, receipts, and Elda's calculator left on the kitchen table. He had never seen her pore over each one, and he imagined her now, with the table covered in paperwork, picking up one bill at a time like they were puzzle pieces, that tiny crease forming over her nose anytime she thought she wasn't really frowning.

"I'll find out about the extra shifts first thing tomorrow, okay?"

They got into bed, both too exhausted to move. Elda slept on her side, facing the door and the hallway that led to the kids' room, but she made a point to press her body close and wrap her feet over his. In this way, they would drift into dreams like two balloons tied together with string, floating apart, but never separated.

She kissed him goodnight and sank into her pillow. This, right here, was Omar's perfect time of day—the beginning and the end, when there was nothing left to do but be with her.

He lay awake and stared at the ceiling, tracing figures in the popcorn ridges. "This is what life should be, lying by your side always." But Elda had already fallen asleep.

# CHAPTER 42

The drought had everyone on edge. There were water restrictions to be followed, designated days to remember when you could or could not wash your car or water the lawn. A thirst swept over the Valley. Local businesses posted "Pray for Rain" on their marquees, and precipitation forecasts were bumped up from the weather reports to the lead stories on the evening news.

The town's water tower, an ever-present giant that hovered just beyond the highway, seemed to shrink each time Isabel drove past it. With every hour (then day, then week) without rain, she would wonder if its reserves could possibly be enough. She would think, *What if it came to that?* Then, *It'd barely last a week.* Until finally, she didn't even look at it, didn't want to think about it. Like all things, it would either be consumed or evaporate.

Other things were not so easy to ignore. One night when Martin was working late, she drove to Elda's house and caught her standing over the ferns in her yard with a running hose in her hands. She held it limply as it emptied into a puddle of mud all around Elda's feet, while she stared at the gray-brick siding of her house. It was not even the right day; a neighbor could have reported her, and she would be fined hundreds of dollars. Isabel left her car running in the driveway to go shut off the hose.

"What'd you do that for?" Elda protested.

She didn't have the heart to tell her the truth. "It's too hot for yard work. Besides, the ferns look beautiful." The ends of their long, feather-like stems had begun to yellow.

"It's this drought. Everything's drying up." Elda threw her hands in the air as they walked the pathway to her door. "What's the date I can water again? It's on the side of the fridge." She took a seat in the living room, suddenly out of breath.

"Wednesday." Isabel handed her a cup of ice tea.

"It's just that this heat is unbelievable." She ran her palm over her forehead, and then looked at it, staring at the drops of glistening sweat. "I can't remember the last time it was so hot. There was that summer we stood in line to sign up for amnesty, but even then, the government had set up tents. They handed out lists of the documents we'd need, and we used them as fans."

"How long were you there?" Isabel sank into the couch, wanting to place her hand over Elda's, but hesitating. Her mother-in-law didn't want to be treated any differently since her sickness, but it had changed her. Or perhaps it'd made her more like the person she used to be, nostalgic and softer around the edges.

"Oh, hours. There were so many of us they had to set up stations, like an assembly line. Bureaucracy at its best. Yessica and I found ways to keep the kids busy, but Omar couldn't stand it. He nearly left. I never did find out if he went through with it, getting naturalized. It would've been easy. I'd set up everything for him. I always did. I guess even that wasn't enough to make him stay."

Isabel placed her hand over her chest. Her heart pounded so hard against her palm, she worried it might give her away. "I can't imagine how hard it was."

"It was a very long time ago."

"But still. You must have so many questions . . ."

"I did. For so long, I did. But now?" Elda crossed her legs and sat up straight against an extra cushion she tucked behind her back. The cushion was rigid and overstuffed; she whacked it several times before wiggling up against it. "Life's too short, and I know better. I have nothing left for him."

"Really?"

She seemed startled by the implication. "What else would you expect? Me curled up in a corner, crying for him? Oh, no no. Those days belong to another person. And it's like they always say: 'Everything happens for a reason.' Of course, it's a shitty thing to say about cancer. Or murder. And war and innocent children getting . . ." She stopped, and Isabel was glad she didn't say it. "But a cheating husband, that happens for a reason."

"Are you sure that's really why he left? That he cheated?"

"What else makes a man leave his family?"

"You all left your family in Mexico. And your friends and everything . . ."

"That was different." Elda gave a sigh heavy enough to swallow the rest of their conversation whole.

Isabel paused to stretch her legs, twisting her feet in small circles that made her ankles crack. "It's been such a rough week at work. I had a patient come in yesterday with a piece of construction debris in his eye. A chip of wood the size of half a pinky finger left him half blind. I asked if there was someone he could call for a ride home, and he said his family's all in Guatemala, and there was no point worrying them."

"That's stupid," Elda said. "They'll find out soon enough when he can't work and stops sending money."

"He said he can still pour concrete with one eye. And he didn't want to make his suffering their suffering." Isabel shrugged. "You'd be shocked to learn the secrets people keep to protect their loved ones. Accidents, injuries, diseases."

"Probably got them from their mistresses."

Isabel tried to stifle a laugh. "I'm serious. I can't imagine going through what they did, what you and Omar did. I can't imagine having to make those kinds of decisions."

Elda stared at the floor, smiling to herself as if remembering an old joke. "Decisions are not the same as choices." She stood up to refill her ice tea. "But enough of that. It's just this drought. It's got us all on edge."

"You're right," Isabel said, though she wished the weather were their biggest problem.

"When's the date I can water again?" Elda emerged from the kitchen holding a glass of ice tea for both of them.

"Wednesday. It's on the side of the fridge." She hid her half empty glass on the side table behind her and thanked Elda for the new one.

# CHAPTER 43

## MARCH 1988

In those days it had become easier to think the boy was well taken care of. That they had switched places—Tomás, gathering dirty dishes in the bus bin and marveling that they never cracked or chipped, and Omar, just a passerby outside the window, catching a whiff of bacon or brisket as he considered popping in for a bite.

Training Tomás had only taken a few hours. When Omar expressed his surprise, Jimmy laughed and said, "What'd you expect?" Then he had told him he could stay the next two weeks if he really needed the hours. Omar knew he was just being kind. Jimmy paused in that way people do when they offer to pick up a tab without meaning it.

"No, it's fine," he'd said, thinking of Elda and the hours they would spend worrying about his next paycheck. Time is money (people here loved saying that). It was always impossible to accumulate one without wasting the other.

Somehow things had worked out better than planned. Omar got the extra shifts he was promised at the office building, until eventually he was working six nights. His pay as a supervisor was the highest he had earned since they had arrived, and he often went weeks without cleaning a thing. He kept track of the staff's hours and productivity, oversaw that their work was up to standard, and kept the building's cleaning supplies stocked. He had a round key chain the size of hand-cuffs, and when he walked through the halls, the heavy jingle of the keys against his hip made him feel important and trusted.

The downside was the schedule. Working a few evenings of the week had been one thing, but with his shifts now back to back, there was never a sense of rest or normalcy. He slept during the day and worked at night, but the transition wasn't as simple as inverting his habits. Elda, the kids, their life: it all went on without him, and when he tried to catch up, it was all a daze. He felt like one of those snow globes Claudita had become so obsessed with; flipping him right side up made his world feel scattered and suspended.

Now that he was home during the day, Omar noticed things he never would have known otherwise. That television programing was terrible in the mornings, and the commercials assumed the women watching were accident-prone drivers. That when Elda and Claudita walked Martin to the bus stop, Martin made his sister walk on his left, so he was closer to the road and moving traffic. Most surprising of all, that Elda became restless in the early afternoons, fidgeting, looking for something to do and always finding it in the kitchen—dishes that needed to be washed, cabinets that needed rearranging or cleaning. She went on like this for one or two hours, usually until the mail came and she stepped out to retrieve it, only to come back looking deflated.

It got to be impossible to ignore. When he finally asked her about it, Elda looked terrified, and then relieved.

"I'm just waiting on more amnesty papers," she said, tossing a pile of circulars into the trash.

"More?" Omar thought the forms and letters they had provided for proof of residence and employment had been plenty.

"There's always something," Elda said. "There's no sense in us both worrying."

She began chopping carrots and celery for the kids' afternoon soup. Now that they had their green cards, their life was an endless wait. If everything went as planned, they could apply to become citizens in three years.

"So we just have to be patient, that's all. Perfect citizens."

He cupped her shoulders from behind. Her muscles were like patches of rocky soil, and even as he tried to knead them, it felt like he was only moving the clumps of stress from one part of her insides to another. A brief moan escaped her, and Elda released her grip from the knife as she rested her head on his shoulder.

"Sometimes I look at our children, and I can't believe something as simple as a birthplace can make us so different."

He rubbed a spot above her shoulder blade harder, until he thought his thumb might snap off. "It doesn't. All this stuff with the papers, it's not real. Not like our family is."

"It's real to Yessica. Real to us if we don't get approved."

"You can't think like that. It only hurts you. And I never want to see you hurting."

Elda took his hand from her shoulder and kissed it. "You should get some rest before you have to go. You were inquieto all morning. Nearly kicked me out of bed."

Omar had no memory of a restless sleep, but no matter how deeply he plunged into his dreams, he could always tell when Elda had gotten out of bed. The sheets turned cold, and there was a vastness that made everything feel empty.

"I was planning on going in early today."

She didn't ask why, and he didn't say. Most days Elda's trust made him feel worse than if he had lied.

When he walked into the diner, it smelled different. Or rather, like it always had, but more pungent, as if time could squeeze particles closer together the longer you stayed away. He hadn't stopped by in nearly a month, and he was suddenly very aware of the plastic odor that rose out of the vinyl booths, mixed with the cinnamon of apple pies and the buttery baked potatoes. He wondered if it ever stayed on him, and if it did, if Elda would recognize the diner on him when he came home.

The hostess, a pale twentysomething with a side ponytail, asked Omar if he needed a table for one. He held his hand in the air and shook his head, and she followed him as he walked past, asking if she could help him with anything. As if he were a stranger, just another customer.

The line cook eyed him suspiciously but said nothing as he walked behind the counter toward the kitchen. The door swung open, barely missing Omar as Jimmy stepped through holding an empty dish bin. "Hey!" He set the bin aside and gave Omar a hug. "If you're looking for the boy, he should be here by now, but he's not. Didn't call in sick or anything."

Minutes later, Omar was back in his car, circling the school and the park before heading toward Tomás's neighborhood. He should have been angry, but he was worried. The boy wouldn't betray his trust, would he? *The boy was not a boy anymore,* he thought.

The streets were quiet and full of parked cars. Omar's engine rattled as he crossed a speed bump but didn't slow down in time. He stopped at the only traffic light on the street and made a left, toward an apartment building with a tower of dented mailboxes near the entrance and a security gate left halfway open.

He saw them as soon as he turned the corner. At first it was no one he recognized, just four bodies kicking at the ground as if they had gotten gum on their shoes, or stepped on an anthill—nothing really worth noticing. It was only a small flash of neon green that made him stop. Tomás had a pair of shoes that color, and as he followed the bright speck through the limbs that surrounded it, Omar realized what he was seeing. The green became a pair of shoes, became a clenched body that rocked side to side in the dirt as countless legs pummeled it. Tomás made no sound, but his body absorbed the impact of each strike with a dullness that made Omar think he might already be dead. He jumped out of the car and left it running, keys still in the ignition, shouting words that were incomprehensible and waving his arms in the air as he ran. It was useless. The blows kept coming faster as he approached. The attackers yelled and grunted and spat at the ground, until one of them bent to lift Tomás's head and punched him in the face. To Omar's horror they began taking turns. A punch in the jaw, the eye, the other eye. His legs burned from running so fast. From the depths of his desperation he pulled out the most threatening words he could think of.

"I've called the cops! They're on their way now."

The group scattered, and Tomás fell to the ground.

"They're gone. I'm here. It's me," Omar said. He hooked the boy's arm over his neck and lifted him up. A mixture of sweat and blood pressed against the back of Omar's head, sticking and slipping as they moved.

He carried Tomás into the car and started driving just to leave, unsure where to take him. The hospital would ask questions. Tomás's aunt would disown him. Omar thought about bringing him home, and though he shut away the thought before it fully formed, the shock of it stayed with him. It commingled with the memory of Elda, curled against a bloodied tile wall. Time had worn away the image until it was just fractured details: Tomás's father, lying an arm's length away, his feet like the hands of a clock, stopped at 1:55. And Elda, so paralyzed that he often wondered if every step she had taken since then protested and ached.

"You shouldn't've done that. Now they'll never be done," Tomás said. He could barely move his jaw, and so his voice sounded like drowning.

"Shh. Hold still and save your breath. Talking will only make the pain worse."

"You're not listening. Ah!" he winced and doubled over. "Where we going?"

"Work. Not to Jimmy's. Mine. It's not far from here." Without realizing, Omar had been driving in that direction. It was the only place that made sense. It was early enough that staff wouldn't have arrived yet, and the building's daytime occupants would have long since gone home. The only person to worry about was the security guard in the main lobby.

"Just wait here."

"Where the hell would I go?" Tomás attempted a smile and coughed instead.

The sky was turning colors now, its glow dimmed by hundreds of grackles landing on the wires strung across the parking lot. Their crows were like thousands of songs playing all at once, noise so meaningless it nearly went unheard.

Omar's plan was simple enough; there was a first-aid kit in the supply closet that he hoped was still stocked with all the essentials. Years ago, one of the staff had cut his hand emptying a trash bag littered with pieces of a broken glass, and Elda had bandaged him up. He made a mental list of the supplies she had used, remembering how the webbed skin between the man's thumb and forefinger had slit in two, how Elda had narrated in a low, gentle voice everything she was doing before she did it. The dab of alcohol, which would sting. The topical antiseptic, which tainted the wound orange.

He wished she were here now, still working with him. Under any other circumstances the bruises and cuts on the boy's face wouldn't faze her. Only Elda could look at something broken and see a million different ways to fix it.

He tried to conceal the small box and a handful of paper towels under his arm as he exited the building, which turned out to be easy because the guard was absorbed in a comic book. Back in the car, Tomás had reclined his seat. He held his arm over his forehead, covering his eyes as if the sun were beaming down on him.

He looked suspiciously at the cotton balls and tape. "What are you, a doctor now?"

"I'm the next best thing. You think any doctor would take a look at you and not assume the worst? They're trained to recognize these things."

"I don't know what you're talking about, man."

Omar raised an eyebrow at the boy, but said nothing as he cleaned off his wounds. Tomás's shirt was stained with blood, and it was getting so dark he had to turn on the car's interior lights. Anyone walking through the lot might look in on them and see everything.

"Here," Omar soaked a paper towel in alcohol and told him to keep his shirt on while he wiped himself down. It felt rude not to turn away, so he stared at the door. "So what does it mean? Blood in? Or were they kicking you out?"

In the reflection he saw Tomás shake his head. "Man, you think you know everything."

"I'm just trying to understand. Maybe they're just a bunch of kids picking on you for no reason." This assumption seemed to offend Tomás the most. "I don't know unless you tell me."

"Then I guess you don't know."

It was too late to drop off the kid at home, and he couldn't stay in the car any longer and still arrive on time for work. Jimmy had always liked this about him. Said he was as dependable as a sixty-degree cold front in December.

"I'll call Jimmy and tell him you're not coming in. He was worried about you. Maybe you should take a few days off."

"Maybe I'll just quit."

There was no point in arguing with Tomás; he was just trying to get a rise out of him. He unzipped his work bag and handed him a canteen full of water and the sandwich Elda made him every night in case he got hungry. A light breeze entered the car as he cracked the windows and took the keys out of the engine. "You should rest. Sleep. You'll feel better if you do."

"You're just gonna leave me here like some pet dog?"

It seemed cruel when he put it like that. "Fine." He got out of the car and Tomás followed. To Omar's relief, nobody asked about the beat-up teenager shadowing him, though plenty paused to stare. After an hour of watching Omar check off inventory lists on each floor, Tomás grew bored. He lay across a set of plush chairs in one of the office's waiting rooms, just like Omar had first asked him to, and fell asleep.

The next afternoon, Omar woke with a sore neck. When Elda asked, he shrugged it off and said he had slept in an odd position, but every time he moved, it was a reminder of Tomás's limp body hanging from his neck.

Elda rubbed it with both hands, then made like she was about to strangle him. "Don't pretend to be tired just to get out of helping with the groceries," she said.

He had completely forgotten he'd promised to go with her. She gathered her purse and keys. When they got into the car, Elda fell back into the seat with a gasp. It was still reclined and she was startled to find it out of its usual position.

"Was someone in the car?" she asked, like it was nothing, meaning it could be everything.

"One of the workers. His car was in the shop." He hated lying to her, but it was less painful than telling her the truth.

# CHAPTER 44

They rarely left her alone for long. Eduardo set up a text group among the five of them, so they could know when one was coming and another was going. Claudia spent most of her afternoons between flights at Elda's, making her enough meals to last for days, while Eduardo always checked on her in the evenings. Martin had arranged to work from home a couple of days a week, and this newfound flexibility meant that he tagged along whenever Isabel had a chance to visit Elda, though she would have preferred a few more attempts at speaking to her alone.

"She seems in much better spirits," Martin said. They had just rushed to the pharmacy, catching it minutes before it closed, and were heading to Elda's to drop off her medication. "Don't you think?"

He did this all the time now. Without saying anything specific, he would comment on some change in his mother's condition and look to Isabel to confirm or deny it. Usually, it wasn't even real, but she didn't see the harm in playing along with his vague observations. "That's good. It's good to see her happy."

He didn't seem particularly pleased with this response. They both knew it didn't mean anything. She was glad they were close enough to Elda's house that he wouldn't push the topic any further. As they pulled into the driveway, they caught Eduardo running out the door. Martin's headlights beamed on him, and he stood frozen in their path, his eyes red and swollen and wet. Too late, he tried to lower his face and cover it as he rushed into Diana's truck, waving at them casually as if to say, *"See you at the house,"* but Martin had already pulled in next to him. Isabel saw the truck's back-up lights come on, then jolt back to just the red taillights as he resigned himself to park.

Martin got out of the car and leaned into Eduardo's open window, scanning the interior like a police officer pulling over a reckless driver. "What's wrong?"

"Nothing."

"Then why do you look like your dog just died?"

"Martin . . ." Isabel put her hand out the window, reaching for him. "It's nothing. We just argued, that's all."

"And you just left her there?" Martin rushed into the house. His shadow scampered across the garage door as he crossed the bright path of light cast by their cars, both of which were still running.

The engine rattled and cracked under the hood after Isabel turned off their car. For a moment she sat in its silence, trying to think of what to do with Eduardo. She had never seen him like this, shaking, holding back sobs, as he tried to sink behind the wheel of Diana's truck. She got out and stood by his window.

"So Diana lent you her truck?"

He nodded.

"How come?"

"I just thought it'd be better if Elda and I talked alone."

"About what?"

He shook his head several times. "I only did what I was asked."

"What who asked?"

"Omar. I thought it might be time."

"Time? Oh my God. What did you—"

"Never mind. Forget I said anything."

"Eduardo—"

"I gotta go."

He rolled up the window and pulled out, leaving her standing in the dark.

Inside, she found Martin bringing his mother a glass of water and a set of pills. Elda sat at the dining room table, her eyes dry and piercing through the glass surface. Black-and-white pictures lay scattered on the floor all around her feet. Some were face up, but most were face down, their yellowing backs blank except for a perfect line of cursive scribbled in fading pencil lead.

She sat still, but stiff, as if she were bracing herself for a blow.

"Here, just relax." Isabel placed her fingers over Elda's wrist. Her pulse raced through her veins. "Martin, get me my blood pressure monitor from the back seat."

"Oh, stop it. Stop it. I'm fine." Elda pushed her away.

"Then what happened with you and Eduardo?" Martin was so upset his voice kept getting away from him. Isabel rubbed his arm and, wanting to make herself useful, began picking the fallen pictures off the floor.

"Don't," Elda said. "Leave them."

"They're beautiful." In her hand, she held a picture of a little girl, no more than four or five, standing next to a water spout and holding a doll, soaked, by the ends of her hair. On the back it said: "Sabrina, cinco años. 1976."

"They're all lies," Elda said.

Martin knelt on the floor next to her and began picking up the photographs. There was Claudita blowing out a candle shaped like a "3" on a cake covered in strawberries. A small version of Martin, with fuller cheeks and fewer teeth, stood frozen on the center of a stage, dressed as a tree.

"That's adorable," Isabel said. "How old were you?"

"Almost eight. It was stupid. The whole play was a disaster."

Ignoring him, she turned her attention back to Elda. "It's nice of you to share these with Eduardo. I wish I'd had a chance to meet her."

"Sabrina?" She chuckled at the mere mention of her name. "She was a stubborn girl, but I loved her. Even after everything that happened, I treated her like family. I never thought she wouldn't do the same."

"Mom, what are you talking about?"

She gathered the pictures and stacked them into a small deck that she placed in a shoebox in the center of the table. "Did you know about this?" She brought out a folded set of papers and handed them to Martin. Even just seeing the back page, with its few lines hand-scribbled in black ink, Isabel recognized the police report. It trembled in Martin's hands.

"Where did you get this?"

"Eduardo brought it. He said I deserved to know the whole story."

He folded the pages back up and held them in the air, pointed at Isabel. "Did you give this to him?"

"Of course not. Why would I do that?"

"No one knew except you and I."

"What are you saying?"

"Never mind. Nothing." He turned back to his mom and knelt by her chair to see her eye to eye. "Are you okay?"

"I'll be fine. I shouldn't have said anything."

"What did Eduardo mean, 'the whole story?'" Isabel said. "Is there more, something that's not in the report?"

Elda's eyes narrowed as she turned away from Isabel and lifted herself out of the chair. She looked down at Martin, tapping his shoulder on her way out of the room.

"You're right about her. She asks too many questions."

"He said that? When?"

"See? Two more." Elda held two fingers in the air and waved them like a stoned concertgoer. Her left leg dragged with every other step, as if her foot had gone numb, but Isabel was too angry to pay it much attention.

"How could you say that?" she asked Martin.

"It was just a joke. A long time ago."

"It's not funny. I'm your wife. I have a right to ask questions."

"You sure you didn't give the report to Eduardo? Or tell him about it?"

Isabel felt her stomach contract, so hard it made her spine crack as she tried to stand up straight. Her throat turned dry and sticky. "You think I'm lying."

"I didn't say that. But maybe you left it out someplace and he found it."

"So this is my fault now?" Her body kept wanting to move, pace, but her feet felt stuck in place.

Martin wouldn't look at her. He kept running his fingers over the crease of the police report. It sounded like a knife being sharpened. "You promised you would keep it a secret."

"And I did. But that doesn't matter anymore, does it?" When he didn't answer, she fell back into her chair. "This isn't going to work."

"What is?"

She lowered her voice, barely managing a word. "Us."

That's when they heard Elda tumble.

# CHAPTER 45

## February 1989

It was a good idea and a horrible idea. That was how Elda described it the night Omar came home from work and found her sitting on the living-room floor next to a pile of textbooks and scattered brochures. When she stood up to explain, he could feel the energy pulsing through her, a foreign thing, like first kisses that are exhilarating in their intimidation.

"I'm going back to school."

"Back?" Omar said.

"Okay fine, not back. But Yessica told me about this test. They were handing out brochures at the library. If you pass it, it's like you went to high school here, and they give you a diploma so you can go to college."

He looked down at the carpet. Two books lay open facedown next to her pink toenails, and Omar imagined the pages and words as living things, suffocating. One was on the basics of geometry and the other one, with its stars and stripes waving in the wind, US history. He turned his head to read the title, wondering if this was really about the diploma or preparing for their eventual citizenship test. Only Elda would worry about an exam years before she had to take it.

"The high school's offering courses." She bent down to pick up a brochure. "You know, to prepare? Which is good, because I don't remember half of this stuff. Maybe we just didn't get to it in my school."

"Which high school?"

"Guerra. The one by where you used to work?" She kept looking around the floor for something, peeking under notebooks and pillows.

Omar felt his breath catch. "With all the kids?"

She laughed as if the question were ridiculous. "Yes, Omar, there are kids there. But the classes are at night. Did I leave a pen on the table?"

Behind him, she had. He clicked the tip as he handed it to her.

"They're three nights a week, starting Tuesday."

"This coming Tuesday?"

"Here, look." She gestured for him to sit on the floor next to her. On a tiny calendar, she had circled all the nights she would have classes. "You work all but one of these days each week. So of course I thought, it's a horrible idea. There's no way, with the kids. But Yessica says she can take care of them Tuesdays and Thursdays. And class is only two hours, so on Fridays you'd only have to watch them for a little bit."

"I can handle our kids longer than that, mi amor." It seemed she had taken everything, including his presumed incompetence with their kids, into account, but had really thought of nothing at all.

"And how would you get there?"

"You can drop me off on your way to work."

"And how would you get home? If class is only two hours . . ."

"I can take the bus." She shrugged.

"But that'll take forever. And you at night, waiting at those stops?"

"We used to do it all the time."

"We. But not you alone."

"You're right. I had our baby with us to protect me, remember?" She stood and walked away from him, pacing in the kitchen while she looked for something to do with her hands. "I don't understand you sometimes."

The lights framed the crevices of her features in dark emptiness. She was breathing heavily, each exhale shorter and slower to come than the last, and Omar could see her deflate. This was not an exhaustion you recover from, but the slow seeping away of a person so gently, it avoids detection until there's nothing left to take.

"It's not a horrible idea, mi amor. It's a great idea, just like you said." He crossed the living room and held her. The world felt very small and so full of things she would soon learn. He tried to imagine if she would ever embrace him like this again.

The first night he dropped her off at the school, he circled it three times in his car before he had to rush to work. Aside from late-working teachers and a few student athletes waiting to be picked up, the grounds and parking lots were empty. Green plastic cups had been squeezed into the fence that bordered the football field. They were meant to spell out "GREEN JAYS 1," but someone had poked out the "J."

The next time, Omar left Elda at the school five minutes early to give himself time to wander. The sky was gray but still illuminated by the last rays of sun stretching past the horizon. It made the school feel hidden, like no one was meant to be here.

Each week he grew a little bolder. He would walk the halls, unsure what he would do if he actually ran into Tomás running into Elda. Sometimes he would be struck by the minuscule chances of it happening, and Omar would leave right away, laughing at his ridiculous paranoia. But soon enough it'd feel real again. In the back of his mind he was always rehearsing what he would say to Elda if the time ever came. Something about knowing she prayed for the boy, and that he loved her so much that he'd wanted to look out for him, in case God had simply forgotten to do it himself.

He began to have trouble focusing at work. He would rush home to ask Elda how class went and could tell just by seeing her smile all he really needed to know. Everything she told him after felt far away, as if he were listening from underwater.

From her enthusiasm he gathered that classes were going well. She made a game of it with the kids: for every A all three of them brought home, she toasted them a Pop-Tart before bed. One night it occurred to him that his family had never been happier. Their lives were like a movie he was watching on repeat.

On the night of a big history quiz Elda had been studying for, Omar skipped his drive around the school and headed straight for Tomás's home. He found him sitting on the black-barred gate that encircled the pool, swinging lazily back and forth as he opened and closed the gate with his foot. Omar hadn't expected it to be this simple. He had planned to knock on the door and tell his aunt that he was an old coworker from the restaurant, and he had found comfort in this half-truth.

But the boy was just there, as if he had always been there. He didn't look surprised to see him. His hands gripped the gate on either side of him, and his shoulders were nearly level with his ears, as if they had swallowed his neck.

"It's a little late to go swimming, don't you think?"

Tomás curled his gaze up at him, silent and expressionless. Omar wondered if speaking to Martin once he became a teenager would be this hard, or if it'd be more natural thanks to the bonds of fatherhood. He tried again and said, "I've been looking for you."

Tomás smiled, then seemed to change his mind and twisted his lips into a pout. "Since when? Not like I'm hiding or anything."

"What's it been? Maybe a few weeks?"

"Try months." Tomás lowered his eyes in embarrassment. For the first time Omar noticed how long the boy's lashes were, how they almost made him look elegant. He hadn't realized it'd been so long since they had seen each other.

"I looked for you by the school. I guess I thought you had sports or clubs or something like that in the evenings."

Tomás pushed himself off the gate, landing like a child jumping off a swing. "Must've gotten me confused with some other kid."

Before he left, Omar asked if he could come by again.

"Do whatever you want. It's a free country."

Omar heard kids toss this expression around all the time, as if it were nothing. "I'll see you next week, then."

They weren't long visits, just a few minutes in between Omar dropping Elda off at school and clocking in to work. But he never knew what to expect from them.

There was the night he found Tomás not at the pool, but in the weight room. It was a sticky-smelling place with rusted dumbbells and poor air circulation. Tomás would lift one weight as if he had lost something underneath it, then move on absentmindedly to the next.

Another night, over sodas from the vending machine, Omar asked about school. Tomás was turning eighteen two months before graduating, and he tried dancing around the topic of whether or not he would finish.

"I guess, if I don't have anything better to do," Tomás finally said.

Omar didn't know how to take this, but he chose not to push it.

The next time, Tomás nearly ran into Omar's car as he was turning into the building's entrance. Tomás had been running down the sidewalk, looking over his shoulder. The boy's hands landed on the hood, popping the metal in and out. He got into the car and somehow Omar knew he should keep driving. They ended up at the parking lot of Omar's work. It felt too familiar to ignore.

"Those guys, the ones that beat you up? Whatever happened to them?"

"They're around."

"They still hurting you?"

"Sometimes," Tomás said, as if he were stating a preference for how often he liked eating tortas.

"I'm serious. You should've told me."

"It's not as bad as it looks. It's just my cousin and his pendejo friends. They think they own some shitty-ass corner of the hood."

"That was your cousin? That last time?"

"One of them, yeah."

"And you weren't joining them or getting initiated or anything?"

"The fuck would I want to do anything with his pussy-ass friends? The last time? They were pissed because I found my cousin's weed. A shit-ton of it, too. And of course my aunt sees it and flushes it, and my cousin lets me take the blame because she'd never believe that her 'all-star track champion' is a dealer. His friends were mad pissed. Said I owed them like five hundred bucks. It took me three months to pay it." He crossed his arms and rubbed his shoulder, as if it still hurt to think about.

"What do they want with you now, then?"

"What do you think? I had to quit my fucking job just so they'd stop stealing all my money. Didn't make no difference."

"What do you mean?"

Tomás's jaw tensed, and he shook his head. "It's nothing."

Omar placed his hand on the wheel and turned toward the center console, like he always did when he was driving in reverse, to get a good look at him. He wanted to tell Tomás they wouldn't move from this place until he told him what was going on. Instead he said, "You know you can tell me, right?"

"There's nothing to tell." His voice turned light and sugar-coated, like the end of a long-winded joke. "I took care of it, viejo." He reclined the car seat and lay back, and Omar knew the conversation was over.

When he returned to his car after work, Tomás was gone. He had popped the seat back up—it was pushed too close to the dash now—and Omar knew he had walked home.

He got the sense Tomás was avoiding him after that. He was always in a hurry, always on his way somewhere else. Omar worried about him so much that he thought the distance growing between them could be a good thing. He wasn't sleeping right anymore. He would wake up exhausted, feeling like he'd barely skimmed the surface of dreams. On nights Elda talked in her sleep, he began to wonder if he ever did the same.

He tried to distract himself by focusing on the children. On their Friday nights alone he cooked them mac 'n' cheese and pretended to die easily when Claudita challenged him to a video game. When she inevitably fell asleep on the couch, he helped Martin rehearse for the upcoming school play.

"There's no reason to be nervous," he told his son. "Ignore the audience and imagine it's just you and me in the room."

Martin stood tall, his arms stretched like a Y over his head, and recited his lines. "I am a mighty tree. My roots make me strong. My leaves swing back and forth with the wind. I give us oxygen to breathe and branches to climb."

When the kids finally went to bed, he would stay up waiting for Elda, watching *The Tonight Show* and laughing at jokes he didn't understand just to unravel the knot deep in his stomach.

On the night of the second-to-last class before she took her test, Omar carried her books down the hall. All the lights in the school were on, and it felt almost selfish that two people were the only ones seeing how the lockers and the laminated posters outside each classroom glistened. He tried to imagine this being the world they grew up in. He thought, *We might've stayed young longer.*

"This is sweet," Elda said, and he wondered if she could see it, too. "I'm almost nervous like I was the first time you walked me home." The floors turned to crunchy orange dirt underneath them, and he looked up as the ceiling turned to sky. Memory made their love feel like an open, boundless thing, and he wondered if this were true or just a trick of life's contrasts—a room darkened by a flash of too much light.

"I'm proud of you," he said.

"For what? I haven't done anything yet."

"You've done everything. You are everything."

A hint of pink flooded her cheeks; he hadn't known they could still do this to each other. She stopped and pointed at her door, taking her books from his arms. Her lips were still touching his when she said I love you and goodbye.

He thought, as she stepped inside the room, about lingering. There were still twenty minutes before he needed to be at work. Instead he left and took the back roads toward downtown.

He avoided passing the old diner and Tomás's neighborhood, because he wanted everything to feel as new and clean as that school. It made him smile to picture Martin and Claudita there someday. It made him feel certain, for the first time, that all was worth this.

Soon his car seemed like the only one on the road. All the houses stood with their backs to the street, and at the end of the block there was a quick mart with one gas pump and a marquee with no numbers for prices.

In the shadow of a phone booth, two figures huddled close together, and Omar's first instinct was to turn away.

But as he approached it became clear. The recognition was glaring. He pulled in and rolled down his window. The air smelled like bitter earth, like a meal no one wants to finish because it has gone bad.

"Tomás?"

The boy seemed irritated to hear his name, but when he saw where it came from a look of terror washed over his face. He pushed the young man next to him away, but the man leaned back in, reaching for something in Tomás's hands.

"Not now," Tomás said. "Get out of here."

Omar couldn't tell which of them he was talking to.

The young man had something crumpled in his hands, and only as he began to struggle with Tomás did Omar notice it was cash. The young man kept saying, "Don't be like that. Don't be like that, man."

Omar got out of the car. As soon as he closed the door he knew it'd been the wrong thing to do. The sound of metal against metal set something off in the man. Tomás pushed him hard enough to make him lose his balance, but not enough to keep him from bouncing back. He stood with his legs spread apart and lunged forward, his arm jutting right into Tomás's side, folding him in half. Like a knife.

It happened impossibly fast. Omar had broken into a run, but he felt miles away. For a moment, as Tomás slipped to the ground, the man seemed to be supporting him, but he only wrapped his arms inside Tomás's jacket before breaking away. Omar ran after him foolishly. Old man is what Tomás had started to call him, and he had never felt that way until now. He was out of breath by the time he got back to the boy's side, and he hated himself that any time had passed at all.

In his arms, Tomás felt as tense as the first time Omar had tried to hug him. His body began to tremble.

"It's going to be fine," Omar said. "Everything's fine." But the knife was still inside him, and Omar didn't know if this was good or bad. The warmth of Tomás's blood was washing over him and leaving the boy cold, and Omar squeezed him and looked at him, into those eyes that always seemed to wish they were seeing someone else's, and he thought he might as well go, too, because he had never felt anything more unbearable than this.

"Everything's fine," he said again, but he knew Tomás could no longer hear him. *Everything's fine,* he said to himself. From nowhere, the lights came on and a pair of arms pulled him away and somewhere dark and small a voice told Omar that he had the right to remain silent.

# CHAPTER 46

In the hospital they stared at her sleeping as if she were a sculpture they couldn't quite understand. When she stirred, it felt like a miracle.

Martin took her hand and said, "I'm here."

Claudia ran her fingers through her mother's hair. She rubbed her fingertips together, oily from the sweat of her mother's scalp. "Can we get the air turned down in here?"

Isabel stood and said she would take care of it. This was not her unit—hers was two floors below—but she could guess from the duplicated layouts where the thermostat was. Still, she asked another nurse, and the young woman looked at her for just a second too long, probably trying to place her. They had likely seen each other before, but without her uniform, Isabel bordered on unrecognizable. It had that effect on people. It was like the superhero costumes in comic books: just clothes, but they changed how others saw them and how they didn't.

She had never walked these halls in these shoes. The rubber soles of her wedges pierced the silence, their whiny cadence vulgar among the sounds of hearts and lungs being monitored.

When they'd heard Elda collapse down the stairs, it had struck them with the terror of an earthquake. They had only thought to hold still, that there was safety in no one moving. It was an instinct that lasted only a fraction of a second, and upon seeing her curled against the tile, Isabel had wasted no time. They carried her into the car and Martin ran all the red lights to the hospital, while Isabel tried to keep Elda calm in the back seat. She asked if she was in pain as she took her blood pressure. Elda had watched Isabel's fingers wrap around her arm, as if her hand were a marvelous thing. "I can't feel that," she'd said. "Not even a little bit."

Now, Isabel thought about visiting her coworkers downstairs before heading back to Elda's room. She was not used to this kind of idleness between test results and MRIs, and she longed for even the smallest semblance of control. They had been waiting for three and a half hours. In five, she would have to be back at work.

On her way to the elevators, she found a small waiting area that she had never paid much attention to. It had an L-shaped brown couch and a circular peony-patterned rug in the center. A flat-screen television hung halfway up the wall, much lower than the ones she was used to seeing, purposely out of reach. Instead of small tables stacked with magazines, there was a bookshelf that lined the wall.

It could've been somebody's living room.

It didn't look like it belonged in a hospital.


She took all her breaks with Elda, and some extra ones, thanks to a few understanding nurses who had already heard that her mother-in-law had been admitted the previous evening. Each time she came back she found Claudia had taken another quick trip to Elda's house. She had brought her pajamas first, then leftovers from last night's dinner. In the afternoon Isabel noticed a bottle of nail polish remover and a set of rose-colored bottles lining the window. Martin was sprawled on the recliner, asleep, and Claudia had left yet again. Yessica paced the room, pausing for long stretches of time to stare out the window or gaze at Elda while she slept.

Isabel took a few cotton balls from inside the cabinets and began dabbing at Elda's nails. The cold scent of nail polish remover filled the room. Hoping to disperse it, she blew on her fingertips.

"You do plan on repainting them, right?"

Isabel jumped at the sound of Elda's voice. It had become Velcro, the words scratching in protest as she pulled them apart from her throat.

"Any color you want," she said, trying her best to sound normal.

They spent the next ten minutes holding their breath, neither wanting to acknowledge how difficult such a simple task had become. With Elda's hands shaking, Isabel struggled to place the tiny, dripping brush on her nail bed with precision. She was a child who could no longer color between the lines.

"Rabbit flesh," Elda said when she was done.

"What?" Yessica looked on the verge of tears.

"Raaabitflesh," she said again, gazing at her hands with a smile as she stretched her fingers toward the ceiling.

Isabel nodded. "They are beautiful."

Sometimes it happened this way. Words misplaced their meanings, mixed them up with others on the path to the mouth from the brain.

"Shiny and red. Like strawberries," Elda said.

Yessica sat by her side and took her hand, careful not to touch her drying nails. She shot Isabel a worried glance across the bed, but Isabel shook her head and pretended not to notice.

It was just one word, Isabel thought. A fluke. She kissed Elda on the forehead and told her she would be back in a couple of hours.

The hallway felt longer on her way back to the elevator. Through the tinted glass of the waiting room, she made out a figure rocking back and forth on the couch. She cupped the window with her hands and almost instantly, Claudia turned to her, sensing she was being watched. She stepped out into the hall to meet her.

"Sorry," she said, looking embarrassed. "I just needed a minute. Is someone with her now?"

"Martin and Yessica."

"Okay, good."

He hadn't woken the entire time Isabel had been in the room, though his eyelids had fluttered as she gathered her purse. Isabel tried to ignore her suspicion that he was only pretending to be asleep.

The sting of his accusations last night had been completely eclipsed by Elda's fall, but had returned in the fresh glare of morning. Now they avoided each other's eyes, even as Isabel squeezed Martin's hands and rubbed his back when she knew he needed a reassuring touch. For now it was all she could give him.

"Be honest with me," Claudia said, pulling her yellow cardigan over her chest. "This is—is this it for her?"

Isabel stared at the buttons on Claudia's sweater, how she kept picking at the top one with her nail.

Not even minutes ago, she had pushed down on Elda's naked thumb, and she had watched it turn white under the pressure, watched the blood take its time coming back, and she had known that this was the body shutting down.

Isabel tried not to be medical about it. More than anything, she wanted to be proven wrong. "I wouldn't be surprised if we haven't even seen a fraction of your mother's strength."

Claudia cupped her face with her hands and took a deep breath. Isabel reached out to rub her shoulder, and with that small opening of her arms, Claudia stepped into them. Her shaking body was a clenched fist, small and rigid against Isabel's chest. She had never seen Claudia cry like this. She had never held her this tight.

"It's going to be okay," Isabel said.

"How can you know?"

She could feel Claudia's tiny sobs receding. They grew quiet, pulling away from one another. Claudia adjusted her sweater and looked at Isabel expectantly, her eyes still asking the question that had gone unanswered.

"Life changes, but it doesn't end. Not for the rest of us. That's how your mom would want it."

Her eyes welled up all over again. This time, Claudia didn't try to hide it. "God. I can't believe you've been with her all this time. It's so good of you. And to think I was such an ass when your father . . ." But she couldn't finish the sentence.

"It's fine, Clau. That was a long time ago."

The elevator slid open, and they stepped back in opposite directions to make room for the people coming out of it. "I'm just really glad you're here, that's all." Claudia wiped her tears with both palms pulling at her cheeks. "Go. Don't let me keep you. I'll be fine."

Isabel squeezed her arm and stepped inside. "Call me if you need anything, okay?"

"Wait! Have you talked to Eduardo?"

Isabel felt the ground rattle as people crowded into the elevator. Everything had happened so fast, she'd forgotten him.

# CHAPTER 47

## APRIL 1989

They said too much that he understood, and too much that he didn't. That he was in serious trouble, that everything he said or did would affect not only him, but his wife and children, that he should think very carefully about the choices he made, because these next moments, just minutes and seconds, could change everything.

Their lives would be compressed to just this.

Omar had understood this reality for years, so now it came as no surprise, but rather as a small comfort. *You cannot scare me with fears I've tortured myself with for so long,* he thought, but didn't say.

He said nothing while the men in thick brown suits spoke to him slowly and loudly, like parents scolding a child. The tall one had a mouth that always sounded wet; his lips would part before words came out, and Omar could hear his saliva stick to his teeth. He paced the room while his partner sat cross armed in the corner with a disappointed expression locked on Omar. Sometimes he would interject with a few words, things like *You don't want this* or *Don't make this worse than it has to be,* as if he imagined himself an extension of Omar's conscience.

He said nothing while the detectives, twenty minutes into their questioning, wondered aloud whether he had understood a word of what they'd said. He tried to keep his breathing steady when the tall one leaned in, narrowed his eyes, and asked, It was just an accident, wasn't it? No man in his right mind actually plans to kill his own drug dealer. Right? He egged Omar on with his slippery voice.

The night's events were only now taking shape for him, and Omar could finally see Tomás through the detectives' eyes. He wished he could tell them all the facts they were missing, all the things only he knew— Tomás's cousins and his friends, how they never stopped, even after he quit the job at the diner, even after they had him working for them on the streets. Tomás and his father, who he couldn't help thinking about, knowing he had been stabbed on the same side.

Omar blinked back tears. He had never meant for the boy's life to become a mirror of his father's death.

So you *do* understand me, the man said. The whole lot of you just like to play dumb.

It felt important then, to say at least one thing: You're wrong. I didn't do this.

The man shook his head and whistled. Well, that certainly clears things right up, don't it, Berg?

They marched out of the room and left him cuffed to the cold table. It didn't surprise him that it felt like hours before they returned. They knew how the waiting weakens.

But they had no knowledge of true endurance. They had never had to rebuild a life, or resuscitate a dead hope. He could tell by how they spoke, as if they knew all the answers to questions they hadn't bothered to ask.

Here's how it's gonna be, they said, if that's the story you're gonna stick with.

There'll be a long, public trial. Headlines everywhere: *Illegal Alien Kills Drug-Dealing Teenager. Boy Found with Knife Still in His Side.* They stretched their hands through the air, writing in invisible blocks.

His blood was all over you, they said. The store clerk saw you rush out of your car seconds before it happened. He'll testify. And because you insist on pleading not guilty, the judge won't be kind when the jury—no doubt—finds you guilty. Twenty, twenty-five years, and deportation waiting for you when you finish your sentence. Green card don't matter if you're a convicted felon. Might as well burn it right now. Heck, we should probably take a look at your home while we're at it. No telling how much drugs your wife's been stashing for ya.

Omar clutched his hands as they started shaking. The air quaked inside of him.

Don't sound so nice, does it? they said. Only one making a mess out of this is you.

He laughed, because they thought they'd gotten him. They didn't know the depths of his real fears. If Elda learned about Tomás dying, she would know how Omar had betrayed her wishes. How he had lied. How he had failed her in the end, because his watching over Tomás had made no difference; he had destroyed their family and their future by making her most haunting nightmare come to life.

That she would never forgive him, fine.

But Omar knew she would never forgive herself.

*If only I hadn't, that night at the stash house,* she would say. *If only I hadn't condemned us all.*

And if she learned about the knife, still in the boy's body?

He begged them, Please, leave my wife out of this.

They pulled up their chairs, their notepads, and papers. Tell us what we need to know, and we might be able to make a deal. Get you a lighter sentence for your . . . cooperation.

The detective stretched out that last syllable, and Omar remembered how confused he had once been by such sounds. He had spelled them out phonetically when he was first learning the language, and to this day these words still conjured the letters *s-h-u-n* in bold blue type in his mind.

Before anything, he told them, no trial. No newspapers. No contacting my wife. Leave her in peace.

They said they would see what they could do, and then they looked at him as if they thought he would begin talking, but he had been in this country long enough to know nothing is real unless it is on paper.

You said a deal. I want it in black and white, he said.

It was another two hours before they returned. The detective who thought himself kind handed Omar a pen.

Omar twirled it slowly between his fingers as he read the pages over. It was such formal language for a life being stolen. His future was spelled out factually, like it'd already been lived by someone else. No lawyers, no trial. He would confess and go straight to prison and in ten years he would be banned from US soil the second he got out.

Before signing, he asked for one more thing. He had seen it in movies, and for this reason he doubted it'd be true, but he needed to try.

I'd like my one phone call, he said.


For the first time all night he checked the clock: 11:00 p.m. Late enough to wake the kids, but not Elda. Without fail she would answer on the first ring to quiet the noise. He would never be ready to hear her voice.

When she realized it was him, she sounded surprised, not worried, and this made him happy, because he wanted it to feel like any other night.

On any other night, he still would have been at work. She hadn't had to wait for him yet. She hadn't had to fear that what has happening had happened.

Still, the call itself was out of the ordinary. "¿Todo bien?" she asked, and he imagined the edges of her lips faltering as she tried to keep the doubt out of her smile.

"Everything's fine. I was just calling . . ."

*To hear your voice,* he thought.

"I was just calling, because I wanted to say goodbye."

"Goodbye?" Her voice plummeted to a place it always seemed ready to go to, like she had always feared this, or a version of it.

"I can't come home tonight. Or ever."

"Tell me where you are, and I'll call a lawyer. They can't do this. We're residents now . . ."

"No. It's not that. I'm leaving. On my own. It's something I've been thinking about for a while."

"You're not making any sense."

"I just . . . I can't stay. I can't do this anymore."

"You've been drinking. Did you get fired and get drunk and think this would be funny?" She didn't believe him, because he couldn't himself, either. He wondered how people who really did this, *did* this, and if they all sounded so coldhearted and clichéd.

"You just have to accept it, mi . . . you have to accept it," he said. "Though it won't make a difference if you don't."

"You're not making any sense." He could hear her crying now, just barely, because Elda was always embarrassed by the first few tears she shed. "Just come home. Come home and talk to me. What is this really about, mi amor? You know you can tell me anything."

Behind him, an officer tapped Omar's shoulder. He heard Elda's voice shrink as she finally asked, "Is there someone else?"

He wished they'd had more time.

"Tell the kids I love them. That none of this is their fault. When they're older, tell them I'm sorry. Please. I'm so sorry, Elda. I have to go now. Forgive me one day, please."

# CHAPTER 48

Come to the hospital, she texted Eduardo when he didn't answer. Room 428. Elda was admitted last night.

It was a relief that he sent her call to voicemail. She didn't have time to explain everything yet again as she walked back to her unit. All morning she had been translating results to Martin, Claudia, and Yessica, trying to keep things simple and matter-of-fact. The mass was growing, swelling inside Elda's brain. "Imagine a raft being inflated inside a small room," she'd told them. "It takes up too much space. It makes it harder for things to function the way they should."

She had heard of it happening suddenly in the younger patients, nearly all at once—parts of the body turning weak, memories coming and going, even hallucinations—but she had hoped Elda was a rare exception. At Martin's request, Isabel glanced at her chart as the doctor explained what he had found in the MRI. It was so devastatingly typical. The only mystery was why it'd happened in the first place.

Half an hour passed before she got a reply from Eduardo, a simple I'm here that sent her heart racing as she checked another patient's pulse.

By the time she headed back to Elda's room, she could feel pockets of sweat sticking to her lower back and underarms. The air in the oncology wing hit her as she entered, cooler than the rest of the hospital by several degrees. Martin stood outside Elda's closed door, staring at the floor with his arms crossed.

"What happened?"

He shrugged and rubbed his neck with one hand. "She wanted to speak with him alone."

"The doctor?"

"Eduardo. Do you have any idea what this is all about?"

She shook her head. "Maybe you should ask him. I would, but you and your mom already think I ask too many questions . . ." In her mind, she had imagined this coming off more gently, reasonable, even, but as the words left her mouth they were full of the hurt she'd been trying so hard to repress.

"Jesus, Isa. You know that's not what I meant."

"Really? Because you made it pretty clear you don't trust me when you accused me of giving Eduardo that police report."

"I was upset. I didn't know what else to think."

"So your first thought was that I went behind your back?"

"I was shocked, that's all. I'm sure there's an explanation."

"Have you tried asking Eduardo? Did it ever cross your mind to confront him? You act like he's so perfect, never any trouble at all. It's like it's easier for you to think I'm the one to blame. Me, your wife. We've known each other since we were in braces, but you give a teenager we hardly know the benefit of the doubt, over me. And you know what? I'm glad your mother knows about your father. He might've gone to prison, but at least he's honest. At least he trusts me, which is more than I can say about you."

"Isa . . ." Martin placed his hand on her shoulder, but it was all control and no comfort.

"I'm done. I can't do this anymore." She turned away from him and saw the door creep open. Eduardo stood at the threshold but hesitated to walk through. She knew just by looking at him that he had heard everything.

"I was just leaving," he said. "I'm sorry."

Later, when Eduardo wouldn't answer his phone, when she and Martin and Claudia had called and texted so many times that he must've turned it off or run down his battery, she thought of all the words she should have said to him.

"I was wrong."

"I care about you."

"You're family."

But when they finally heard from Diana that he had been pulled over, Isabel wished for only one.

Stay.

Stay.

Stay.

# CHAPTER 49

## APRIL 1989

The night after he left was laundry night. Elda watched as Claudita sorted the dirty clothes into piles—her father's long white socks into one pile, his blue button-up uniform into another. She looked quizzically at her mother's striped blouse.

"That one goes in a third pile," Elda said. "But I'll wash it by hand."

She had Martin sort his and his sister's laundry, and when they were done, they each carried a hamper down the stairs. The plastic baggie full of quarters jingled against Martin's thigh as they descended; she had tied it to his belt buckle because he always asked to be in charge of the money.

"If there's leftover, can we go to the vending machine and get a Coke?" he asked.

"Only if there's enough for you and your sister." She held the door open for them and nodded at the empty machines in the corner. "A ver, what do we have total?"

Martin scattered the coins over the washing machine, stretching his arm over the edges to keep them from rolling off. He sorted them into stacks of four, counting seven dollars and twenty-five cents.

"Each machine costs seventy-five cents," Elda said. "And judging by how much clothes we have, we'll need to do five loads."

Martin did the math against his thigh with his fingers, his lips moving in small whispers as he carried the numbers. "Three seventy-five!"

"To wash. And to dry?"

"Twice that." His shoulders drooped as he realized they wouldn't have extra change for the vending machine. He checked and double-checked. "We're seventy-five cents short."

"We'll see what we can do." Elda opened the first machine and began placing the whites inside, plucking out pieces here and there. She did the same for the darks and mixed colors, and when she was done, she had filled four machines instead of five. "We'll do the rest next week."

She thought this would make Martin happy, but he only glanced at the stack of discarded clothes she had set aside. It was all Omar's.

"When's Dad coming home?"

"Soon. It depends on his boss." She reopened the machine and pulled out a pair of her own jeans and a large T-shirt she often wore to bed. Into the other pile they went. "How much change do we have now?" she said as Martin turned back to the stack of coins. "Four loads. Times seventy-five cents. Times two."

She gathered four quarters while Martin busied himself doing the math. When he got the answer right, she gave them each fifty cents. "Don't take too long." She doubted they heard as they ran off.

The sounds of water running and clothes tumbling filled the room, the air thick and warm. She stacked her empty hampers, placing the one full of Omar's clothes on top as she picked up the tub of detergent. Everything felt heavier than usual.

Halfway out the door, Elda slammed the hamper onto the floor. She searched through his dirty clothes for her jeans and pajamas, then tossed them back into the washing machine. The kids would be asleep by the time she would have to switch the loads into the dryer. They always were.

*Nothing has to change,* she thought. Nothing really had.

Omar hadn't even bothered to come back for his toothbrush or a clean set of clothes. His things still took up half the space in their closet, and his watch lay face down on his nightstand. Everything was in its place, except for him. She resented this most of all—that he could leave her and leave so much of himself behind.

*He'll be back,* she thought, when it'd only been a day or two. But then the calls started coming, and she felt her convictions waver under the weight of her own lies.

"He didn't tell you?" Elda told Omar's boss. "Something didn't agree with him, and he's been vomiting for days."

To Elda's small relief, he didn't fire him. She thought of how Omar would thank her for this when he came back. In these daydreams, she would lash out at him, but he always said something that made things right.

She wanted to believe that there existed a combination of words powerful enough to undo this. It was the only way she functioned at all. She dropped the kids off at school, like she normally did. She studied, and took her GED exam, and passed, and when she got her diploma, Yessica came over for dinner with a cake that said "Congratulations!"

When she called her mother to share the news, Elda made up a story about Omar cutting his finger as he sliced the cake. "Thank God it didn't go too deep," she said. "And the kids think it's hilarious he used their Flintstones Band-Aids." She laughed, but when she lied about him now, he bled. By the time Elda had to pick up Omar's last paycheck, his sickness had gotten worse, and his only hope was a liver transplant. By the end of the month, when she had no choice but to move into Omar's parents' apartment upstairs, Elda told the kids that she and their father had parted ways.

"And he's not coming back?" Martin said.

"No, my love."

He pushed her away and called her a liar. For weeks, despite his father's obvious absence, Martin was convinced Elda was wrong. Even minutes before curtain for the school play, Martin told his mother that Omar would be back. He went onstage and searched the crowd for Omar's face. The silence stretched into anticipation. People cleared their throats as Elda pushed back tears, praying that he would get through this. The realization seemed to hit the auditorium all at once, in one unbearable second: her poor boy had forgotten his lines.

Martin ran off the stage as a new wave of students replaced him, thunderous in their song.

"He's not coming back," Elda said, though not even Yessica, sitting next to her, heard. That night, she allowed herself to take up both sides of the bed. She cried into Omar's pillow, then threw it across the room in a quiet fit of desperation. By dawn, she decided to mourn his disappearance as if he were dead. It would be easier this way. His absence would no longer be a question she had to answer.

# CHAPTER 50

Sometimes when Elda woke, she would hear them talking about her as if she were already gone. Perhaps it was that her eyes took so long to open.

Perhaps it was that sleep already felt like another place.

On the first day, she asked, how long was I asleep? They said fifteen hours, but for her it felt like nothing. It had not been like sleep at all. Not a long stretch of darkness that she later remembered, not time accelerated by dreams or nightmares. It was a blink; it was so unreal. A lonely emptiness, a void that barely existed between a life and a death. She couldn't place herself there, in between.

She felt better later. More complete. She wanted nothing but for them to be together, even if they didn't speak. Come, sit, stay, she told them. But they didn't want her to feel crowded.

She imagined them tiny, tucked under her arms beneath the white sheets, like Claudita and Martin used to do when there were storms, or when the neighbors got too violent. They had been so afraid then, and they were children again, afraid now.

Everything will be all right, she said, but they had stopped believing her words years ago. It'd been the price of growing up. Now it was the price of growing old. They no longer thought she was lying; they looked at her like she believed the wrong truth.

As proof, she held up her hands to show Claudia and Martin her red fingernails. They were vibrant and fresh, like she felt.

When I get home I think I'll paint them orange, she said.

Claudia offered to go back to the house for the nail polish. Yessica told her to stay; she would bring the entire collection for her.

Don't, Elda said. It's not necessary.

Her daughter insisted. Any excuse to leave, it seemed. She supposed she couldn't blame her.

Do you want to watch anything? Martin said. They had had the TV on mute all day. He searched for the remote, not knowing it was the same one used to control the bed. She tried handing it to him but he didn't see. She tried turning up the volume, and like some old sitcom, her bed went up, and then down, channel up, channel down.

It made her and Yessica laugh so hard her eyes welled.

Everything in here is hooked up to something else, Elda said. When will hospitals go wireless?

She was still smiling when she heard a light tap at the door, and Eduardo poked his head through. He waited. Did he think she would throw a shoe at him? Then she remembered the night before, and she understood everything.

Give us a moment, she told Martin.

You sure?

When did you start talking back to your mother like that?

He said nothing as he left the room. Yessica offered to get them coffee.

So. Eduardo. Those were some terrible, serious things you said last night. I don't know what you hoped you'd accomplish.

He placed his hands on the beige bar that bordered her bed. A barricade.

I'm sorry, he said. It's my fault that you're here. I never meant to upset you. I thought you'd be relieved to know he didn't do it.

Relieved? She let out a loud, deep *ha!* and he was so taken aback, she felt sorry. I don't know what it is, but it's not that, she said. How do you know it's even true?

Eduardo looked like he wanted to hide. In all their time together, she had never seen him so vulnerable. Not even the first time she had held him, the day she offered Sabrina money to help them cross the border. Even as a baby, he had puffed up his chest, mimicking his mother's defiance as she said, *Why do you even care? After everything my brother did to you?* All Elda could think to say was she couldn't turn her back on family. As he had to all of them.

Well? How do you even know it's true? she repeated.

He looked down at his hand and said, He told me.

When?

I don't know.

You do.

I don't want to talk about it!

She could understand, because her pain was fresh, too.

He regretted all of it, Eduardo said. Until his last days.

The room grew so quiet, all they could hear was the sound of Isabel's voice outside the door. Eduardo moved closer, looking back at Elda like he expected her to stop him.

But suddenly she was very cold, and tired. She rubbed her arms and pinched her skin. She marveled at its elasticity, how it slowly breathed itself back into shape, like a ball of dented dough.


She slept again. She just wanted to go home.

How long have I been here? she asked the nurses and the doctors and anyone who would answer.

Five days.

Six.

Seven.

Once, she heard someone say that they would just have to be strong and patient.

She nodded and said, Yes. Patience is a process that births forgiveness.

Her body had begun to feel ephemeral, like a twitching light bulb that any second would grow tired, blink, and never turn back on.

The cruelty of it was, she didn't feel ephemeral. Her thoughts were as young and robust as the day she first fell in love, as the day she held her first child. She was so aware, clinging to these moments, resenting their passing. Words ached inside her head, trying to break through, and when she opened her mouth, nothing came out, or something else came out, and she couldn't always tell the difference.

I'm here, Martin kept saying.

I'm not blind, she wanted to shout.

Can you hear me? he said.

Yes, goddammit. I'm not deaf. Are you?

The nurses came in and changed the sheets with her still in them.

Goodness, where are your manners? she said.

They won't see you anymore, but I do, a voice said.

Go away. I can't talk to you right now.

He smiled as if she had said something kind. She felt warm, and calm, but a part of her was in pain, and she couldn't understand why. A part of her sensed he knew the answer.

I'm not ready, she said.

I'll wait, mi amor. For you, I'll wait always.

# CHAPTER 51

## July 2016

Marisol could not have imagined it would come to this. All these years of sacrifice so her daughter could do anything and go anywhere she wanted, and they were back where they had started.

"Your abuela would never approve of this," she told Josselyn as they walked up the stairs, each carrying the few boxes they could manage from the truck. She calculated the move would take all day; it'd be worse than the drive out of state had been. They knew no one they could ask for help, or at least, no one they could ask without Marisol dying of embarrassment. Thirty years of not calling could do that to a friend. There was no welcome committee for her in McAllen.

"What? My job? I think she would've been proud," her daughter said.

"She had big dreams for you. A doctor. A lawyer. A mother, at least."

They set the boxes down in front of a red door at the top of the stairs. Josselyn sighed as she slid the lone key she had picked up from the leasing office into the knob, stopping just short of opening it. "You promised."

"I'm sorry, mija. Okay. I'm sorry."

"You always say that, but I'm serious. If you can't accept how I'm living my life, then maybe it's time we stopped living together. You had a perfectly beautiful house back in Florida."

*"But you left it,"* she wanted to say. Until Josselyn had children of her own, Marisol knew that she would never understand the pull that made her follow her daughter back to Texas. Back home, her little house had a mango tree in the backyard, and a pool that Marisol cleaned herself in exchange for lower rent. Her fingers were forever smelling of chlorine concentrate and pH tablets, but if it hadn't been for their regular visits to the pool supply store, Josselyn would not have gotten her first job. She kept it all through college, becoming store, and then district, manager, and when she had gotten her business degree, Marisol was convinced no other student had as much experience as her daughter.

Now all these years later, she had gotten an even fancier graduate degree and quit. Marisol had been so supportive then. It made sense for her daughter to pursue bigger opportunities. Instead, she had traded it all in to be an assistant to some bureaucrat. Here, of all places.

"Yes, but, whoever heard of a mother being so far from her daughter? It's not natural," she said.

"You and Abuela did it."

"That was different. We had no choice. You, of all people, should understand." Her chest tightened as she tried to hold back a string of tears that came out of nowhere.

Josselyn took hold of her shoulders. "I know, Mom. I understand. Why else would I be here?"

She opened the door, and they carried their boxes into the new apartment. It smelled of fresh drywall and damp tile grout. The appliances were all shimmery steel and smooth glass surfaces, but the kitchen cabinets looked identical to the ones in their first studio efficiency. They had only recently been painted gray.

"They said this is the biggest of the two-bedroom floor plans," Josselyn said. "What do you think?"

There was not even a balcony. They faced south, and she knew they would barely get any sunlight through the living-room window. "It'll feel more like home when we finish unloading the truck," Marisol said.

There was hardly time for them to settle in before Josselyn's new job took over her life. The calls would come at dinner, at three in the morning, even when they were at church. She would sense her daughter fidgeting with the phone in her pocket before excusing herself to take it. They began sitting at the ends of the pews.

"Again?" she would say.

"If it was your child, you'd want to know."

Then Josselyn would be gone for hours.

It was no place for a woman. Marisol stayed up evening after evening, imagining the worst. Why would her daughter choose to retrace those same steps through the desert, all to find nothing more than corpses they could no longer help? Sometimes, when they found migrants still alive, but barely, Josselyn would race to them, accompanied by Border Patrol. This only worried Marisol even more.

"You can't trust anyone out there. It does something to people. It feels godless, like no one's watching."

By the end of the month, Josselyn had helped recover twenty-seven bodies. One had a phone number tattooed on the inside of his upper arm, and so contacting the family had been easy.

"Well, not easy. You know what I mean," Josselyn said. The rest were catalogued in a database Josselyn's group shared with Central American consulates. It was Josselyn's job to document as many details and personal items as she could, to help families search for their missing. Most of her records were sparse: a case number, the date found, the person's sex, and a clothing description were usually all the county sheriff's office could glean from a body. On the rare occasion that she also found a name, Josselyn would come home and tell it to her mother.

"Ermenegildo Garcia-Paz. He was thirty-four. His mother answered the phone shouting his name. She must've seen the US phone number and thought it was finally him, calling after all these months."

"I can't hear this, mija."

But the next night, Marisol would listen as Josselyn retold their stories, and she would hold her daughter close. Sometimes they would cry. Sometimes they would say nothing at all, because the border had left nothing behind but silence. Sometimes they would fall asleep on the couch, Marisol's hands still holding her daughter's head in her lap, until the phone startled them both, and Josselyn grabbed her keys and kissed her mother goodnight.

In those hours, a familiar loneliness crept back in. One night Marisol pushed aside her shame and called the one number she still knew by heart. A young man answered and told her his mother had passed weeks ago. She was too late.

"And your father?" she asked.

"Gone, too."

"Did they die close together?" She remembered how the young couple had always seemed to be embracing, even when they weren't. The young man said they hadn't, that they had died years and miles apart. "I'm so sorry," she said. "Omar once saved my life."

"He did?"

The young man listened as she told him the story, never once interrupting, and Marisol knew she was no longer alone.

# CHAPTER 52

## July 2016

On the day they released Eduardo from the detention center, Isabel tried to arrange his room back to normal as best she could. It was hard to remember what it'd looked like before. It was hard to remember anything. There were seventy miles between the hospital and the detention center, and despite driving them countless times while Eduardo was detained, Isabel had few recollections of each trip. She had spent most of them staring out the window, not knowing what they were passing, how they were getting there, what they would do, why.

Diana had come with them on the first trip, the one where they were turned away. Visitation times for detainees with last names beginning with *A* through *F* were Saturdays between eight and noon, the officers had said. Isabel thought they'd had until four, but the officers explained those were the weekday hours. As if they all should have known. She and Martin had not slept since hearing of Eduardo's arrest, torn between going to him and staying at Elda's side. Isabel could not have kept track of the days and hours if she'd tried.

On the next trip she had brought Eduardo a sweater that the officers didn't let him keep. It'd been just her and Martin that time—Diana had gone on her own—but they had driven mostly in silence. When she tried to say anything at all, Martin only begged her to let him think. "One problem at a time," he kept saying. Except they had all blurred together in her mind.

She made Eduardo's bed and cleared her toiletries from the top of his dresser. She took her work shoes and a set of scrubs from his closet and placed them on her bed to put away later. She had been careful not to use his nightstand or his drawers, hoping that the day would come when he would reclaim them. In the guest bathroom, she replaced the towels with fresh ones and took his toothbrush, body spray, and face wash from the cabinet, displaying them next to the soap and lotion meant for guests.

He and Martin would be home any minute now, followed by Claudia, Damian, and Diana, who had asked if they could be here to welcome him back. That was the word they kept using—"welcome"—as if they were convinced the worst was behind them, and the judge would allow him to stay.

They hadn't seen each other since Elda's funeral. The house was quieter now, and sterile, and she worried it would give her and Martin's separation away. If anyone asked, she decided, she would say nothing had been the same with Elda and Eduardo gone. They were still adjusting to being alone again.

She made sandwiches and placed plastic cups and plates on the table. It reminded her of the first time she had met Eduardo; they had had sandwiches for him that day, too. Claudia had offered to bring chicken and grill some fajitas, but Isabel wanted to keep things simple. It didn't feel right to celebrate yet. Lately, every happy moment was relative; they no longer stood on their own, but next to an overshadowing sense of despair that insisted on being there first. This was how she had tried explaining grief to Martin, now that she could recognize it. Grief is never really gone; it is just a darkness you eventually adjust to. It was the only thing they had really spoken about, because it was the only thing in their lives that felt uncomplicated. She held him when he needed to be held; she rubbed his back when he cried. Some nights he played old Spanish ballads that she knew reminded him of Elda, and Isabel sat next to him on the floor to listen. They mourned together, even when everything else was tearing them apart. Then they would go their separate ways to bed.

It wasn't long after she had set the table that Eduardo and Martin arrived. He seemed taller to her—could he really have grown in just two weeks?—and when she hugged him, there was less hardness in his muscles, as if his body had been pulled a little, stretched. She looped her arm over his as they walked into the house.

"Don't worry about anything. The important thing is, you're home, and we're going to take care of everything."

Martin followed quietly behind them. Together they stepped into his room, and Isabel sighed.

Eduardo sat at the foot of the bed and bounced a little. He smoothed the comforter and looked around, taking in his surroundings as if they were new.

"We'll give you some time to settle back in," Martin said, tapping her on the elbow to indicate they should both leave.

"Isabel?" Eduardo poked his head through the door as she was making her way down the hall.

"Yes?"

He handed her a long, black cable and her cell phone. "I think someone's texting you."

"Right. Thanks." She couldn't believe she had just left it there, plugged into the outlet behind Eduardo's desk.

After dinner he told them he would be sleeping over at Diana's. Her parents had offered him a couch in their home until he sorted things out. When no one, not even Martin, seemed to object, Isabel asked to speak to them in private.

They left Claudia and Diana clearing the table, while Damian made the unfortunate mistake of asking Diana about their search for a new apartment. Martin and Eduardo shuffled into the master bedroom, looking bewildered.

"But you have a room and a home here," she said, once the door was closed. She was fully aware of how whiny she sounded, but no longer certain that she cared.

"He knows that," Martin said. "I'm sure he and Diana just want some time together, right?"

"I just thought, since we don't know how the trial will go . . . maybe these next couple of months are all we've got."

"You can't think like that," Isabel said. "Everything's going to work out. They let you out, didn't they? That has to count for something."

"I'll pay you back for that. I promise."

"Don't worry about the money. That's how a bond works," Martin said. "We get it back after your court date."

"And that's not what I was getting at," Isabel added. "What I'm saying is, we have to be reasonable. Why would they deport you for a traffic violation? They're more interested in sending real criminals back."

"To them, we're all criminals. You saw what it was like in there."

She wished she hadn't. She'd been sure they had gotten the directions wrong when they pulled up to a building encircled not just once, but twice, with a chain-link fence and barbed wire. She'd been afraid to ask about the bloodstains on Eduardo's blue jumpsuit. He had asked for soap, Eduardo told her, so the guard threw a bar at one of his cellmate's head, pointed a finger at Eduardo, and turned his back while two guys in orange kicked him to the floor.

The colors of the jumpsuits were supposed to set the first-time offenders apart from those with more serious charges. But there was so much orange. On their way out, she had watched the men pacing the grounds. It was like seeing fire swallow drops of water.

"That's exactly why you should be here. In your own bed," she said.

"It's fine, Tía. I don't want to cause any more trouble." He seemed anxious to get back to the living room.

"I didn't mean what I said that day." Her voice came out louder than necessary. "In the hospital."

"I know. You already told me. But if I hadn't showed Elda that report, she might still be alive. Diana didn't even want to ask for it at the police station. I'm the one that insisted."

"None of this is your fault. You understand?"

Eduardo looked around the room. The pile of clothes she had brought in earlier was still sprawled over the bed, a mixture of dresses, pants, and scrubs on their hangers. "I'm just trying to give everyone their space. Me and Diana, too." He walked out and closed the door gently behind him.

Martin pulled her close, rubbing her shoulders as he looked down into her tear-stung eyes. "You have a room and a home here, too. You should take our bed tonight. I'll sleep on the couch if you want."

She didn't know how to respond.

Martin sighed. "That day at the hospital. What you said about my father? You're right. I should've trusted you." He took a step back and sat on the edge of the bed, his hands pressed together between his knees. When he looked up at her, his forehead squeezed into grooves that stretched all the way to the corners of his eyes. "It's just that you've always had these amazing memories of your father, and I can barely count my good ones on one hand. I didn't tell you, because I was afraid you'd think he was a horrible person and think less of me. Then he shows up on our wedding day, and I just thought, he's gonna ruin this, too. All the best things in my life, he fucked them up. So I blocked him out. I never meant to block you out, too. You've done nothing but try to keep our family together. My crazy, fucked-up family that you never asked to be dragged into. And I just made things harder for you. I'm so sorry, Isa. I don't know what else to say. You had every right to be upset with me."

She sat next to him, and together they stared at the blank television against the wall. The dresser was covered in unmatched socks, pieces of junk mail, and receipts emptied from Martin's pockets, but along the edge lay a single dried rose from Elda's funeral. He must've kept it when he went to place roses over his mother's coffin.

She wondered if, like Omar, Elda could feel what she was feeling now. If she could understand this aching hesitation that made love burn and run scared in circles, because the only place that could cradle all her hurt was the same place that was causing it.

In her last days, so little of what Elda said made sense, but it didn't seem to matter so long as she was heard. She spoke of plans for her children and their future, and arrangements for her own. She spoke of trips home, and bags that needed to be packed, and sometimes she spoke without vowels, without sound, with just breathing.

Isabel had clung to all of it. There was the illusion that if she held on to her hand tighter, or if she listened harder, she could make their time last a little longer. It felt futile, until Martin left them alone for a short moment. The doctor had come in to check on her, but Elda only looked away. With a clarity and volume they hadn't heard in days, she had looked at the empty chair across the room and said, "*Yes. Patience is a process that births forgiveness.*"

And then she had called Omar's name. Just once and so low, Isabel wasn't sure if she had imagined it.

Isabel placed her hand on Martin's. She couldn't look at him yet, but she told him the only thing that felt true. "Give us time."

# CHAPTER 53

## November 2, 2016

## Year Four: Fruit and Flowers

It was almost a normal day: four years exactly since they were wed. In preparation for Day of the Dead, Martin had built an altar for his mother using a chest of drawers he had found in her closet before they sold her house. It was the one he had had in the family's first apartment, back when he and Claudia still shared a room. He told Isabel how he had climbed it, pretending to be the president of the United States delivering a speech. Omar had walked in just as Martin was raising his arms and losing his balance. "You could've died!" he said. "If I ever find you up there again, te mato."

The chest was just four wooden drawers, stained and stacked, one on top of the other. Instead of knobs, it had handles carved into the edge of each drawer, like a half-moon cuts into the sky. Isabel used these slots to hold flowers she had made out of tissue paper. She hung a banner of Elda's pictures over the wall and draped the top of the wooden surface with her silk scarves. Next to it, she had converted one of the living-room side tables into an altar for her father.

She was alone now. Martin had taken the day off, but this morning he had gotten an email on his phone and said he had to rush out for a quick surprise. An hour passed, and there was still no sign of anyone. Isabel played one of Elda's old records, lit a few candles, and waited with her eyes closed.

It felt silly. She knew better. She knew it never worked like this.

The strum of guitar strings faded as the record player sent crackles into the silence.

"Sorry to take so long."

She smiled, opening her eyes to see Martin, hands full of bags, unloading them onto the kitchen counter. The next track began before she could say anything. It filled the room with the sob-filled voice of a singer mourning his lost love and strength. Isabel turned down the volume and joined Martin in the kitchen. "What's all this?"

"You'll see." He took a couple loaves of pan de muerto out of a plastic bag. "Took me almost half an hour to get these. The bakery was packed." He moved between the cabinets and drawers, pulling out plates of different sizes and a knife. "Then I went to H-E-B for some of these"—he showed her a bag of oranges and began slicing them down the center—"and I went by the games section, thinking I'd kill two birds with one stone, but everything there was so new and unused. It didn't feel right. So I stopped by the flea market and got this."

He held up a blue-and-yellow tin, not much bigger than a phone. It was dented and rusty along the edges.

"What is it?"

Martin gave it a shake, and she heard a deep, quick rumble, like dozens of pieces with not enough room to move. He tucked the box under his arm and grabbed the plates of pan de muerto and orange slices, signaling for Isabel to follow him to the living room.

"This," he said, placing the plates and box on the altar, "was one of my father's favorite pastimes." The tin popped as he opened it, revealing a set of black-and-white dominoes. The plastic tiles had been stacked perfectly, with their yellowing faces looking up, their dots like eyes that hadn't seen light in years.

Isabel ran her fingers over the ridges. "I don't get it. Are these his?"

"Well, no. But they could be." He took out a few and placed them in a short line. "Ever since Eduardo left, I've been thinking about all the questions I never asked him. All the things I assumed would be too hard for him to talk about." A look of sadness came over him, when only a moment ago he had been smiling, and Isabel understood, because this was how they had both felt it. Eduardo's deportation had been like a flood coming in from under them. They had prepared for everything but its force, how quickly it left them with nothing.

"I realized that I never asked Eduardo about the good stuff," Martin said. "The memories he probably wanted to share. All I really know is that he loved my father. He says he was innocent. And he spent a lot more time with him than I ever did."

She was beginning to understand. "So this is all Eduardo?"

Martin nodded. "I called him last week . . ."

"But his phone keeps going to voicemail." She had been trying to reach him for weeks, imagining the worst, leaving message after message, begging him to call back. She didn't even know if he had received the money they'd wired.

"So I emailed him. It turns out he couldn't pay his cell phone bill this month."

"But I told him—"

"I know. And he's grateful for it. He says he wouldn't have been able to move to DF without it."

She couldn't bear to think about him alone on a bus, navigating the capital. They had tried to visit him when he first arrived, but with the amount of time they had taken off of work for Elda, they couldn't afford to leave. It was the worst kind of helplessness, sending nothing but money every couple of weeks. Isabel worried it would make him a target of the gangs all over again.

"So he's settled in okay? What part of town is he in?"

"I don't know. But he has a roommate, and he just got a job."

"A job? Where?"

Martin smiled and picked up another domino. "I promise I'll get to that. My point is, I emailed him to ask about my father's altar. What he'd put on it, if it was him. He said he and Omar used to play dominoes and eat oranges outside Sabrina's restaurant. That's how they spent their breaks."

The tiles clinked together as she shuffled them over Elda's green-and-yellow scarf. She couldn't remember the last time she had played dominoes, and she was surprised by how light and fragile each piece felt in her hands.

"You wanna play?" Martin said.

She shook her head. It was enough for her to just leave them here. Something told her that Omar would appreciate it, but that he wouldn't make it today, or ever.

She thought of him and Eduardo playing dominoes, sharing a few oranges on a warm day. It made her feel like she might drift to somewhere peaceful, but like always, her sorrow sank, and then buoyed her with each breath. Her and Martin's happiness would be wholly theirs, but it would always be incomplete. As long as Eduardo was far away, they would be floating to him in the backs of their minds, carrying this emptiness together.

"I'll be right back," Martin said. He kissed her forehead and disappeared into the garage. When he came back, he held a large gift-wrapped box. She shot him a stern look as he placed it in her lap; they had agreed not to do big gifts.

"It's not what you think," he said, helping her tear away the paper. It was a Blu-ray player, just like the one they had, except the box said that it connected to Wi-Fi in big, gold letters. Isabel tried to hold a convincing smile as Martin dug into the box.

"Happy anniversary," he said, handing her the instruction manual.

"I don't get it."

"Listen." He took out his phone and dialed the number on the bottom of the manual, putting the call on speaker. A machine answered, and before it could run through the call menu, Martin pressed zero and told the operator he had just been disconnected from a call with Eddy.

The connection came and went as they were transferred. A machine reminded them that the call would be recorded for quality assurance purposes.

Then a voice came on the line:

"Thank you for your call, this is Eddy. How can I help you today?"

She felt it in her chest before her mind put the sounds together: that same English he had learned from Omar and nearly perfected with them over dinners and drives and days and days in school. His accent, of course, lingered. It was in the vowels, in the way the sounds tucked themselves underneath his tongue, like a mother tucks her child into bed.

"Hello?" Eduardo said. "Are you there?"

Martin mimed for Isabel to say something. She covered her mouth and uncovered it, trying to keep calm, even as her hands and voice began shaking. "I'm here," she finally said. "My name's Isabel. My husband, Martin, just bought me a DVD-player for our anniversary, and we don't know how to connect it. We're a total mess lately. I can't tell you how happy I am to hear your voice."

# CHAPTER 54

## October 2012

He called out Eduardo's name into the jungle and heard nothing but the mocking hiss of the cicadas in return. Omar followed the dirt path carved by the feet of so many migrants before him back to the shelter. It'd be nightfall soon, and he and Eduardo had been resting since the previous morning, but now Eduardo was nowhere to be found. Maybe the boy had finally gotten the energy and the gumption to do it. He had been threatening to go back for his mother ever since they had left her doorstep. But that was weeks and hundreds of miles ago.

He scanned the faces of those who still remained outside the blue-stuccoed building. Most had either gone inside for the night or headed out for the railroad, but a few sat with their backs against the wall, legs stretched and feet bare, holding plates of rice and beans against their chests. A young man lay under a tree, his face covered with the corner of the same towel he had propped under his head for support. Omar kicked his foot lightly.

"Eduardo?"

The boy startled awake. There was always fear at the corner of every restful moment. Omar apologized for confusing him with someone else.

He could feel the panic start to swell in his chest, as row after row of beds he checked turned up nothing but unfamiliar faces. The only thing he recognized was the braced alertness in their eyes, how quickly it shot out of them at any sound.

"I'm looking for my boy," he told anyone who would listen. "About my height, dark, straight hair to his ears. Ojos claritos."

"You really don't know the color of my eyes, Tío?" From behind the portable toilets, he heard a cheerful voice. It belonged to a different place from this.

Eduardo stepped over a set of cinder blocks and metal weights, rubbing his palms against his jeans. Omar didn't know what to make of the slack expression on his face. Eduardo had always looked up to him. Then, just this past summer, out of nowhere, the boy grew taller, and his body began tracing the outline of a teen, and he had been clumsy in his attempts to fill it ever since. In his disbelief, Omar had told his sister it had never happened that quickly when he was Eduardo's age. She had only laughed and said, "You know how it goes. It's different when it's your son."

But he hadn't known at all. What was worse, he and Sabrina were not the only ones taken by surprise. Suddenly Eduardo was fair game for the Zetas in their neighborhood, no longer an innocent boy they had no use for, but a moldable recruit. After three of their younger members had threatened him with guns made out of PVC pipes on his way home from school, Sabrina made Eduardo begin working at the restaurant. She asked Omar to tutor him with books checked out from the library. Eduardo was insolent at first, arrogant and unconvinced that Omar knew what he was talking about.

"You spend ten years dodging Maras and 18s in prison, you learn to love every book in the library." He never told Eduardo much more about prison than that, not even when he begged, claiming it would help him stay out of trouble. But Omar knew better. The only way to stay out of trouble was to get the hell out.

"We gotta go," he said, handing Eduardo his bag and a fresh bottle of water. He looked at the exercise equipment scattered across the ground. Ever since they had seen a boy his age get pulled under as he had stood straddling two cars, Eduardo worried he would be too weak to hold on to The Beast. "How many did you get this time?" Omar asked.

"Twenty reps with the twenties. Ten with the thirties. Stronger, but not tired."

Omar laughed like he always did whenever Eduardo echoed one of his made-up expressions. It was nice to know that he listened. But the boy didn't seem amused. He grew quiet and morose, the closer they got to the tracks. Like every night before this one, they had no idea when the train might pass, or if it'd pass at all. They simply waited in the dark brush with the others.

"Remember, just commit. No hesitating."

Nearly three hours passed before they heard the horn, and soon after, like lightning, they saw its lights. Even from afar, it was a giant, and it seemed to only accelerate, indifferent to them as it approached.

"This is insane," Eduardo said.

"Stop thinking. Just go."

They started running. The ground vibrated and grumbled beneath them. The train rocked side to side, so loud Omar thought it'd explode. Its wheels turned in fierce rhythm, and he tried to time it, tried to feel its pulls and jolts in his limbs. It was a deadly dance, and they had only seconds before he knew it'd be too late.

He saw Eduardo's arm stretch. It flailed in the air and then it latched on. Omar followed and jumped. He took hold of something sharp and cold, then felt the wind trying to pull him under. Everything was speeding past, but his body was slipping slowly. He cried out and didn't hear his own voice. He felt something grab at his arms, like it might rip them out of his shoulders. In an instant, he was inside. Four men and Eduardo breathed over him.

The train shuddered with the massive force of steel railing against steel, its thirty tons of cargo now so much heavier with the souls of those it carried. One by one, the migrants drifted off to sleep. Some hugged the side of the car as they switched to another, or climbed onto the top.

Eduardo sat in a corner, shaking. Three times now they had jumped onto this line, only to flee when the police or cartel came to raid it. They could never get used to the shock of the ground hitting them, or of the train leaving them behind. But he knew that so far they had been lucky. There were those who had tried seven, eight times. They were beaten and robbed and left in the bloody grass without a cent to buy food or water. Somehow they still found the strength to climb back on.

"Here. Drink," he said, handing his water to Eduardo.

He took a sip and looked him straight in the eyes. "You almost died."

"You saved me."

"I don't want to do this anymore. I want to go back."

"There's no back, Eduardo."

"There is. There's my mother. How could we just leave her?"

That was exactly what Omar had said to Sabrina when he had learned of her plan. He had insisted she come with them, but she wouldn't hear of it.

"You know what they do to women on the trail," she said. "Like it's some sick tax they have to pay with their bodies. Here, at least, without the restaurant and Eduardo, there's nothing more they can take from me."

"There's your life," he said.

"That's worth nothing to them."

They both knew this wasn't true. The only excuse the Zetas needed was that she would bleed.

"Please come. Eduardo and I will protect you."

"You'd die trying."

After that, he knew there was no changing her mind.

"This is what your mother wanted," Omar said now, for what felt like the hundredth time.

Eduardo shook his head. "I'm not jumping next time."

"You don't mean that. You've come too far."

"Right. All this way, and we're still here. This kid at the shelter? He's been trying for a year and a half. But he says his mom's in Tennessee, and he's going to find her. At least he has something that keeps him going."

"And you don't?"

"What do I have?"

"A better life." It was the only thing Sabrina wanted for him. It was the only promise she had ever asked Omar to keep. Even when he had finally come home, his sister had asked nothing of him but to help her look out for her baby. Eduardo had been barely a year old then, and Omar felt tainted next to his innocence. He'd told Sabrina where he had been the last ten years, unable to explain more beyond his charge and his sentence, and she had interrupted him and said, "You didn't do it. I can see it in your eyes you didn't do it."

He could feel in his heart that Eduardo wouldn't keep going, and it scared him more than the tracks screaming beneath them.

"What can I do?" he asked.

Eduardo pushed a stone off the side of the car with his foot. "Nothing. You said so yourself. When we get to the border, I'm on my own."

"That's because I already missed that train. I can't go back. But you have to keep going forward."

"See? That's what I mean. You were there. You had a life and a family and everything and you still ended up back here. What's the point?"

There'd been a time when Omar had asked himself this same question. He was nearing the tenth year of his sentence, and he was convinced that the only good thing about life was that it ended. In the weeks before he would be freed, he would daydream about who he might pick a fight with, who might kill him the fastest, if he just asked for it.

And then Martin came to visit. His only son. He was grown, and he was strong and healthy and he had such conviction in his eyes. It didn't matter that he wouldn't talk to him, because Omar had never felt prouder. Here was the man Elda had raised: his son, who was decent and good and had found him.

"Want to know my secret?"

Eduardo wiped at his eyes and nodded.

"There is no point. Life is shit, but it's fucking beautiful."

He made him promise never to tell. He said there was no other person alive who knew his story. "I'm trusting you, got it?"

"Got it."

He told Eduardo all of it. The happiness and the pain, the regrets and the moments he would never change. There was no need to whisper, because the roar of the train swallowed everything.

# ACKNOWLEDGMENTS

This book would not have come to fruition without the unwavering support and encouragement of its first readers: Demery Bader-Saye, Everlee Cotnam, Kate Cotnam, and Barbara Sparrow. Thank you all from the bottom of my heart; may all writers find friends as true and advocates as fierce as you.

My endless gratitude to ire'ne lara silva, Kendall Miller, and Alex Layman for their guidance and insights along the way. To my agent, Laura Dail, who made me believe this book could really happen, and then made it happen. Thank you for seeing something special here, and telling me so. To my editor, Vivian Lee, for seeing and hearing and embracing this story. I am so incredibly lucky it landed in your caring hands. To Maggie Sivon and the entire team at Little A, I cannot thank you enough for all the hard work you've put into my books. Thank you also to Ginger Everhart and Callie Stoker-Graham, without whom I would not feel 100 percent confident that this sentence is grammatically correct.

I'd like to thank Adriana Dinis, Carlos Betancourt, Marialy Gonzalez, and Elvia Ramirez, who took the time to share the nuances of their work with me. Words cannot express how much I admire your tireless dedication to the immigrant community, as well as your kindness and compassion. To Nora de Hoyos Comstock: thank you for bringing us comadres together and always, always amplifying our voices. And to all who know what it is to leave your home in search of another: may you find a world of open arms and hearts. To those who shared their stories with me: I am grateful for you and your bravery. I am grateful you are here.

I began writing this novel on a warm November first on the second floor of the Faulk Central Library. I still remember looking over the stairwell as I thought of the very first line. Thank you to Austin Public Library for providing harbor for the imaginations of readers and writers alike.

They say writers will always be writing about the same things, in one way or another. This is true—even when I don't realize it, every word I write is in honor of and made possible by my family. My parents, Ceci and Ramon, sacrificed so much for the life they dared imagine for my sister and me. Ceci, thank you for being my hero in more ways than I'll probably ever know. Ramon, thank you for always believing I could do this, even (and especially) before I did. My sister, Ursula, never failed to nurture and encourage my desire to write, even in the crucial beginning when, as a timid teenager, I'd drop a poem in her lap and run out of the room, desperate for validation and approval. Thank you for giving me this and more.

Muchísimas gracias también to my amazing in-laws. Rey and Kathleen, your unconditional support never escapes me; it is a rock, and I'm forever grateful. To Odalis; I cherish you, your loving wisdom, and our heart-to-hearts so very, very much.

I wrote this book mostly in the early morning hours, and I don't know how, but Maggie always knew exactly when to wake me, and Pita always knew when to crawl onto my lap. So much love and so much thanks for these two little ones.

And Eric! You are always there to remind me of all the reasons not to give up, until I have no choice but to quote Carrie Fisher: "You're right, you're right. I know you're right." Thank you for this love and this life, and for every day I get to create more of it with you.

And finally, to every person reading (and this far, too!); I am so honored and grateful for the time you've given these words.

# ABOUT THE AUTHOR

*Photo © 2017 Eric Sylvester*

Born in Lima, Peru, Natalia Sylvester came to the United States at age four. As a child, she lived in Florida and the Rio Grande Valley in Texas before her family set down roots in Miami, where she received a BA in creative writing from the University of Miami. A former magazine editor, Natalia now works as a freelance writer in Texas and is a faculty member of the low-residency MFA program at Regis University. Her articles have appeared in *Latina* magazine, in *Writer's Digest*, in the *Austin American-Statesman*, and on NBCLatino.com. Natalia's debut novel, *Chasing the Sun*, was named the Best Debut Book of 2014 by Latinidad, and was chosen as a Book of the Month by the National Latino Book Club.